MESSA...
PRIME MINISTEF...

It is with great pleasure that I received a copy of your book, 'Daughter By Court Order.' Congratulations for your efforts. I am also thankful to you for your kind words for my speech on 15th August.

Women have a very important role to play in the development of India. It is the need of the hour to make women equal and integral part of the decision making process at every level. I have said it repeatedly then whenever there is any instance of harassment against women, we are overcome by a sense of despair. It is nothing but a national shame. We need to collectively work to bring about a positive change. I also agree with you that society needs to change its mindset and attitude when it comes to rights and dignity of women.

I hope your book is able to drive the change that you aspire. My best wishes for your future endeavours.

Narendra Modi

New Delhi
30 October, 2014

LETTER FROM
RATNA VIRA TO THE
HONOURABLE PRIME MINISTER

Shri Narendra Modi
Prime Minister of India

Honourable Prime Minister,

It is with great respect and hope that I write to you, particularly after hearing your heartfelt and wonderful speech at Independence Day. I, along with the rest of the nation, am deeply grateful for your victory in the recent Elections and hope that this brings a new era of prosperity for all the people of India.

I was, in particular, touched by your many references to the rights of women and that mothers should ensure that they treat daughters and sons with equal respect. Close to the time of your victory in the General Elections, my debut novel, Daughter By Court Order, was published and launched in Delhi at the end of May 2014. This book deals with important issues relating to the rights of women and daughters in a seemingly forward looking but otherwise feudal family, set in a modern North Indian context. The issues raised by the book might be of interest to you, specially as I have tried to show that laws and courts are not enough – what is required is good enforcement and administration, accompanied by a change of attitude.

These issues, I am aware, are close to you as well and I draw encouragement from your initiatives in bringing greater transparency and accountability to the administrative and judicial processes. I also draw encouragement from your call to the nation to treat its women well.

I do hope you will find the time in your busy schedule to read my book, a copy of which is enclosed with this letter.

Respectfully,

Yours sincerely,

Ratna Vira
23 August 2014

Ratna Vira holds a masters degree from the London School of Economics and Political Science, as well as a masters in English Literature from St Stephen's College, University of Delhi. She also holds an MBA. She is the daughter of senior journalist, Nalini Singh, and SPN Singh.

Ratna juggles her corporate career with her writing and her love of art. She lives in Gurgaon with her daughter and son, where she is at work on her second novel.

New Edition 2015

Published by
FiNGERPRINT!
An imprint of Prakash Books India Pvt. Ltd.

113/A, Darya Ganj, New Delhi-110 002,
Tel: (011) 2324 7062 – 65, Fax: (011) 2324 6975
Email: info@prakashbooks.com/sales@prakashbooks.com

facebook www.facebook.com/fingerprintpublishing
twitter www.twitter.com/FingerprintP, www.fingerprintpublishing.com

ISBN: 978 81 7234 521 1

Processed & printed in India by HT Media Ltd., Noida

DAUGHTER
BY
COURT
ORDER

RATNA VIRA

FiNGERPRINT!

'Fiction is obliged to stick to possibilities. Truth isn't.'

-Mark Twain

In the loving memory of my *nani*.

————∞ ∞————

For my children, Suhasini and Shauryya,
for they must know why.

The Moving Finger writes;

And, having writ,

Moves on: not all thy Piety

Nor Wit

Shall lure it back to cancel

Half a line,

Nor all thy Tears wash out a

Word of it.

-Rubáiyát of Omar Khayyám,
translated by Edward Fitzgerald

ONE DAY. ONE MOMENT.
LIFE STOPS.

'Memories warm you up from the inside.
But they also tear you apart.'
— Haruki Murakami

▼

Life changes in a moment, but we don't always see it coming. Aranya, or Arnie as everyone called her, didn't see it either.

It was just after eight on a particularly hot summer morning. Angry at being disturbed, and that too so early in the day, the woman did not attempt to hide her annoyance at seeing Arnie in front of her. Her tacky nightclothes were in sharp contrast to the ultra chic black chiffon sari flung carelessly by the foot of the bed, the blouse merely a string bikini revealing more than it covered and glistening with Swarovski crystals that winked and teased as they caught the morning light. The flimsy covering was still damp with her perspiration and her perfume taunted Arnie for her naïveté. She knew the woman must have been all smiles, sophisticated and soft-spoken, bejewelled and dressed to kill at the President's *At Home*. Arnie had seen it played out several times before. She watched her now, mesmerised, this woman whose resemblance to Goddess Kali was striking. The large red *bindi*, the heavily-kohled eyes even at this hour, the long hair flying and blowing out in all directions in the blast of the air conditioner right behind her, loose strands of hair framing her face like irate serpents, reminding Arnie of Medusa. The woman's pencil-thin lips had disappeared behind angry words as she screamed at Arnie for asking stupid questions. She was in a terrible rage, and Arnie, trapped by her hypnotic snake-like eyes, stood helplessly rooted to her spot, feeling smaller with every passing second, her stomach tightening into a ball.

Her words were like physical blows and they hurt just as much, but Arnie heard them with a slight delay, as if there was a bad DVD running with the lip sync off by a few seconds. The woman kept shouting and hurling abuses at her.

"*Kutiya!*" the woman screamed. "You want to put us on the road? I am still alive! And I will not let your evil plans succeed, you hear? You will not succeed, *haramzadi*. You should have died in that bloody incubator. I would have done it, but my father warned me that this would not go unnoticed in France, and that bloody social worker person made life miserable asking all those questions. And then Baby Singh came to get you. She's made you just like her, the bloody bane of my existence! She has gotten her revenge! I am left with an imbecile, an idiot like you."

She was shouting so loudly by now that Arnie feared she might have a stroke.

"I know who you are!" the woman continued with her tirade. "A trouble-maker and a bitch. *Pleez*, if this is about your Stanford, or that Sloan School of whatever, then some other time. I have important calls to make! The government might fall any minute; that famous director wants to cast me in his next film, do you see how much work I have? But here I am, wasting my time with you and your obsession with two hundred-year-old universities! Grow up! At least let your children go to new colleges!"

It didn't take her more than a fraction of a second to destroy Arnie's hard-earned academic success, demolishing Queen's College, the oldest in Delhi, hacking at the University of London, and beheading Stanford in the process, and all in the same sentence.

"Shrey want to *eshtudy* laws at *Yay-el* and that no good daughter of yours has many talks about going to some Rizvi. Yudi told me." Her carefully maintained accent had lapsed into the familiar Punjabi dialect as she screamed.

"Rhode Island School of Design, RISD, not Riz . . ." Arnie began, but the woman cut her short, the ensuing angry monologue successfully ripping Arnie's life apart, putting her on the defensive as her children were brought into the conversation, as was intended, and reducing her to a blabbering idiot.

But I've always known that she's a master manipulator and strategist, Arnie thought to herself, and giving herself a sharp mental kick, she cut in, "Is there a case regarding Civil Lines? Are we in court in Ranchi? What is it all about?"

"Nothing to *dooz* with you; no *sport* needed," the woman hissed back angrily.

"You mean 'support'," Arnie corrected her instinctively and immediately bit her lip for having done so. Having started though, she was not to be deterred. Mustering up courage she didn't feel, Arnie persisted. "There must be something going on. A friend of mine, he is in the civil service, hinted at something."

"I not need to tell you *aaanything*. You So-and-So, you nobody. How you question me like this, huh? After I suffer in this *mizzrable* house for forty years? You are just like your Chhoti Phua, always looking at us, eyeing us. Go fight with your in-laws and you will have my full s-u-p-p-o-r-t!" the woman enunciated the last word carefully, as if taunting her with the correct pronunciation. "Now let me get back to my newspaper. Get out."

Her dismissal was typically abrupt and disparaging, but Arnie was determined to get her answers. "Is there a case going on in Ranchi? Please, just tell me," she pleaded, and without waiting for an answer, Arnie plunged blindly into her carefully rehearsed lines, "I know my place in the family hierarchy. I have repeatedly told you that. All I want is to be treated as a part of the family. I have

17

even said this in my emails to you, but you are too busy to either talk to me or reply to my emails!"

She had been speaking for about a minute when the woman suddenly got up quickly, walked over to where Arnie was nervously perched on the arm of a sofa, and yanked her up. Shocked, Arnie was unable to resist the woman and she allowed herself to be pulled up and dragged to the door. "Get me a bloody paper, a document that you have any rights, you haramzadi!" The woman's face was a frightening crimson now, distorted with anger and hatred. She was literally frothing at the mouth like a rabid dog. "Why should I give you anything?" she gesticulated wildly. "Civil Lines is mine! Just like everything else is! Everything belongs to ME and I will do as I want. You are nothing but a bloody cockroach that I will stamp with my *jooti*."

And with that, Bang! The door was shut on her face; shut with a finality that stunned. Arnie found herself on the outside. Just like that. One of life's changing moments. And she never saw it coming.

Arnie did not know how long she stood there, leaning against the white pillars of the verandah of the house she grew up in, the house she called 'home'. She continued to look, gazing at the line of majestic mango trees near the boundary wall. She saw the sun shine weakly through the aged trees as she strained to catch the song of the *koel* and take in the heady smell of rain on dry mud, for nature had matched her silent downpour of tears with its own.

She closed her eyes and went back in time. A long time ago, almost a lifetime.

Arnie remembered running barefoot on the cold marble floor of the verandah and the red brick uneven ground of the *aangan*, playing hopscotch, as she would count "One . . . two," squinting to see the parakeets perched on the tall mango trees. Now, through her veil of tears, she saw the manicured lawn dotted with frangipani trees and endless beds of flowers. She watched in silence a row of Ashok trees sway in the breeze, rain-washed and emerald green, a sharp contrast to the brilliant yellow Laburnum.

Someone thrust a glass of water at her and Arnie took it with gratitude. She looked up and saw the embarrassed yet sympathetic face of the *chowkidar*; he had witnessed the drama. He finally walked her to the waiting car. As the car pulled out of the portico, Arnie looked back at the majestic colonial house, giving in to the tears she had held back until then.

Meetings with her mother, Kamini, had never been easy.

1

'You never know how strong you are,
until being strong is your only choice.'
– Bob Marley

Memories and thoughts . . . the pulse of a quiet mind.

Arnie went back to the days of her childhood, remembering how she would sit for hours in the alcove across the *sheesham* gates, waiting for Dadaji's car to drive in so that she could perch on his lap and play with Chhoti Phua, her father's youngest sister. She loved to hear her aunt's clear voice as she told stories, almost singing rather than speaking. Her lilting voice cocooned Arnie in a world in which her grandfather was always the hero and her father the favourite son. It was magical. It was her introduction to a world of song and story, of myth and imagination. Arnie would clap her little hands as her aunt blew the special white conch, invoking the blessings of the gods to protect her niece as she did for Dadaji every morning. This was a past filled with joy, where Arnie laughed and giggled.

"Your Dadaji sent both his sons abroad. You could say that they were exported to study. The older one failed miserably and squandered his time and our father's money, while your father, the prodigal son, graduated as an engineer from Cambridge University and began working in Paris."

Her aunt would enunciate each word slowly, making Arnie repeat them after her, as if trying to impress upon her the magic and the grandeur of the places and the people she was talking about. Paris was a fairyland in these stories, a big and beautiful fairyland right out of Arnie's storybooks, and her father's life, a dream. Chhoti Phua often told Arnie that if she were good, then she would live there with her father and her brother. Her father's stories were told with great pride tinged with a little envy. He shopped only at Le Bon Marché, one of the biggest shops in the world; even his vegetables came from there. He had a bevy of foreign girlfriends, lived in the posh 16th Arrondissement, and was a regular at the Indian Ambassador's parties, because Dadaji knew His Excellency, and he was one of the chosen few who were invited for dinner whenever Prime Minister Nehru visited Paris.

"Are Ambassador cars in Paris big enough to host a birthday party, Chhoti Phua?" Arnie had asked innocently and her aunt had burst out laughing, the sound still an echo in Arnie's ears. The Ambassador in Paris was Dadaji's friend, an important man and not a simple car.

"So you are married to my Dadaji?" Arnie would often ask her. Her reply was sad. "No, Dadaji was married to your dadi but she is a star now," she would say, pointing to the brightest star in the sky as Arnie nestled close to her, lying in the bed placed outside in the aangan and reaching out for Dadaji's hand until her eyes were heavy with sleep. They slept outdoors under white mosquito nets stretched over their beds. The baby cot was dragged out every night into the aangan but Arnie always crept into Chhoti Phua's bed, so her cot was used to store water and extra supplies of the mosquito repellent which was burnt every evening.

It was a time long ago, when the city was safe and children slept under the stars without fear. There were so many memories; Arnie could stay trapped in the past for a long time. She no longer had time for such indulgences; she had things to do and places she needed to be at. The morning had been traumatic and she fell asleep as the car sped across the city.

The car rushed down deserted roads, devoid of office commuters, as it was a national holiday and then screeched to a halt at a red light. Arnie opened her eyes for a moment but dozed off again, sinking into a fatigue-induced sleep.

She stirred uneasily a little later as her dreams changed into a nightmare.

Dadaji is dead and lying on the floor. He looks small and shrivelled. She breaks into a cold sweat because she can hear Chhoti Phua's shrill voice over that of her father and his brother.

"We have to take him to the cremation grounds before the sun sets."

"We have to follow the customs laid down in the Hindu *shastras*."

The solemn cavalcade leaves Civil Lines. Representatives of the Indian government and relatives accompany them, many of whom Arnie can't even recognise. They speak of Dadaji's achievements and in hushed voices talk about the warring sons as they drive along the dusty roads of Delhi to the crematorium.

Arnie sees her Dadaji's lifeless body lying on the rough wooden logs as his sons, her father and his elder brother, fight. The arguments reach a crescendo as they jostle with each other in public over the right to light the funeral pyre. The screams get louder and more abusive as the rest watch in absolute horror. They shout, attack each other, and wrestle to light the fire that would mark the end of a majestic life. Arnie sees her mother egg on her father to light it and he leaps into action. He grabs the lit log from the surprised Brahmin's hands whose voice wavers and tapers off as he loses balance.

In the ensuing struggle, the pyre is lit.

Arnie sees the smoke bellowing, the flames licking Dadaji's body hungrily, and she wonders if the dead watch their last rites. The Vedic chants rise to the skies and then gently fade away. She sees the flames rise higher and higher as the sky dissolves into crimson and violet. And suddenly, it is dark. Does it hurt, she wonders? She feels the chill as the sun sets and the December wind bites; but it is not the cold that chills her heart. She looks back as she leaves and the fog descends, her vision blurred by tears.

With headlights on, they negotiate their way out of the crematorium as impatient honking robs the moment of its dignity. It is her mother, as always in a hurry to reach her cocktail party, standing on the horn of her car. Arnie sees her cribbing to her father and speaking on the mobile at the same time. She pats his arm with mock pride and Arnie hears her say that she wished Randeep, Arnie's brother, had been in India to witness his father's heroic actions.

Arnie realises that the fight had been about money and control, not about the funeral pyre or lighting the fire. She watches sadly as her father looks out of the car window, apparently pleased with himself. Tears collect in the corner of her eyes as she wraps herself in her pashmina shawl. She looks back one last time as the car pulls away but cannot see much; the tall *peepal* tree obstructs her vision. She wants to linger, she doesn't want to leave him alone. She wants to wish him well for the journey he has started, but her thoughts are disturbed again as Yudi mama, her mother's illustrious brother, pulls up near their car and gesticulates to her mother. Arnie hears her mother's incessant whining as she relates another endless list of complaints to him and she is glad when the traffic moves, cutting her mother short in mid-sentence.

And just like that, Dadaji is gone . . .

Aranya woke up only when the driver pulled up in front of her apartment building. Startled and a little disoriented from her dream, she stumbled out of the car; she was home. She ran up the stairs, two at a time, and rang the bell, telling Aida, her house help, to get hot masala tea.

"Lots of green cardamom. Crush it and infuse the tea with it," Arnie said, settling into her favourite chair. The television news played its continual drama in the background as she sipped her tea

24

slowly and watched without really seeing. Finally, she walked up to the large bay window and looked out. The condominium *maalis* were scurrying along with their wheelbarrows. Little children played on the swing merrily, while the older ones enjoyed their cricket and the maids gossiped. She smiled as she saw her neighbour's teenage daughter exchange coy glances with the college-going son of the Malaysians on the ground floor. The older aunties were doing yoga stretches together in the green patch as their young daughters-in-law went jogging past. She waved to all of them and smiled. Life was all around her and she was part of the action.

Household chores and grocery shopping, a quick sandwich at the coffee shop and a leisurely stroll through her favourite bookshop took up the rest of the day. Arnie filled the time with mundane activity to distract her mind.

Evening turned to night. Arnie picked up the piles of paper lying on her desk and brought them to some semblance of order; she had been working late. Exhausted, she lay down and immediately fell asleep. And she dreamed . . .

The gates of Civil Lines are slowly closing behind her. They are no longer those warm wooden gates; instead strong and cold iron bars have replaced them. She can no longer see through them as she did when she was a little girl hopping in the garden, chasing squirrels. She runs forward and bangs against them, just to be let in. She can hear Chhoti Phua turning the rusty key in the lock and her mother hollering that Civil Lines belonged not to Dadaji, but to them.

"Civil Lines is ours. OURS! O-U-R-Ssss . . ."

She continues to bang on the gates but their combined might, her mother's filthy abuses, and her father's betrayal are impenetrable. Refusing to admit defeat, Arnie jams the gates with her foot to prevent them from closing on her. She continues to hammer on the gates while they try to push her away. Her father and his brother and then other relatives join Chhoti Phua and her mother. Arnie sees her brother, his wife, and her cousins. The crowd continues to swell. They beat her back and she falls away. Suddenly Arnie realises that she is not alone. There is someone beside her, a child. Her daughter, Sia. She has been with Arnie all the time, pushing the iron gates, her little hands pounding along with Arnie's. She realises that Sia is pointing to the papers on the desk and is looking beyond them. Arnie looks up and recoils because she is no longer in front of Civil Lines and can see the imposing Court building.

Her daughter, Sia, brought Arnie back to now, to this moment. There are no secrets. Arnie knew exactly what the dream meant. It points her to what she must do. She cannot find a resolution without joining the dots that connect her past with her present. Strangely, the force of her troubled mental, physical, psychological, and emotional state seems to be far greater than their combined efforts to barricade the gates. Slowly but surely, she feels the gate shift slightly . . .

The incessant ringing of the alarm on her mobile phone woke Arnie up. She groaned and hit the snooze button, but it rang again and she woke up and walked to her children's room. It was six in the morning on a weekday and they needed to dress for school. She walked into their room and realised that her son had left the FIFA-11 game playing on his computer. She bent to switch it off but then hesitated. Something made her sit and Google her grandfather's name and she smiled as she remembered it was his birthday. 'Sir Eshwar Dhari' filled her search screen as she found over a thousand matches for him. She opened the Wikipedia article and began reading:

'Sir Eshwar Dhari was a freedom fighter, a secular humanist, a politician and administrator, and an educationist who founded schools and colleges with a special focus on educating women. Sir Eshwar Dhari was the Vice Chancellor of the University of

Ranchi. His support led to the development
of post-graduate courses at the university.
As the university did not have enough room,
he donated family land in Hanumannagar to
build a campus extension.
'He was an able administrator and was appointed
the Chief Minister of Madhya Pradesh. Dhari
was honoured with the Ramon Magsaysay Award
for Public Service.'

Arnie remembers him being sworn in as the Chief Minister of Madhya Pradesh. She can see him dressed in a white *bandhgala* with his favourite diamond cuff links, not fazed by the morning's newspaper headlines that had screamed, 'Octogenarian CM go back'. She can still hear his voice as he took the oath, clear and articulate as he pronounced each word with the same thoughtful deliberateness as he chewed food, one word at a time. He was a handsome man, but not beautiful. It was apparent that he had been quite the rage in his youth, for his charm and presence made him attractive and people flocked to him. He was elderly by the time Arnie truly came to know him and he had lost much of his vigour. But he was more than a match for his family and even the political hierarchy of the country could not ignore him or sideline him.

'He was a close friend of Pandit Jawaharlal
Nehru.'

The line caught Arnie's attention and flooded her mind with memories. It was Indira Gandhi, who had chosen Dadaji as the Chief Minister of Madhya Pradesh when she had come to power, but things had changed drastically in the years that had gone by. Madhya Pradesh was a divided state now. And so was her family.

2

'Truth, like diamonds, has many facets.'
– Chitra Banerjee Divakaruni

Randeep's grip is tight and Arnie struggles to free her hand. She manages to reach up with her free hand, grab a clump of his hair, and pull it hard. Her brother's hair, thick, straight and falling over his forehead boyishly, is his weakness. He spends hours in front of the mirror, brushing it to get the swish just right. She has heard that the girls in his school swoon when they see him, dimples, floppy hair et al, but his heart is set on someone else, and not on a girl at all.

"Let go, Randy! Ouch, please!" Arnie begs as he shakes her and twists her arm, towering over her small frame. Spasms of pain shoot up her arm and she begins sobbing. Her brother is a bully, but only at home, for he is a wimp outside the house and many a remark are passed at school, even to his face, about his limp handshake and his affected behaviour.

The fight is broken up by the shrill angry voice of a woman telling them to stop.

"*Bas! Chhod do usey*, son. I will not put up with this wild and outrageous behaviour in my house. So unlike the Sharmas!" Arnie's tormentor, their mother, comes charging into the aangan and pulls them apart. She is trembling with anger.

"What has gotten into you, Randy? She is beyond redemption, but what about you, fighting so shamelessly? You are above such things, superior to that lowly creature," she said, pointing at Arnie menacingly with her finger and muttering, "This *kutiya* will ruin everything."

Arnie's mother had decided a long time ago that she was a *besharam* creature; brazen, a burden, and stupid. Randy could be chided in this way because he was intelligent; so unlike his sister.

"She was reading this without your permission!" Randy said as he hastily retrieved the latest issue of *Fringe* magazine from the floor, bending to pick it up. It had slipped out of Arnie's hands during their fight.

The cover was plastered with an oversized close-up of their mother's face, wearing her trademark red *bindi*. Her big charcoal eyes and the crimson-red fake smile stared back at them from the magazine. "She was asking questions, embarrassing ones, about how you did not know that the journalist was recording the interview to print it." Looking over her shoulder, their mother quickly retreated with her beloved son, her *aankhon ka tara*, resisting the urge to slap Arnie. The Punjabi curses, intertwined with Hindi swear words, were sacrificed as she quickly surveyed the scene and fled across the aangan. All the while, Arnie could hear her muttering under her breath that the journalist would have to pay for writing lies, for her lack of professionalism and that she would enlist Yudi's help if needed. Through all of this, she continued to shake her fist at her daughter.

Surprised that her mother didn't slap her then and there, Arnie turns around to find Chhoti Phua standing at the other end of the aangan, a copy of *Fringe* clutched in her hand. From the expression of seething rage on her face it is clear that she has not only witnessed the scene but also knows exactly what had been written about Kamini, Arnie's mother, in the magazine.

'From rags to riches, from bahenji to bombshell. Kamini
teaches every woman to battle for victory!'

Arnie looks at the magazine cover as she holds it up and winces. She reads and re-reads each word and attempts to deconstruct the title of the article. When was her mother a pauper or dressed in rags? Arnie would have been glad to get some of those 'rags' handed down to her! And when did she become a princess? Arnie makes a mental note of the term '*bahenji*' and other references to her being a 'persecuted wife' so that she can ask her grandmother, *nani*, the encyclopaedia of family information. She doesn't quite get the meaning or the context but moves on to 'prima donna' and then to 'bombshell with a dulcet voice'. Her eyes glaze as she stares at it in disbelief. Since when were screaming banshees described as having a dulcet voice? The journalist must have either been drunk or incredibly naive, Arnie thinks, as she tries to link the woman in the article with the person she sees every day. In the real world, words and foul expletives in Punjabi were not enough. Arnie bore scars and scratches all over her body that she would have liked to show the journalist. These scars were not from the playground, but were proof of her mother's foul temper and quicksilver anger. For when annoyed, she vented on Arnie and hit her with anything she could lay her hands on. The water bottle, pencil box, bunch of hard iron keys, the cooling iron in the corner or even her pointed heels.

Arnie takes the magazine from her aunt and reads the article for the hundredth time, internalising the shame and preparing to brazen it out at college the next day. Her mind grapples with the worst and the most humiliating parts, which she will need to defend when her friends laugh in her face. The only word that jumps out is 'princess', but that is so not true. If her mother is a princess then Arnie also is. She too, should be living the dream life, but she is not. That is not her reality.

Back to the article. She glosses over the bit that eulogises her mother's academic excellence and moves to the description of her 'designer clothes'. The words 'unlimited jewellery and unlimited clothes' take Arnie into a world of fantasy and imagination, where her teenage mind readily believes descriptions of emeralds as large as eggs. The magazine drops as she pulls her chair closer to Chhoti Phua. She knows all the gossip and is quite happy to repeat it to open ears. Arnie asks whether the emeralds her mother referred to were the size of chicken eggs or those of quails.

"Size makes all the difference," Chhoti Phua chuckles as she reaches for the fizzy drink placed below her chair.

Imagination is a magical thing. Arnie's takes her to a dream world where emeralds are the size of ostrich eggs and at least one has her name on it. This wasn't too much to ask for, was it? After all, the princess had dozens, so wouldn't the daughter get some? Chhoti Phua had often told Arnie that family jewellery is passed down from mother to daughter.

Chhoti Phua is speaking again. This time she conjures up visions of jewellery that could compare with the famous Nizam jewels— ropes of pigeon-sized, lustrous black, grey, and salmon pink pearls from Basra; a heavily chained cummerbund; thick, braided gold bracelets; a solid gold *hasli* carved with a scene from the Ramayana— and Arnie could see herself draped in a soft delicate chiffon, showing off the jewellery with élan, much like the royalty she had brushed shoulders with at Lake Bhawan in Bhopal when Dadaji had been the Chief Minister.

But her dream world disappears when Chhoti Phua gives into her rage. "How do you think we feel?" she hisses, waving the magazine around almost manically. "A rewritten Ramayana is what this is! Kamini is now the *apsara* and we the ugly brigade of *asuras*!?"

"I arranged this marriage!" Chhoti Phua is not done yet. "I brought this upon Babuji, upon our family. It is all my doing!" she laments. "I insisted on bringing her into the family and Babuji gave in even though he hadn't been sure of her at all. His astrologer too, had warned him against the marriage. The *kundlis* did not match. But rejecting everything, every single inauspicious sign, I forced my will on Babuji. He agreed to the alliance only because I fasted for three days and drank water only when he reluctantly agreed to my wishes. How I wish now he had not let me convince him!

"We had proposals from the best families of northern and

western India. In fact, there were proposals from many of the erstwhile royal families of Punjab as well. But what did I do? I chose her! I saw your nani, the epitome of decency and class, and assumed that your mother, her only daughter, would be just like her.

"The Sharmas were not paupers," she continues, almost pre-empting Arnie's question. "Your mother is wrong in that article, very wrong," she says, waving her bejewelled hands to emphasise her words. "She has talked about torn school uniforms and shoes with holes. Blatant lies! Her father was an honest police officer, not a *chapraasi*. Your mother and her brother, they got the best of everything. The Sharmas were known for their good name and their honesty, but your mother! She stands out from them; she does not belong to the Sharma clan! She is not a patch on your nani, swearing and cursing like a street harlot."

Ancient history, even that of her family, bores Arnie, and after a while she begins to look distracted. Her mother is her mother and that is her reality. There is nothing she can do to alter that, and the scheming of an earlier generation is not the concern of a young girl. The emeralds were much more interesting.

Chhoti Phua has shifted gear without Arnie really having registered the transition. "We are *zamindars*," she was saying, "and your Dadaji loved fine jewellery. He took personal interest in selecting the fifteen sets of jewellery we gave your mother. Each piece was unbelievably exquisite. There were bangles of solid gold; exquisite diamond strings held together by a Burmese ruby clasp; a traditional *navratna* choker; amulets carved with parrots and peacocks and studded with precious stones and strung with Basra pearls. Each gem, each piece of precious stone had travelled from far. There were Columbian emeralds and Sri Lankan sapphires wound together in a braid that sparkled in the dark. The stones were that good, they sparkled. But it was the big emerald ring that was Babuji's favourite, a deep, mesmerising green, and flawless. And *jaante ho*, even her *sindoor* box was gold. I had it made myself.

"As for her wardrobe, that was no less either. A hundred and one saris came in especially from Banaras. Weavers had spent months creating yards and yards of rich silk with incredible designs woven in pure gold. There were five saris, I remember, which we had ordered inspired by the beauty of the tie-and-dyed fabrics. The makers added embellishments and embroidered sacred motifs. The result was gorgeous but those five saris had required much effort. There were old *jamevaar* shawls that had been bought through our friends in the Kashmir royal family. Heirloom pashminas in every possible shade were given to her."

Arnie wonders, as Chhoti Phua goes on with her fantastical descriptions, when, if at all, she will ever wear some of these pieces.

"Your father was the youngest in the family and Babuji's favourite. It was a given, therefore, that his wedding would be lavish. But the reality was far grander and richer than the planning. Everything dripped money and class and your Dadaji insisted that it be so. After all, it was the last wedding in our generation. Everything he ordered had to be large, larger than life. The wedding reception was held at Hotel Chanakya, which had recently been inaugurated. The building, with its many floors, towered over the Delhi skyline in those days. And it was in those ten acres, surrounded by manicured lawns, right in the centre of Sardar Patel Road, that Dadaji got your father married.

"The wedding itself was a blur of endless events and celebrations; days merging into nights and nights into one long, unforgettable extravaganza. The finest of wines were flown in from the Mediterranean slopes. There were blindingly bright lights, tinkling chandeliers with a waterfall of diamonds, a thousand guests dressed in the richest of silks, and the heady intoxicating scent of tuberose and marigold mingling with rose *itar*. Prime Minister Nehru attended the wedding, his signature red rose tucked into his *achkan*, and so did President Rajendra Prasad. All roads led to Hotel Chanakya that evening." Chhoti Phua lapses into a momentary silence, reliving those days of her brother's wedding.

"Tell me," she asks Arnie, "have you ever seen the sari Kamini wore at her reception? The one your Dadaji gave?"

Arnie shakes her head, gesturing to her phua to continue talking.

"It was woven with pure gold thread and had dancing peacocks embellished with real Basra pearls and precious stones on it. But of course, she hasn't mentioned this in the article, has she?

"There was a revolt in the house after your parents' marriage. The other daughters-in-law sulked, jealous of all the money spent on the wedding. Dadaji had to appease everyone with gifts.

"We used to live in Sardar Patel Road those days. It was the loveliest locality in Delhi, with rambling old houses surrounded by peppermint green lawns bordered by flowering shrubs. When your Dadaji bought Civil Lines, the entire family had to move there. We missed our old house, but Civil Lines was so grand and large that we soon settled in. Babuji bought property spread over numerous cities. A *haveli* in Lucknow, a house on the banks of the Ganges in Varanasi, and even a villa in Goa. Do you think that your father or our elder brother could have paid for even one of these places? No! Not in a hundred years!" she says.

Arnie quickly rises in defence of her father, pointing out that neither could Chhoti Phua nor her sister have done as much.

But Chhoti Phua disdainfully emphasises that Kamini could not have dreamt of such an address while growing up in the government barracks in Hissar. "We made her a princess and look how she has spoken about us! She has hurt all of us and made us caricatures of ourselves. And all this while your Dadaji is still alive!

"And your father, he was the most promising of all of us. My heart breaks to see him now." Chhoti Phua's voice has dropped down to a whisper, her grief evident in the tears pooling in her eyes. "He has reduced himself to being nothing but Kamini's minion. He gave up everything. Le Bon Marché for Khyber Market, suits for kurta pyjamas, and working in that big office in Paris . . . I forget the name of the road," she says, touching her forehead for a clue as she loses her train of thought. "It has been so long now, but I still remember seeing your father's Paris office," Chhoti Phua sighs, her voice reflecting a mosaic of emotions, raw pride tinged with loss. "He gave up his life there for what?!"

As she listens to her aunt lament, Arnie realises that the man Chhoti Phua is describing is not the father she knows. She is bewildered and fascinated. He has never worked a day or brought home a pay cheque as far as she can remember. Never. All that she can remember, instead, are his requests for the thick white envelopes with his share from the family money that were sent regularly from Ranchi. Would her father have been more in control of the family if he had a job?

"We don't understand what happened," Chhoti Phua shakes her head with genuine disappointment. "All of a sudden he gave up everything and returned to India. Initially we thought it was a holiday, but then months turned to years and years turned to decades and your father stayed here, doing nothing.

"Babuji even got him a Congress ticket to fight the state legislative elections from Madhya Pradesh. He had always been interested in politics, and we thought this would reignite his interest in life, but it was not to be so. Such was the pro-Congress wave that year, in the aftermath of the assassination, that even a donkey would have won! Your father seemed not to care as he lost the election and started sinking deeper into his lonely world. I am not blaming your mother, but I have to say that she could have supported him better. The odds were completely in his favour in 1984, Aranya. Dadaji couldn't believe that your father did not win and the election loss haunted him."

Elections in India are an exciting affair. When Arnie's father stood for elections, the entire joint family shifted base to Madhya Pradesh to campaign for him. It was summer; that summer when Arnie and her brother watched movies non-stop on an old borrowed VCR and she had experienced her first crush—the hero of *Love Story*. The Asian Games had recently come to Delhi and brought with them colour television broadcasts, so they felt most privileged to have a state-of-the-art entertainment system. A decade later, Kamini would pack the music system and disconnect the television set when her son left for his studies, even though Arnie was still living at home.

"The election loss destroyed your father and he never recovered. Your mother was quick to exploit his loss. She wrote an article that Chanakya would have been proud of. Full of complicated descriptions of closed-room meetings and strong-arm tactics, all aimed at an alternative history of the elections that only *she* had been clever enough to understand. And she wrote that wretched book with the photographs . . ."

"All *jhoot*; lies! She took our family retainers and photographed them as political goons for her book!" She is almost spitting out the words now, little pellets of hate smattering against a target that was not even there, as Arnie tries to control her laughter. What a hullabaloo about Kamini and her ghost-written book. This was the well-crafted emergence of Kamini from the shadows of her in-laws. One story after another. Lies after lies. Today it was a book on corrupt politicians, tomorrow a piece on empty promises made to government school children. "This must be jealousy," Arnie thinks and protests vehemently to defend her mother. She gets up to leave, wanting to avoid the conversation from turning rancid. She is acutely aware that her mother's rising career was a touchy subject in the Dhari clan. The other women in the family would do anything to demean and discredit Kamini. As she walks away, Arnie hears her aunt say that she would find out for herself some day because the truth could not be hidden forever.

Arnie shrugs off the lingering unpleasantness and runs across the aangan. She has her own struggle, that of facing sniggering friends at college the next day.

It would be decades before Chhoti Phua's words would come back to Arnie . . . words about the lies and falsehoods of her mother and that the truth would eventually emerge.

3

▼

Having seen the children off to school, Arnie flipped through an old family album she had. She stopped at a family photograph taken years ago in the aangan of the Civil Lines house. The sepia image had captured the romance of those times, making everyone look younger, nicer. Her mother was there, of course, holding Randy, her little prince, up for the world to see. Her father, however, was missing from the picture. Arnie looked for Chhoti Phua and spotted her standing next to Dadaji as she herself, a little girl then, peeped out from behind her sari, a Bengal Tangail that was her aunt's favourite.

Chhoti Phua, or Baby Singh as everyone else knew her, Arnie remembered, enjoyed a commanding presence in her father's house, like the uncrowned queen of the Dhari castle. To be in charge of Sir Eshwar Dhari's official residence, to accompany him on tours, to be the General of the Dhari household. It was a role Kamini yearned for and believed should be hers, being the daughter-in-law married to the 'favourite son'.

Married off at fourteen to an extremely wealthy but much older oncologist, Baby Singh had been shipped off to Jamshedpur immediately after the wedding. At eighteen, sickly thin and continuously complaining of nausea and stomach cramps, she returned to the Dhari household for a holiday. The doctor was summoned immediately, and upon checking, he declared that Baby Singh was 'in the family way', as pregnancy was demurely referred to in those days. Eshwar Dhari's joy was boundless and Baby Singh got back her Babuji's attention and the comfort she had missed so much at her husband's house. The delivery was routine and brought a much-coveted male child, but Baby Singh's elation was short-lived. She was disturbed by her porcine husband's growing fondness for his step sister-in-law. Suspicion, anger, and resentment festered, and eventually, there was no way the marriage was going to survive, and her father brought her back home, well before the first birthday of her son.

Not everyone was as welcoming, however. Mother and son were constantly humiliated by the rest of the Dhari household. They were 'returned goods' dumped at their doorstep, not worthy of even their table's scrapings. But Chhoti Phua, undeterred, clenched her fists and set out to ensure that she and her son would never be ousted from her parental home.

Baby Singh had always had her father's ear, and this privilege, mixed with her determination and cunning, was a powerful combination. Before anyone realised what was happening, she had become Eshwar Dhari's conduit of information within his little family and fiefdom. She consolidated her position strategically but with a quiet innocence, playing her cards carefully, making sure that she appeared gentle and non-threatening so that her sisters-in-law, in contrast, appeared shrews to her father who liked his women to be feminine and docile. As the patriarch of the family, and clearly, the epicentre of power, he took all the decisions, even when it came to his nieces and nephews, arranging marriage alliances, securing jobs, and dictating terms.

The entire family curried favour with him. A nod here, a smile there, a gesture now, and an expression then, everything fought over, coveted, argued about, and dissected for hours. To be in Eshwar Dhari's good books meant instant elevation in the family hierarchy, and, most importantly, it meant closer access to the family wealth.

The brothers competed with each other and their two sisters to please and appease Eshwar Dhari. But, like a temperamental god, Eshwar Dhari neither smiled nor showered them with the importance and the money they craved for. Only Baby Singh was in complete control. She held the keys to his safe. And even to his heart.

Time and chance saw a growing closeness between Baby Singh and Phool Kumari, her elder sister who, like her, was spending more time in the family home along with Betu, her son. Little was known of her reasons, other than an ill-defined sickness, because Phool Kumari refused to talk. And for once, even Baby Singh could get nothing out of Eshwar Dhari. However, she had her sources and kept her ears open. Eventually, she heard whispers that Phool Kumari's husband was openly spending time with a lower caste woman he was besotted with. This woman, rumoured to be his servant's daughter, was pregnant with his child. 'That woman' had obviously done some '*jadoo tona*', some black magic, to control the man, Baby Singh thought to herself, otherwise why would he even touch that lowly slut? Surely he would not want to face her father's wrath? To take on Eshwar Dhari was to provoke the very gods themselves! And that too, for some promiscuous lower caste woman?! Impossible, she told herself, slyly pouring some whisky from the decanter in the drawing room and settling down for the evening.

Arnie wiped the black-and-white photograph and closed the dusty album. The Dhari daughters had always been treated with more affection than the Dhari daughters-in-law, but did she, herself a Dhari daughter, feel as special as Baby Singh and Phool Kumari?

Restless, she got up and walked over to the French windows of her flat, opening them to let in some fresh air. She could hear the distant sounds of a *baraat* procession passing somewhere close by—the rhythmic beating of the *dhol*, the ritual shouting and screaming, the playing of popular Bollywood numbers by a typically out-of-tune brass band. Who marries in *maagh*, in August, in any case? Arnie frowned, trying to remember the auspicious months for marriage as mentioned in the strict Hindu calendar. The noise of the marriage party brought up memories, overwhelming her, as if the shutters of her mind kept opening to a time, a time not so long ago.

"No, No! I will not go for Deep's wedding. Not if *She* is invited, that *kutti*, that shameless slut! Is it not enough to have her in the house and see her control Eshwar Dhari every day every hour? She has taken what is rightfully mine! What business does *She* have, eyeing a share in my property?"

Arnie had walked into her mother's room and overheard her mother speaking to nani on the telephone. The 'she' in her mother's tirade was, as always, Baby Singh, the real threat to her position in the house because Kamini felt that she deserved Eshwar Dhari's attention and complete control of his purse strings, for she was the entitled one, the one married to his favourite son, and a graduate unlike the other women in the household. And reinforcing her self-belief was the fact that she had given birth to a male child, her Randeep, her handsome son. Arnie was, of course, considered a scourge and an enduring burden like her phuas.

But Baby Singh could not be dislodged so easily from her father's house or heart. Eshwar Dhari was protective of his daughters and suspicious of his sons' wives, especially Kamini. He instinctively disliked her, curling up his toes and clenching his fists whenever she bent to touch his feet to seek his blessings, as was customary.

So strong was Eshwar Dhari's determination to protect his daughters' interests that when he bought property in Civil Lines, he put his heart and mind ahead of tradition and insisted on putting the names of both his sons and his daughters on the property deed. The daughters-in-law protested, especially Kamini, but he held firm and got his way. "Lead by example," he had said, aware that his action was highly unusual for its time. "I will show India that sons and daughters are equal," he had remarked, while inking the deal.

But little did the grand patriarch know that several years later, his actions would live up to the promise he made to himself. Had it not been for him, Arnie knew her life would have remained bound to the cradle, the cooking pot, and finally, the grave, because her own mother had only craved for a male heir.

Kamini, she had been told, had been bitterly disappointed that her firstborn was a sick and frighteningly bluish-looking baby girl, weighing less than four pounds at birth and almost continuously ill after that. She had been irritated and humiliated beyond measure and had rejected her at birth, hoping that Nature, having let her down once, would now do the needful.

Her grandfather, however, had shaken his head on seeing a photograph of her. She, a wee little mite just a few weeks old then, had caught his attention, and he had declared that it was going to be a miracle if she ever came out of the incubator. He could sense Kamini's rejection of Arnie and he knew that he would have to keep a watch over her. His resolve was strengthened when he overheard family gossip about a letter from Yudi, Kamini's brother, exhorting her to abandon her child and join him in New York where he was doing extremely well. The brother's complicated devotion to Kamini bothered him as did the twisted logic of snuffing out one life to begin another. He sent Baby Singh to Paris on the pretext of a holiday, ordering her in secret, as the head of his feudal family, to bring the baby back with her. "Bring my granddaughter back to India," he had thundered, "she will grow up in my house, in front of my eyes!"

4

'Be so good they can't ignore you.'
— *Steve Martin*

Arnie smiled fondly as her silver grey Skoda Laura stopped in front of her alma mater. The familiar red brick structure with shafts of sunlight streaming in, the hourly chiming of the big clock, the well-kept lawns, everything took her back to the seemingly carefree days she had spent here. She often visited the college café for its mince cutlets, toast, and coffee. And as she stepped out of the car and walked into the college grounds that morning, memories came tumbling out of her mind's closet, transporting her back to the day the results of her school-leaving examination were to be released. A day that was etched in Arnie's mind . . .

"Please, God! Don't make me need Her to intercede on my behalf to get me admission. Please give me Queen's College because of my marks." She had been praying all morning, trying to strike a deal with the Almighty, with the Universe, with any passing angel willing to spare her a minute. "Please God, I will be beaten to pulp. Be with me just this once!" A little later, having literally dragged herself to school, when Arnie finally stood in front of the notice board where the marksheet was pinned, she stared at it, stunned.

She looked at it again, tracing her name and checking the

numbers printed against it, and then looked away in disbelief. She rubbed her eyes and then focussed on the marksheet again, this time placing a ruler against her name and tracing the marks again, just to be sure. But no, it couldn't be! She couldn't have stood first! And that too in the whole country!

She could see the gates of Queen's College opening up for her. She was overjoyed; she had done exceptionally well. Brilliantly, in fact! Arnie was ranked first in the whole of India. She had cracked the system. Broken out of the mould her mother had so kindly, oh so kindly, set up for her. She could see the wrought iron gates of Queen's College open up for her.

However, her happiness was momentary; the fire in her belly extinguished by her parents and extended family. They poured water on Arnie's dreams and her aspirations. She was reminded of her place in life, reminded that she was a girl and that they had other plans for her, plans that did not include her studying in a college of her choice. "But, it is the very best, Chhoti Phua! Yudi mama studied there," Arnie exclaimed more than once, her agitation visible.

"*That* is exactly my point. What good has come of your *mama* studying there, huh?" Chhoti Phua retorted. "Nothing. No! No buts. Believe me, I know what happens when girls and boys study together. I have seen the world." Chhoti Phua paused for effect; a long and calculated pause. "Girls from families like ours just don't study in a college with boys. It leads to things that are sinful! Talk to your nani if you think I am wrong," she said before triumphantly stomping across the aangan, for she knew that Arnie's nani and she were one on this issue.

Arnie did call her grandmother a little later and begged her to support her desire to study in Queen's College. But nani's answer was as firm as was her disapproval.

"I love you very much," she said, "but this cannot happen. *Kaddo nahin*! You know what happened to my cousin's daughter! It was a monumental scandal; we have still not recovered from the shame! And it all happened because that girl just did not listen to us.

"The boy was the son of a rich man and had the world at his feet. It was a short-lived affair. He said he was in love with her, but as soon as his father threatened to disinherit him, he agreed to an arranged marriage with a rich man's daughter. The dowry at that time was one lakh rupees. I am talking about the 1960s, when you could buy houses for that amount and still have money left over. As for her, she had to be married off in a hurry; the family name had been tainted by the affair. See, it is always the woman's name that is sullied. Her father struggled to find a match for her and then for her younger sister as well. He died, finally, an old heartbroken man.

"Your *nana*, Sharma sahib, will never agree to you studying with boys. He will be horrified if you so much as talk to a boy. It is best you study in a girl's college, with no unwanted distractions. You'll get good results, good marks. Sharma sahib will be happy. I am talking to you because we are Punjabis; our family is open-minded. Your Dadaji will not even discuss this! That whole family is backward and conservative in its thinking. So, Arnie *bachche*, *ab bas*. You have to live by their family norms. Don't break your heart over this, dear girl."

Arnie had taken her nani's support for granted. Unnerved by this opposition, she began to cry over the phone. "If-if-if this is how you fe-fe-felt, nani," she spluttered, "th-then why did you ask me to study so hard? When Randy chose to swim instead of playing cricket as you had wanted, you said that we had to encourage him. You let the family believe that he was the only hope of his school making it to the Nationals. Even you would have been surprised if he made it to the other end of the pool. It was fortunate that he cut the sole of his foot on a broken tile in the school pool. Everyone was able to save face. But here I have the marks; I did it on my own, nani! Why is no one happy?"

"Bas! This is no way to speak to elders. And boys are different, you should know that. Anyway, I have to go now because your nana needs the phone."

And that had been that.

Her parents too, for that matter, were on the same side on the issue, united in their disapproval of her desire. It was rare for them to agree on anything. Mostly, it was Kamini screaming and her husband nervously trying to escape, having long given up the desire for a quiet routine sans all the drama.

"There is no question of discussing this any further. It is decided that you will only go to a girls' college," Arnie's father said firmly, flush with Kamini's approval. And then, to make the most of the moment, he paused and added, "Even Babuji will approve of this decision."

"Not that you are a genius," Kamini added mockingly, "standing first in a language is pathetic! What are you so happy about anyway, huh? When people ask me what course you are considering, I change the topic because I am embarrassed. It isn't as though you are planning to read Economics or Mathematics! Those are the real subjects of tomorrow; *they* reflect brilliance. As for English, paah! It is only a language. No relevance in the real world, just the indulgence of a weak mind!" She spat out the words, demolishing Arnie's achievement so skilfully that the girl began to doubt herself.

"You think you have done well? It is just luck, that's all. These days the exam are so easy that anyone can crack it. You think that you can match Yudi mama? Let me remind you, he did Mathematics and not this *English-Vinglish* that will get you nowhere. It is better to do it quietly at that convent college and then get married. Abandon these dreams. Get real. To fail in the college that still remembers Yudi will be shameful, and fail you definitely will. You will bring disrepute to our Sharma name."

They raved and ranted in front of her, but Arnie held on to her desire. Kamini even used the grief Arnie's decision would cause her old parents as a card. "You know it will raise nani's blood pressure because she will be uneasy until you come back from college. The university is unsafe and the coffee shop there a den of vice. This is *Kalyug*. What's more, there can be a bomb under your seat in the bus! You never know with the way things are in Punjab these days, the terrorism," she continued, getting no response as Arnie hung her head and listened silently, fighting back her tears and feeling herself topple into her mother's guilt game. Bitter disappointment scoured her soul and she felt small and diminished.

Finally, Kamini used her trump card, Dadaji, smug in the knowledge that Eshwar Dhari, with his feudal mentality, would never agree to Arnie's studying at Queen's College.

"Speak to your Dadaji if you have the courage. Let him decide," she said with a self-satisfied smirk, pointing towards the aangan. "But remember, you cross him and you will have hell to pay," she said, her voice thick and ominous.

Eshwar Dhari, dressed in a starched *bandhgala*, a Gandhi topi perched on his head, sat reading in his favourite chair, wrapped in old-world charm. Trembling, Arnie walked towards him, her face hot and burning with shame and streaked with tears. She felt so little, ever so tiny as she approached the man who had led Madhya Pradesh until recently; a man who was iconic despite being exiled a few years after Indira Gandhi's assassination, as her son relied more on his own band of cronies than on veteran politicians; a man who was larger than life, elite and enlightened.

She had rehearsed her little speech over and over and over again in front of the old bathroom mirror. But now that she stood in front of him, this man who was her Dadaji, she forgot the lines, the words, the letters. Everything was a blurry haze.

She mumbled a soft "Dadaji" and bent to respectfully touch his feet. He looked up and smiled, his eyes grey like old glass. A sudden unexpected spark of optimism hit her as his eyes twinkled and he winked at her affectionately. She felt warmth radiate from him, and it gave her courage. "Dadaji, you have to let me go to Queen's College.

Please! It's the college of my choice. I have stood first in India, Dadaji, even though it is only in English Literature . . ."

Her grandfather stopped her with a gesture of his hand. "What does Kamini's father, that Sharma, have to say about this?" he demanded authoritatively.

Arnie looked down at her feet and told him, her voice small and bereft of hope, that her nana was totally against her going to a co-educational institution. "Dadaji, nana and nani, they say that I cannot even have coffee at the co-educational college because it will put bad ideas in my head, and that no one will marry me," Arnie burst out, her feelings an assortment of shame and fear as she wiped away her salty tears. "They say that you won't allow it," she finished.

She looked up slowly, hesitantly, as if afraid of the refusal she would no doubt see on her grandfather's face. But instead, it was a roguish glint in his eyes that she saw.

"Sharma was always, always a coward!" her grandfather exclaimed, "Preoccupied with society and *izzat* and his honour. It is his wife, your nani, who holds the family together. I wish your mother were more like her. Tch!" he clucked his tongue in annoyance. "Anyway, tell him that you are my granddaughter and your marriage is my responsibility, and it will happen after *you* complete *your* education. That too, from the college of *your* choice!"

"Listen to me!" he bellowed as Arnie stared at him, stupefied. "Do not let people run you down, especially people who have failed at the very subject you wish to pursue! Now go."

Arnie wanted to ask Dadaji who these 'people' he was referring to were, but her dismissal was final. As was the seal of approval on her fate for no one, not even her mother, dared challenge Dadaji's decisions.

Dadaji had known for a while that Kamini favoured the boy, her son. Age and experience told him a story no one dared to narrate in his presence. He had seen the sign—a neglected granddaughter and an increasingly withdrawn and moody son. He had watched his

47

son transform before his eyes and was saddened by what he saw. A confident young man, educated in England, was now retreating into a shell, brooding and inaccessible. He had heard Kamini shout and had heard the daughter cry. He had to watch out for them, his son and his granddaughter.

That was then, a long time gone. So much had changed; even India had made a long and stumbling journey from telegrams to Twitter, from Kodak photographs to Instagram and Facebook. The last sip of her now tepid coffee brought Arnie back to the present. As the cafe started filling up with students, Arnie paid her bill and left. It was just another day for them. At home a little later, her shoulders hunched, her face showing signs of fatigue, she picked up her daughter's clothes from the floor where they lay discarded in the rush to get to school on time. She noticed how small they were. At thirteen, her daughter was still a child, Arnie's child, too young to bear the burden that her mother had carried at her age. Arnie wondered what she would make of it when she looked back on it several years from now. "My story will not be hers; she will have a different life," Arnie prayed.

5

'The past is never dead, it is not even past.'
– William Faulkner

The location was the Maurya Sheraton coffee shop. Arnie knew she turned heads in her chic black linen Zara dress and the stylish Omega on her wrist. It was an evening in May, the year her life turned on its head.

She sat drumming her manicured fingers on the marble counter top in anticipation. Anticipation of what, she was not sure, but anticipation nonetheless.

The day had begun normally enough for Arnie before it took a rather bizarre turn. It started with her phone ringing in the middle of a meeting, as it always seemed to do. She had to rummage through her bag to find it, already irritated with whoever it was who was calling. But the familiar voice that responded to her brusque "Hello" drove all thoughts of the meeting from her mind. Surprised and startled, Arnie had struggled with herself, wanting to disconnect, wanting not to continue, wanting not to have a conversation, any conversation at all, but curiosity got the better of her. After all, it was Chhoti Phua calling her unexpectedly after fifteen years of silence.

She introduced herself with the only words that she could have ever used. "I am Baby Singh, your Chhoti Phua." She paused for a heartbeat, as if waiting for a reaction, and then continued, "I want to meet you tomorrow, but only if *you* want to see me. It can be after work, or after the children are back from school. The choice is yours, though evening will be good for me because I can then come straight from my meeting."

Arnie had chuckled mentally, wondering whether Chhoti Phua's supposed meeting was with a jeweller or a property broker. The woman didn't seem to have changed at all, still lusting over *daulat* and *makaans*. "*Tauba tauba*," nani would have exclaimed, "at this age too, she is like this!" There was, of course, only one real option Arnie had, and so, she had agreed to meet Chhoti Phua the next evening. She had rushed home to change after work, remembering to wear her Omega and her diamond earrings, knowing very well that Chhoti Phua would definitely notice them. Arnie desperately wanted her to know that the little girl who used to run barefoot in the aangan had grown up and was doing well, well enough to indulge herself.

Reaching early, Arnie had chosen a seat next to the bay window, and as she sat there waiting, she was transported back to those long summer afternoons when her aunt would tell her stories in that lyrical voice of hers she had so loved. And what a rambling bunch of muddled up reminiscences it used to be.

"Babuji was an accomplished politician, both revered and hated by his four children and their spouses. Our mother died quite early, but Babuji did not remarry, even though he was naturally popular with women and there were many who would have eagerly accepted his proposal. He singlehandedly presided over a full house of people, all vying for his attention and favour. I secretly think that he enjoyed the family jostling thus for his affection, but he was a good father. After your Badi Phua, my sister, came away from her marital home, he immediately launched her in politics and got her an election ticket and even wrangled the Zila Parishad chairman's post for her. He sent me to the best cooking school, Cordon Bleu, but I did not set up a business. I regret that now.

"Jaante ho, your Badi Phua and I often spoke in Bengali, because language, in the Dhari household, was a secret weapon, a tool of power, and both of us conversed in Bengali. Babuji also knew Bengali. And the three of us would complain and curse with abandon, our language isolating the daughters-in-law of the house and the house itself echoing with Bengali banter, Hindi insults, and the occasional use of *Hinglish* as we spoke to each other or called out to the maids who were at our beck and call those days.

"The men of the Dhari household, including your father, did not work, and they derived their importance and self-worth from the reflected glory of Babuji. They were, after all, Sir Eshwar Dhari's sons, and *that* should've been enough for the world, shouldn't it? Their fortunes hinged on his whims and fancies, and the tide in their affairs rose and fell like choppy waters, depending on who the 'chosen one' of the moment was. Babuji's estate, like his formidable reputation, was spread over many Indian states, and he had portioned it out to his sons to manage and run.

"Jaante ho, Babuji had been mesmerised by the world of cinema, and enthusiastically, he had set up undivided Bihar's first film production and distribution business. It was a big thing back in 1946 and the state had been abuzz with excitement. He had hoped that his sons would see the grand plan, the blueprint, and grow the business into an empire. But much to his dismay, his sons thought only of the sultry, seductive actresses in the movies. Both father and sons dreamt about size. The only difference was that while the father focused on the size of the business, his sons concentrated on the size of the heroines' breasts. In both cases, however, bigger was better!

"The family lusted after the trappings of power. An invitation to a government dinner was like a shaft of happiness. Each one of us wanted to be the one chosen to accompany Eshwar Dhari. The resident *dhobi* would be summoned and the family's expensive clothes would be ironed—delicate petticoats, heavily embroidered blouses, georgette saris, *tussar* kurtas, silk handkerchiefs. The air would be thick with anticipation. Over evening tea, which was at around four, Babuji would casually drop the name of his darling of the moment, and after that, the rest of us would be left to grind our teeth in frustration. No one had the courage to dissent or to question, even though we all feared that it might not just be about a dinner, and, instead, be a symbol of times to come with the heir apparent already chosen. There was enough for everyone in the Dhari estate, but so great was the feeling of scarcity and insecurity, that the joint family was always brittle and on edge."

There were only snippets of her conversations with Chhoti Phua that Arnie still remembered that lay embedded somewhere in the recesses of her memory, faint traces, like candy floss, she could almost taste it, but it would melt and vanish if she tried to hold it in her hand. But everything seemed to have happened in another lifetime. Had she been gullible as a child? Or had their life actually been as her aunt had described it to be?

6

'But at my back I always hear;
Time's winged chariot hurrying near.'
— Andrew Marvell

▼

A dark, bewitching Chhoti Phua walked in, fashionably late. She looked just the same! How did she do it? Arnie wondered. Let's pray some of those genes have found their way to me, she hoped. In her crisp white sari, with diamonds sparkling in her ears and fingers, Chhoti Phua was resplendent. She was a haze of chic white perfection, and Arnie felt a sudden gush of affection for her aunt. She got up to greet her, giving her a long, warm hug.

"Chhoti Phua, so good to see you!" she exclaimed as they sank into the soft cream sofa. "You look just the same," she said, reaching out to touch the familiar rings on her aunt's long fingers. Big diamonds, rubies, sapphires, and amethysts that had been the cause of much controversy and jealousy within the household now winked at her in the muted light of the coffee shop.

Chhoti Phua smiled and said, "Jaante ho, my meeting started late; I am a Buddhist now and I attend regular chanting sessions."

Arnie simply nodded her head in response.

"I am eighty years old," Chhoti Phua continued, emphasising on the number, "and I have never dyed a single strand of my hair. But, but I feel my age now, though I must tell you that your hair will not grey and you will not wrinkle prematurely like so many others because you are a Dhari. Your own mother, she started dyeing her hair at thirty-five! Imagine!"

Arnie grinned and it struck her just how much she had missed having her aunt around. The hostess interrupted them just then to take their order and they took a good twenty minutes to place their order, studying the menu thoroughly before making their selection. "Times have changed so much! Chai, for me, was merely soppy Marie biscuits washed down with hot sweet tea, and now look!" Chhoti Phua exclaimed as they pored over the menu.

Arnie smiled indulgently, happy to hear her aunt's lilting voice again. It was like the old times, going happily back and forth like two little birds lost in their own world. They looked at each other as the hostess scurried away with their order, relieved that they had finally decided what they wanted to eat. Arnie looked at her retreating backside and remarked, "Girls are so thin these days; I wonder how they do it?"

Chhoti Phua smiled at her niece. "You are not bad at all yourself. I wish your mother could see you in that dress."

So much had changed. And yet, nothing had. Chhoti Phua was hurting; her pain and humiliation were still clearly raw, and Arnie knew where it all came from. It came from the last time they'd met, the day of the Big Fight. Years ago.

With wide chestnut eyes, Arnie watched in stunned silence as her mother hurled abuses at Chhoti Phua. She knew that imploring her father to intervene would have no effect as he only tried to make himself invisible, literally merging into the white walls, dressed as he himself was in a white kurta-pyjama. As for Dadaji, he had been too ill to do anything.

Her mother was in a rage the likes of which she had not seen before.

"Stealing *kutiya*," she shouted, "*thoz* diamonds are mine. *Aall* of it belongs to me! You are nothing but returned goods, you hear? And your son *ij* growing up in MY house!" Her words were like bullets loaded with venom. "I *vill* place my throne on your evil *haart* and rule this *leetal* kingdom one day!" She was screaming and shrieking, her English having slipped back into its natural idiom.

Throughout this vile tirade, Chhoti Phua had stood quietly, flinching as the words hit her one after the other, relentless in their cruelty. To be accused of ruining her niece, of wanting to take her away from a so-called 'doting mother', of wanting her life to end up like hers, in a divorce, it was more insult than she could bear. But Kamini had gone on and on that day until Chhoti Phua had finally withdrawn from the aangan, walking further and further away from Arnie, closing her *jaali* doors behind her and disappearing into the darkness, which was for once what she needed. She never once looked back towards Arnie. Her door was firmly shut now, leaving Arnie alone on the outside, never to be let in again.

Until now . . . perhaps?

"When did you last see your father?" Chhoti Phua asked, breaking Arnie's chain of thoughts. "And why have you stopped coming over to Civil Lines, *beta*? Why don't you send the children? Your daughter used to look at me from across the aangan, just like you did. Her mop of curly hair and her soft features reminded me of a tiny rag-doll," she droned on, "but I haven't seen them in years. They must be grown up now. Which class are they in?"

"Seven and five," Arnie replied automatically.

"So the boy is in seven?"

"No, my daughter is the elder one, just like me."

"Hmm . . . Does she also look like you?"

Arnie knew exactly what that meant and smiled. "Yes, Chhoti Phua, she has my complexion. But these days it really doesn't matter."

"The world is a tough place," Chhoti Phua said, shaking her

head sadly and mumbling about how fair skin was still a mark of superiority, a symbol of being the 'crème de la crème' of society, a colonial hangover from the Raj.

"Those who spoke fluent English got easier access to all the embassy parties in those years," she spoke wistfully. "I am talking about the seventies, mind you. Babuji had kept an Anglo-Indian tutor for us. While your Badi Phua and I giggled through the afternoon classes the tutor conducted in our house, your mother was cleverer than us. She learnt quickly, spent hours practicing before the mirror, and even had a little diary in which she noted clever English phrases to later impress people around her with. But even today, her accent drops back to Punjabi when she is agitated. She has worked hard and improved considerably, no doubt, but still, all those articles of hers are still ghostwritten. These days, she even has a Bollywood dance teacher and a hairdresser on her payroll! And to think that she is nearing seventy!"

Chhoti Phua broke off suddenly, as if mentally debating whether she should continue telling Arnie more about her mother's antics or not, and with barely a pause, continued, "Jaante ho, we saw her shimmy and dance at the minister's son's wedding last month. She did a horrific imitation of Katrina Kaif in *Sheila ki Jawani*." Chhoti Phua shuddered.

Arnie looked away, embarrassed at the thought of her sixty-seven-year-old mother competing thus with the sixteen and twenty-year-olds for attention.

"I feel bad for your father," her aunt added after a moment. "He has reduced himself to such a state that even Kamini's driver looks smarter than him! We all blame her for turning him into such a spineless man, but then even he did not stand up for himself at all."

"Babuji died heartbroken, you know, because Surya Dhari, his favourite son, who had once excelled at Cambridge and had such a bright future ahead of him, that boy spent his days idly watching life go by. His world shrank to the chipped brick walls around the Civil Lines property. He did nothing but watch quietly as time ticked along. He sat frozen, his face a complete blank as the babies of the house played with their *ayahs* in the garden in front of him. He watched the toddlers driven out of the gates to nursery schools, watched as his children, now young adults, walked out of the same gates to college. And he watched with the same vacant expression as we greeted the wedding processions for the *betis* and *bahus* of the house." Arnie knew that there was little exaggeration in what her aunt was saying. She remembered only too well, how nothing ever changed for her father, how time and life eclipsed him. And that long verandah was his refuge from it all.

Almost as if reading her mind, Chhoti Phua added, "To get away from it all, to escape Kamini's screeching voice and her fierce temper, he would escape to the verandah. Your mother's soft voice was reserved for her male friends. I saw everything from across the aangan. I see your father every day even now, hovering nervously outside on the verandah and entering the house only after her car drives out of the gates.

"This is a tragic curse, no man after Babuji has had the spirit or the strength to carry his mantle forward. No spark, no burning passion in any of them. Not one has ever held a stable job or pursued a profession!"

Pointing out the case of Chhoti Phua's own son who was a successful consultant in Norway, Arnie argued that she was generalising a little too much.

"But he is not a Dhari," Chhoti Phua retorted right back. "And while the same logic applies to your son Shrey, look at your brother, Randy!" she continued. "Like a typical Dhari boy, he is repeating a now familiar pattern. He married Alok Punjabi's daughter, and that girl is as domineering as your mother. And her father, that thief, made a ton of money while he was in the government. He was quite handsome and had a weakness for liquor, ladies, and land, so a little extra money always helped. Rundee, that poor bastard, is truly in a jam with your mother crushing him from one end and his wife from the other. I saw him the other day, he has begun to stoop and looks shifty. Jaante ho, he is fat as well now!"

Misplaced loyalty made Arnie protest. "Chhoti Phua, his name is Randeep, so it's R-A-N-D-Y when you shorten it. It was bad enough because he was teased in school and called horny, you, at least, should not distort it any further!" Undeterred, and with a mischievous smile, Chhoti Phua disagreed. "My English is not good, so RUNDEE!"

"But that means prostitute in Hindi!"

"So, isn't he just that? He has prostituted himself, hasn't he? Nothing escapes me. Rundee's wife still carries on with her childhood sweetheart while ruling Rundee with a firm hand. He believed her when she claimed she was a virgin. What were she and her boyfriend doing all this while then? Playing house-house like kindergarten children?"

The hurt of Kamini's words years ago was still raw and Chhoti Phua couldn't resist the temptation to stick the knife in. "What goes around comes around. Kamini had the guts, the guts, to call us returned goods, but look! She got a daughter-in-law who is still making out with her 'ex-boyfriend'; her goods are still in the market. Who is the *used-maal* now?!"

Her aunt's acerbic words were evidence of her wounds still being raw and she continued venting as they ate, describing the petty humiliations of everyday life in the Civil Lines home.

"I am tired. Your mother has troubled us relentlessly. For half a century now, we have been the evil in-laws. She lives in our father's house and makes life hell for the rest of us, shouting without provocation even if my grandson and his friends kick their football into her lawn. Does revenge not have an expiry date?

"I am trying to atone for all the hurt that I must have caused earlier, Aranya, but whatever I did was prompted by the need to survive in my father's house with my little son. My brothers' wives, they were convinced that my sister and I were usurping our father's love and, more importantly, his money."

Perhaps it was age and a sense of mortality, or perhaps it was something deeper, Arnie couldn't be quite certain of her motivation, but Chhoti Phua seemed filled with a depth that Arnie didn't remember her having.

"I remember telling your mother several years ago that Kamini, I will someday meet my Creator and I do not want any negative karma. But she just would not let things go. She crushed your Dadaji's spirit even as he had lain ailing in his bed. It is her corrosiveness that singes and scorches the family even today. I have watched my own brother waste away in front of my eyes, and you, look at what she has done to you!"

"I am fine Chhoti Phua, I have survived," Arnie said, pushing back the tears that had inevitably welled up in her eyes, for her aunt was right.

"You have done better than survive," her aunt insisted. "When Krish left you, your children were not even as tall as her dining table!" Chhoti Phua sighed and lapsed into a momentary silence before excusing herself to go to the washroom.

Arnie nodded blindly, her eyes full of tears and her mind having already taken her back ten years to that unfortunate Diwali. A burst of firecrackers, anger, confusion, grief. A painful memory.

7

▼

All it took was a moment, a flash, and Arnie's life changed forever. One moment everything was as fine as it could have been, and the next minute, it was all over. Her marriage was finished, done with.

Arnie had come through the complicated relationships, the petty jealousies, the deep insecurities, and the political jungle of her growing-up years with great strength and had turned out to be a fine young woman. She had thought of her marriage to Krish as an escape from her horrible life with Kamini. In the days before the wedding, it was all she could think of. Her future with Krish

But life had other plans for her. Should she have seen the end coming? Should she have had a hint that her relationship was going sour? But Arnie knew that she had truly not seen it coming.

There she had been, left with a fourteen-month-old baby Shrey, and Sia barely three; almost keeling over with a heavy mortgage for the flat she and Krish had bought together.

There had been fights and arguments, yes. But they had all been over things like the colour of the curtains and the upholstery to be used in the children's room. A mix of candyfloss and powder blue, colours perfect for a nursery, but

Krish had insisted on a splash of buttercup yellow, "for a dash of something more," he had said.

Everything about that horrible evening when things first started unravelling was indelibly imprinted on Arnie's mind.

She was returning from Bangalore with her two babies and as she walked out of the airport, she spotted Krish standing at the far end of the arrival lounge with his parents behind him. There! Right there! Even from afar, she could sense that something was wrong, but try as she might, she could not put her finger on it. Its probably fatigue, she had thought to herself as an irritated Shrey had pulled at her hair.

In the car, the air was thick with a heady concoction of Rexona soap, tension, apprehension, and the stink of manipulation. Arnie sat frozen in the backseat, slightly confused and scared even as Krish cooed to the children as he drove. He kept throwing accusatory glances in her direction for he had had to run the house in Arnie's absence. "All because of your job and career," he muttered. From the corner of her eyes, Arnie could see his mother gloating as she played with her grandchildren.

Once home, Krish strode into the master bedroom, gesturing for her to follow, and there he began listing his ailments—ill, depressed, and sick, all in one. Confused, she had stared at him. To her he had looked well, in fact a little overweight.

"This is a nightmare," she had thought to herself. Her tired mind was crying for a cup of chai, for a bath, for sleep, but there she was, held captive in a room by her husband.

Trin-g-g-g.

The ringing of his mobile phone cut through the air and Arnie heard a shrill feminine voice on the other end. "Is that my brother's wife?" she asked incredulously.

With a curt snap of his fingers, Krish gestured to her to be quiet. "It's my guru's daughter, she understands me, knows when I am stressed," he retorted, implying that Arnie lacked these skills.

"But she sounded like Dolly!" Arnie insisted, unable to control herself. But Krish simply got up and left the room. He returned a few minutes later, and as if galvanised into action after his brief conversation on the phone, he pulled out a suitcase and began hastily packing his things. His mother stood at the doorway of their bedroom, watching with approval.

"What are you doing?" Arnie asked him, dreading the answer. But Krish chose to ignore her. When it became evident that he was leaving, she begged him not to go, to think of the children, of their lives together. "What happened?" "Stop!" "Stay." "Please don't leave us!"

"It is your temper," Krish finally responded. "You had to have your way in everything. And your mother interfered incessantly in our lives. You are blind to her ill treatment of you. Did you not see what it was doing to me?" he shouted, even as she stood transfixed, staring at her life that lay shattered like broken glass.

"His mother looks at Arnie accusingly, urging her son to hurry. His mother, the same person who gave Arnie fake bangles while she helped her son apply sindoor to Arnie's forehead to solemnise the marriage. The same lady who, without shame, totally unabashed, hung her lacy panties and frilly bras to dry in the middle of the living room while Arnie looked away, too timid to pick them up. The same woman who had asked for the jewellery, as she performed the rituals to welcome Arnie, her daughter-in-law, into the marital home. "Give it to me, I will keep it safely," she had said as Arnie looked at her, unsure of her status in the new family, unsure of her husband who she had met only a few short months before the marriage."

Little Shrey had pushed his face into her neck and had begun whimpering, as if he could sense the tension in the air.

"We will take the children," Krish's mother had suddenly spoken up. "Come to *dadi*, darlings."

But Arnie had picked up the courage, and through her tears, she had refused to let go, clutching on to her daughter and holding the baby boy tight.

"I won't goed with you!" Little Sia had screamed. "I won't goed without my mumyee."

"Krish don't go, please!" Arnie had tried for the last time. "I beg for forgiveness. I know I haven't been a good wife; I am so sorry, but let's try and work it out. I will do anything you want. But don't, please don't do this to us."

But in the end, Krish's car drove off in a cloud of smoke and dust.

"Bhaiya gaya?" Aida, her house help asked, equally shocked, for she had seen them in happier times. She scooped up Shrey and bundled him up to the house, leaving Arnie to trudge up the stairs with Sia.

"I told," Sia muttered, meaning she was cold because she could not yet pronounce 'C'. Arnie looked at her tear-stained face and her heart sank. "How will I do this on my own? How will I be a mother and a father? How?"

She stumbled into her bedroom, the children demanding her attention, climbing all over her. Shrey wanted a feed while Sia tried to wipe her tears, asking, "Why did Papa goed away? He loves dada-dadi more? Gandi dadi thu thu."

Arnie had called her mother then, but it hadn't been long before Kamini had started blaming her for everything.

"You are a bloody bitch," she had ranted. "You are incapable of doing anything vell, you should have kept his bed warm, have you learnt nothing? How can I sport you, haramzadi?"

Kamini's mad rage, her vile abuses, Arnie's own lack of reassurance had caused her to start trembling then, making her unsure, unsure of herself, her life, her future.

In a trance, she had walked around the house, déjà vu hitting her as she opened Krish's cupboard, touched his clothes, his shoes, his camera still lying on the table. She wandered from room to room. Her mind raced to their first date after the marriage had been fixed, when Krish had lovingly pointed to the full moon and said, "Every time you look at it, think of me." She broke down then, her body racked by sobs.

After many nights of wandering around the suddenly frigid house in a trance, watching night turn to day and day to night, she had finally packed her bags to go back to Civil Lines. She had collapsed into her mother's arms, sobbing hysterically, but Kamini had been far from sympathetic.

"Pick up your bags," she had shouted, "because we will stuff you back in his house. You have to be like me, put your throne on his heart and rule. Look at what I have done to your father and his bloody sisters; be like me, do it for the money."

But Arnie knows that she can't possibly do that. She isn't like her mother. Yet, she has no one to turn to. Nani was in the hospital once again and Dadaji was long dead.

Kamini, meanwhile, expertly manipulated the situation, drawing all sympathy and attention away from Arnie. Even in this tragedy, she was the victim, the one dealt another blow by life, she was the doting grandmother and the worried mother. All the while, Arnie wondered how she was going to manage a job, a mortgage, and the children.

It happened a few days later, when she finally sat down in front of the old computer in Civil Lines to check her emails, hoping that there would be something from Krish. What she got, instead, were a couple of sinister emails revealing dark truths.

> 'Hi, Don't get scared, i am a friend to you! That bastard ur husband is having an affair with my girl. He has hurt her bad and is taking her job away.
> Today is our engagement party and we are getting married now. Will keep her with me!!!!!'

And then, as if in a volley, the emails begin flooding her inbox.

> 'she loves krish she wants 2 use him he has cut her off i cant let go of her and was using her 4 sex now am in love live and work

64

```
with her and see her all day want herf with
me shes with me and will stay'
'She decided to ruin Krish's reputation and
name. want him to die a slow death. He shoudl
kill himslef now and save trouble later'
```

Without really thinking about it, Arnie shared the emails with her mother, and hell broke loose after that. The theatrics that her mother indulged in, the screaming and the shouting and the humiliation of her own life, finally made Arnie decide that she had to move on, that Krish was out of her life forever, that her mother's heart was clamped as tightly shut as her purse, and that she, Arnie, no longer cared whether the moon remained in the sky or crashed to the ground.

Someone tapped on the table, making Arnie snap back to the present. Chhoti Phua. She was back from the bathroom. "You are lost. What happened?" she asked, settling herself down on the sofa once again.

But Arnie just shook her head and smiled. It was all in the past. It was gone now.

8

'In three words I can sum up everything
I've learned about life: it goes on.'
— Robert Frost

C hhoti Phua had a purpose in meeting Arnie. What she
 said then would cause a tidal wave in Arnie's life and
finally lead to the fateful morning encounter with Kamini
the following week.

"Listen carefully, beta. I'm not going to tell you what to
do, but I'm leaving it to you to make what you want of it,"
Chhoti Phua said matter-of-factly. "There is a court case, a
partition case for your Dadaji's properties in Ranchi." She
rolled her eyes as she articulated the next few words carefully.
"But Kamini, your 'mother', has blocked the hearings to
harass us. She doesn't fail to point out in every conversation
that I am old and that she will see me into my grave. I am
only thirteen years older than her and not a hundred and
thirty as she believes, but that is a separate issue."

Arnie nodded. She had heard something. A friend from
her college had stayed at the Dhari house in Ranchi and did
mention some case. Arnie had, at the time, mustered up the
courage and asked her mother, even emailed her, but was
rebuffed for being greedy.

"But this was last December, Chhoti Phua," Arnie told
her aunt, looking into her eyes as she realised that there was
more to this story than she could understand now.

Chhoti Phua took some time to get her thoughts together, wondering how much she should tell Arnie. "The point is that I am tired. I'm just tired of this endless litigation and these frequent trips to court." Arnie presumed that her aunt was talking about the case in Ranchi and nodded in sympathy.

"Must be really tiring to make these trips to Ranchi," Arnie said, her voice full of empathy.

Her aunt looked at Arnie long and hard and her words were like fire. "At all times, you must know that you have a share equal to that of your brother in your parent's property, and I am not talking about Ranchi. I am referring to our fight to divide our self-acquired property, Civil Lines."

Arnie sat there rooted to the spot and looked at her in stunned silence, as Chhoti Phua decided to talk.

"We know that you worked hard to bring up your two children, to be both mother and father to them. We watched as you struggled to pay off that huge mortgage and were aghast that she did not help at all. In fact, she went on a shopping spree, buying herself flats in upmarket colonies. We had hoped that she would let you live in one or at least rent it and help you with the loan payments. But not she! We hung our heads with shame when she lamented publicly that you had let her down and that it was our influence, implying that I had manoeuvred this upheaval in your life to make her miserable, that my father was to blame because he had ensured that you grew up in his house rather than die in that incubator in Paris. The nurse in the hospital in France told me that your mother did not even *look* at you or hold you all those weeks before I arrived. The first time you were held was when Yudi picked you up and his wife held you close."

"Yes, I have heard this story before. Yudi mama was in Paris en route to America," Arnie added. "Yes, you were really small but full of life when I brought you back and gave you to your Dadaji. He was waiting anxiously at the airport. He was not known to show his emotions but that day, he cried with relief."

Arnie understood now, understood that her aunt's heady cocktail of love for her, hatred for Kamini, contempt for her weak brother, and the weight of her own mortality had made her seek out her niece.

"Don't say anything, just walk me to the lobby." Arnie nodded mutely as emotions washed over her, for the importance of the older woman's words hit her as she saw her aunt to the car.

Arnie rushed home after meeting Chhoti Phua and logged on to her computer to read the emails she had sent her mother.

'Attention: Kamini Dhari
Dear Mom,
I would just like to make a few things very clear that came up in a recent conversation. I vividly remember one of my last conversations with nani. Asking for my ancestral property, which is rightfully mine, does not make me greedy. I'm not writing this to compromise but to get what is and what has always been mine. I want nothing more than my rightful share.
Having a career is demanding and it has been a struggle to manage it and to bring up the children. My children's happiness is a priority for me.
You as always bring Yudi mama into the conversation, invoking his name to intimidate me, but today I want to understand how Yudi mama fits into this equation.
Civil Lines (being my paternal grandfather's property) is rightfully Randy's and mine. I am ready to sell you my share, but I repeat, I want what is rightfully mine with minimum hassle and squabble.

I respect family and unlike you, do not want court battles; unlike you it does not excite me. I do not want, in my old age, if I am alive, to see Randy's child in court. Let us resolve matters once and for all and finally move on with our respective lives.'

There were so many unanswered questions. Was it possible to sell Civil Lines when it didn't belong only to Arnie's father but to all of the other family members as well? What did 'self-acquired' mean when you had no earnings to buy it in the first place? When no one in that generation actually held a job or ran a business?

Dawn broke. Nothing had changed, it was just another school day and Arnie woke up with a jolt. Chhoti Phua must have twisted the truth yet again, thought Arnie, trying to console herself. Kamini knew the truth that Dadaji had purchased Civil Lines.

Arnie pottered around, making herself some tea. The children rushed in to say goodbye and were stunned to see her tear-streaked face. She flashed them a weak smile and kissed them, muttering, "It will be all right, I am okay. This has to be a misunderstanding. I will call my mother later today."

Sia urged her mother to talk to Yudi. "He always knows what to do, Mum; he is so wise. Promise me that you will," she said. Shrey instantly cheered up and clapped his hands. "Enough," Arnie said, as she nudged them to the door and hurried them along for school.

Picking up the phone nervously, she stared at the mobile screen for several long minutes, mustering up the courage to dial Kamini's number. She punched in the first four digits and disconnected. The time had to be chosen with care, she told herself. It could not clash with Kamini highlighting the headlines in the morning newspaper. It could not clash with her daily party sessions and nightly soirees.

Oh those extravagant night-long parties!

As a child, Arnie had watched from behind the dusty *jaalis*. She had seen the bright lights, felt the beat of the music, and breathed in the mounting excitement. Fur coats, heavy gold jewellery, and rich silks in plum, avocado, and coffee, the air a heady mixture of Chanel and *itar*, of loud laughter and hollow tittering. She had seen the rich and the famous in flesh and blood, but always from afar, from behind those dusty *jaalis*.

And her mother, her mother would flitter and flutter and speak in dulcet tones to seduce one sucker after the other.

Kamini had few friends, for her entire life was about networking and contacts had a shelf life. Names and numbers would vanish from her address book as soon as they ceased to hold on to their important corporate jobs and government portfolios. They would become the fools she no longer cared to suffer. Her eyes were always on the lookout for someone important and powerful, as she flitted in and out of parties.

"I have to get this right," Arnie told herself sternly as Chhoti Phua's words came back to her. She picked up the phone and had just dialled the first two digits when the phone began ringing, shocking her. It was Jaya, her childhood school friend. She was going to be in Noida later in the day and wanted to know if they could meet for lunch. Arnie distractedly said yes to her friend, and then just before she disconnected the call, she blurted out the news to Jaya.

"You met Chhoti Phua?!" Jaya exclaimed, familiar with Arnie's aunt. "Must be after decades, na? How does she look? How old is she now? Are her diamonds as big as they seemed to us in school? Why are you quiet? Is she ill?"

"Something terrible is happening, Jaya," Arnie whispered into the phone, not bothering to answer her friend's questions. "I don't quite know what is going on, but it's as big as Miss Matthew's class."

At the mention of their teacher, Jaya instinctively did a quick imitation of Miss Matthew's soft, wispy voice, transporting Arnie back to their school days, back to Miss Matthew's classroom. They cracked up laughing, remembering the stairs in their school that Kamini had tripped down in unspeakable shock, or was it shame, because Arnie had stood fifth in Class IV.

Jaya suddenly fell silent, remembering how Arnie had stood cowering at the bottom of the stairs as her mother had stomped off angrily. She knew hell had awaited her friend at home that day. But had no one ever stopped to see how Arnie had coped with her mother's abuse? She knew that in spite of the torn uniforms, the holes in her shoes, and the bruises on her arms, Arnie had believed in magic, escaping to a warm fuzzy place in her mind when things became too much to handle. She had tried to hold on, by the tips of her small fingers, to a world where she did not belong, hoping that her mother would love her. That someone would love her. Arnie had always been hungry for a kind word, for the smallest gesture of affection, and often for food. Jaya knew how much Arnie had loved her nani. She used to long for Sunday mornings because that was when they would go over to her nani's house. Arnie would go running to her beloved nani for a hug, hiding her face in the folds of her *Chanderi* sari, as she heard her grandmother laugh at her school stories, making Arnie's little world whole again.

"Don't you have to go to work?" Jaya asked Arnie. "Carry on with your day and make sure you call your mother only after lunch," she cautioned. "Get on with thee," she added when Arnie said nothing, making Arnie giggle.

Arnie began scrambling to get ready for work, having ended the conversation with a promise to call Jaya after speaking with her mother. "Promise," she repeated to herself again before stepping out of the house.

9

'Now that I have opened that bottle of memories,
they're pouring out like wine, crimson and bittersweet.'
— Ellen Hopkins

The dreaded phone call did not take place that day. Or the next. It would take Arnie time to build up the courage to have a routine chat with her mother. And that only happened a week later. The words from that meeting still rang in her head.

She dressed reluctantly for work that morning, filled with foreboding. "This is a habit," she told herself. It was caused by years of being physically beaten up and manipulated by mind games, where Kamini was always the victim and Arnie was blamed for her problems.

Her mother's attitude caused Arnie to go through incredible stress. When she was reading for her CFA professional degree, for instance, Arnie had to drop an accountancy paper because nani had had her first heart attack; she had collapsed in a heap right before her, gasping for air. Kamini, quite typically, had claimed that her mother was merely seeking attention and that she, Kamini, did not deserve such nonsense. When did she ever, for that matter? It was, as always, about her and how India was going to suffer if she stayed away from work, all because of her delusional sense of self-importance.

Arnie's consequent poor result in her accountancy paper dented her confidence, but her mother did not notice.

Arnie's nana was the only one who could see no fault with Kamini and he indulged her beyond reason. Only he, in his eighties at the time, could have said, "*Shabash*" and kissed Kamini on the head when she stole a contract from a rival firm. Did he know that she had used her feminine charms and done things that would have made him cringe in order to secure the deal? Did he know that she had played with his good name and family *izzat*?

Of course not. For the righteous Mr Sharma, nana, the boundaries between right and wrong always got blurred when it came to Kamini, his beautiful daughter. Where he otherwise stood up against injustice, his guilt at having arranged Kamini's supposedly 'hateful' marriage made him partial toward her. He felt he had to be the one to protect her from the world, from her 'evil' in-laws. They were the perfect father-daughter duo, assuming to always know better than anyone else and considering themselves a cut above the rest. Nana had ingrained in his little family unit the value of being a Sharma, repeating again and again that the family name and *izzat* were of supreme importance.

The *izzat* was, however, selective, and Arnie, the only granddaughter of the Sharma household, was to wrap it round herself like a *burkha*, shielding herself from the outside world. Rules that weighed her down didn't seem to apply to others. "Don't jump that high," "Don't talk to boys," "Don't answer back," "Speak softly," "Don't chew with your mouth open," "Don't look there," "Don't wear that," "Don't cross your legs." On and on and on went the list of instructions, and Arnie was forced to conform to them all.

It was time. Time to make that dreaded call. Arnie tried her mother's number, not the full number, but just the first few digits again, and disconnected. "Nothing has changed," she shook her head. "All these years and she still has the same impact on me.

Even today!" Disgusted with herself, she looked at her reflection in the mirror and noticed the red, sleep-deprived, swollen eyes and the tense expression on her face.

She couldn't go on like this. She must call. She had to, and it was best done now even though she was still at work.

"Hello!"

The sound of the all too familiar voice made Arnie freeze. Her mind turned to fudge and her voice was a scared whisper as she said, "Hi, this is . . ."

"I knows who you are," Kamini cut her off, already sounding irritated.

"I-I-I don't want to be in court in my old age," Arnie fumbled. "Let's please sort things out and settle matters. Let's do the right thing. I-I will gladly accept whatever dregs from the family pot that you give me. I will sign away any future rights as well. I may not see Randy these days, but I do wish his family well. I am not the evil aunt, the *badmash phua*. With me out of the way, you can continue your legal battle and settle scores with your in-laws."

Did her mother understand her jumbled words? Could she connect it to the property cases? And what really did she herself expect to hear? That her mother was taking care of her interest? That Chhoti Phua really was a troublemaker? That Arnie should not be concerned about family matters because the elders really did know best and would look after everyone, including her and particularly her vulnerable children? That she should smile and go for lunch with Jaya, secure in the comfort and support of belonging to a family that owned her up?

No, Arnie had not expected this, but neither had she expected what followed!

It began with abuse. As it always did.

"Get me a bloody paper that SAYS you exist, you haramzadi. DO YOU UNDERSTAND? Why should I give you anything? I will do as I want. And yes, Randy will get his due, even though he

74

still bleats about you, that foolish boy. Saying I should give you that plot in the outskirts, which I had told everyone, was for your children when Krish left you. But those were only words, do you understand? I will do as I want! And you are no one, no one at all!"

She was sobbing openly by now and her mother could hear it.

"*Hari mirchi*, always crying! You could not even handle your husband! Did I not tell you that you are an abject failure, a disaster at all relationships? Who told you to marry a struggling artist, huh?"

It was blind anger, Arnie knew, that made Kamini forget that it had been arranged and that it was she who had rushed Arnie into the marriage. And Dadaji, overcome with Alzheimer's, had not been consulted. "And now you talk about your share? What share? I will see you cremated before I give you anything. Everything is self-acquired, even Civil Lines. And I can do what I want. Not even the door latch belongs to you, you haramzadi! Get me a paper, one single sheet, to show me some proof of these rights that you are talking about, you bloody bitch."

"Please! Please think about my children!" Arnie begged her mother.

"Your daughter!" Kamini snorted. "She is a lost cause just like you. Even your son is no good. You are dead to us. All three of you. You should do what my friend's daughter did! Hang yourself and spare us!" she yelled before disconnecting the phone.

The flat tone of the disconnected phone hummed alongside her mother's echoing words in Arnie's head, crushing her strength and deflating her spirit. Time passed. She barely noticed that it was late afternoon.

It was quite late in the afternoon when Arnie snapped out of her stupor and left office, wanting only to get home as soon as possible. As she drove into the condominium, the *dhobi* accosted her but she didn't engage with him, quickly climbing the stairs to her first floor apartment. She reached home, closed the main door, and called out to her children, holding them close, drawing strength from them.

"Papa is here," Shrey announced, wriggling out of his mother's embrace.

"Oh, good. Good," Arnie muttered.

"Is it that wicked witch who has made you sad again?" Shrey asked angrily, sensing his mother's mood. Hurt at being disowned by her, the children had resorted to calling Kamini the 'wicked witch'. Sia shut him up with a glare and taking Arnie's office bag from her, marched her to the living room where Krish was seated.

While Krish and Arnie were still estranged, he had increasingly come back into the lives of the children, and into Arnie's as well. He was making great effort to build back his relationship with his family, prioritising them over everything else. He had taken to spending more and more time with the three of them and the children derived stability and comfort from his presence. Arnie and he were rediscovering a new equation that was difficult to describe. But given the trauma of the moment, Arnie was glad that he was around and she let it out, trying to make sense of it all as she narrated the entire incident.

"Chhoti Phua was right. It is over! There is some court case going on and they are going to sell my Dadaji's house," she moaned. "The house that I grew up in, from where I went to school and college, from where I was married to you. My Civil Lines." She rocked herself back and forth, feeling utterly hopeless and helpless.

"Well, what are you going to do now?" asked the ever-practical Krish. "Is it going to be the same as before? Or do you have a plan? This is your family and your home, so the decision is yours. Do something, or walk away. But stop crying because crying will not solve anything."

His words acted like an unexpected catalyst and in a moment's clarity, Arnie realised that she had to take charge of her life. To decide the way forward. To do something. Anything. But what she didn't know at that moment was that the decision she would take as the setting sun broke the sky into shades of vermilion, lilac, and crimson on that summer day, would be the biggest and the most important one that she would take in a long time.

As Virginia Woolf said:

'You cannot find peace by avoiding life.'

10

'Honesty is a very expensive gift.
Do not expect it from cheap people.'
– Warren Buffet

A poem that she had once read on the Internet resonated in Arnie's head. A young girl, Tara, had written it:

'Not knowing what's wrong or right,
For me I was my only battle left to fight.'

Strangely, however, it was Her voice that Arnie heard repeatedly, egging her on to fight. Kamini's motto was to crush rather than be crushed. To never give in when there was a battle to be fought.

Arnie knew she had to stand up for herself and take the issue head on, not run away from it. The fight was for her children, for her grandchildren, and, finally, for herself. She could not let them crush her spirit. She would not give up without trying.

"Krish, I have decided to fight," she said quietly, feeling the weight of her decision with every word. "I am going to do this because I need to be at peace with myself."

Fight and peace. A strange juxtaposition, but one that defined the essence of her life; one that would ensure that she was not going to let history repeat itself with her children. She would not allow Kamini to crush her children as she had tried to destroy her, her own daughter. Arnie would not allow it. Never. "Are you absolutely sure?" Krish asked.

"Yes Mamma, are you sure?" Sia questioned, her small face scrunched up in worry as she wiped Arnie's tears.

Shrey clutched her hand and kissed it. "Mamma, we have everything, we are happy. We don't need anything else," he said. "And don't fight if it will make you unhappy. You are not good at fighting anyway. You cry too much and worry too much."

Arnie tried to smile through her tears, but it was difficult. "This is for all of us, and for me," she said, trying to explain it to her small children. Her soul felt wrenched into two by her decision. On one hand was the family she had grown up in, and on the other was the one she had created. Sia and Shrey. Arnie knew that she owed it to them, as much as she owed it to herself, to break the pattern and to prevent Kamini from stealing a brighter life from them.

"She continuously referred to some piece of paper this afternoon," Arnie said, suddenly remembering her mother's words.

"Are you sure?" Krish persisted. He had been fiddling away with his iPad and Arnie had been a bit upset with his apparent distraction at a time when she needed his full attention. But he turned to her in triumph now, waving his iPad excitedly. "Look what I found!" he exclaimed, thrusting the tablet at her.

Arnie took the iPad and stared at the screen. It was a number.

Seeing her exasperated expression and before she could berate him, he explained that all court cases were tagged with a reference number and were available on the Internet. "So I found your case! I found it on the High Court website!"

The four of them huddled around the small screen and looked at the case details that appeared under the case number. Boring details, legal terms, adjournments, orders, and rulings on things that Arnie didn't understand. Towards the very end, she saw the name that she had been looking for. There. As large as it could be. Suddenly making everything very real and immediate.

"Hey, that's my dad's name right there," she said jubilantly, pointing to a name on the order. So they had the right case! It was a small beginning, but a beginning nevertheless.

"But who is this Anil Dhari person?" Shrey asked. "Have I met him?"

Arnie ignored the question and addressed Krish. "What do we do now?"

But Krish had already started dialling some numbers on his phone. They ended up calling almost all the lawyers they knew and each one turned them down. Some said that Arnie was too late in coming to them. She should have decided to enter the case much earlier on. Others pointed out that Kamini was known to be nasty and powerful. They were almost at the end of their tether when a lawyer friend finally agreed to get a certified copy of the case file for Arnie, but he was adamant that he would only advise her and not appear for her in court.

"Are you sure about what you are doing?" the lawyer asked.

"No," answered Arnie, "but I have to do this, and I have to win. The consequences of losing will be too terrible to bear."

"Well, I am not too sure of your chances. Procuring the papers is the easy part. Entering a case that has been going on for so many years, and that too without any evidence or documents with you, that is going to be difficult. I would advise against it."

But Arnie was quick to jump up and show her resolve. "I am going to fight this case. Either with you or without you. I appreciate your assistance, but if you can't help me, if you can't get me the papers, then tell me. I will look elsewhere. But fight this case I will!"

"I wish you well," he replied quietly, "and I would help you if I could. But I cannot appear in court for you. As for the papers, you'll have them by next week. I will read through them and we can discuss it, but that is about all that I can do."

"Thank you," Arnie said, accepting his help. She was sure that it would be a long and arduous journey ahead.

An entire week passed before the lawyer got back. "I have sent the papers with my driver," he told Arnie on the phone. "It doesn't look good, the case I mean, it looks messy. I flipped through the papers and the matter is quite complicated. Read the papers and then let's talk," he said, transitioning from friend to lawyer. "Whatever you decide, remember that legal cases often take a long time, even decades, to get resolved. Have patience. Do nothing in a hurry. No *jaldbaazi*. Don't react in haste and repent at leisure. Also, talking is often the best option." He paused for a while, as if mulling over something. "In your case, however, I guess that is not possible. Your mother . . ." He left the sentence incomplete and they hung up because both of them understood the reality perfectly.

Nothing, however, had prepared Arnie for what she saw in the legal file and she was glad she was sitting when she found that one piece of paper that explained her mother's supreme confidence in being able to deny her everything. It was an innocuous piece of paper, stashed deep inside the file, with a simple, equally innocuous looking chart on it. A simple family tree that summed up Arnie's non-existence. She looked through the branches, through the leaves, and down under at the very roots of the family tree before her. Once. Twice. Thrice. But she was nowhere.

How could that be? Her mind screamed. Years and years of the case going on and no one had pointed out to the court that one person was missing from the genealogy? Everyone else was there, all the men and all the other women, but not Arnie.

Desperate to make some sense out of what lay in front of her, Arnie called Jaya and told her everything.

"Jaya, tell me why? What did I do to deserve this?" she asked, her voice a barely audible whisper. "My own mother and the brother I brought up and protected from older cousins have done this to me. I just cannot drown out the noise in my head, Jaya. I can't. It feels like my heart is breaking and my head will burst. And when it does, a big 'why' will pop out."

"I am sorry, Arnie, but your mother has always been mean and nasty; she is pure evil," Jaya said angrily. "But this is just too much even by her standards. What are you going to do now? She is so bloody powerful. Will Yudi mama step in? He has always been upright and he loves you, surely he can sort things out? Don't cry. Think! Where is Krish? Call him. He has seen them closely. They made his life miserable as well. And consult a lawyer. Immediately. Don't talk to anyone from the family before you have spoken with one."

"I will," Arnie said, her heart shattering into a thousand tiny pieces, just like the empty water glasses Kamini used to fling at the wall in rage before turning her anger on her.

She had learnt to recognise the pattern, and she would hide every time she sensed her mother's anger. But Kamini always found her. And then it would begin. She remembered clenching her little hands into tight fists and squeezing her eyes shut, preparing for the beatings to begin "One, two, three" . . . she would count minutes until the familiar darkness would descend and she would pass out from being thrown against the wall. A little midget, slumped on the floor, bleeding, dishevelled, long hair sticking to a tear-stained face, her fringe, whatever had not been plucked or pulled out, stuck to her forehead. The entire night would pass in a haze of pain and tears, and the next morning, she would be shaken awake by the maid, dragged from her hiding spot under the bed, and hurried through the routine of getting ready for school. And with a child's optimism, she would skip to school, hoping that it would be a better day, but it never was.

Her mind had taken Arnie back to the past and Kamini dwarfed her yet again. This was an unequal war; Arnie was not up to her mother's mind games. "I cannot battle with my mother, my parents," she muttered to herself, shaking herself out of that unpleasant memory and then indulging in a bit of dreaming. "They will be so embarrassed when they find out that I know the truth. They will fly across the city and sort it out. They will probably give me less, but they will want to settle with me. We must do as we always do, save face, cover up, and move on. We are, after all, a family in the public eye! The Sharma family is an icon for the emerging middle class."

Publically, Arnie knew it would be presented as a misunderstanding. Kamini would browbeat everyone into declaring that she was looking out for her daughter and that her mother's heart stopped her from involving Arnie in a protracted legal battle. "Arnie, the poor girl, she has enough going on in her life without us dragging her into court-*kecheri*." That would be the public line.

But things were not going to run by the usual script, and Arnie's story took on a life of its own.

She started by calling lawyers, but one after the other, every one of them seemed to feel that taking on her case would be futile. Her mother was just too powerful to challenge. And to add to that, she had no evidence to back her claim that it was her grandfather who had bought the Civil Lines house and not her father or his siblings.

Arnie drowned her anxiety in action. She had exhausted her list of lawyers and decided to reach out to a wider circle. She called an ex-colleague, now a corporate biggie, and after small talk, Arnie got to the point. "I need help," she said, "legal help. My family, my mother to be more exact, is doing me out of my grandfather's property, and the case is difficult. Not one lawyer wants to take on my family and I simply don't know what to do!"

Arnie's friend heard her out quietly and then, after thinking for about a minute or so, she said, "I have a close friend who is a lawyer, quite fearless at that. He does not shy away from a fight.

Let me speak with him and find out if he will see you. Give me an hour."

And in less than an hour, she had not only spoken to her lawyer friend, but she also made Arnie talk to him, and before Arnie knew it, she had an appointment to meet Ramesh, the lawyer!

Full of anticipation, Arnie rushed to his office a couple of hours later.

"I have been briefed by your friend, but I need to see a copy of your case file," he said the minute they met. "Meanwhile, tell me all that you know."

Ramesh was shaking his head by the time Arnie got to the end of the story. "As I see it, you have a story, but no evidence to support it. And from what I can make out, the money came from your grandfather's adoptee parents. Where is the adoption decree? Any idea?"

Arnie nearly gave in at this moment. Her grandfather had been born at the turn of the twentieth century. How could she ever access an adoption decree from then? Did it even exist? And where would she look for one, even if it existed? From what Ramesh seemed to imply, without this one piece of paper, she had no hope of proceeding. She was, at best, clutching straws! Arnie felt completely demolished.

"Don't look so defeated," Ramesh said, sensing her despair. "First thing you need to do is write down everything you know in a chronological order. That will help us get a clearer picture before we can begin with the actual work. I need everything, the names of your grandparents, the names of your grandfather's real parents, and those of his adoptee parents." Seeing Arnie start to panic, he tried to put her at ease. "You might be underestimating your own ability to recall events; mull over it tonight and we will talk tomorrow."

Krish had driven Arnie to the lawyer's office. On the way back, she asked him, "Should I turn to Yudi mama for help?"

"Yudi Sharma!" he exclaimed. "He will go off on a different tangent altogether. 'Forget about material things. Such a life is futile. Meditate!' And such rubbish," he scoffed.

Arnie giggled at the absurdity of the thought. "Do you remember that he had actually asked me to do exactly that—meditate?" she asked, reminding Krish of an email that her uncle had sent two years ago.

When they reached her apartment, she switched on her laptop and scrolled through her inbox looking for that email. She found the message without difficulty, but this time, when she read the words again, Arnie felt the ground give way; what had been an innocent-sounding email took on a different meaning now.

He had been her hero, a bit strange and cuckoo at times, but he had always been there for her.

Or had he?

The email was no longer as innocuous as it had seemed. It was a distraction, an attempt to guide Arnie down the wrong path and to convince her that she was jumping at shadows and seeing ghosts where there were none.

Dear Aranya,
I'm extremely heartbroken on receiving your oh-so-depressing email. Money has no meaning in today's world . . . what you truly need is inner peace. This will be beneficial to you and your kids . . . Do start Bikram hot yoga and meditation. It shall help you immensely. Follow my lead . . . I meditate anywhere and everywhere, in the bath, in office, after office, in the car. Just keep meditating. It brings ecstasy and inner calm. Forget matters of the past and the future, just FOCUS on that chakra surrounding you.
You have beautiful children who will have

ample wealth and luxuries when they grow up . . . All you need to do is take care of yourself . . . have a good diet. Vegetables, fruits, cereals in the right amount, they are all integral for your well-being. Stay away from sugary and overly salty food. Even caffeine is a big no-no. After all, a healthy body leads to a healthy mind.

Harness your mind, Aranya. It is like a wildly bucking horse. Pull the reins and forget everything else.

Please go to the market and immediately get *The Miracle of Mindfulness* by Thich Nhat Hanh. He is one of the great teachers of modern times and his book will be of immense help to you. You must also see a counsellor. You must realise the power of following my example of keeping high standards. And appreciate the acts of moral instruction. It does tire me that you are such a slow learner.

Will call you in the evening.

Love,

Yudi mama

PS: Sometimes we tend to read more into events than necessary. For instance, it is only now that I learnt of the baby that Randy and Dolly are expecting—wonderful news, but why should we have been told of the baby earlier?

Krish, who had been reading the email over Arnie's shoulder, guffawed and muttered, "'Meditate,' my foot! More like 'masturbate', the pretentious bastard!" But the look on Arnie's face shut him up.

"Krish, he fooled me!' she cried. "He distracted me! I knew there was something going on which is why I had asked him for advice. Two years is a long time. If only I had gone to court two years ago, I would have been in a better position than I am in now!"

Arnie fell silent. She could remember the context of the email clearly. It was about Randy, her brother, and the thought made her grimace. They had been close once, but, over the past few years, coldness had swept over the warmth they had shared. Arnie had been told only a few short weeks before his little baby was born, that his wife had been expecting, because she had, in their minds, assumed the role of Baby Singh, the evil aunt. She had turned into a bad omen for them.

As always, she had reached out to Yudi mama then, seeking a reason for having been kept in the dark. "Did he know?" she wondered now, a niggling doubt emerging in her mind that he had played her. And manipulated her. The deception, the enormity of it all washed over her, wreaking the same damage as a tidal wave.

However, years of conditioning and unflinching belief kicked in the next moment, making Arnie surrender to her image of him. In her mind, Yudi mama was this God-like being, completely devoid of greed and malice and any human failing whatsoever, a divine being with a halo of virtue and brilliance and unmitigated goodness around him. He was her saviour at all times, her dear Yudi mama, and she chided herself for thinking otherwise. "Yudi mama always does what is right, strictly upholding the Sharma values," she told herself. She could always call him, like she normally would have, and seek answers, but for some reason that she couldn't explain to herself, she decided against it and sat staring, instead, at the computer screen blankly. "Where do I even begin?" she wondered. She had no dates, no fixed definitive details, just a vague memory of their family history.

Krish had left soon after having dropped her home. After seeing him out of the door, Arnie had walked around the house in a daze. She vaguely registered the children coming home from the park and all of them sitting down to eat dinner. Did she eat or not? She wasn't quite sure. She sat by the big French window in the living room for a long while, taking in the view passively.

Arnie's mind went back to her memories of security and happiness in an otherwise troubled childhood. Memories of her nani who was the centre of her world, and of Yudi mama. Arnie learnt early on that she could laugh only at his jokes when with him. She hated Urdu couplets because she couldn't understand them but had to look impressed when Yudi mama burst into one.

'Sarkash hain jo darakht un par samar nahin
Pur samar hain jo darakht uthate voh sar nahin.'

It was much later that Arnie realised that the oft-repeated verse was said with a purpose. She had to be like the humble mango tree bent with fruit, never daring to lift her head. Whereas her brother, like the lofty eucalyptus, could be haughty and hold his head high.

"Enough for today," she told herself sternly after a while, and getting up, she went and snuggled up with her little children. But the conversation with Ramesh played in her mind. She remembered his perplexed expression as she had narrated her story. "What is behind this? Is she your real mother?" he had asked incredulously. Arnie had nodded and looked down. "There must be someone who can reason with them?" he had continued, and then, giving up, he had told her to email the details starting from the beginning.

So, what then was the beginning? The beginning! Arnie's tired mind wondered whether it was when she was born or when her grandfather was. Or was it when he died? Or will it be when she dies?

11

'You have power over your mind, not outside events.
Realise this, and you will find strength.'
— Marcus Aurelius

It was difficult for Arnie to deal with work while she was still grappling with the enormity of the situation and trying to answer the questions Ramesh had asked. She had slept uneasily the night before and had woken up with a headache. She had somehow pushed herself to get ready for work, but she was having a particularly sluggish day.

"Perhaps I should Google for answers?" she thought as she sat staring blankly at her computer.

Strange how the world had changed. A company that was unknown until a decade ago now had its name used as a verb! Google Maps to begin with, Arnie decided. She quickly opened the application—India was there, of course, and she zoomed in on Delhi, and then down to Civil Lines. There was a long winding road with strategically placed houses, and then she spotted a school she remembered from those days marked out on the map. Arnie sat back. She could still hear the loud gong of the school bell that had become a marker for her day.

A loud burst of music brought Arnie back into the present.

A shot in the dark
A past, lost in space
Where do I start

David Guetta sang out loudly from the BlackBerry. The song was Arnie's ringtone for incoming calls. It was an unknown number. Arnie picked up the phone and before she could even say hello, a muffled voice spoke from the other end:

"Civil Lines has been sold, you are too late, Aranya."

And click, the line went dead.

Stunned, Arnie sat frozen for a full minute before she snapped back and tried redialling the number, only to find it switched off. Panicking, she called Ramesh and then Krish, but neither of them was reachable. She left them a million frantic messages. Was it actually over? Her mind raced. Snippets, flashes, memories. Panicking, she called Jaya. Jaya would understand. Jaya knew about her attachment to that *jhoola* on the old mango tree in the aangan and those chipped red brick walls and the weed-filled, mossy gardens. It was her home. Her Civil Lines. Jaya would know what to do.

"Jaya ... Jaya ... Jayaaaa!" Arnie cried out the minute her friend picked up the phone.

"Arnie! What is it?!" Jaya exclaimed, alarmed at the agony in Arnie's voice.

"Civil Lines has been sold, Jaya! It's sold! It's gone! My Civil Lines is gone!" Arnie shrieked into the phone.

"What? How do you know?"

"I got a call. Unknown number. Some strange person." She shuddered as she spoke. "He told me that Civil Lines has been sold. I am still shaking, Jaya. His voice was sinister. And h-h-he called me Aaa-Ran-Yaa! Carefully pronouncing my name. Each syllable!"

Arnie suddenly began feeling extremely suffocated. Her breath was coming out in short bursts. She felt trapped in quicksand, sinking deeper as she desperately struggled to get out. "He-he-help me, Jaya!"

"Arnie, calm down," Jaya instructed, sensing that her friend was having a panic attack. "I will call that number from my landline and find out in a minute who the person was, okay? Have some coffee until then."

But Jaya couldn't get through the number either. "You have to call your lawyer or Krish or anyone else who can help because this number does not exist," she told Arnie gently. "And remember," she said just before hanging up, "a big house like this cannot be sold in a day. Not even your mother can manage this. It's not a family tree drawn on a piece of paper."

Arnie felt incredibly lonely after Jaya hung up. She had urged her to hurry. But hurry and do what? Go where? Her soul felt oppressed by the weight of the past even as the present held her in a vice-like grip, squeezing her harder and harder, drawing the very breath out of her body. The veins at the side of her head throbbed, as if keeping beat to the blood rushing in her ears. Squeeze, squeeze, matched by swoosh, slosh. She stared at the lines on her palms.

Our destiny lies etched in our hands. "Destiny; what is destined for me?" she wondered.

Back when Jaya and she had been in kindergarten, they had often sat on the roof of the *barsati* overlooking the aangan of the Civil Lines house, surrounded by tall mango and neem trees. They would look at the lines on their palms. At the twists and turns. The little branches. Wondering about their future. And on a lucky day, the *totawalah* sat with his cards neatly arranged in front of him and a squawking parrot next to him. As he waited patiently outside the wooden gates of the house, they'd go rushing to him to have their fortunes read. And on his command, the parrot would swagger out and pick up a card that would determine their future. They would squeal with delight as the *totawalah* would recite their destiny. "You will marry a fat man." "You will face an embarrassing moment." "You will be the mother of ten children."

Today, looking down at those very lines on her palm, Arnie still believed that what was hers would be hers. No soothsayer, talking parrot, or fortune-teller could change her will to survive and her desire to live life on her own terms.

Like in most traditional Indian households, any kind of superstition was an integral part of the Dhari family routine. There were omens of good luck and of things that could go wrong. A new moon. A horseshoe. The nut of the *rudraksh* tree. All these were good. The old bungalow perched on Civil Lines faced south. In *vaastu* terms, this was lucky. Dadaji, being a strong believer in tradition, would start his mornings with prayers. Bare-chested, in his white *dhoti*, the sacred thread, *jeneu*, across his chest, wearing *kharaon* or wooden clogs, he offered water to the sun as he did the *surya namaskaar*. *Havans* would be performed once every month to ward away all evil from the house. The family would gather around the crackling amber flames while the priest poured spoonsful of *ghee* into the hungry fire.

Arnie smiled to herself because her prayers were so simple. She prayed that she would not annoy her mother and became a good girl so that her mother would love her. Chhoti Phua had, on one occasion, found Arnie sobbing in the corner of the aangan and had tied a black thread, strung with an *Aum* locket around her neck. Arnie had clutched it when Kamini shouted at her. The cold metal had clung to Arnie's chest. She didn't know then or now if it was Chhoti Phua's mindless brainwashing or her blind faith, but she had felt protected. Arnie wished she had it now; she really needed protection and help.

The mobile phone rang. It was Ramesh. She had a sense of

foreboding, of urgency and apprehension, as she just stared at the blinking phone that flashed her lawyer's name. Anxiousness at hearing about progress was mixed with anxiety. She felt anxiety and apprehension as she bent forward to pick up the mobile and raised it to her ear as though in slow motion.

"Hi Ramesh. Is there any news?" she asked.

"Aranya, I just got your messages. Don't worry. Things cannot move so fast. It is a court matter and these things take time. I will find out the exact status of things and let you know, okay?"

"Hmm . . ."

"We have several options open before us," he went on. "We can try to enter this matter or we can file a new petition of our own."

Arnie lost track of what Ramesh was saying after that. She just slumped into her office chair, feeling small and afraid and tired. Ramesh eventually hung up, saying he would call her back later. The room felt dark around her in spite of the sunlight pouring in. It was a hot summer day outside, but Arnie shuddered as if the cold was seeping into her bones.

The rest of the day went by in a blur as Arnie mechanically went through the motions. Nodding, smiling, attending meetings and reviews, even cracking a joke to ease the tension, making the children do their homework, having dinner, listening to them chatter. An attempt to distract herself.

The call came much later that night, after her children had gone to bed.

"It is over. Civil Lines will be sold by court order!" It was her bhabhi. "All the parties have given it in writing that they will come up with a scheme for the sale. We'll be free, finally."

Arnie held her breath as she spoke, diving into a cesspool of emotion and emerging with a fistful of questions. "When did this happen? Today?"

"Don't ask!" her bhabhi exclaimed. "It was a miracle

because both of *them*," she was referring to Chhoti Phua and Kamini, "did not resist or argue. I was stunned, and even the lawyers were stunned when these two did not raise any absurd objections! There was complete silence as the judge dictated the order for us to come up with a scheme to sell the property," she said jubilantly.

"Who is the buyer?" Arnie asked hoarsely, her world crashing around her.

"The court has asked everyone to submit bids if they have buyers. So we will find out soon enough who the buyer is," she rambled on as Arnie inhaled deeply, spluttering like a diver emerging from the bowels of the deep dark sea.

"So it is true," Arnie repeated to herself again and again. "I am late, very late!" Without pausing to think about the time, she dialled Ramesh's number.

"I was just going to call you," Ramesh said the minute he picked up the phone. "There have been certain developments in the case," he continued, not waiting for Arnie to say something. "They're not good, not in our favour, but all is not lost, not yet," he said slowly and deliberately.

"But what will you be doing?" Arnie spoke up for the first time. "Is there anything that can be done or have I lost before I even started?"

"Well, to be honest, things are quite bad. But you must understand that as a lawyer, I have seen the most improbable scenarios turning around, confirmed winners suddenly losing everything. *Jungle ka mamla hai, kuch bhi ho sakta hai.*"

"But what is it that you plan to do?" asked Arnie, interrupting him. "These are fine words, but do we have a strategy? What are the steps that I should take? What are my options? Will we ever actually get before a judge?!"

"All you need to do is answer all my questions honestly and find me the name of your great grandfather and that adoption decree," Ramesh said, as if what he was asking for was the easiest thing for Arnie to do. "We will talk tomorrow after court, and relax a little, Aranya. I'm on it!"

Arnie called Jaya after Ramesh hung up. "Jaya, I should have done something earlier. It is too late now!" she said, telling her about the imminent sale.

"It is never too late until it is over," Jaya retorted right back, typically practical and composed. "I understand your grief, and even I am shocked, but go to sleep for now. You are exhausted right now. Things will look different tomorrow."

"But Jaya, where will I begin tomorrow? The damn lawyer wants an adoption decree." Arnie almost spat out the words. "Do you even know your great grandfather and *his* father's names?" she asked to prove her point.

"Yes," Jaya replied smugly. "I asked my mother about it this afternoon, much to her surprise. Remember that the writing on your forehead cannot be changed. No one can go against what is in your destiny."

Arnie groaned. "Jaya, please! I need help! I need my great grandfather's name and my grandfather's adoption decree. Any idea where I should begin my search for a faceless, nameless ancestor?"

She giggled the next instant, exhaustion giving way to laughter as the absurdity of her situation finally dawned upon Arnie. Jaya joined her the next moment, and they both collapsed into peals of helpless laughter. A weak goodnight was all they could manage through their giggles when they hung up a little later.

A slight sudden tap on her shoulder a minute later made Arnie shriek with fright. It was Shrey, looking scared and frightened, and clearly having just had a nightmare.

Arnie grabbed Shrey, taking him into her arms and reassuring him that all was well. He moved to the centre of the bed, closer to Sia, and Arnie curled up beside him, grateful for the familiar warmth of his little body pressed against hers and the gentle clasp of his hand as he drifted back to sleep, content and safe.

Peace radiated from her sleeping children and enveloped Arnie in a deep soothing embrace as she struggled to sleep. "You cannot take more, you cannot give less," she chanted to herself until eventually, sleep claimed her.

12

'Not all those who wander are lost.'
– JRR Tolkien

▼

Arnie sat in the office canteen trying to eat but couldn't. A rather familiar smell made her look up from the plate in front of her to see who had brought *aloo ka chokha* and *achaar*. It reminded her of the Civil Lines aangan. There were always large jars of freshly made pickle kept out in the sun in the aangan. Sweet and sour mango pickle, plump red chillies, sharp bitter lemons, mixed vegetables. The sun would beat down on the glass bottles, and after six patient months of waiting, the bottles would be opened and the pickles enjoyed with stuffed *paranthas*.

Arnie got up and left the canteen, the pleasant memory of all those pickle bottles in the sun a welcome distraction. Back at her desk, she Googled *aloo chokha* and read the recipe, smiling as she remembered Chhoti Phua's regular arguments with the family cook about his mechanical style of cooking. While he would carefully measure cinnamon, milk, flour, *ghee*, and sugar, Chhoti Phua would literally fling chilly powder, cumin seeds, a fistful of onions, and salt into her famous *Jhal Machli*. The sizzling oil, the constant bustle, and the spicy gossip made the kitchen a very 'happening' place in the house with pots and pans constantly being moved around, and *garam masala* hurled into *karahis*. And all of this would be accompanied by Baby Singh's bantering with the family retainers, the topic of their conversation always remaining the same. Complaints about Kamini. And Arnie, she remembered listening to them intently even as she watched the live fish thrash in the *Dalda* tin before they were plucked out of the water and thrown into the smoking oil.

Ramesh called her a little later in the day. If nothing happened over the next few days, he said, the High Court would break for its annual summer vacation and that would give them more time to prepare for the case, to strategize, and gather more background information. He wanted the fact sheet from Arnie as soon as possible, even if it was an incomplete one. He also suggested that a litigator should represent Arnie. Not knowing any better, she readily agreed and they decided to speak again in a couple of days.

Krish, meanwhile, was in far off Bhutan. Beautiful, idyllic, remote, and isolated from the rest of life, from Arnie. She needed to speak with him, to use him as a sounding board and she cursed her luck that he was out of contact. He might as well be on a mission to Mars for all the help he could give at this moment. In any event, she sent him a text message, pressing the send button and launching her words on the strength of a silent prayer, hoping they got to him before he boarded the return flight.

The next few days passed in a daze. Arnie was anxious when Ramesh called and said that there was a court hearing the next day! However, he had found a senior lawyer who would appear on her behalf. "I have seen the fact sheet you sent," he said before Arnie could panic, "and we have made progress. I found a litigator who has agreed to appear for you. I have briefed him. He will appear in court tomorrow and listen to the proceedings, and if things go out of hand, he will speak on your behalf.

"It is difficult, you see," Ramesh continued. "We have no supporting documents. And getting more papers from the court seems daunting as it is, and to get them by tomorrow is impossible.

So let's hope there is no action in court and we can use the vacation to our advantage."

"How did it get so bad?" Arnie asked herself later that night. 'There is a tide,' the Bard had said, but in her case, it was more like a tsunami. She felt disoriented, her thoughts galloping wildly into the past and dragging her away at the same time. Her story had begun unspooling with a great speed that she could no longer control it.

Night turned to dawn and the pewter moon faded somewhere into the lightening sky.

"So today is the day," Arnie told herself as she walked over to the bathroom and stood looking at her reflection in the mirror, noting the dark circles under her eyes, her face taut with tension.

The day dragged on. Arnie noted the hours pass on her wristwatch and kept checking her mobile phone every other minute for messages and missed calls. But it wasn't until almost seven in the evening when Ramesh called. His tone told Arnie that the day had not gone well. Hope faded with the setting sun.

"Everything happened very fast," he began. "They came to court prepared, ready with an agreement that has been put on record now. The judge passed an order which states that the sale of your Civil Lines house has to be completed within three months. All parties who are interested in finding buyers are to submit sealed bids to the court. And the winning bidder will have controlling right over the matter. He or she will decide what to do and will have to apportion the money out to the rest of the family members. And, the court vacation begins from tomorrow."

They both fell silent. Arnie tried to frame a response, but found herself unable to think of a single thing to say, and they hung up eventually.

On her way home a little later, Arnie passed the malls that she drove past every day. She watched the glittering lights as always. Yet, today it all seemed different. She saw people walking out, loaded with packages, smiling, talking to each other, hurrying along, happy with themselves. How she envied them!

When she walked into her apartment, Sia ran to her and hugged her. "What's for dinner?" she asked innocently and then reminded her mother about her dance performance the next day.

Arnie groaned and found herself telling Sia that it all depended on the meeting with the lawyers; it was a phrase that would be repeated again and again in the days to come. This was just the beginning.

Arnie's BlackBerry rang just then. It was Chhoti Phua, her voice laced with obvious relief.

"Jaante ho, *aaj* order pass *ho gaya,* beta. Civil Lines has been sold. One of the family members, maybe your parents, will arrange the sale and pay us a court-determined price. They will buy us out. I thought I should give you the good news. Finally it is all over! We will get our money. Civil Lines is sold! Aranya beta, why are you so quiet? What is the matter?"

Feeling dejected and broken, Arnie was at her wit's end, but she refused to give up, and mustering up enough courage, she decided to nevertheless ask her aunt for information regarding the family history. After all, if Ramesh had said they would talk later, surely then, there could still be possibly some way out!

"Nothing, Chhoti Phua, I just started thinking about the house," Arnie hastened to reassure her aunt. "Anyway, Sia has to make a family tree for a school project and she needs to start with the names of Dadaji and Nana's fathers. Unfortunately, however, I really don't remember their names. Could you please help me out?"

Chhoti Phua, God bless her, had an excellent memory, and she promised to help Sia out with forgotten details about their family background.

Once she put the phone down, Arnie felt a strong yearning for some comfort food—her nani's famous *sooji ka halwa*! Quickly going to her study, she rummaged through her papers until she found it, her nani's old cookbook and there, scribbled in a neat running hand was the recipe for *sooji ka halwa*.

"Aida," Arnie called out to her maid. "Aida! We're going to make lots and lots of *sooji ka halwa* today!" she told her, beginning to read out the recipe.

Heat *ghee* in a pan and when hot, add 1 and 1/2 cups *sooji* and mix well.

Roast the *sooji* (stirring frequently) till it begins to turn a very light golden brown and gives off a faint aroma. The roasted *sooji* will have the grainy consistency of wet sand. Now add plenty of almonds and raisins to the *sooji* and mix well.

In a separate pot, and on medium heat, bring a mixture of 3 cups of water, 1/2 cup sugar, and 5 pods of cardamom to a boil, stirring often.

When the *sooji* is roasted, gently add the water mixture, stirring all the while to prevent lumps from forming. Cook the mixture till it thickens and begins to come away from the sides of the pan.

Arnie took her first spoonful of the *halwa*; the soft, warm, granules melted in her mouth. She took bites of happiness, savouring the memories that came with each bite. Her nani used to make the *halwa* only on special occasions, like birthdays and Diwali. "Today, nani," Arnie whispered, "is special, for today my fight begins, and I won't back down, no matter what they say or do."

13

*'You can break down a woman temporarily but a real
woman will always pick up the pieces, rebuild herself
and come back stronger than ever.'*
– *Anonymous*

Krish was back from the Mountain Kingdom. Hearing him come in, Arnie rushed out desperately, feeling the tension leave her when he walked in through the door. "All seems to be lost, Krish; there is a court order allowing Civil Lines to be sold off and apparently my parents will arrange the sale and pay the other family members a court-determined price," she said.

"Calm down, calm down!" Krish cut her off, sounding quite terse. He appeared to be trying hard to control his anger. Forcing Arnie to sit down, Krish looked at her and said, "I will speak to the lawyer later, but first you have to listen to me." Reaching out to take her hand in his, he continued, "You must believe that all has not been lost. That you have a right. And that we have to find a way to get it . . . okay?"

Arnie nodded and looked away. "Do you think my mother realises that I know?" she spoke up suddenly. "How do you think she will react when she finds out that I know? You know, I have tried to think back and find a reason for her extreme dislike for me and figure out when and why it took root."

She looked up at him with tears that told their story of abject despair and rejection. Restless, she got up and began pacing the room. She opened cupboards, shut drawers, rearranged chairs, papers, books, everything.

Ramesh called just then, and Krish spoke to him, fixing a meeting for a little while later. They sped towards the lawyer's office in Krish's car soon after. At India Gate, they got stuck in a traffic jam because of VIP movement, and Arnie, with nothing else to do, looked out of the window towards that magnificent archway built in blocks of the finest sandstone, each stone engraved with the name of a martyred soldier. She noticed the huge beehives under the arch only as they inched closer towards the monument, beehives as big as jackfruits.

"You know, Krish," Arnie spoke wistfully, "when I was in school, Jaya and I would sneak out in the evenings, just before my mother came back. Not that she cared where I was, but well, we used to go to Kashmere Gate. It would be pulsating with life in the evenings—balloon-sellers and toy-makers peddling cheap products; lantern-shaped streetlamps haloed with insects. The highlight of our trip was an ice cream if I had managed to get a few coins from Chhoti Phua. It is amazing, Krish, what happiness these memories bring. I would take out a 50 *paise* coin and pay for both Jaya and me."

The traffic moved as the light changed and Krish speeded up because they were running late. Arnie continued with her stories in an attempt to contain her nervousness.

"Krish, I remember those Sunday mornings when Chhoti Phua would be in an adventurous mood; it used to be so much fun. She would pile us into her blue Standard Herald and whisk us off to Lodi Garden. She would insist that her son and our older cousin also join in. You know, Krish, until kindergarten, whenever I was asked to draw a picture of my family, I would show my parents with three sons and me on the side. For me, they were my brothers, just like Randy. It was only after my mother threw my sketch into the dustbin and slapped me across the face that

I reluctantly drew only Randy." She stopped only for a second, letting the pain wash over her face momentarily before continuing with her reminiscences again.

"Chhoti Phua would point out the nuances of Mughal architecture, from whatever little she knew, as we walked through the garden. And the picnic, oh Krish! The picnic in itself was such an elaborate logistical exercise. Tailing our car would be a dirty, dusty vehicle, packed with servants who carried everything from a large thermos of spiced sweet masala chai to a *durrie* to cricket bats and what not. The picnic basket was a huge wicker trunk lined with a red checked cloth, which would be strapped to the roof of the car. And the driver, he had quite a task. Every time he would use the brakes, Chhoti Phua would yelp and admonish him to be careful, for the basket was loaded with goodies that could spill and fall, and we would giggle as she clucked and shook her head all the way. There were endless turns on what seemed like a never-ending dusty road to the garden, and all the way there, we would count the passing cows, the red lights we crossed, and the hundred honks and the thousand songs we heard.

"Chhoti Phua would stuff tiny finger sandwiches, stuffed potato and pea samosas, and small pies and muffins and a hundred different kinds of sweets and savouries into the picnic basket. After eating to our heart's content, Randy and I would run around the garden. Playing. Hiding. Chasing each other.

"I was fascinated by the two central tombs, and I remember begging Chhoti Phua to read what was written on the stone blocks, the finely etched slender Islamic script. I used to be so disappointed that she couldn't because I believed that she could do almost anything. But it was not her, it was Yudi mama who was invincible and knew everything."

Arnie had paused, in thought. Family members had played different roles in her life. Chhoti Phua had been the person with whom she did things, while Yudi mama had been her hero. The thought had vanished almost as soon as it bubbled up.

Still caught up in her sepia memories, they finally reached the lawyer's office. They waited for Ramesh in the reception area, chatting quietly. Arnie opened the case files and began flipping through the pages. These papers held the answer to her questions; if only she could find the relevant parts. Turning to the detailed list of properties attached towards the end, she began to read them out aloud to Krish.

"Hanumannagar, Ferozepur, Civil Lines, and . . ."

Krish grabbed the list from her, looking unnecessarily excited. "Did you say Civil Lines? Did you?"

Arnie nodded, a bit irritated. "I not only said Civil Lines, but also Hanumannagar, Ferozepur, and acres and acres of orchards and farmlands scattered all over. Civil Lines is the most obvious property, yes, but look at the rest of the list. It is really quite a lot."

The receptionist called them just then, gesturing that Ramesh was ready to see them.

"Good stuff," Ramesh said as they walked into his chamber. "Much progress, I say. I have read the revised fact sheet, and the jigsaw seems to be falling into place, bit by bit. But we have to file immediately after the court reopens if we want to prevent the sale."

Krish jubilantly pointed out the list of properties attached to the case file, and Ramesh looked visibly pleased after he scanned through them. Sinking into his chair, he ordered a round of coffee with a flourish. "You have found a smoking gun," he said with satisfaction.

They discussed strategy and Arnie took Ramesh through the family history, struggling to come to terms with what her parents had done.

"There is not much else," she said towards the end. "I was always told that I was ordinary and not good enough, although I did do reasonably well in school and college . . ."

Krish interrupted her at that point. "Reasonably well? Ramesh, she topped CBSE, studied English Literature at Queen's College, and then got a full scholarship to London University! She has single-handedly built a career, brought up two kids, and paid off the mortgage on her flat." Then, a little softly, "She has been let down by everyone in her life, including me. But at least I regret what I have done and want to be there for her, unlike those brutes."

Arnie flashed him a small smile and reached out for his hand. "This is not about us, Krish, and the past is just that. The past. It's over. And I am not applying to Ramesh for a job," she quipped, trying to lighten the mood.

"Well, this is not an ordinary case and these are not ordinary people that we are fighting. As a lawyer, I have seen all sorts of family fights, but this is rare even for me—a mother doing out her own daughter—Aranya, do you have proof that her ill-treatment has a pattern? That this action is in continuation with past hostility?"

Arnie nodded and took out her laptop, wanting to show him the email exchanges between her mother and her.

She scrolled down her inbox until she found the one particular email she had in mind, and then turned the laptop towards Ramesh, feeling sad as he read it. She buried her nose in the cup of cold Cafe Latte in front of her.

```
Subject: Re: Heartbroken
After an important day at work and key
meetings I have arrived home, only to read
your email. In response to your email I
have to bring forward points of my own.
How you say that I didn't understand your
pain? When for so many years I myself faced
the same devastation caused by your bloody
Chhoti Phua? You have always accused me of
```

being 'wicked', 'power hungry', 'plastic', 'unfaithful'.

YOU are ready to believe that it was me who caused evil into your life. YOU want to point up finger at me for crushing you, my little daughter. YOU are willing to believe that all that hate in your life was pre-planned by me and executed in cold revenge. YOU are determined that it was my mission to hurt you and get pleasure . . . and then party? YOU say this is truth and this is what YOU want only to believe.

As you say goodbye, I want to say how simple it will be to say 'sorry' falsely to you to stop this countless emails.

Why you drag Randy into this. You two were deeply affectionate beings. Why you say that you and Krish were only there for him? In truth he was there for you and flew to meet YOU. YOU have to realise why me and Randy's behaviour changed regarding YOU. With your mean sms, msg, mails you have furthered us all and made talks with you next to impossible.

It was me who went for Grandparents Day, to Sia and Shrey's school. Encouraging their small talents.

I never expected this partition day to come . . . But it so has and it's horrid and bad but that's that. You have told us to let you be and we are willingly agreeing, so be it. But remember you told US.

If this farewell's your meaning of 'closure' then so be it . . . I know absolutely certainly that I, Daddy, and Randy will always love you. Randy's little daughter will be told

107

about her phua for sure when she grows up a
bit but will also be spared your evil nazar.
You are too much like your Chhoti Phua and we
are listening to you to stay away from your
litter. Remember no fault of ours; we do as
told so that you are happy.

I pray this farewell gives you the happy
times you wished for, increase your happiness
levels and double-multiply your future
dreams. May God's hand guide yours.

P.S. That wealthy famous actor-politician who
I had lunch with today was giving me powerful
insight on today's fickle, materialistic,
selfish generation which I'm giving talk on
Vee Stars channel at 4 today.

"Unbelievable! Your mother has conveniently blamed her
actions on the world and on some Chhoti Phua, and that too so
cunningly that even I am amazed!" Ramesh exploded. "She is
writing for effect, measuring every word before writing so that
there is nothing legally binding! What did you write that made her
reply in such a manner?"

Arnie looked up at him, her eyes watery, her soul drooping,
and head throbbing. There was a long letter that she had written,
but she could not bring herself to share its contents with Ramesh
just yet. She tried explaining everything to him and told him that
she had, in her letter, referred to the brutal beating, the verbal
abuse, and the humiliation and deprivation of her childhood that
extended far beyond anything explainable, and which was now
threatening to consume her children too.

Ramesh was angry. "I would have done a lot worse for what
she has done to you in the past and which, from what I can see,
is criminal."

Quietly, Arnie filled him in, telling him that she had wanted to run away from all the drama and had said so in an email. She had wanted closure, and hence the 'goodbye' Kamini had referred to in her email, but all of this had been even before she knew the extent of what her mother was capable of. Finally, she opened the email she had written and gestured to Ramesh to read it.

Subject: Heartbroken

Mom this is my last and final attempt to express my feelings to you. I don't want your diplomatic 'official' replies. I just want my MOTHER to read this mail.

The never-ending questions and 'WHYS' festering in my mind are becoming hard to silence so I write this mail to you not in spite nor with bitterness, but to silence those voices. To silence that pain and rejection that has eaten its way into my mind. To silence that feeling of being inferior or not worthy enough.

Today, I am a mother and have supported my children SINGLE-HANDEDLY. In all honesty, it has not been easy. I too, have faced my share of ups and downs. And by no stretch am I a perfect mother. I'm human.

So, I write this letter to the human being behind the thick caked make-up, glitzy jewellery, designer costumes and glamorous roles. I write this letter to my mother.

When I close my eyes the most vivid memory of my childhood flashes before me in black, white, and red. Mom, why, WHY was I thrashed, thrown against the walls for no fault? WHY was I your venting-bag?

I still feel the pungent sting of your comments. Bright like the red lipstick, brighter bindi and dark like the stubborn kohl around your eyes and your trademark flowing hair. I watched as you struggled to wash your makeup every night, slathering your face with anti wrinkle serums. I remember your face covered with black streaks as the kohl smudged; my life has similar streaks of pain. Can you recommend a serum for my broken heart?

As a child I was conditioned because you repeated that I, I was a failure, an evil being, incapable of doing anything right (including something as simple as tuning the radio in the car or switching on the TV, for which I was thrashed on numerous occasions). My hunger for warmth/love drove me to contemplate committing suicide on several occasions. I can still taste the heady yet intoxicating concoction of Moon Drop or your Ogee shampoo swirling its way through my body. But nothing seemed to get your attention. I was never . . . NEVER good enough.

And so, Mom, after pulverising me, you would repeatedly wash your hands to get the blood off your fingers! Even today you brush your teeth ten times a day to wash out the venom. Sitting there, trembling in the corner I waited . . . I waited but no one came to save me.

Your shock at my not getting best grades in class four is still unfathomable. I just wanted someone to hold my little finger, to guide me. Instead, you terrified me. I was friendless, wore torn uniforms and I can still feel those sharp hunger pangs. Hunger not only for food, but also for a kind word. I was humiliated time and again when I had to stand in the dustbin because you had not paid the school fees.

Nani was my guardian angel in every sense. She was THERE, simple as that. Something which every child needs. She was there to hold my hand and catch me when I fell. My shield against Dadaji, Daddy, and then you. For you successfully wedged a knife between Dadaji and Chhoti Phua, making them the enemies in your 'US-versus-the-evil-world' game.

Nani was my security blanket, to keep me warm, happy and fill me which the much-needed affection and food. She stitched not only my torn school uniforms but also my confidence. Grow up, Mom. Take responsibility. Stop blaming Chhoti Phua and then nani for 'brainwashing' me.

At times I still feel like the young girl pacing up and down to make sure your Chevvy left before I entered the house to avoid getting assaulted. And I remember how you would, in the middle of beating and cursing, transform into a diva, speaking softly as you giggled into the phone when that minister friend called.

I still feel that tingle at the nape of my neck and a chill on my spine when I hear your voice.

Mom I know that I AM to blame—I was too short. Not pretty. Too thin. Later, too fat. Too ugly. Too 'chaloo'. NEVER good enough.

NEVER. I was 'untrustworthy' for misplacing your nail cutter. Sia has misplaced a dozen nail cutters and a bunch of my keys but I can assure you, I haven't and will NEVER react in the same way you did.

But Mom, as we all know, you are ALWAYS right. Your version was the only one and anyone who challenged it was rebuffed.

I tried to pretend everything would fall into place and that I would get my fairy-tale life. Still. STILL trying to get your approval. Despite getting into Queen's College, I was still an embarrassment.

Nani sent delicious food when Amita di's servant ran away so that her columns mentioned your parties. The carefully packed meals were ferried to her house by Yudi mama's office car so that every column mentioned you; such was the support you got from your doting family.

After shopping for Sia's 11th birthday present, I picked up 'Pretty' by Elizabeth Arden. My 21st birthday flashes before my eyes . . . I remember mustering the courage to ask you for a perfume, 'Chance' by Chanel and I was dumbstruck when I ACTUALLY got it. To date, I can't figure out why the bottle read 'Change by Channel'. Just maybe you were implying you wished to 'change' me or was it a fake?

My college fiancé reminded me on several occasions that my state was not much better than your battered Chevrolet Impala—all your cars were gifted to you by nana; you were lucky to have a doting father.

But I was exploited, tired. And would eventually be discarded when of no use, like the old Impala. After my engagement broke, my marriage to Krish was forced due to your ultimatum and threat of 'cutting me off' if I went to study abroad and I fell for it. You wanted me married. You wanted me OUT of your 'picture-perfect' life. Meanwhile, you grinned from magazine covers and pontificated about women's rights. Unlike the numerous cuts that you can do and undo on your article drafts, the way you treated ME, Mom, is irreversible.

YOU were the one who scolded me for talking to your political friends but you conveniently (oh-so-conveniently) failed to mention my scholarship and academic achievements to them.

Mom, were you not proud of me? Or was that just a cover to hide your age?

Mom, did you ever wonder how I adjusted to small-town life post my marriage? And you conveniently guest-starred in my life, swanking in and out of my in-laws' house at your own whim and fancy. No, not to enquire about how I was adjusting or if I needed help, but mainly to parade your designer bags and jewellery. Did you ever, just EVER realise the wedge it created between Krish's family and me?

Irrespective of everything, and I mean EVERYTHING, Krish and I were there for you (the genuine kind of 'there'), from hearing your aches and pains and highly exaggerated physical ailments to bouncing on and off scooters to copy a friend's kurta 'same to same' (as you put it) for your photo shoots . . . to driving down with Krish to help you with your program recordings. But ironically, Mom, Randy was seen as the 'prodigal' son. Parties were thrown in his honour. Making him a director of your company was a given as being a 'son' OBVIOUSLY granted him these perks. In case you were wondering Mom, this is the 21st CENTURY. Wake up . . . smell the coffee. You may live in Civil Lines, in a 'posh' and 'modern' area, but if you ask me, your mind-set compares with that of a village woman—same to same, in your words.

When Sia approached you for an interview for her school newsletter (which I'm pretty sure is the BIGGEST interview you have got so far), you acted like your 'important' busy self. As usual. YOU ARE HER grandmother. You should have made the time. Sia was so right when she said that it would have been easier to interview Tom Cruise.

Diwali came with a bang. And this 'bang' for me was not the deafening firecrackers bursting outside, but when I was forced to close my doors on Krish. BANG! The doors of my mind, my heart, my home. Mom, did you realise that I needed you the MOST at that time? Being left with my two children and saddled with a heavy mortgage, I was forced to move back home. Ironically, I felt like a stranger.

Mom, did you ever think of how the children and I slept on one bed with that razai mapped with holes? I still wonder why you didn't stop Dolly when she gossiped about me with the maids or made me dust my OWN house or buy vegetables she needed . . . Instead you played a 'double role' and talked about me behind my back. Just by the way, one of the texts you sent to her, mocking me, reached ME. Was that deliberate to let me know my place in life?

My life collapsed in a short span of months. All you did was shovel more rubble and try to bury me under your accusations and constant blame. When Sia and Shrey arrived home ravenous from school, HOW could you tell them that my kitchen was run by you? HOW COULD YOU? Meanwhile you continued with incessant partying and you continued blaming me for anything and EVERYTHING which went wrong or that was missing.

Mom the pain persists . . . you blamed me for Dolly's miscarriage. That hurt and still does. And Mom, this blemish cannot be covered, unlike the layers of makeup you slap on your face to hide your aging skin.

As for the kids—Shrey and Sia are still so young and impressionable. I want them to believe in happy endings. Their excitement knows no bounds when they receive an over-sized parcel from you. But how can I explain to them that the name on the card is someone else's and is not a mistake but a 'sasta' useless present passed on from you (oh-so-kindly). And now, NOW my children aren't good enough for you . . . History is truly repeating itself. Did you know that your incessant violence and physical abuse drove

3-year-old Sia to almost call the police
when we were at Civil Lines? You can count
your lucky stars that Aida was there to stop
her just in time.
This is life, Mom. Not a movie. YOU have
failed. Mom, for you this world and our life
was really a stage and I, YOUR DAUGHTER was
merely a player . . . You've exhausted all
your takes.

There was complete silence in the room after Ramesh finished
reading the email.

"Give it to me. Forward it," he said after a while. "It is too
much to digest; I haven't seen a woman like this!"

Arnie and Krish took their leave after that and drove back
home.

The door opened even before Arnie rang the bell because
both the children had been glued to the kitchen windows,
keeping a lookout for Krish's car. They looked anxiously at her.
Krish winked at them and they launched into a dance, relieved
that there may be a breakthrough in the case and singing at the
top of their lungs, "If you are happy and you know it, clap your
hands, Gangnam style," combining the Korean hit with a much
older classic. "Gangnam style, Gangnam style," they screamed,
throwing up their hands in the air and pretending to ride a horse!

"Calm down!" Arnie almost shouted over the noise.

"This is a turning point for you!" Krish said. "Your link with
Civil Lines and your grandfather has been established by what we
found and discussed. This is really invaluable!"

But the import of his words was lost on Arnie, what with
the dancing children and the frantic buzzing of her BlackBerry. It
was Chhoti Phua, calling to give Arnie the details about her great
grandfathers that she had asked for. "Bharat Bhushan was the man.
He and his wife adopted your Dadaji. As for your nana's father,

Prem Nath was a small-time politician and a local muscle man. I will tell you more later. My son is calling, and you understand how it is with international calls. I will call you later, *achcha?*"

"I have my great grandfather's name," Arnie told Krish after putting the phone down. "It is not much to go on, but I guess it's still important enough. But, Krish, isn't it too late?"

"Never too late," Krish muttered, writing down the names. He walked off and sat in a corner with his iPad and kept muttering to himself.

"Stubborn bugger!" Arnie thought. She sat and stared out of the window, for what else was there to do?

An hour went by like that before some mumbling from Krish's corner caught Arnie's attention.

"Hey! I've been talking to you! What are you daydreaming about?"

"What does he think I am dreaming about?" thought Arnie.

"So, Bharat Bhushan, yes?"

"Of course YES, idiot," Arnie thought irritably.

"This ancestor of yours, was he a pious man?" Krish continued, not bothering to wait for Arnie's response.

"How would I know?"

Krish was beginning to get irritating now, but clearly, he was nowhere close to done with his questions. "If yes, then we have something."

That was it! "Woah," Arnie exclaimed, as memories suddenly came flooding into her head. She remembered there used to be a secret family password for opening safes and lockers. A phrase that linked religion with her ancestor's name. 'Bharat Bhushan'. Yes! That was it! She remembered that Randy and she used this in their games, especially those inspired by Hindi movies. They had picked it up from the adults. It was entrenched in their psyche, something so taken for granted that she had never mentioned it to Krish. So how did he know that Bharat Bhushan was a pious man?

117

She turned to question him and found him with a smug and triumphant look on his face. "Once you got the names from the old lady, I did some research on Google and found it. I have found it!"

What had he found? Dadaji had been born at the turn of the century, at a time when computers and the Internet were not around.

Krish stunned her with his next words. "I have found the High Court order confirming and upholding your grandfather's adoption!"

Rendered speechless, Arnie blinked as he handed her the printout of the decree. Mayhem broke loose after that, with Arnie dancing and shouting, the children jumping up and down excitedly, and Aida, happy to see the tension ebb away, pouring endless cups of tea for everyone.

"That is it," Arnie thought to herself. "I have the information I need to show the lawyer. To prove my existence!"

Krish explained the significance of his find to Arnie. "Your lawyer had asked for the source of your grandfather's assets and for his genealogy. And with a copy of this court order, by which your grandfather's adoption was upheld, you can answer both the questions. It is clear now that your grandfather inherited his wealth, and that seems to be important for Ramesh."

"Oh my God!" Arnie exclaimed as she realised the full import of what Krish had stumbled upon.

Night came with a gentler sleep than Arnie had had for many days. The next day, she had to meet Chhoti Phua again, at the Trident Hotel this time. What new secrets would tomorrow bring? What new intrigues would the day reveal?

14

Arnie watched Chhoti Phua alight from the big car ahead of her. She smiled to herself, seeing her aunt's familiar figure and her diamonds sparkle in the sun. She felt a sudden rush of affection for her aunt and ran to help her go through the security check.

Chhoti Phua looked at Arnie and smiled, as though reading her mind, and then said, "You will be fine, beta. We are built differently." She tightened her grip on Arnie's hand as they walked into the hotel together. "My mother was not too well and had too much red chilli when she was carrying me. That is why I am dark, but we still have the same blood," she said.

"You are sexy Chhoti Phua, and I am sure that when you were in France, you must have had quite a fan following," Arnie teased her, adding that she was absolutely fabulous now and that she hoped to be like her when she was older.

"Pretty ring," Chhoti Phua remarked, noticing the big emerald ring on Arnie's finger. "The diamonds are good, but in our time, your Dadaji insisted on Golconda diamonds."

Arnie was almost bursting to ask where his diamond collection was, because a ring or two would surely help her at the moment. However, better sense prevailed and she bit her lip, steering clear of controversial family topics, for Arnie remembered the bitter fights that had been waged over Dadaji's fabled diamond collection.

They settled into an easy conversation, having chosen their table and ordered the wine. Relaxed, they sat back and looked at each other, joined by familiarity and memories, which made it all a bit fuzzy and warm. Arnie looked at her own mortality mirrored in the lines on her aunt's face and her greying hair. Chhoti Phua told her that she had nothing to fear; age sat well on Dhari women. She then added wistfully, "If only I had your complexion and your education."

Arnie noticed with amusement the order of her aunt's wish list. So typical of Chhoti Phua. She reached out for her hand across the table and smiled as the large diamond on her aunt's finger dug into her palm. Chhoti Phua knew that Arnie too, appreciated fine jewels.

Over lunch, Arnie asked Chhoti Phua all the questions that she needed answers to on Ramesh's fact sheet and she was amazed at her aunt's clear recollection of the past.

"Chhoti Phua, I met someone through a friend, who claimed that we were neighbours once," Arnie lied, trying to get information. "But Chhoti Phua, you know I grew up in Civil Lines, with all of you around, so this can't be true. Help me, because I foolishly made a bet and I will lose my ring if I cannot give her the address of our homes before we shifted to Civil Lines. This happened at a party after a glass of wine when I wasn't really paying attention. I took a chance because I knew we were going to meet and I know you remember everything. Actually, you can show me the house itself, can't you?"

"Of course I can!" Chhoti Phua said dismissively, and then, turning her attention to the ring on Arnie's finger, she said, "That ring is beautiful; the emerald is good but the diamonds are ordinary. So, I will not only take you to the house on my way back, but I will also get these diamonds changed by Chota Jain.

Jaante ho, his father was Dadaji's jeweller and he would always stand when Dadaji was in the room, much to my amusement. He is expensive, yes, but he will not cheat us." She clasped Arnie's wrist in her hand, examining the Rolex that had been worn for her benefit. "I have the same model, but with a black dial. I am happy you are doing so well for yourself, Aranya."

"Yes, Chhoti Phua, I live a good life. I work hard, very hard, but I also try to enjoy the moment. I remember you once told me that even when the times were not so good, Dadaji always wore his Rolex. He never let on to the outside world the turmoil within, living life to the fullest and holding his head high." She was referring to his last years when Alzheimer's overtook his mind but not his spirit, which remained his very own until the last.

"And that is what you have, isn't it?" Chhoti Phua said slowly.

"Yes. I have managed to keep my head above the water even though no one has ever come forward to help me. I am scared to fall ill even for a day, Chhoti Phua, because this little life that I have built with my children will come crashing down. I am vulnerable. And I am dependent on my job for my life. My savings are limited; I pay for everything myself. I have no financial support whatsoever. I have scrimped and saved to reach where I am today. It took me years to take my children for a real holiday, but they are good kids, Sia and Shrey, and they do not complain. Things are better now, but they are so only as long as I work."

They both fell silent, sipping their wine and wondering about the whys and hows of their lives. Chhoti Phua nodded as she listened and then spoke after taking a sip. "Kamini brought both your brother and you to believe that we were bad, that my father was evil. Nothing in life, beta, is black or white. The Sharmas did not arrive on the backs of angels dusted with piety and Dadaji was not dropped into the world cavorting with the Devil."

Arnie buried her nose into her glass, fearful that her eyes would betray her. She had stumbled on to the truth but she did not want her aunt to know it. It was too early and there was so much more that she needed to know from her.

"So, where did we live before Dadaji moved us to Civil Lines?" Arnie asked after a while, trying to steer the conversation back. "And why did Dadaji buy houses in the names of his children?" she asked innocently and Chhoti Phua immediately began giving her answers to all her questions, joining the dots and filling in the blanks about the past. Over dessert they talked about the court order sanctioning the sale of the Civil Lines property and of the life her aunt was looking forward to. "You can visit me freely now. She can do nothing. After all, she won't be there!" Chhoti Phua told Arnie triumphantly.

Noticing her subdued reaction and sensing her internal agony, she looked at Arnie and said, "Mark my words, the lines on your forehead, your *kismat*, means that no one can take what is yours. No one, beta, can change that. I believe in this, and life, as it will unfold for you, will prove me right. I cannot show you how to get there because you are far smarter than I am. I cannot even speak English fluently, and I rely on common sense alone to take me through life. But be positive, beta, and life will look up for you. You, like me, have to bring up your children on your own."

Arnie opened her mouth to speak, but Chhoti Phua cut her short with a wave of her hand. "I had Babuji to take care of me, financially and emotionally, but you have no one. Babuji saw to it that his daughters had enough and were nicely provided for. However, life has been harsh for you. Kamini has been an absentee mother from the time of your birth. First it was Babuji and I who brought you up, and then it was your grandmother, Mrs Sharma. And now you live by your talent and your courage. You make me proud, Aranya!"

As Chhoti Phua spoke, Arnie felt a sudden stinging rage grip her as years of conditioning kicked in. She heard her mother's voice ring in her ears, telling her that the Sharmas were good and that the Dharis were bad, and that Chhoti Phua was the worst of the lot. But it was all wrong. Arnie knew that her aunt was right, but her mind continuously tried to make her dismiss it. "How did she get the order, Chhoti Phua, and that too on the last day of court when nothing substantial happens?" Arnie asked, wanting to not get sucked into old mind games. She was aware that her question might let on that her sudden interest in the past was not a mere obsession with ancestors long dead and buried.

Her aunt looked up, her expression one of disapproval. "It is embarrassing how your mother wraps a thin *dupatta* around her neck like a scarf and sticks her chest out at the judge, showing more than should decently be shown. And jaante ho, she wears padded ones, the cheap ones that you get everywhere."

Stunned, Arnie stared at her aunt, unsure whether to laugh or scream, torn between receding loyalty to her mother and the desire to laugh at the naked rivalry that still existed between the two women. She laughed until tears rolled down her cheeks and Chhoti Phua, who was amused at the reaction to her joke, joined her.

They drove to her flat so that Chhoti Phua could meet Arnie's children. Both Sia and Shrey, when they met Chhoti Phua, were on their best behaviour, completely taken in by the fact that their mother had a relative who, unlike Kamini, actually wanted to see them. And Chhoti Phua's delight on meeting the children was too genuine and heartfelt to be doubted.

"How is Krish?" her aunt asked as they sat sipping tea in Arnie's living room.

Arnie knew Chhoti Phua was not enquiring after his health but about the health of their relationship.

"He has worked hard to reach a certain level of friendship. We are not back together in any sense, but Krish does spend time with us. I was unwell, a few years back, and I was asked to get a biopsy done. My mother knew about it, but, as always, she was too busy partying to care about me. It was Krish who calmed the children and took care of everything, and since then, he has been around."

"So sweet, your children," Chhoti Phua said as they left Arnie's flat and drove towards the old family home a little later.

Arnie listened to her aunt talk. A big piece of the whole affair would fall into place once she knew exactly where the house was. And as they approached it, a confident Chhoti Phua directed the driver to the crescent where they had once lived.

"I often have lunch at the Chinese restaurant around the corner from the house, and I think about it every time I eat there," she said.

They got out of the car and Arnie followed her aunt to the gate of the house. "We owned this house," she pointed out, "the one next door, and the one after that. Your Dadaji was not an ordinary man." Quietly, she then opened the gate closest to her and walked in, stopping next to the majestic mango tree right alongside the gate.

"Your Dadaji planted this tree," she said, running her hand lovingly over its bark. "He loved mango and lychee trees. He was passionate about trees and he had many orchards . . . Specific instructions were given to Bhaktiram, our *maali*, to grow different varieties of trees, especially fruit trees. Bhaktiram, I remember, was this muscular tanned hunk who would work shirtless in peak summer, shovelling the earthy soil, watering the shrubs, and plucking the fruit. But Babuji was forced to sack four gardeners, including Bhaktiram, due to Kamini and her cheap antics. I knew everything then, I know everything now. Nothing escapes me."

This was what you call a moment, a moment when Arnie felt the present allowing her a connection with the past. She felt a gentle breeze caress her face and she breathed in the magical scent of the summer, and in it she saw optimism and hope. All was certainly not lost. And in that brief fascinating moment, she vowed not to give up. Ever.

15

'It's not what you say out of your mouth that determines your life; it's what you whisper to yourself that has the most power!'
— Robert Kiyosaki

"It all adds up," Arnie told Krish excitedly. "I have all the information for the fact sheet. Dadaji sold three adjoining houses on Sardar Patel Road and used the money from that sale to buy the Civil Lines property. Chhoti Phua showed me the houses and then even pointed out the bank where Dadaji held accounts! But more importantly, I have the answer to why Civil Lines was bought in the name of the four children. Apparently, Dadaji did this all the time, buying and selling houses in the names of his children, and moving them around like plastic pieces on a Monopoly board. The houses that Chhoti Phua showed me, they were all bought as joint property under the names of my dad and his brother. Dadaji then sold these and bought a bigger family property in Civil Lines. As his daughters were living with him, they too, had their names added to the property deed. All of it makes perfect sense now."

"Slow down," Krish teased her. "I am getting old and it takes me time to process stuff, so don't bombard me with so much good news," he chuckled and then, on a more sombre note, told her that they were scheduled to meet the lawyer later that evening.

For once, Arnie looked forward to the meeting. She

dressed meticulously, applying mascara with care and curling her eyelashes, and noted that her dark circles no longer looked like Portobello mushrooms; her eyes glowed with life and sparkled with mischief. She generously dabbed her favourite perfume, Chance by Chanel, taking in the fragrance and imagining the day she would win. Finally, she had hope.

"You look good," Krish told her when she came out of her room. "And you radiate confidence, that's great. No matter what the outcome, Aranya, remember who you are as a person, and keep the faith."

Arnie smiled and wistfully asked him, "Why can't I be the happily-ever-after person?"

"You will be," he assured her.

When they reached Ramesh's office, his receptionist told them that he would, unfortunately, be unavailable because he was busy in some arbitration case. However, undaunted, Arnie refused to let the cancelled meeting spoil her day, and as they drove back home, she and Krish reminisced about old times. One thing led to another and Arnie ended up talking about her brother. "You know Krish, I often told my mother that as Randy's children grow up, she should tell them that I wish them well and that I am not the evil phua."

"Seriously?" an incredulous Krish asked.

Arnie nodded and continued. "Can you imagine, I was such a loser that I actually told my mother that I would not want to appropriate Randy's children's rights and in fact, would give ours to them willingly. But I did put my foot down on recycled gifts and stale cakes. Supporting my kids, paying a mortgage, running a home, paying off the car loan, and managing a hundred other things means that I do not have any savings; loan collectors have hounded me on several occasions. We are struggling a little even now, but we do have self-respect and we do not deserve recycled gifts and stale food. I told my mother that although life was

126

difficult, I would not stand for being humiliated. So, when she asked me for the one gold bangle that she had grudgingly given to me at our wedding, I told her that if she wanted whatever little she had given back so that she could give it to Dolly, she could have it! Today, I even question whether my brother and I were ever as close as I thought we were."

They were quiet as Krish pulled into China Garden, Arnie's favourite restaurant. As they waited for a table, Arnie reached out for the newspaper on the table in front of her and scanned through it, stopping at an article that spoke about women having different market prices in the matrimonial business according to their fairness, beauty, and their educational qualifications—all things that the in-laws could later brag about. In some parts of the country, girls were forced to study medicine with the sole purpose of getting a better 'match'. Once married, the medical degree was abandoned and forgotten.

"Nothing has changed over the years," Arnie commented. "My mom was most reluctant to sell me off . . . Actually, who am I kidding? She would have 'given' me for free *and* thrown in a couple of hundreds from her own pocket for whoever would have come along and taken me off her hands!"

Krish agreed. "She is a real piece of work. Remember, I was an upcoming artist from a small town when she readily agreed to our marriage, all because she wanted to get rid of you."

Arnie wanted to cover her ears to block out Krish's words, but she knew he was right.

A bevy of girls had been produced for Randy. Some were from extremely eminent families, some were well qualified, some fair, and some breathtakingly beautiful. But no one, NO ONE, had been good enough for Randy because Kamini had vowed that she would rest only when her son had found the best and nothing less.

The procedure was always the same. The poor innocent girl

would enter their living room with her family, and before they had even seated themselves, Kamini would start raving about Randy's endless achievements, all nothing but a web of poorly-crafted lies.

"In actual it was Randy who inventor the y-phone, but Mr Apple stole his ideas from hims . . ." she would begin.

What an evil plot on Steve Jobs' part, Arnie used to laugh silently, watching them in action.

"You see, Randy recently was offered title of Bittu's Most Wanted Bachelor. But modest boys that he is, outright he refused its."

Arnie would crack up when her mother reached this particular point, because the only so-called modelling campaign Randy had ever been selected for was for his tuition centre, where they required a geeky, scrawny 'nerd' and Randy fitted the bill perfectly.

"Randy is vary helthy conscience." And Kamini's definition of 'helthy' meant feeding her beloved Randy with custard, full fat milk, and a diet of 'solid' non-vegetarian food. "Randy is a very lovable boy." As far as Arnie can remember, the only person who had found Randy loveable was Rajni, Rajni Prasad Pandey Lal. Their bromance had continued for quite some time.

Kamini and Randy had practised this drill for oh-so-long, perfecting themselves so brilliantly, that they could communicate with each other through simple eye movements. A slight widening of Kamini's eyes was code for the girl's family being suspicious people who were not to be trusted. A single blink implied that there was a possibility for a future. And a double eye blink meant that the girl would definitely be part of the Dhari household. However, pursed lips and a single raised eyebrow, which most girls were greeted with, meant the girl was a catastrophic disaster!

Even the memory of this made Arnie cringe, as she too had a daughter and would hate it if she were treated like this; her little princess cut to pieces by some asinine idiot.

She focussed instead on the evening ahead of her. It was only when she returned home and sat down to check her email that she found the day was to result in more drama.

Beti Aranya,

Just STOP! Stop focusing on wealth and land. Stop filling your mind with toxic sludge, it will corrode you. In my last mail, I told you, and I repeat, meditate. JUST MEDITATE. Your children need you. Make them your top priority. Don't make them reliant on ancestral wealth and property. They should be self-sufficient. This inheritance will be a load on their little shoulders . . . Look at me for instance, I'm swimming in so much money that I am left with major storage issues. There are only so many cupboards and safe deposit boxes in a house na? So, I'm FORCED to spend the money on cars, houses, and land. But it's such a burden.

Stop being so materialistic and focus on the larger picture. Cutting off your mother, your brother, and your family will do you no good. Family is the backbone of everything. After my marriage, I moved into my sister and her in-laws' house to stay close to her until your nana built a spacious bungalow.

Beti, it is for you to take the onus of your life. Stop blaming others. Focus on yourself. Focus on your Karma . . . Change the colour of your Chakra . . . you, YOU can heal your life.

Yudi

P.S. Our guru told us to take a short vacation in Singapore. He believes that this will cleanse us of all negative vibes. So I will be leaving for Singapore shortly. And now, I have to go for a sitting as my portrait is being done. I must say, it is coming out well.

P.P.S. We are also purchasing a new car as Guru ji believes it will help us to drive to 'abstraction'. Follow our lead and stir your life into peace. But you should focus on a simple life, the cars and the comforts are for us, at our age. Worship your mother, she needs everything life has to offer, *bechaari* has gone through so much. STOP sending her emails as this will hurt you in the future.

Arnie stared at the computer screen. She just sat and stared. How, just HOW could her hero betray her like this? When, just WHEN did he change sides? WHEN did he stop loving her? WHY was his writing laced with fake sympathy? Had he always been like this? Perhaps she had seen him only as *she* wanted to see him—as a role model, as a saviour, as her personal God.

Confused, Arnie forwarded the email to Ramesh. It would be good to get his reaction to the email. They had discussed the family in detail and Ramesh understood the inter-personal dynamics within the family members. He particularly understood the high esteem in which Arnie held her Yudi mama.

Ramesh called a while later, having read the email. "Disgusting, this does not show him as fair; quite on the contrary, and so very different from his public image. He is trying to prevent you from getting closer to the truth. All along, you've only spoken of how great he is. How could you not see through this?! The man is trying to not only distract you, but also discredit you; he is almost implying that you are neurotic by referring to emails and messages you sent to your mother. And there is a threat there, if you read between the lines, which suggests that there will be dire consequences for your children and you if you do not toe the family line. Incredible! He's like the head of a *khap panchayat*!"

Ramesh told Arnie that they needed to urgently get the case papers from the Ranchi court where the litigation had been going on. "A lot depends on what has been filed already and the orders that have been passed. Meanwhile, we shall firm up the strategy." Then, getting no reaction, he said, "Please talk to your phua. Keep her engaged and get as much information from her as possible. We need her support, so more lunches with her are necessary. And yes, do not let on that you are being guided by a lawyer. She might clam up. We need more on your father as well. Where did he study? What was his work? What was he doing when you were born? I need facts. Courts rely on verifiable facts. You have to be brave. I know this is difficult, but relying on emotion and appealing to the 'better side' of your family has taken you nowhere. Your family has used your emotional side against you. It is time to outwit them with bloody facts. Meet your aunt because I get the sense that she knows everything."

They rescheduled a meeting for the following day, and when they met, Ramesh mapped out the future course of action. Arnie then told him about her plan—to go to London for a holiday.

"By all means, please do go," Ramesh said. "I will work on filing a 'suit' in the ten days that you will be gone. And I'll keep you updated about everything through emails, so don't worry at all."

Arnie left Ramesh's office feeling much better than she had when she had come in. There was a roadmap now. And she still had a case. And the trip to London for the summer, that, thank God, was still on. The despair lifted and she felt better.

"Let's discuss our London holiday," Arnie declared happily to the kids as soon as she reached home. They hugged her tightly in response; their happiness so contagious that it set her spirits soaring.

It was like old times, before she'd seen the family tree where one branch, hers, was missing.

"Mamma, what did you do to make your mother so angry? Were you a bad girl?" Sia asked suddenly.

But Arnie had no answers for her daughter. "I don't know, sweetheart. I have struggled with this question every day for the past many days, but I just don't know," Arnie replied honestly. "I just don't know, Sia . . ."

The children fell asleep very late that night and Arnie fell asleep even later. Her dreams were a kaleidoscope of broken bits of the past, all colour and no sound. A message in a bottle, a yellow parchment scroll in a green bottle. Corked. Floating away into the distance. Into blue nothingness. The rain outside. The lines from a song. *'Raindrops on roses and whiskers on kittens, bright paper packages tied up with strings. These are a few of my favourite things.* Packages in different shapes and sizes. Wrapped up in crisp sheets of gold leaf, cobalt blue, deep burgundy, coral, and teal. The delicate smell of her mother's favourite perfume. Chhoti Phua's dressing table. Crowded with big bottles, tubes of red lipsticks, white compact powder. Her chubby five-year-old hands holding a bottle. And then, the bottle crashing to the floor. Arnie woke up with a jolt, an intense longing for those days when she was a little girl running around in the aangan, giggling, laughing, took hold of her. But strangely, every nightmare, every dead end in her life always left her in the same place—the place where she had started, shocked, scared, alone, and without any answers.

16

'Everybody is a genius. But if you judge a fish by its ability to climb a tree, it will live its whole life believing that it is stupid.'
– Albert Einstein

A week later and Arnie was still searching for answers, for evidence of anything that would help connect the dots of her family history. Nothing was making sense any more, and desperate for some comfort, she called Monica, her colleague, her friend, and her soul mate.

They huddled together in Arnie's office room. "Let me check the case details on my laptop, wait a minute," she said, as she got the Wi-fi network going. "She is unbelievable, man, totally mad-d-d-d! I have always found her strange, but this, this is just weird and sick."

She found the case online and went through the Dhari family tree. Arnie's name was missing. "But look, some girl cousin of yours is here. You too could have been shown." She clucked her tongue in irritation.

Arnie suddenly began to laugh as she read the girl's name on the screen.

Monica looked up. "What's the joke woman, I don't see anything." In between hiccups, Arnie painted an image of her obese cousin hanging from a branch of the family tree, which, under her weight, was about to snap.

"Huh?" Monica grunted. "What about hanging your mother from it?" she asked, not mincing her words or hiding her aversion. "Is she for real anyway? She is the worst rendition of any stepmother in any story ever told!"

Monica had tears in her eyes. They were joined in grief for Monica remembered her mother, lost to the ravages of incurable illness, and Arnie grieved for her mother, a woman she no longer knew, a shadow from her past. Life had dealt Arnie a blow and she was not sure that she could stand up again.

"And look at you, her daughter, but so bright, so beautiful, and taller than me!" They two women looked at each other and smiled. It was their little joke. They were of similar height and stature. All the years they had worked together, they had borrowed clothes, exchanged jackets and skirts. But, Arnie always thought of Monica as being the taller one.

Height was always a concern for Arnie, her own height, that is. Kamini had made Arnie believe that she was a midget, that she crawled the earth to cause her mother shame. Everyone, just about everyone, was taller than she was. Monica was taller, of course.

Monica realised how mean Kamini had been. She had undermined Arnie's confidence. Her abuse had been like living with a sound that could not be switched off. Arnie used to cover her ears, bury her head in a pillow, yet she was unable to drown out her mother's screams. Even today, she doubted herself because of the way her mother preyed on her self-confidence and singed it with her hate.

Monica was enraged on looking at the court papers.

"You know you can't let her get away with this," Monica said after a while. "Let's expose her. Let's peel off her bloody mask. There has to be something. Why will people not believe you? Let us show them those eleven pages, the ones that you emailed to her and the ones which made me want to murder her?"

"Those eleven pages," Arnie thought to herself, "are, most probably, my mother's weak point." Those pages are the truth that will not remain hidden and will, over time, expose who Kamini was as a person.

"The lawyer asked me many questions," Arnie told Monica. "But I don't know where my father went to school. I don't even know when he graduated and from where, before going to Cambridge. I don't know where he was born or where he grew up. We spent all our time fawning over my mother and completely neglected him, and now I don't know how to figure this out.

"He was always in the shadows and we were made to feel guilty if we spoke to him. Everything was about my mother. If my mother began to yell, so would we. As small children, we were unaware of our surroundings and would just clutch on to her sari. If she cried, I would begin to wail and Randy would join in, and we would glare at my father, as though he was to blame. We were always doing that to him, leaving him out. Feels awful now, I wish I could go back on it. I wish I could turn back time and be kinder to him. I wish I had stood up to her door-banging tantrums."

"I know," Monica said quietly. "But we need to get to the facts, so let's focus on that. What about that Chhoti Phua? Surely she knows which school her brother went to?"

Arnie shook her head. "I have to choose my questions carefully. I can't spook her."

Monica thought for a while and then, brightening up, asked, "Hey, what about the time when you were going to Stanford? *Arrey*, when the I-20 came with your name backwards? Remember how I pulled your leg for ages after that and you threatened to kill me?"

"Yeah," Arnie smiled wryly. That time had been like the golden period of her life, when the Sloan School of Management and Stanford was all she could think of.

"Well, at that time you had said that your father gave you some papers about his French work permit."

What was Monica leading up to? Arnie wondered, looking at her friend quizzically.

"Well, you are a true *angrez*, Arnie! Anyway, you needed documents to prove that everything was legitimate and he gave you something, wasn't it? Some documents from his side?"

"Oh my god, Monica!" Arnie exclaimed. "You are right! He did give me papers that would help with my visa, but he asked for that packet back over the winter saying he needed them for a case in Ranchi."

"Crap! It's the same court case with the bloody tree, the one they forgot to hang you from!" Monica exclaimed, making the connection faster than Arnie. "Where is that fucking packet? What does it have? Get up, get up, get up!" she yelled, pulling Arnie out of the chair and pushing her out the door. "We are going to your house right away!"

Her excitement was infectious and they ran out giggling. "Two heads are better than one," Arnie told her, laughing all the way to the car. "No, it is not that. Do not run yourself down as always. You have done so much with your life. The only time I want to claw you is when you undermine yourself. Just because some bloody bitch who doesn't deserve to have a daughter like you drilled crap into your head. It is a miracle you survived. And now the same bloody bitch wants to steal your money and rob your children of their future."

"Easy, don't pull the steering so hard else it will be in your hands. You are driving a car not riding a horse," Arnie teased, as they pulled up in front of her condominium.

They ran up to the apartment, rushed right past a surprised Aida, heading straight for the cupboard where Arnie stored all her important papers. They literally tore the cupboard apart, pouncing on the old khaki envelope. Longish in size, frayed at the ends, and thick. Almost like a package. The wax seal was still stuck to the now open flap.

Arnie's fingers trembled as she slid the contents out.

The papers fell to the ground, astonished, perhaps, at themselves for having seen the light of day. A blue, hardbound passport; a degree certificate from Cambridge; an Indian university paper too. Taking it from Monica's hand, Arnie shook the manila envelope to see if there was anything else in it. Out floated a pale green sheet of paper. It was madam Kamini's Senior School Certificate marksheet. She had failed English and got a Conditional Pass in Math!

There was stunned silence before Monica, unable to hold back any longer, exclaimed, "She failed! She bloody failed! And she claims to be a writer and a social commentator of national fame! She behaves like she could teach the bloody Queen a phrase or two, and she failed!"

Perhaps this is why she had run her down, Arnie thought. Because she reminded her mother of her own failure. That is why her mother had said that *English-Vinglish* was a waste. Arnie's mind raced back to Dadaji's words on failures. He had been right. Yudi mama, nana, and even nani had never let on about her mother having failed. Their collective loyalty to her mother was greater than their love for Arnie.

Disappointment filled her soul and dampened her spirit. If only she had stopped to listen to Dadaji, her life might have been radically different. She would have seen her mother as she was, rather than live in fear of her.

She called Krish and told him she had found the papers, also telling him about her mother's marksheet.

Krish burst out: "She's absolutely fake, and will have to pay for it! Always superior and grand, always talking down to the rest of us even as she single-handedly ruined your life, and that too, while pretending to be a feminist for all the world to see. She destroyed your self-confidence, but no one would believe you because you were pitted against the Goddess herself, the paragon of virtue, with that self-righteous brother beside her. I had great respect for Yudi Sharma despite his vindictiveness towards me after I left you. I always dismissed his behaviour because it reflected what I foolishly believed was love for you and the children. Unbelievable, man!"

"Have you finished venting?" Arnie asked tersely. She continued when Krish muttered a yes. "Nothing is random, Krish. Everything happens for a reason and we recognise the pattern much later. It's like the curtain lifting to reveal the grand set in a musical, but only that particular section lights up at a time which we are supposed to see, and we figure out the whole story only later."

But Arnie's metaphor about the world being a stage was lost on Krish. Seething with anger over a woman who had ruined their lives, he hung up the phone.

Packages of different sizes come into your life at different times. As the late Pete Seeger sang, '*Little boxes on the hillside, little boxes made of ticky-tacky*'. Some large and glitzy and showy and wrapped in the finest of paper, and some small yet valuable ones. Good things most definitely came in small packages.

Smiling, Arnie clutched the now disintegrating khaki envelope and held it close.

17

*'The flower that blooms in adversity is
the rarest and most beautiful of all.'*
— *Walt Disney Company*

Misfortune and heartbreak have a way of uniting people, as does a shared enemy. For a part of her family, Arnie was a ticking bomb waiting to blow their well-crafted reputation apart. That was her life, a tragedy and a potential scandal.

The night turned purple as Arnie sat back and took a sip of white wine. It tasted bitter and strangely, like cardboard. Everything had a strange aftertaste for her these days. "Will my decision to fight them leave me similarly bitter?" she wondered. She sighed, suddenly feeling weary and overburdened by responsibility, by decisions taken, and those yet to be taken.

Once she signed the papers taking her extended family to court, life would be a roller coaster. Could she risk losing? Arnie knew that she would, in any case, be kicked out, stamped upon, and hauled over the coals. She would be spurned, scorned, and blamed. If she lost, she would be pilloried from every pulpit and their judgement condemning her would be final. No one needs to explain anything if they win, for the world loves a winner. If she lost, which was a very real and frightening possibility, her family would crush Arnie completely.

Once she set the ball rolling, she would have to carry on, for the one thing she did know without a doubt was that if she quit, she would lose.

"My children and I will be shunned publicly. I am already the black sheep of the family, the outcast, but can I put my children through this? The exaggerated sighs once used for my father will be used for me."

A shiver ran up Arnie's spine although it was a hot June night. Life seemed a burden and she felt much older than her years as she slumped sideways at a corner table near the window.

Pandit Nehru had written to his daughter even from jail. Her father, however, never had, not from anywhere. Her maternal grandfather did though, but not exactly in very maternal terms.

Arnie pulled out her nana's letters to her and wished she had destroyed the correspondence years ago. She cringed as she read the letters again. They held a different meaning now. Arnie had been vulnerable and gullible. She was to do as they said and be the person they wanted her to be. Her happiness was sacrificed at the altar of family reputation, to uphold a tradition that she had never seen and which protected neither her children nor her. How were they any different from the Taliban? She was meant to be seldom heard and never seen.

The letters smacked of betrayal. There was an unstated compact; with conformity came protection. It was an unsaid promise that if Arnie conformed to the rules of this family, she would, in return, get to bask in the reflected glory of their great Sharma name and would be protected if she came to harm in the future. This belief had made her sacrifices her happiness over the years.

Her life was similar to pre-partition India, under her family's strict gaze, wearing clothes covering her in a modesty that the rest of the country had long shrugged off. Arnie had silently borne the insults of sniggering friends. Petrified that she would not be allowed to complete her graduation, she had stuck to her group of girls, shying away from exchanging even pleasantries with the boys in her college.

Yet, in spite of everything, she had loved nana and had believed that he, along with Yudi mama and nani, loved her back. The life she once had had been so simple; the Sharmas were good, the Dharis bad and she was on the side of the angels. But now, she felt nothing but despair as she read her nana's familiar scrawl once again.

Bitiya Aranya, dear,
Again, on bended knees and touching your feet, I am pleading with you . . . our family has very good reputation. Everybody says good words about our family members. I beseech you, with folded hands, to kindly make special efforts to maintain this reputation and further enhance it. You can do this. Please do this.
Firstly, I have now learnt with great agony that you have distanced yourself from your mother and father. Whatever the circumstances, bitiya, ones mother and father are always precious. Nothing is more important than your mother and father. If there are any differences, kindly say to them, "I am sorry." Apologise to them. Whatever the circumstances, the words "I am sorry" and "I apologise" are the most precious words in the world. Please give them strength and your love and your deep regards. ALSO, NEVER TELL ANYONE WHAT THE FAMILY HAS DONE TO YOU OVER THE YEARS. Keep our izzat. I gave my daughter the same advice and now I am telling you as well . . . India

has changed, but traditions in families like ours are sacred.

Secondly, I hope some day you will pick up the telephone and ring up your mother-in-law and father-in-law and convey to them your apologies and your love. Your mother-in-law has spoken to me and has cried copiously on the telephone. She pines to see Shrey and Sia. She cries again and again.

I don't know where Krish is. I have never had the opportunity to talk to him or meet him properly. If there are issues you have with him, please, you have the capacity and knowledge to correct them, overcome them with love . . . think about the little children.

Beti, nani and I are on our way out. I thought we might not last this Diwali. Nani has unfortunately become helpless because of age.

Bitiya dear, there is so much in your hands to save the family and its reputation. Please do something. I once again implore you on bended knees and touching your feet.

I am sending some more sweets etc. for the children. Give them our love.

And, here are three hundred rupees. Please give them to your ayah and driver.

Your loving nana.

Even a decade later, his words were like acid, burning her soul. It was not his love for her, his granddaughter, which jumped out from the letters. It was a preoccupation with his good name, his *izzat*. He implored Arnie, begged her. All ways and means to play with her and make her do what he wanted.

Arnie had sobbed on the phone to nani and had wanted the comfort of her mother who had abandoned her and was busy partying and buying property. Nana would hear no criticism of his daughter, the beautiful Kamini, and thundered at nani.

Another letter followed his outburst.

Arnie took a sip of her wine and looked out, her heart clogged like the gutters outside. She watched a fly search for an opening, battering itself against the glass pane, frantically looking for an escape. She turned her attention to yet another one of nana's letters.

Dear Bitiya Rani,
I am writing these few lines with deep anguish in my heart. In my last days, and also nani's, I cannot help but express this anguish.
Your behaviour last Saturday is the cause of this anguish. Both nani and I needed to go to bed at 2 p.m. Could you not have come earlier?
But that is not what grieves me. What grieves me is that in your self-importance you chose to heap this insult on me and nani. Despite this, I chose to deliberately record "message" on your mobile, tending apologies and going to the extent of touching your feet, which, of course, I will do any time. My anguish is mainly due to the fact that you have alienated your mother, your father, your in-laws, and also, obviously, your husband. You have not cared to abide by the adage "give and take", and respect for others.
I have poured out my heart. I will continue to touch your feet in my endeavour to persuade you to see reason and be considerate and

respectful to everybody. I have spent my
life doing this.
I hope you recognise in this letter the
anguish of a person who is in his last days
and who wants your life to become better.
Yours affly, Nana.
P.S. Your curtness last evening, on phone,
has compelled me to pour out my heart this
way.

There were happy memories too. Arnie was reminded of nana's
great love of photography, of chasing clouds with him as he ran to
click them. He enjoyed photographing old colonial buildings, capturing
remnants of the British legacy. Nana would stop at the *gol-chakkars*
on the major roads, with their inner radius of picture-perfect gardens
and seasonal flowers. He would leap out and photograph the snow-
white alyssum as Arnie plucked candytufts, often jumping over the
flowerbeds to do so. She loved the pansies and would make faces
at them. He would point at the tall and elegant Delphinium larkspur,
with their feathery green leaves.

Bored and irritable, Arnie would demand and get an ice cream.
Their outing would usually end with her in tears because nana
would have photographed the flowers and the clouds but not his
granddaughter in her pretty white frock. Tired and hungry, she would
fall into nani's arms. As always, nani would have been in the car for
hours, quietly waiting for nana.

Nani took Arnie in every time her mother hit her excessively
and threw her out of the house. Arnie would pack her few clothes
into a rough bundle, clutch her school bag and take an auto rickshaw
across the city to nani's house.

She had studied at the prestigious Kinnaird College but nani never
spoke about it. She had moulded herself to the Sharma specifications.
Arnie never found out any more than what nana told her as nani had
closed that part of her life forever. Her sisters completed the circle,

like crabs in a well, pulling her down and hoping that this would enhance them, for she was 'bahenji', and thus nothing more.

Nani meekly accepted her life. At first, her sisters took her for granted. Then her husband did and finally her son. Lines were clearly drawn. It was all right for nani to cook the dinner for Yudi mama's parties, but not for her to attend the same party, although it was held in her house. Yudi's wife felt nani was not chic enough. Arnie had seen Yudi mama stir a drink for his mother-in-law, who lived with them and was always a VIP, but not for his mother. Arnie saw it all, nani's humiliation and her quiet dignity. Nana would brusquely switch off the lights and fans so that the guests would not know that he was home. His hurt was palpable as he was left out along with nani, but he always made excuses for his star son and gorgeous daughter-in-law, and no one dared be critical of them.

At such times, he would console himself with his favourite Urdu couplet:

Tundiye mukhaalif se na ghabraa e akaab, Yeh to
chalti hai tujhe unchaa udaane ke liye . . .

It was years later that Arnie mustered up the courage to ask him what it meant.

'Let not the raging wind unnerve you, O Eagle.
It blows just to take you higher.'

"So here I am," thought Arnie aloud. "I am the lone eagle, grappling with hostile circumstances and struggling with your legacy, nana, the good and the bad."

What advice would he give his daughter today? Had he not taught her that stealing was a crime? That leaving your daughter out of a family tree did not mean that she did not exist? That grandchildren were precious and you could not and should not steal their future?

Not for anything in the world would she give up on her children, Arnie knew that. She would not be like Kamini. Neither money nor the good name of the family would ever make her sacrifice their happiness. Nana was right. Her children were special.

18

'Doesn't matter what you do or how you do it, your neighbours are going to talk elsewhere about you, anyway.'
— Felder Rushing

▼

On her way to a meeting in Delhi, Arnie took a detour. "Drive past the gates of my house in Civil Lines, the one that has a boundary wall that spans the entire road," she told the driver, her voice tinged with pride, loss, and sadness.

He was sitting there just as Arnie had known he would be. She was looking out for him through the open gates and her eyes welled up with tears when she saw him there, sitting on the verandah, staring vacantly as always. Dust and grime hung heavy around him. Everything around him spoke of neglect—the verandah, the garden, the aangan, and even the trees, their once green and shiny leaves now coated in mud and black soot.

Arnie's earliest recollections of her father were of him sitting on the verandah, just as he was now. "How did he get to be this way," she wondered. For the handsome, Cambridge-educated favourite son of Eshwar Dhari to reduce himself to this state must have taken some doing. It had always been difficult for Arnie to reconcile Chhoti Phua's stories of the high life that her father led and the great work he did, with the person she had grown up seeing. In her memory, her father was forever ensconced in the safe clutches of his familiar surroundings, the verandah. It became his Times Square and his Central Park. His empty durbar and his self-made prison.

The verandahs in Civil Lines were large. They extended across the entire frontage of the house and were as wide as rooms. An entire modern apartment could've fitted into one of them. And the house, the house was as long as the road itself. Space was never an issue, not even with the large extended family that lived there.

Every day, when she left the house, first for school, then for college, and later for work, Arnie would wave to her father. He always sat at the same spot on the verandah, dragging his chair slightly here and there as the sun moved, either to shield himself from its angry glare in summers or to follow its apologetic path for some warmth in the winters. It was always the same routine, and, depending on where his chair was on the verandah, Arnie could tell the month and the time of day.

Nothing changed on the verandah, but Arnie had. She had changed from a jumpy girl in pigtails chattering to him about school, to a young woman running to work, muttering under her breath as he strained to catch the rushed sentences. He was still there, years later, wiping a tear from his eye as he watched her drive away as a young bride with her new husband.

A puff of smoke and she was gone. But he, he remained there. He was always a magnet that drew Arnie, and she would stop for a moment next to him even as life would fly by. The trees would grow, from saplings to tiny shrubs to tall, towering trees. And then they would die. The cycle would repeat itself. And he would still be on the verandah.

The driver had parked strategically so that Arnie could look through the gates without being seen herself. An old *peepal* tree grew near the verandah. It was 'the tree of spirits', and under its boughs were kept little idols and figurines of gods and goddesses. Arnie squinted, trying to see from the distance the little *diyas* that

148

were placed in the recesses of the roots. The ochre and russet thread entwined around the sturdy trunk looked faded and frayed. She remembered her *ayah* telling her in her Bihari-Hindi accent, that if she put a tiny paper in the trunk of the tree, her wish would be granted.

What did little girls wish for? Dolls and dresses perhaps? But every time, Arnie's wish had only been to be a good girl and be loved by her mother. And the wish didn't change even when Kamini beat her, for she would just limp to the tree and write her wish on a leaf and place it in the cavity of the trunk. Looking at the tree now, decades later, Arnie smirked at her own naiveté; the *ayah* had clearly taken her for a ride, for the totem had obviously never worked.

There was a mighty banyan tree near the servants' quarters and Arnie smiled as she recollected that the servants called it '*banyaan*', a vest. The roots hung down from it, forming a lattice and making it look like an old wrinkled witch. She could see the resemblance as she looked through the gate. There was her long nose, there the wicked eyes. Oh! And there was her pointed hat right on top, like a witch. "Like my mother," Arnie murmured rebelliously.

Her eyes searched for the vultures that once sat majestically on the tall mango trees around the periphery of the house and remembered that Krish had once told her that these scavenger birds had all but vanished from Delhi. "If they still existed," she wondered, "would they swoop down and prey upon *her* body, pick on the flesh and leave it lifeless? Just as she is doing to me . . ."

This sprawling, living, vibrant, noisy house, with its six gardens and long verandahs, had been home to a menagerie of relatives. A blush came to Arnie's cheeks the next instant as she remembered the many scandals and hidden dalliances that had happened within the house. To describe all that went on in that house, she would have to marshal her thoughts room by room.

The Verandah.

The house was constantly bustling with activity and literally sizzling with gossip, mostly alleged affairs and infatuations. It usually started with cousins mocking and teasing the 'victim'; then the aunts and uncles would jump into the fray with their priceless tips and personal anecdotes. The parents of the victim, however, would be in damage control mode and would try to hush up the issue. However, the final say always rested with Dadaji. The verandah was his courtroom, and the verdict would come in his roaring voice, causing the jury of immediate family to hurry off, while the army of servants, drivers, cooks, and hangers-on delighted in the family spectacle.

There was a time when, from the verandah, one could look and see Delhi's silhouette and breathe a lung's worth of fresh air. It was on the same verandah that was later on going to be the definition of his failure, that Arnie's father had spent his best times. Those were the days when animated discussions on politics had preoccupied the aristocracy of North India. Differing political ideologies were not tolerated; Dadaji's perspective was the only relevant one. And Arnie's father was always at the centre of these discussions and could be relied upon to bring up one conspiracy theory or another. But that was all before his thoughts turned to finding buried treasure and sitting on the verandah, waiting for unicorn-drawn chariots bearing untold wealth and glory to come and place them at his feet.

The Kitchen and the Servants' Quarters.

'Scandal' was the other name for this den of vice, sex, affairs, and controversies. The place of amorous sounds and erotic glimpses. Kamini walking into the laundry room and finding the maid snuggling with the thin puny driver; the young girl 'brought' or better still 'bought' by the cook for his entertainment, running from one room to another in her negligee, without his wife and children knowing.

The Bedrooms.

Shhh ... everything was hushed here. Walls, as they say, have ears, and the air that curled its way around the cracks in the doors carried tales with it. This was a time when Bollywood movies used two flowers, quivering and shaking, to depict kissing scenes, and blushing heroines emerging from behind trees were an indication of covert intercourse having happened off-camera. The word 'sex' was not used in polite society. When the doors were closed, the world was a different place.

Arnie's bedroom shared a wall with that of her parents; this was before Kamini stomped out of her husband's room, preferring to sleep alone.

Arnie's ears turned red as she remembered that one peaceful morning, a long time ago, when she was sitting in her room, sipping chai and gazing out of the window. A sudden loud BANG from behind the wall she shared with her parents' bedroom almost made her drop her hot tea. And then, the first bang was followed by slower and slower bangs. Arnie almost died of shame, when, the next instant, she heard Kamini's voice moaning and groaning in obvious ecstasy. "Ohh my Ram yezzz yez." Dumfounded and embarrassed, she didn't know whether to run or to hide. Oh my God! She had caught her mother having sex with her partner in the export business!

The Bathroom.

There was a time in the distant past when women papered over their periods, pretending stomach cramps were caused by food poisoning that occurred every month. Distant past? Hah! Nani's sister had once said that she slept in another bedroom on 'those' days because her mother-in-law considered her 'impure' and ordered her to do so.

The Dining Room.

Meals were accompanied by the occasional gossip session with cousins with Chhoti Phua adding the extra *tardka*. *Playboy* was not freely available in Delhi back then, and *Fifty Shades of Grey* was yet to be written. Sex was an obsession with both men and women, and everyone gossiped, but in covert ways. As the servants scooped out the delicately spiced *aloo chokha* on to their plates at mealtimes, they too, would pitch in, adding spice and rumour to the Bollywood scandals they knew of. A superstar of that time running away with his girlfriend, the leading lady of his films, and ending up with two wives; stories of the 'Dream Girl' and her Jat husband, both the darlings of the camera and the audiences; actresses who had used the casting couch to get a lead role; actresses who had had a threesome with sleazy directors; plastic surgery, and Bollywood.

These rumours were subtle hints intended for a particular person at the table. And though everyone knew who it was, the name was never mentioned it. Except for that one time when the name slipped out of the bearer's lips: "*Voh* Kamini madam . . ." Time made Arnie forget whether he was referring to her mother's nose job or the bum firming, but the next day, she remembered, poor Bahadur had been sacked.

The Garage.

The rest of the spaces in the house were tame in comparison. The large, dusty garages were where the real fun was to be had. It was where the young daughters-in-law of the family flirted with older brothers-in-laws, and it was where older male cousins made passes at younger girls, be they relatives or daughters of the servants. Chhoti Phua, it was said, had once caught Kamini emerging from her Chevvy Impala, scandalously dishevelled, her hair tousled, and the windows of her car fogged up. And then, from behind her, the Swiss *angrez* had emerged. Seeing Baby Singh, he had run off and wasn't seen for a while after that. Then Kamini started her foreign trips, her flights always hopping through via Switzerland no matter what her destination was.

Kamini's office.

A line of finely placed and perfectly potted *Cordyline fruticosa*, with their lush purple leaves, led straight into Kamini's so-called office. This room had many avatars. At first, it used to be an export office, but it rapidly transformed into a branch of 'Woman Alive', because feminism was in vogue, and then to an AIDS office. Arnie had no idea what it was used for at present, whether it was foreign aid for the development of the impoverished millions or a public relations centre for the latest business venture of a powerful politician, but 'work' seemed to carry on at all odd hours and the visitors mostly preferred to slink away, hiding from the light of the lamppost at the corner. No one was quite sure whether the grants-in-aid were for sericulture or for Kamini's nocturnal activities. A convenient snip and a tuck to uplift . . . more than her spirits!

This isolated office was not enough. Kamini needed greater privacy and a place to get away to, so her doting father gave her his retirement home, not far from Civil Lines. It was a getaway for his gorgeous daughter and the parties she held there, to 'unwind from her stressful life', were definitely rocking! "Get away and do what?" Arnie had wondered when in school. Nana had provided a roof for Kamini, a security, which, ironically, Arnie struggled for even today.

The interesting rooms were not restricted to Civil Lines alone. Arnie smiled as she remembered the pious and godly Yudi mama's office.

There was quite a hullaballoo when nani's maid had suddenly gotten pregnant, because her husband lived in the village and they hadn't met for over a year. She was known to be quite a recluse and didn't venture out of the house either. So it was someone from within the Sharma household whose hormones had been active and at work. What was even stranger than the whole affair was nana's stern dismissal of the whole scandal. No one dug deeply into the matter, but there was needless justifications that Yudi mama, the ever dutiful son, had "nothing to worry about."

The saintly Yudi mama had his office in an outhouse on the Sharma property, totally cut off from everything else and overlooking a beauteous garden. A large mahogany desk, plenty of books, a small fridge in the corner, and a comfortable bed with a thick, soft Rajasthani quilt which made it quite definitely the perfect place to 'sleep on' . . . or maybe 'sleep with' someone!

Was it the proximity and the lack of privacy within the joint family system which meant that sexuality was always in your face? Perhaps yes. Perhaps every joint family had secret places for dalliances and affair, and more than a few skeletons in their cupboards.

It was all such a long time ago. Having had enough of reminiscing, Arnie asked the driver to move on. She looked out of the window as the car sped back towards her house. Gone were the days of the spacious verandahs, large garages, huge unending gardens, and the extra spaces in houses and hearts for relatives who had fallen on bad times. Civil Lines, as she had known it, was an anachronism now.

Arnie's journey into Delhi, however, had been pointless. She had reached the Delhi ridge forest when her phone rang and she was told that the meeting she was to attend had been cancelled. She sat back and took in her surroundings before deciding where to go. She had a few hours to kill before her next appointment, which was another meeting with Chhoti Phua.

Arnie drove into the Promenade Mall in Vasant Kunj and headed for Nandos, first floor, left wing, table 18. She was early. But a little bit of window-shopping, two mojitos, and a twenty-minute wait for a table took up some time before Chhoti Phua arrived, as usual fashionably late.

19

'Being weak doesn't make you worthless.
Being strong doesn't make you invincible.
But having those two sides makes you, you.'
– Danielle Baker

The Portuguese lunch at Nandos may not have been to Chhoti Phua's liking, but the wine she ordered made up for it.

"So when are you leaving for your holiday to London with the children?" she asked.

"In a couple of days," Arnie replied, sipping her mojito.

"Good. By the time you come back, I will have finalised my new home. I want to get an 800 square feet plot in Shanti Niketan. I have seen it and the house is nice; just like the ones I see abroad."

A wicked grin crossed Arnie's face. If Ramesh, her lawyer, had his way, then no one would be moving into their new houses in a hurry. If she was lucky, that is. A big IF. Enjoying her glass of wine, Chhoti Phua began her ritual updating Arnie on the family gossip. "Your mother, what can I say about her? Jaante ho, her expensive lawyers are able to buy her time while she scouts for potential buyers. There is enough for everyone, but she still wants more. Her greed defies logic. Every afternoon, she brings people across the aangan to show them the house. She thinks that I will be asleep, but I make it a point to be awake at that time. I watch her showing off my father's house. What gives her the right to show the house to anyone? Which drop of Sir Eshwar Dhari's blood flows in her veins? I wish your father had not been such a wimp. She struts around, but she cannot bypass me. I am always there, and she eventually has to cross the aangan and introduce me to the buyers. They might think that I am a doddering old woman, but I am sharper than they assume and I get all the information I want. Particularly how much they are willing to give for the house. Your mother is trying to have a side deal and make lots of money in cash . . . we know it all."

Her voice trailed off. If she were younger, she would have fought. Being eighty and weary of a long court battle, she was willing to settle for the agreement that she had secured.

They talked about the children after that and Chhoti Phua asked Arnie to buy their favourite books.

"Okay, I will, Chhoti Phua," Arnie replied, wondering why her aunt wanted her to do that. "Next time, we will meet at the Suzi Wong restaurant with the children," her aunt continued. "I love Chinese food!"

Over dessert, and much to her amusement, Chhoti Phua gave Arnie her London shopping list. "You will get all these things at Harrods. And while you are there, remember to get me mint chocolates. You will find them in the corner after the fragrance section. Anyway, we will meet again next week, just before you fly off. Please get me the children's favourite books, don't forget. Gift-wrap them and give the packet to my driver. I want to present them to the children, but you help me by buying them."

"Yes, Chhoti Phua," Arnie replied, walking her to her car where they said their goodbyes.

"The driver talks to your mother, you know," Chhoti Phua whispered just as she was about to get into the car. "Next time, I will get Bhabhi's car because she has a new driver who's neutral. We need to be careful, *bekar ka jhagda*, no point darling. And that Swarovski crystal ring doesn't suit you." And with that, she was gone.

Arnie watched the car drive out of the mall parking, amazed that at eighty, her aunt was still all there, ticking her off for not wearing what she considered fine jewellery.

Her car drove off and she waved regally, like a queen. Arnie was left standing there, under the *sheesham* tree. The tree was strong, sturdy, and straight. Rooted. Able to withstand the harshest of storms and the toughest of weathers. Protecting, shading, and shielding. The wind howled, rustling its jade leaves. The *sheesham* stood there in all its glory. Unperturbed and fearless. She had to learn from it.

Arnie was glad that she was finally piecing it all together. She called and filled Krish in on the details on her way home. Dadaji had included everyone in his estate, all the children and even the grandchildren. She was the only one who had been left out, and not by him.

When she walked in to her apartment later in the day, Arnie saw the children crowding around Krish.

"He has found exciting information," Shrey announced, pointing to the iPad even as Krish pulled her closer and made her look at what he had found. It was a court order relating to a tax dispute over family property, put by Eshwar Dhari in the names of his sons.

"This is an important order, and if you scroll through all of it, you'll come to that one amazing fact that will make your day. Your uncle, Anil Dhari, has shown the money trail starting from early properties and ending all the way at Civil Lines! That too on oath!"

Arnie's disbelief was apparent. "Again Google? When I have some money to spare, I must buy shares in Google! But where is it? Show me!"

"Of course, where else? And I have done a summary for you; your lawyers will be pleased." Arnie read it once and then again but seemed to be missing the point of significance. "Where is it Krish? And tell me the relevance because I am tired."

"Here," Krish said, pointing at a particular passage with his finger, urging her to read. "Anil Dhari has not disclosed the means and resources available to them. He has then claimed that they had sufficient cash with them as they were old zamindars."

"But where does it say how much he had? And how did you make the link with Civil Lines?"

"Well, keeping it really simple, he says, on oath mind you, that Dadaji and your family were old zamindars and they had lots of money. So they didn't need to earn anything and they could buy many properties. And he said that all of this was ancestral wealth."

"Oh my God, the dead do speak!" Arnie exclaimed. "Let's call Ramesh and tell him all this. Wow, this is huge. If this was ancestral wealth, then I have a share in it too. If only we can get some proof beyond his words, it would be super." She grinned and clapped her hands, inspiration striking her suddenly. "The Lloyds Bank branch they used for the transaction! It's just across the road from their house. I know because Chhoti Phua had pointed it out, remember I told you about it?"

Krish nodded his head. "But there may be a problem here," he said. "Lloyds has been through several mergers and acquisitions, and though they may have kept records through all this, but don't bank on it."

Muffled giggling caught their attention then, and they turned around to see both children laughing because they found the pun on the word 'bank' very funny. "Don't bank on the bank for help, don't bank in the bank, don't bank with the bank or bank on the bank," they chanted, and their laughter suddenly brightened the atmosphere, easing Arnie's tension.

"It has to be ancestral wealth. I know my father did not work and neither did anyone else in the family. And suddenly, now that time's running right past them, they realise that they are old and that's making them desperate to sell Civil Lines. They want to enjoy the money for what is left of their lives. They would not have dared to lie so blatantly while my grandfather was alive. He would've slapped them soundly, especially my mother since he never liked the way she exploited his name while running him down." Arnie paused for a second, before continuing again. "Do the dead get angry? Do they get homesick? Will Dadaji miss the house that was so closely identified with him once they sell it? Will he hit them on the knuckles for lying, for claiming that they bought the house? Does he feel sad as he watches them bicker? Who, when they have divided up the spoils, will take the *koel* that sang in the summer every year? Will they divide her too, into precious little bits?" Arnie asked, swallowing her emotions in a big gulp.

Krish looked at her, his steady gaze not leaving Arnie's face. "Your Dadaji is with you. Look at the timing and be grateful that you have pieced together events that you were unaware of. He is watching over you."

"And my nani, too, for sure," Arnie added, wanting to believe that her nani had loved her, that someone had, because her life, as she had known it, was falling apart.

The three grandparents that she knew were no longer alive, but they did love Arnie. She slumped in her chair trying to remember them as they once were, full of life. Not so much for the memories of their passing, the hospital wards, Alzheimer's, and the end. She was blessed that they had loved her and she believed life would have been different if they had still been around.

Arnie's present was shadowed by a past that continued to darken her future. Nothing mattered today, not her degrees, not her scholarships, not the repeated invites from the Sloan School of Management at Stanford, and not the career she had painstakingly built.

Was the transition similar for her Cambridge-educated father? The transition into despair and defeat? For like him, she too, felt like crawling into a hole and pulling the covers over her, shutting out the world and withdrawing from the struggle.

Arnie could still see him, her father, sitting in the verandah, older and huddled, being harangued even now by Kamini. She could picture all those times when her mother had humiliated him through her brother. They had sniggered, the two of them, egged on by Kamini as she lamented her fate and either mocked him or stayed completely indifferent to his presence. But nothing ever caused him to lose his temper; it was as if he had vowed to bear it all. No one really knew what went on in his mind. Whenever someone was weary, rushed or overworked, they would automatically look towards his room and raise their eyebrows or shake their heads at his apparent lethargy and inactivity. Quite often, he was looked at with burning contempt for not working, and Kamini and her father fanned the flames of this behaviour.

In their father's hearing, Arnie and Randy, his children, were told not to be like him. Eshwar Dhari was not spared either. Kamini would spit out, "Be different, break the mould, and never be mean and vicious like your Dadaji is." She did this as often as was required for her children to internalise the message. They became ashamed of Dadaji and learnt not to speak about him in their mother's presence or in front of the Sharmas. They saw him, their paternal grandfather, as a thief, a rogue, a bandit. Everything good and positive resided in the Sharmas and they had to be like them—honest and forthright, devoid of greed and overriding ambition. They had to rise above their genes and fool their DNA if they were to succeed in life. The irony was that slowly, they began to see themselves as Sharmas, even though they stayed with Eshwar Dhari, in his house, their entire lives.

The brainwashing and the rewriting of history was a well-thought out and coordinated act. It was not that the Sharmas took an opportunity that had presented itself and then made themselves holier-than-thou. They actively went out and created a reality that worked for them. The Dharis, renowned conspirators and powerful individuals in their own right, were outclassed and outmatched by the cunning and persistence of a perfectly matched brother and sister combination, Yudi and Kamini.

Arnie remembered Yudi mama running her father down, with Kamini playing the perfect victim. Animated conversations between Kamini's parents and her brother were sprinkled with anecdotes about Arnie's father's grand life while he worked. These conversations always ended with their signature exaggerated sigh and a heavenward look.

Arnie and Randy would be reminded that their father had responsibilities towards them, while they were being primed to shout at him. Arnie, in particular, always needed to prove her allegiance to the Sharmas, for they were never sure on which side she would come down if she were left on her own. Arnie would start rather timidly and uncertainly, forgetting the lines she had been taught by her mother, caught between the crossfire of warring adults even at the age of five. By fifteen, however, her voice became steadier as she recited Kamini's list of woes by proxy. But her father's lack of response then, as now, was inexplicable and in his silence, there was something more tangible than words.

What a giant of a man he could have been, her father! He had been a tiger, full of promise, a young Cambridge engineer reeking of power and grace, the son of a rich and powerful man. Not just any son, the favourite son. The world waited for him to bloom and flourish, to leap forward and seize the day. It was difficult to write him off. He had far too much going for him. He was like a sleeping tiger, ready to leap forward like the Asian economies that were emerging and taking on the older commercial power centres of the world. Returning from the West, he had the trappings of success and the arrogance of old money. And the backing of Sir Eshwar Dhari, his father. He assumed an aura of intrigue and had a sphinx-like status, mysterious and enigmatic. His apparently hot temper was talked about in the backdrop of money; his reclusive temperament was attractive because he belonged to aristocracy. His wearing kurta-pyjamas was seen as becoming, just as was his leaning towards religion. The last was explained as him reaching for his roots, having seen the vagaries of the West and, much like the Beatles, leaning towards the mystical East. He had the world at his feet and, any moment now, he would step forward and claim his place in the firmament.

But he never did take that step. And over the years, the society that was slow in its condemnation of him, suddenly forgot him. A complete amnesia.

When the sun began setting on the grand old man, Eshwar Dhari, the very people who supped at his table and fought for his attention, suddenly crossed over to Kamini's side, buying her story that she was the victim, her version of life sprinkled liberally with big lies. And when he was gone, Kamini had it all. Doting parents, a fawning brother, a pliant husband, and a dead but powerful father-in-law. She went to parties hosted by the President of India on invitations addressed to the dead patriarch. She exploited fully the slowness with which government databases were updated. She successfully encashed his legacy, while cursing his son. She did what she had set out to do, set her throne on his son's chest, suffocating his family, burning with revenge for ills meted out to her in an era gone by and by people long dead.

Arnie shuddered. "Does revenge not have an expiry date?" she wondered, echoing the words of Chhoti Phua from a long time ago.

20

'Fiction is the Truth inside the Lie.'
— *Stephen King*

Delhi is one of the fastest growing cities in the world, unconstrained as it is by any geographic barrier to a seemingly boundless expansion. With its population come the vehicles. Black swirls, toxic gas, pollution-covered trees and children with respiratory problems are commonplace in this capital of India.

It was not always like this. There was a time not too long ago when vintage and classic cars negotiated the roads that were used largely by Ambassadors, Fiats, a few Heralds, and a number of scooters. Buses were well ventilated and the trucks had been going since the Second World War. Then came the younger son of a doting Prime Minister and the Indo-Japanese marvel of Maruti Suzuki was born.

Nana had used his influence to hand over the keys of a shiny white Maruti 800 to Kamini. He had jumped queues and used contacts for his beautiful daughter who, to his mind, always deserved the best. Part of his busy day was pre-occupied with her; getting her cars, investing in commercial properties, and buying the best plots in the suburban city being developed by his friend.

Chhoti Phua and Arnie met often these days. She was the only link Arnie had with her extended family and she enjoyed the relationship that they had rediscovered. She was running late today for their meeting at the new hookah place in Saket. But Chhoti Phua walked in just as Arnie got there, resplendent in a designer chiffon, Carrera dark glasses, a Louis Vuitton handbag, and reeking of Dior.

"Wow, you look good," Arnie gasped, looking at her with open admiration, bedazzled by her large diamonds. Her aunt was dressed to kill.

Pleased that she had created the desired impact, Chhoti Phua casually slipped out a shoe from under her sari and said, "Handmade Chinese," as she waddled across the room to a suitable table.

"Why are you walking like that?" her niece asked, trying to keep pace with her.

"I have had knee replacement surgery on both legs," her aunt replied, attempting to hitch up the sari proudly.

They ordered double-mint green-apple-and-grape *sheeshas* and settled down.

Chhoti Phua immediately slipped into a now familiar conversation pattern, her pet peeve being Kamini and her irritating ways. "Why is her salwar always a bit yellow? It is never as white as her kurta or that miniscule scarf she wraps around her neck. *Dulhanji*, as the maids used to call her when she was a new bride, was very nicely turned out, but her innerwear was not always clean. Your mother has not changed at all. In court, I always look for a dirty salwar and that is how I spot her in the crowd."

Arnie was in splits because she vaguely remembered that her mother's kurtas were always sent for dry cleaning, but never the salwars. She laughed and reminded her aunt of the days when she herself pinched her hair into waves using frightening clamps.

"That was the fashion in those days, even Greta Garbo used them," Chhoti Phua defended herself.

"And what about the tons of whitening powder you used?" Arnie teased.

"I used all those creams to lighten and brighten my complexion; why not? I wanted to look good, I wanted a life."

"Of course, Chhoti Phua. I remember watching you as you dressed to go out, fascinated by your jewellery."

"I had tons of jewellery so I wore it. In life, do what you want. I had it, so I flaunted it. Kamini sniggered then, but look at her now. She hangs three pairs of earrings, one hoop and from it a dangler. Now I laugh at her."

Arnie remembered her aunt's boyfriends and teased her about them. "Jaante ho, I lived life and I lived it on my terms in my father's house in front of these manicured vultures," she said, referring to her sisters-in-law. "The worst was your mother. You thought that we had all the human failings and that the Sharmas were gods. Let me tell you, they were no less."

The *sheeshas* arrived and they inhaled a puff. Releasing swirls of grey smoke, Chhoti Phua continued. "Did you know that Sardar Saheb used to ogle at Yudi Sharma's wife? He openly flirted with her and even dedicated a book to her? But it was tolerated because Yudi was still trying to establish himself. And what about all the young nubile attendants that come and go in a steady stream, signing disclaimers that Yudi Sharma is like their father? Never heard of this in any other household! What is the necessity for such declarations," her aunt asked smugly.

"And let's talk about your nani's brother-in law, the one in the airlines, who was in bed with his wife's own niece. *Arrey*, I am talking about the one who was an airhostess, Miss Long Legs and Short Skirts."

Arnie was thoroughly enjoying herself by now.

"We saw all three of them at your parents' wedding, the man

groping the young girl openly while she giggled foolishly and the wife's anguish as she clutched her little child's hand . . . nothing was lost on us. The affair carried on and it was an open secret. Everyone, including your Yudi mama, looked away. Your nani and her sisters gathered around the woman, consoling her, pumping her up so that she stayed in the marriage. Those big diamonds presented in front of everyone as a declaration of undying love from her husband-dear, they did not deceive Dadaji or me. We are neither stupid nor blind. The Sharmas and their obsession with self-respect amused us.

"Jaante ho na, that is why they got her married to that IIT engineer in America and packed her off, but they forgot the uncle was a pilot and travelled all over, so the scheme failed. And now I hear she is back in Bangalore because her husband heads some big American multinational which is setting up a base in the city," she chuckled. "I see his photograph in the newspaper, giving awards, hobnobbing with leading industrialists, and I always laugh to myself."

"Can't be, Chhoti Phua, I know who you are talking about. They seem so nice."

But Chhoti Phua waved her objection aside with an impervious shake of her hand. She was not even close to being done.

"Did you know that Mrs Sharma's youngest sister was famous for her dalliances on the side? While her husband was posted at the border, defending the country, she had a field day with the junior officers. It was *vande maataram* of a different kind in that house. Did you know that Dadaji found out about it because his Principal Secretary was the same batch as the officers? Kamini denied it, of course, and Mrs Sharma shook her head, but I told her to her face that her sister was popular with the staff and that her stories were legendary.

"This family always had a lot to say about others, but the way they treated their own was pathetic. They called us *jungli* because

166

we were from Bihar; we were the *adivasis* and we belonged to the jungle. We were supposedly backward in our thinking. But it was your mother's first cousin who liked her. But we were the evil ones? Why? Because we had the guts to live life and not wrap it up in some social propriety?

"I am talking about a time when there was no Facebook, no mobiles, not even television. When women could not look at a man who was not a relative, let alone speak to him. These things happened in every household. You studied English Literature; you tell me, was incest invented today? Yes, Dadaji married his children into good families and chose his daughters-in-law with care. We changed the names of our daughters-in-law because it was a tradition in our family. We regret not doing the same for Kamini. Maybe it would have turned out differently for your parents.

"We have been very particular that we do not want working women in the family because your mother has been an awful experience and we do not want anyone like her to marry into our family in the future. Your Dadaji always said that a woman could either make or break a family. Look at what your mother has done. Your father has been ruined and none of us has been spared. Would you marry your son to someone like your mother?"

Arnie's expression revealed her horror at the thought of Shrey marrying a girl like Kamini. The very thought made her want to throw up.

Chhoti Phua continued her tirade. "We, unlike the rest of India, have not been fooled by the Sharmas and their facade of goodness. Unlike them, we do not barter our daughters for houses. Your nani's middle sister arranged the wedding of her stunningly beautiful daughter to a fat underachieving oaf because his parents owned a big house in Maharani Bagh. Even your mother married you off in a hurry because your in-laws had that house in South Delhi. She never bothered to check that it was rented and not owned by them! Do you think I don't know? Huh!" Chhoti Phua snorted. "Do you remember that millionaire you were almost married off to? That man was twelve years older than you were and about a decade younger than your mother. The one from Australia. Do you remember him?"

"Yes," Arnie nodded.

"She slapped you, calling you a whore because he had wanted to marry you because he liked you, but it was she who was in love with him. She complained bitterly that you were at fault, but we all knew the truth."

Realisation made Arnie sad and she felt conflicting emotions as she reached out to hold her aunt's hand. There was a connection between them that the years had not diminished.

"We got good offers, proposals, asking for your hand, but Babuji was too old to fight your mother and we did not want to be insulted or abused. I could never tell you how relieved I was to hear that you liked someone from your college and wanted to marry him. We were heartbroken when your engagement was called off, though it was not surprising because I had heard how your mother insulted him when he stood up for you. Do you remember how Betu had crossed the aangan and offered to pay for your wedding because at that moment we had thought that money was the issue? We had tried to stop him from interfering because we feared your mother, but he had gone across nonetheless, clutching his chequebook in his hand.

"Do you think we gloated when you were miserable? I saw your stunned expression when she ruthlessly began exhibiting you within weeks of the break-up, and we knew that you accepted Krish's proposal in order to escape her. And you did escape, and we watched and prayed that you would be insanely happy because Krish was different. Your mother and her brother made us feel unwelcome at your wedding, turning outright hostile, but we participated enthusiastically for you were our daughter, a daughter of the house and we owned you up. We felt their animosity, but we opened the gates of Civil Lines and our hearts to welcome the groom's family. Those gates were symbolic of how strongly we felt for you because we risked Kamini encroaching into our space, but we put our fears aside so that your wedding would be spectacular. We know that you saw everything, but did not acknowledge it because of the years of conditioning. But still, we did our best by you."

Life teaches difficult lessons, Arnie thought. The Dharis had been there for every part of her wedding, but Arnie had avoided and ignored them. Today, she could see the mysterious twists and turns that life had taken and how her loyalties had gotten horribly entangled.

"You have not met me for years, but I see some of your Dadaji in you. You have the same aquiline nose and the same high cheekbones as he and your father had. Three generations with the same birthmark on the face. You carry yourself like him, straight, with chin lifted, and with a slightly superior not-to-be-crossed air about you. Your eyes have a twinkle and like me, you love watches, perfumes, and a good life."

"That is true," Arnie agreed. "I love perfumes, and Dior reminds me of you, the fragrance that wafted across the aangan every time you passed. I remember all your favourite perfumes. My affair with fragrances began at your dressing table."

"Your Dadaji used expensive *itar*, mixed specially for him in the most famous shop of that time, and his *achkan* had expensive diamond buttons. Your mother made earrings out of his cufflinks. I learnt a lot from Mrs Sharma, but I taught your nani about perfumes! She used, let me think, that Main Grief."

Arnie burst out laughing. "You mean Ma Griffe, Chhoti Phua, in that green and white packaging, right? I remember that."

Chhoti Phua looked Arnie up and down and seemed to like what she saw. "Look at you! Well-tailored clothes, expensive perfume, and sparkling eyes. You are a Dhari, one of us," she proclaimed. Perhaps it was the smoke or maybe it was the discussion, but both their eyes were watery, red, and blotchy.

"Aranya beta," Chhoti Phua said, serious all of a sudden. "I am proud of how you have turned out. You are the brightest and most intelligent of all the Dhari grandchildren and you have built a career for yourself. I know that life has been a struggle for you and that you have not had any support, but you are more than a survivor; you are a winner!"

She was not finished. "After the sale, I want to ask Kamini something. I want to ask her that she might hate you with the same intensity with which she dislikes us because you, her daughter, are one of us. But then whose son is Rundee in that case? Does he not have the same blood? I want to understand the cause of this discrimination!"

A question had bothered Arnie for a long time, and she decided to ask her aunt about it now. "Chhoti Phua, you did not seem happy when I got admission to Queen's College, and had it not been for Dadaji, I would not have gone there. Why did you not support me at that time?"

Chhoti Phua, to give her credit, did not whitewash her own deeds. "I am not a Sharma and I cannot pretend that I was happy that you were doing things that I wished for my son. My thinking was clouded when I saw you strutting around as a Sharma. I am a mother and then a phua. I was jealous of your success. I wanted my son to study English Literature at the same college as you and then prepare for the civil service examination."

"Yes, I remember," Arnie spoke after a while. "You were very keen on him sitting for the Civils. You used to interrogate young probationers and their fathers in the Chief Ministerial days in an attempt to squeeze the secret recipe for cracking the civil service exams," Arnie teased her.

"Not everyone is brilliant, and brilliance often is not enough," she replied as Arnie nodded in agreement.

Dadaji played favourites and Arnie was lucky to be amongst his most favoured ones. Her brother was not in that select group. Randy had to sit at the back with the security at a Madhya Pradesh government function while she sat in the front row with Dadaji. She had felt bad because her brother had looked so small and joyless. It had torn her to walk to the front without him.

Chhoti Phua could recall the incident and did not hesitate in laying the blame at Kamini's door. "It was your mother's fault, sending him like that, without the proper clothes for such a function. You were a girl and I wrapped a beautiful *dupatta* around your shoulders to hide the fading *salwar kameez* and made you wear my earrings, but I could not do anything for him as he had just arrived from Delhi. Dadaji liked you and overlooked a lot where you were concerned. He was a man, not a Sharma pretending to be God," her aunt continued. "Your nana, on the other hand, was very middle class in his thinking. He was tall, stern, frugal, and puritanical. He shoved his old-fashioned values down everyone's throats until we all felt like vomiting. Every time I spoke to your father, I was the evil sister-in-law trying to manipulate him, but Yudi's obsession, that was not malicious? When we asked for something, it was 'dowry', and when he gave his daughter a gift, he was the doting father. My sister was the Zila Parishad Chairman, and the furniture that you grew up with, the beds you jumped on, your study desk, everything was provided from her government quota, meant for her house, but she sent it across to you. All that we did was left unsung and unnoticed because it was my father's responsibility to not only provide the house but also the furniture and pay the school fees and run your kitchen. Yet, he was the villain and you were brought up to think of him as evil. Would you do as much for as little?

"You have children and some day they will have babies. Do you look forward to them running away when they see you, as your brother and you did when you saw us? You peeped, smiled, and waved, and were beaten up mercilessly if you spoke with us. Do you think that your Dadaji felt good when he heard your screams from across the aangan when she beat you at the slightest pretext? Do you remember that it was Bhabhi who covered all your schoolbooks with brown paper for as long as you were in school? You gave your pile of books to her instead of your mother. And we were bad?

"Do you know that your father, fed up with your mother, had asked her to leave? Dadaji sent me to her parent's house to get you and Randy back. I told him that both of you would be looked after by all of us, but he had insisted that you needed a mother. Some mother she was to you! I used to smuggle money into your skirt pocket because your tiffin was always empty, though never your brother's. She screamed when you innocently asked her for money and let slip that I indulged you. From that day on, you had no money and no food either."

Arnie nodded because although she had buried the memory like so much else from her childhood, her friend Gursharan, now a successful doctor, had jokingly told her that it was payback time for sharing her tiffin through school. It was true.

"That Diwali, when Krish left the children and you, we watched in shocked silence as you gave your gold bangles to Dolly as a rite-of-passage, trying to pander to her. But Dolly's mother had exploited your vulnerability and asked for the matching necklace to complete the set! Disgusting! And I hear she is a shopaholic. What is eating her up? Guilt at destroying your life or her daughter's brazen display of self-indulgence?

"Your mother, in that famous article in *Fringe* magazine, accused my father of sending a servant to your side across the aangan to kill her. Your Dadaji was old and very ill when that article came out, so she got away with it. Sometimes, I feel it was good that Alzheimer's ravaged his memory, for is this what he deserved? He forgot the slights, but I cannot forget. He was the same man who stood up for you and he deserved better."

She gestured to the waiter, "Coal *badal do*," and he rushed with the burnt orange coal aglow in a yellow light and rekindled the flame. The mixture inside the *sheesha* bubbled.

"Do you remember the CM's house, Lake Bhawan? In the times he lived in, your Dadaji was a giant. He was the head of his family and extremely protective of you. He knew his responsibilities. Do you remember the number of times you got into his car, feeling important as you rode alongside him? Every summer for five years, you escaped from your mother for two months, the entire duration of your summer vacations, and flew in his private aircraft to the state where he was Chief Minister. Can you call for her car with the same ease with which you climbed into his? Can your children swivel in her chair in her not-so-grand office that stands on his property, as you did on his chair when he was CM? He owned you up. I hear your mother was the chief guest at your children's school and spoke for twenty minutes without once referring to Sia and Shrey, thus belittling her own daughter's children and carrying her imaginary battle to a school field?"

On a roll, Chhoti Phua carried on. "Your nani was different. She looked after her own. She was the reason we married our brother into the Sharma family. She was my friend in Hissar. I learnt so much from her, but it was sad to see her suffer towards the end. She was a remarkable woman, I have to admit, even if I dislike her daughter."

There was truth in her observations. These two remarkable people, Dadaji and Nani, were the ones who had looked after Arnie, and she felt their hand on her even now, years after they had passed on to better places, far from these families of conflict and viciousness.

"Mrs Sharma would have been embarrassed if she could

see your mother stick her chest out at the judge and pretend to be nineteen. She can fool them all, but she can't fool me. Jaante ho, she has orange hair now; after all, you can dye white hair any colour because the colour catches well, and her eyes are blue."

"Come on, Chhoti Phua," Arnie said, almost choking with laughter at the image her aunt had conjured up. "She has dark, almost black eyes!"

"Nothing escapes me; it just means that you have not met her for a while, because she started wearing blue lenses after Katrina Kaif wore lenses in that item number. But your mother, with her blue lenses, looks like a reptile, cold, cunning, and calculating, like a crocodile waiting to pounce on a kill and beat the life out of it."

"Ugggh," Arnie shuddered because it was true. She had secretly called her mother the Iguana Woman for years, but it was surreal that Chhoti Phua had used a similar analogy without them ever having spoken about it.

"There is a God," Chhoti Phua continued, "and some day her ill deeds will catch up with her. I may not be there to see it, but you must learn from that."

It had been a long day and Chhoti Phua had been full of stories. Arnie realised that Kamini had done a brilliant job of ensuring that she was seen as the victim. She had a hold on the men of her family, her father, her brother, her husband, and later, her son. All of them had scrambled to help her. She was always right and would not tolerate any contrary views or uncomfortable questions.

Both of them were quiet. They heard the buzz of insects and were tired by their breathless and animated conversation. The waiter arrived with the bill. A swipe of Chhoti Phua's Visa card and they were done.

The room was almost claustrophobic; pools of thick, flavoured smoke-puffs were everywhere. Swirls suddenly seemed to rise around her but she could see clearly again. Chhoti Phua had opened her eyes. Arnie was no more that little girl running across the aangan.

"They had to leave as Arnie was taking the kids for a holiday the next day." As she trooped out behind Chhoti Phua, steadying her as they got into the elevator, Arnie's mind was clear and a different perspective shone through. They emerged into the courtyard and Arnie blinked as a flash of the raging sun through the surrounding trees blinded them. The sun, as Arnie looked up at the sky and noticed, was peeping from behind the tamarind tree, weighed down by its own dull-brown fruit, both sweet and sour, just like her meetings with Chhoti Phua.

21

*'A daughter may outgrow your lap, but she
will never outgrow your heart.'*
– Anonymous

A rnie and the kids were vacationing in London when
Krish surprised them by joining them. The happiness
of the children was apparent at having him stay with them.

"So what plans, guys?" Krish demanded as he walked
into their room and the children squealed with delight.

"Coffee would be a good start," Arnie said as both the
children stared at her in disbelief.

"But Aida *didi* always makes you morning tea," Sia said.

"I am on holiday, so croissants with coffee for me,"
Arnie asserted.

Shrey leapt up with a mischievous glint in his eyes, ran
into the kitchenette, and came back clad in a tartan apron to
assist with the cooking. Arnie remembered the lovely Mother's
Day breakfast Sia and he had whipped up a few years ago and
how she had crunched into the burnt whole-wheat toast with
runny scrambled eggs and savoured every bit of it.

While preparing breakfast, they discussed what each of
them wanted to do in London. Sia wanted to shop, for she
was increasingly getting interested in design and the finer
things in life, while Shrey, the foodie in the family, wanted his
holiday to revolve around restaurants and food, filled with
the boisterous banter that made a vacation fun.

London would always have memories of juicy, glistening, rare to medium steaks with fries at Angus Steak House; of Mamma Mia's Spaghetti Carbonara drizzled with extra virgin olive oil, sprinkled generously with Parmesan; of apple-roasted chicken from Marks and Spencer's; honey-glazed Peking Duck from China Garden, and, finally, burgers at Garfunkel's on the way out at Heathrow.

Sia made a list, hypnotized by the sophisticated charm of Oxford Street's stores. Primark, Top-Shop, H&M, Forever 21. Shrey was an 'old soul' in every sense and wanted to visit Greenwich, the Science Museum, and, of course, watch a football match; the last being at the top of his agenda. "And, oh yes! Food, food, and more food," he squealed, scanning the London guidebook.

"What about you?" Krish asked Arnie as she looked away.

"It may sound strange, but I want to go to Mayfair and walk by Princess Ann's Hospital," she said quietly.

"What can we get there?" Shrey asked innocently.

"Nothing, but a fistful of lies," she whispered, ever so softly.

Krish looked up, sensing her pain, and held her gaze without flinching. "Mamma was born in Paris but was very ill and was brought here to London for treatment, to this hospital. She is trying to put the pieces of her past together," he said softly, trying to fill the deafening silence.

"What does she mean by a fistful of lies?" asked Sia.

"You were a beautiful baby," Krish began, gazing lovingly at Sia with that very warm look that Arnie had craved for from her parents as a child, only to be interrupted cheekily by Shrey. "Take a closer look, Papa!"

"Shut up you monster," Sia glared at Shrey while Krish continued.

"As we put our fingers into the clenched fists of new-born babies and open out their little fingers, we make them a promise.

A promise to look after them, to help them dream, to keep them safe, and to be there for them. Mamma was given a fistful of lies; she has been let down time and time again."

The children looked at Arnie. "I was an incubator baby," she said, "tiny and shell pink when I put on some weight, and she, she hated me. When I got better and went back to Paris, I was rushed to India because Dadaji feared for my life. Sometimes Krish, I look at these two as they sleep next to me and wonder what would make me say things like one is not mine or for how much money would I think of selling my child? And every time, my soul, my very being, revolts. Never will I dash their hopes of having a future, of having a chance at love and life!"

"Don't you worry, we will fight for your rights. We will talk to the lawyer later in the day and read the petition," Krish said, quietly beating the eggs for Shrey's breakfast, furiously venting his frustration on the contents of the bowl.

Arnie found herself with Sia at Oxford Street a little later. Sia pushed her towards the fragrance counters at all the larger-than-life stores. Arnie felt her relationship with 'smell' rekindle. Smell. Something so powerful. So deep. More importantly, something that had left an imprint on her mind. Different phases of her life were associated with smell. Even if she tried, she could not forget the smell of wet paint in her room, the smell of petrol at the fuel station, and the smell of freshly baked cake wafting across the aangan as Bhabhi brought it out of the oven.

Sia insisted and Arnie gave in, dabbing different fragrances on her slim wrist. Some old classics, some new ones. However, all seemed to have a pungent after smell, a lingering smell of betrayal. Clouds of Chanel Number 5's feminine sophistication, suddenly drowned by hints of citrus in Guerlain's Shalimar, further spiralling into the air, infused by the spicy carnation in L'air Du Temps, gradually camouflaged by her personal favourite, Dior's Poison, with its honeyed tuberose.

"Mamma, see White Linen," Sia said, dragging her mother to the Estee Lauder counter. "Your childhood stories always had the description of White Linen."

"You remember?" Arnie was touched as her daughter repeated her stories from the past. Tales about the grandeur of the Darbar Hall where men wore *bandhgalas* and the women dressed in their Indian finery.

She closed her eyes and was transported back to a train from Delhi. Three compartments had been booked exclusively for family and friends to attend Dadaji's swearing-in ceremony when he took over as Chief Minister. Arnie remembered running from one end of the train compartment to the other, chased by older cousins and her younger brother. There were festivities and endless discussions about clothes; joyous laughter echoed through the compartments. Chhoti Phua was teased, with everyone singing the popular Hindi film song '*aaj kal paon zameen par nahin parte mere*', with even the daughters-in-law joining in and singing along with the daughters, jealousy and envy forgotten. What she remembered most clearly were the smells, a heady cocktail swirling in the air and in her mind.

"You said that your Chhoti Phua wore White Linen then, and that you could identify perfumes worn at these parties because of her collection," Sia said enthusiastically. The smell of freshly laundered clothes and starch came back to Arnie as she nodded and told Sia that she could identify Dior even before she could spell it.

"Those were fun times. On occasion, I can even recall years of my life by the fragrances in vogue."

"Let's try and find them, and you tell me what you remember," urged Sia. Arnie nodded, giving in, but cautioned her daughter. "Some you just won't be able to find, like MoonDrops and Charlie," she said, ever so confidently.

Not one to give up, Sia found Charlie and Arnie recognised the fragrance. "Well, Charlie is woody, mossy, over-powering. It takes me back to when I was a little girl."

"And MoonDrops?" Sia interjected.

"Its sandalwood and musky warmth reminds me of being naughty and of a stomach wash, so I guess pain and anguish," Arnie replied.

"Wow, this is fun, and what did your nani use?"

"Leftovers and hand-me-downs from her daughter and sisters, and if her daughter-in-law felt generous, then a gift from her. It was a splash of citrus sunrise, eau de cologne for a long time, and then Ma Griffe's delicate hints of Lily of the Valley. No one ever asked her what she liked. They just plied her with the 'extras', telling her it was special. Her sisters would condescendingly hand her their unwanted *'bahenji'* scents. Despite the constant taunts, nani accepted these bottles with grace, with class."

Arnie knew the difference between fine fragrances and cheap plastic ones, having learnt to walk holding on to Chhoti Phua's dressing table which was loaded with the most expensive and the best of perfumes.

As she grew up, Arnie realised that her beautiful nani was seen as *'bahenji'* because it suited her sisters. They could not bear that nani's little unit was doing well, that her husband had risen in stature and that her son was studying in America. Her sisters were full of envy having seen the jewellery given to Kamini at her wedding. Nani always scrambled to be a loving mother, doting aunt, and even an affectionate grandmother to her extended family, holding the delicate web of relationships together and making personal sacrifices.

Tresor! Aah, she loved it even today, a mysterious heliotrope that reminded her of a cousin in senior school. And her huge eighteenth birthday party! The preparations could be seen from across the aangan. With longing eyes, Arnie had wanted to be part of the festivities, the fairy lights, the music, the boisterous voices of friends, and the smell of warm fried food delicately floating through the air. She shared her joy, but silently. At the back of her mind was a twinge of sadness for her neglected birthday, just a few years before.

The mother-daughter bonding at the perfume counters continued. "My mother never bought a single bottle of perfume for me, buying many for herself instead. I used to spray tiny bits on now and then because fragrances uplifted my soul. I would collect money and beg my friends to buy me some when they travelled abroad."

As they came to the Calvin Klein section, Sia saw Arnie cringe and quickly walk past. The little girl tried on Eternity and said, "This is divine, try some." But Arnie shook her head and sighed when her daughter asked for the story behind it. The sweet violet, pink sandalwood with a musky overtone took her back to her wedding, she said, for that was when she had first used it. At that time, she had believed that marriages were forever, eternal. That Eternity was a hymn of eternal values, of love, family, and peace. "I could never buy it now," said Arnie.

The Ice Green Poison bottle at the Dior counter brought memories of Arnie's final year of college. Its mysterious, hypnotic smell had intoxicated the world. She had begged Kamini to get some for her twenty-first birthday and had felt incredibly small when her mother had handed her a knock-off while she sprayed herself generously with the original, laughing in her face. "Too expensive for you *kutiya*, and where will you use it? To get into beds, you whore!"

Clutching her mother's hand, Sia asked, "So is that why at Diwali you always give her expensive gifts, mocking her shrunken and shrivelled heart?"

"Nope, that is only half the reason. I fear for my father; he feels the cold more acutely after his illness and no one cares, so I use Diwali to gear him up for the winter without starting an argument."

"What fragrance did he use?" Sia asked.

"Nothing, I guess," Arnie replied after a moment. "I associated the smell of cigars with him when I was very small. Hmm, and then no particular smell, except that of sweat and *beetel* juice. He had no access to aftershaves and I could only give one to him much later, when I got my first job and travelled abroad. In India, it was not available freely and he had no money in any case."

Sia drooled over the clean citrus, orange, and mandarin wafts arising from J'Adore, which reminded her of Arnie. "If I close my eyes and smell the woody, spicy Dolce Vita, I imagine you going to work, Mamma." Arnie grinned because Sia knew her very well, her little girl.

Soon enough, it was time to leave and join Krish and Shrey at Angus Steak House, where they enjoyed platefuls of steaming food accompanied by Arnie's favourite drink, Pimms. As they tucked in, Shrey declared that he wanted to jump over the timeline at Greenwich, and that they were headed that way after lunch. Arnie groaned in mock protest, but was out-voted. She looked up and saw Sia pecking at her food, but she didn't want to check her just then and looked away.

"Have you heard from the lawyer?" Arnie asked Krish and he shook his head. There was no news from Ramesh. Arnie was disappointed, but she tried to lose herself in the children's banter; she didn't want her past to cloud the gaiety in the room. She got up and rushed to the washroom. She washed her face and touched up the blush, but nothing could fool Sia when she walked back to their table, and the little girl held her mother's hand through the rest of the meal until finally, Arnie gathered the courage to speak.

"I am late in the whole process, I have no documents. Even my lawyer is dragging his feet. So where does it leave us? The ancestral estate will be sold if we do not file when court opens in a fortnight."

"Nothing of the sort," said Krish brusquely.

Arnie held back her instinctive reaction to argue, to contradict, to rage. Instead, she remembered that it was her friend who had introduced them to Ramesh, and she decided to send her a text message. She handed Krish her BlackBerry after drafting the message. "Is it okay?" she asked.

"No, it isn't because you cannot vent on her. Let it go for now."

They walked around after lunch. Arnie's mind was still preoccupied and her brain wrinkled with worry. "I will look a hundred if I don't watch it," she said out aloud.

"And be in a hospital soon, if you don't take care," added Krish as an afterthought.

"So do cardiac units also mend broken hearts? Hearts that have been attacked by the patient's mother? Hearts that have been fed lies and robbed?" Arnie retorted.

"Hmph!" Krish grunted in response as they walked into Barnes and Noble.

The 'After Death' section drew Arnie and she flipped open a book that explained present life trauma as a payback from the past. She could not help giggling because Monica's theory was explained clearly in the pages before her. "Hey, read this," she called out to Krish. "According to this, there is something that I must have done to deserve this mounting injustice and continued misery in this lifetime, for this to happen to me. The author claims that I must have been a witch in my previous birth."

"The leader of the entire evil pack," Krish said, and Arnie added, "Yeah, of international fame!" They grinned at the all too familiar phrase used pompously by Kamini to describe herself.

Arnie's self-doubts had not gone away and she clutched Krish's elbow for support. "I cannot do it; I will lose what little savings

I have along with my sanity. I am up against a wall. My mother and her ruthless brother have money, power, and the influence to finish me off. She meant it when she said that I was an irritating cockroach and that she would pulverise me."

"A good metaphor, because after a nuclear bomb, the only life form that survives is a cockroach. So have respect for a cockroach," Krish added irritatingly, bringing in another one of his quirky factoids.

"I cannot do it, I cannot gamble the future of my children, I just cannot," Arnie whispered. "Even gamblers take calculated risks and I am clutching at straws; I have nothing."

"One fucking lawyer does not respond and you give in? You taught me to live, brought up the kids on your own, and built a career . . . all this to give in now?"

But his argument did not convince Arnie and she was still lost in thought as they headed to Waitrose to pick up a takeaway dinner. They waited in the frigid cold as the sun set quickly, finally inking the London skies black, until Shrey popped out with stuffed carrier bags almost as large as him. They piled into a cab and headed to the service apartment.

Once back, Krish and the kids warmed up dinner as Arnie jumped into the shower, wanting to cleanse her mind of everything. Five minutes later, there was a faint knock on the bathroom door; it was Sia.

"Mamma," she said from outside, "don't give up. We haven't given up on you and neither has the Universe you speak of. Mamma, Mamma, Mamma," she sobbed as Arnie quickly dried herself and stepped out, gathering her daughter in her arms. "We only have you, Mamma," Sia spoke brokenly, "don't get depressed or sad Mamma, please sweet Mamma. I want to be like you when I grow up, not like that dragon with claws. Definitely not like her."

Emotion was stuck in Arnie's throat like a fishbone as she struggled to console her little daughter. She had never denied Sia the right to be a daughter, unlike in her own case. And she hugged her tightly now, the embrace filling their souls and making the small bathroom warm. Arnie's heart swelled and expanded as she gently urged Sia to step out so that she could get ready for the evening.

Over dinner, they watched a serial on television and Sia watched Arnie from the corner of her beautiful eyes, attentive, alert to her mother's fragile state.

"I am okay, my sweetheart," Arnie assured her, pulling Sia closer to herself and holding her little hand just as nani used to while talking to her when she was growing up.

At bedtime, Arnie cuddled up between her children and kissed their sleepy faces and small hands, repeating again and again, "I love both of you and nothing can change that, nothing."

A letter rested next to her pillow when Arnie woke up the next morning, a headache having kept her in bed later than normal. She picked it up and saw that it was in Sia's writing. Curious, she opened it and began reading.

Hey Mamma,
I know that you've been upset lately because of all that's been going on . . . but seeing you upset is making me upset. I want you to know that I love you so much and you're the strongest person I know. Growing up, Shrey and I didn't have the adoration of our grandparents, the support of aunts and uncles, phuas and chacha-chachis, the friendship of our cousins, and for a long time, the presence of our father. But all that didn't matter because you filled in for them all and gave us more love than all of them ever could have. You're not only my mother, but also my best friend and role model (and also

my shopping partner, movie buddy, and much more). You inspire me to take the good with the bad, live life to its fullest, stand up for yourself and for what you believe in, and not take shit from anyone. I know you've been let down but you've never let that get you down. You always pick yourself up again. So Mamma, I know you're having a tough time, but you're standing up for your rights and that is so inspiring. I am by your side and always will be (so will Shrey) and you've come too far to give up, Mamma. You're strong and you can do this, so we'll make it through this together.

Sia

Arnie was glad that she had been honest with her children and had told them about the case. For the shameful truth was that her family was denying her very existence.

"I promise we will make it through, my darling," Arnie whispered, hugging a still asleep Sia. "We will."

She walked over to Krish's room, handed him the letter, and told him determinedly that she would not give up. His face clouded with emotion as he read Sia's letter. "I will do all I can to support the children and you. Just be brave."

Arnie and Sia opted out of the science museum excursion that Krish and Shrey had planned the next day and headed to a pub instead after a lazy morning. Sia enjoyed her lunch and Arnie ordered a Pimms. She felt herself relax. It was good to be away, away from it all, she told herself. She noticed the sexy shoes worn by the lady on the next table and pointed them out to Sia. "Have to get those," she mouthed to her daughter, who giggled and nodded, quietly taking a photograph.

"Look at that dress, it is really sexy," she told Arnie, pointing out to a fat woman stuffed into a gorgeous red dress. "Such a waste because she has no waist," she whispered and they giggled conspiratorially. "Oxford Street in the afternoon and Bicester Village tomorrow," they planned enthusiastically, all concerns suspended for the moment as they chuckled, mother and daughter footloose in London.

"You have to check out this really cool song, it describes your relationship with your mother perfectly. Listen to it Mamma, just change the word 'dad' to 'mom'," said Sia, clamping her headphones on Arnie before she could resist, and she listened, mesmerised, in the middle of HMV on Oxford Street. The words washed over her in waves as she heard the lyrics of 'Perfect' by a new band called Simple Plan.

Hey dad look at me
Think back and talk to me
Did I grow up according to plan?

Arnie yanked off the headphones because she had started crying. Sia immediately pulled her closer, hugging her, the roles reversed for a bit, her daughter comforting her and Arnie knew in a song that Sia understood perfectly what she was going through.

I try not to think
About the pain I feel inside
Did you know you used to be my hero?

Arnie's lower lip quivered. Sia understood that she was thinking of Yudi mama.

"Yudi mama was your hero, right Mamma?" she asked. "We used to like him too. I miss him and so does Shrey. We feel we are not his own anymore."

Arnie grabbed her, almost smothering her in a tight hug, because they both felt the betrayal, but only she had spoken of it aloud.

I can't believe it's hard
Just to talk to you
But you don't understand
'Cuz we lost it all
Nothing lasts forever

Arnie rewound the song and listened to it again, soaking in the words. She was haunted by the years that had gone by, but she was determined not to repeat the same mistakes with her children.

"Okay, enough. Let's go to Primark, we have the whole day to ourselves," Sia announced as she raised a poster that made Arnie laugh because she modified the contents as she read it out aloud. "I want to be the girl you want me to be, I want to be the girl you would want your son to date, I want to be classy like you; anything but trashy like her or flashy or as pathetic."

They burst out laughing as Sia's eyes twinkled with mischief, and then she did a mock performance of '*Sheila ki Jawani*', oblivious to the people around her and Arnie laughed like she hadn't in years.

22

'The living owe it to those who no longer can
speak to tell their story for them.'
– Czaslaw Milosz

With a heavy heart, and completely confused about the future, Arnie boarded the flight back home. As they took off and the London skyline became a blur, she prayed that her life would also take off with the same speed and that somehow she would jet ahead in the case.

Once the children had settled down, Krish and Arnie talked about the case. Krish tried to get her to relax, and as they sipped the wine served on board, he asked her how her parents had more than their share of the property in their control. Arnie smiled wryly for her mother's modus operandi was extremely simple.

Kamini gradually encroached on all open spaces. She believed that every inch was worth fighting for, and once it was in her control and occupation, she fought bitterly to maintain the status quo. Krish and Arnie too, in the days before their separation, had stupidly helped Kamini extend her office.

Piecing it all together, Arnie marvelled at how Kamini cleverly manipulated everyone; they were unsuspecting and clueless. She made Civil Lines her registered office with their co-operation and active participation. She transferred the electricity connection to her name; all small steps towards establishing ownership. Arnie was never truly trusted, for like Chhoti Phua, she was a Dhari and therefore suspect in her mother's mind.

Krish looked at Arnie and said, "Fall seven times, and stand up eight! This is a Japanese proverb."

"Nope, curl up and die is the line they left out. Forget the Japanese, fuck my family and the whole damn world," Arnie replied through her tears. Tears that fell furiously and fast, like rain pelting down her face in huge drops. "Keep calm and do no *kaam*! Why is the damn petition not ready yet?" she asked. "It was meant to be with us by now. What use will it be if the house is sold and the money scattered all over the place?"

Arnie had been sharp with Krish, but she was feeling raw and on edge. Her only hope was Yudi mama. "He loves me and will definitely counsel my mother. He has always been there for me, defending me, protecting me. He said I was like his daughter. He loved my children. He brought them gifts from all over the world when he travelled. He was the one who built the first toy train for me, using matchboxes. He took my brother and me to the zoo for the first time.

"This is an aberration; they cannot do this to me, to my little children. It is insane." Arnie paused to wipe her tears and continued, "My mother is wicked, but not evil. She loves me less, that I can handle, but does she not love me at all? What could have made her do this? What? What have I done to bring this upon me, upon the children?" She felt rejected, heartbroken. She felt a chill creep along her arm and asked the stewardess for another blanket.

Then she whispered, "What about Randy? We were so close before his marriage. What could have changed? How can he stand by and watch this? He is a good person, albeit a bit weak. He can take more, but why stoop to this? He is completely blind, but his wife, surely she understands that stealing is a punishable crime? Will this end? If my life was a book, I would love to flip to the last page."

Seeing her despair, Krish reached out and held Arnie in a tight hug. "All will be well. I don't know what else to say. Go to sleep now, you are tired."

Arnie nodded and curled up, falling asleep within seconds.

"Wake up, they are serving breakfast," Krish woke Arnie up, handing her a cup of steaming coffee.

Sipping coffee, she searched for something on her iPad and gave it to him quietly. "Krish, I want to show you something. This email exchange was in February, when I thought I was part of the family. I haven't quite figured out the disconnect. Here, read this."

Subject: from Yudi Sharma
Dear Aranya, my fingers are tired dialling you. Phones these days don't seem to work. Wish you and the children the happiest of birthdays and happier ones to come. Here is every good wish in the world for each of you and hope your phone works.
Your aunty had to be airlifted to Pune. She was with the doctor. Is improving.

"At which, I had rushed across, chequebook in hand, ready to hand over my meagre savings, can you imagine? Contrast it with what they are doing!"

"Hmm, I did not know of this; sounds serious. So, your aunt did get better, right, because I saw his photograph at some book launch recently and she was there. Did you attend it? The write-up mentioned your mother and brother being there."

Arnie shook her head. "I wasn't invited, isn't it strange? What is happening, Krish? Yudi mama has always been there for me, and is extremely fond of the children. Why was I left out? In February, we had this email exchange and a few months later, he starts totally ignoring me? Do you think my mother has finally got to him, Krish?"

There were no answers to the questions in Arnie's head as she grappled with conflicting thoughts. She ignored Krish and continued talking, almost to herself. "It is strange because this is not a property tucked away in the wilderness. It is a place he has visited often, he has been there, and more importantly, he was well over forty when my grandfather bought it. So he knows the truth."

They looked at each other in silence. Arnie tried to find a justification. "He is the best uncle in the world, absolutely the best."

"Sure, but he did light into you when you emailed him on that super work assignment, cutting you to size, and destroying the moment for all of us. Show me the email," Krish said.

"Why rake up the past?" Arnie asked, refusing to show Krish the email. "Guess he has his difficult moments, must be tough to play God all the time."

Krish was amazed. "Wow, this is the first time I've heard you say something tinged with sarcasm about him. It has always been irritating, this blind adulation. Show me his email because it says something about him and what he thought of you."

The reference was to when Arnie wrote to him, telling him that it was very difficult to get a foothold in a ruthless and competitive corporate world. She struggled with being a single mother. She had written to Yudi mama that she had joined as Country Head of a new organisation. He maintained, in his reply, that Arnie was overtly preoccupied with designations, but she dismissed his comments as him being menopausal. When he lit into Arnie for renovating her flat after eight years of moving in and called it materialistic, she was hurt. "I did not get gold pots and pans. All I did was tell him that I had painted the flat and bought new curtains, but yet again, he had called me greedy and dismissed it as *maya*."

It had been difficult when Krish left her and Arnie had needed to confide in someone. Yudi mama had seemed to be the one stable point in an increasingly illusionary and changing world. Both children were less than two feet tall and still in diapers. She had a divorce case pending, hostile in-laws, an unsupportive brother, and a mother who vented her anger every evening. Arnie was advised to sell her flat, but she resisted and somehow survived those early years. Yudi mama advised Arnie not to talk about her life at work, which she had done in an unguarded moment, because the Sharma family *izzat* was paramount. Begging his forgiveness, Arnie had requested Yudi mama not to judge her by that incident, which was an exception.

Unlike her mother, Arnie didn't vent at home and didn't take her frustrations out by beating her children, or playing favourites and beating one while cuddling the other. She didn't terrify them by shouting or screaming at the maid. She came home and helped them with their homework or to revise for exams and still managed to have birthday parties for both.

"Krish, read what I wrote to Yudi mama. I told him that he was free to think of me as materialistic, but that he should also pause to reconsider. I had a lump and lived with the fear of cancer on one side and the growing demands of my children on the other. I had started a scholarship in nana's memory for a woman student at college so that another vulnerable girl like me would have an easier time. I did not, Krish," Arnie said, "want understanding or sympathy, but wanted him to stop referring to me as materialistic."

Yudi mama was always so warm whenever Arnie wrote about the children, and she opened another email, this time from him about Sia.

```
Re: Sia
Goodness gracious! The little girl has grown
and is such a lady! Shrey's picture is
blurred. Will show mami photographs. Yudi
```

In the next one Arnie opened, Yudi mama was raging again, so Krish made his limited point in one succinct word: "Complicated."

Aranya, stand up for yourself and have a
mind! Why are you trying to read into my
mind? My open talk silences you. I am a
straight man, known for it. You suspicious,
your problem. So, just meditate.
Yudi

"Why were you grovelling all the time and what kind of love
is this?" Krish asked, annoyed.

Arnie replied, "You are right, I am the blithering idiot. I grew
up in a household where he was taken as being next in line to
God. My nana-nani spoke about him in hushed tones; he was
revered by all of India, so who was I to think otherwise? I was a
little girl lucky to be growing up in his shadow. I don't know what
happened, Krish, what did I do?"

He completed Arnie's thoughts. "You have fallen from grace,
but it is unfathomable. Maybe he was the protector you turned to
when vulnerable, but as you steadied your life, both professionally
and with the children growing up, he lost importance, and he
doesn't like it. Can't you see, his importance has reduced over the
years? And over the same span of time, you built yourself up."

"Impossible. Not my Yudi mama. In fact, as soon as he finds
out about this great injustice, he will sort it out for me. I am
certain that he doesn't know. And when he does, he will reach out
for family peace and their great reputation."

"Time will tell; hope you are right, but do not count on it,"
Krish said softly.

Arnie tossed and turned in her seat, feeling ashamed, with an
odd sensation creeping up in her stomach. Something told her
that she was wrong. That irrespective of what she did, she had
not been good enough for Yudi mama. His sermons always had
an undertone of criticism, telling her that she should have done
things in a different way, his way.

23

'In the midst of winter, I finally learned that there was in me an invincible summer.'
– Albert Camus

▼

They finally reached home after a longish wait for their luggage at the airport. The intercom crackled when they were in the middle of unpacking. Aida spoke to the guard and turned to Arnie, "There is someone at the gate; she wants to meet you. She says she is your relative."

"Send her in," Arnie told the maid and rushed to get ready.

But no one came. Strange. Tired from the flight, Arnie forgot about it and continued with her day.

A text message on her mobile phone from her boss interrupted her a little later and she groaned on seeing it. There was a launch event and he wanted Arnie to write the internal compliance part of his speech. He needed it in an hour. By the time she went to office and then got home much later in the evening, Arnie was exhausted.

"Hey Mamma, how was it? Ooh, you look good and that is J'Adore," said Sia, crinkling her eyes as she gave her mother a hug. "It reminds me of beautiful you, Mamma."

"What is that?" Arnie asked, spying a large yellow manila envelope on the table.

"Someone dropped it off," Aida told her. Soon after Arnie left for work that morning, a 'madam' had given this envelope and told Aida to hand it to Arnie.

"Strange," Arnie thought, kicking off her heels and tearing the packet open. Out popped old letters and faded photographs of people she didn't recognise, in clothes that belonged to a different era. Stranger and stranger still!

"Wow, what is this?" Arnie looked at the photographs closely. "Get me a magnifying glass, Shrey. The one from your detective kit. Hurry!" Sia and Arnie peered at the pictures. Sia was, as usual, talking nonstop and some of her jabbering got through Arnie's concentration. "Look, she is pretty and has long hair like me, Mamma, and that old woman staring into the camera has your nose and your mother's large forehead."

"Shut up, Sia. These are unknown people, long dead, and will haunt you tonight for your blasphemy," Arnie told her, giggling, "Hey, I love her *salwar* and look at that lace. My next *salwar kameez* will be a variation of this," Arnie told Sia who was staring at the feet of the man in the picture.

"Mamma, look, he has the same deformity as your nana, his toe. And look, he has the same prominent nose and deep set eyes as well."

A few letters and documents had fallen out of the envelope. They had things written in Urdu on them, which she could not read. As Arnie looked more closely, a torn bit in English caught her attention. The writing was familiar, scrawl-like, as if an insect had fallen into ink and run across the paper. She sensed something, not quite sure what, but shrugged off the feeling and waited for the magnifying glass. "Who is this woman?"

Shrey finally brought the magnifying glass and Arnie squinted, looking at the photograph through it. She could not recognise the women, but the man seemed strangely familiar. His feet, pushed into *peshawaris*, kept catching her eyes. There was something recognisable about them. Were they Yudi mama's feet or her nana's? Did either of them act in a period movie or play? Not that Arnie could remember. "Obviously this isn't meant for us," she said, and put the contents back in the envelope. She was far too tired to figure out this new development and wanted the packet kept away from the children so that they would not ask any more questions.

Ramesh had requested for a meeting, so Arnie took the next day off from work and drove to his office. Her arguments, according to him, had inherent weaknesses from a legal standpoint. He needed much more information before he could do anything for her. "I will support you as best as I can," he said, "but I can't do anything without more documents and court papers. You need the court records of the case your family has been fighting in Ranchi and you will have to get these. I suggest you look for another lawyer who can get you the papers as this matter is beyond me."

Arnie was devastated and stepping out of Ramesh's office, she called Krish. "Ramesh has refused to carry on with my case. I found this lawyer with such difficulty. Where will I get another one?" she asked. But Krish had no answers for her.

Every lawyer on her contact list, on her LinkedIn profile, and on her mobile phone got a call or a message from Arnie that day. The legal head of a large overseas pharmaceutical company responded almost immediately and asked whether she was well. "Yes, but I need some case papers urgently from a local court in a place I have never been to."

"Don't worry," he reassured her, taking the details. "I will call you tomorrow and the papers will be on your desk within seven days, I promise."

This was followed by a couple of friends who called, responding to her messages. One said that he was close by and would be happy to meet for a coffee and discuss the case. He met Arnie a short while later, but he was not encouraging. "Look, I am going to be blunt; this is very late because several orders have already been passed. Why were you sleeping sweetheart? Buggers, not showing their own daughter on the family tree. Is it a joint family? Look, check on that because you are a coparcener, a member by birth, and the law is quite clear on this. Imagine people like *them* are doing this; shameful! They can be seen everywhere taking the high moral ground, almost as the conscience keepers of India. You can depend on me, I will help," he said. "But remember, you are in it for the long haul. This will take years. Civil cases take time, and I mean it sweetheart."

"My mother, at sixty-nine, is the youngest of the extended family, so the rest, being much older, don't have the luxury of time," replied Arnie.

"Holy cow, sixty-fucking-nine! I saw her dance to '*Sheila ki Jawani*' at the minister's party just a few weeks ago." His parting remark, as they left, made Arnie smile.

Gathering her thoughts, she called Krish and updated him. Krish said that he would come over so that they could discuss what to do next.

Dinner was tense as Krish and Arnie argued furiously. "You are an emotional idiot for believing your family will be embarrassed at finding out that you know about their shenanigans and will settle with you. If that was so, why did they do this? The case was filed almost a decade ago, long enough for them to remember that they have a daughter. It is not as if you were lost at sea!"

His earnestness was so appealing that Arnie couldn't be upset with him for long. Suddenly she remembered the large manila envelope that had come in the day before. "Long lost relatives," she told him as he opened it and the photographs popped out. "A joke of some sort, perhaps, a woman dropped it off yesterday."

"Come closer," Krish said, staring at the photographs, "for this looks like your nana wearing period clothes and with a moustache that clearly doesn't suit him. And his large glasses look odd."

"Really, you can see a resemblance?" Sia had also said something about the feet, Arnie recalled. The magnifying glass was whipped out again and they looked at the photograph, peering into the past.

"Let it be," Arnie said a few moments later. "I have had enough excitement for one day. This is just a prank. Let's not lose focus. I have to find a lawyer and file a suit within the next fortnight and we have to follow up on the court papers. I am convinced, Krish, that my mother is not evil. That she does have a heart buried deep down; she doesn't love me, but I am sure that she cannot do this, aware as she is of my struggle to bring up the children and pay the bills. This is, however, unbelievable! Even I have begun to wonder whether I am a stepchild or adopted."

Krish said matter-of-factly, "As long as your father is a wimp, there is no hope because she will continue to bully him. However, even if you are her stepdaughter, your grandfather and father remain the same. It makes no difference. I looked up the law and it is the same for all, no exceptions." He then asked a rhetorical question and answered it himself, much to Arnie's surprise. "What do you think she sleeps in? A coffin! Never mind, bad joke. I really don't know how she sleeps at night."

Arnie noticed a message on her mobile phone just then. "Hey, I have a text message from some Sanjeev telling me that he has found the Ranchi Court papers and would like to meet tomorrow." It was the lawyer referred by her friend in the pharmaceutical company. At least something was moving forward!

"Good, confirm and ask him the time and venue for the meeting. Now sleep, even if it is the last thing you want to do," said Krish as Arnie walked him to the door. After he left, she texted her boss that she would not be working in the second half of the next day and cancelled all meetings post lunch.

The next afternoon, leaving early from office, she walked into the lobby of the Taj Hotel for her appointment with Sanjeev. "I have no idea what Sanjeev looks like," she thought to herself. But a gentle tap on her shoulder and Arnie turned to face a young man wearing large sunglasses who introduced himself as Sanjeev. They shook hands and sat down. Propping his glasses on his head, he handed her the papers.

"Aranya*ji*, I have taken a look. Good case. As soon as we file, I guarantee you that within a week they will be here to settle. Right here, sitting on this very sofa, no problem."

Arnie looked at him, unconvinced, and opened the file. "This is in Hindi?"

"Not a problem; will get it translated." She got up to go after thanking him and asked him about his bill.

"*Aap* paper *dekh lo* and I will call you later about the payment," he said, as they waited for their cars to pull up.

Once in the car, Arnie called Krish. "Hey! I have the court papers from Ranchi. I am actually holding the file," she almost screamed in excitement, adding that it was mostly in Hindi. She didn't know why she was excited as she didn't even know what the papers said. All she knew was that Ramesh had wanted these papers and they were important according to him.

"Not to worry. You know that I am completely bilingual; you are in luck." Krish had also arranged for Arnie to get a second opinion from a friend of his. While waiting for her call, Krish had gone through his school and college alumni directory and found a few lawyers. They agreed to meet in the Green Park market and drive together to see his friend, a corporate lawyer. The emotional strain was telling on Arnie now, particularly since she could see Randy's signature in a few places in the court papers, so she knew that her brother was in the loop and there could be no denying that she had been deliberately left out. This was no oversight.

Once Arnie was in Krish's car, she handed him the papers and he quickly scanned through them. They walked into Krish's friend's office a little later and showed the documents to the lawyer. Krish's friend made notes as he turned the pages of the court files. The silence got louder as Arnie waited for him to speak.

"Interesting," he said after a while, "this is obviously deliberate and their intent is mala fide. According to the law, you have the same rights as your brother Randeep and your father."

Tears rolled down Arnie's cheeks and she apologised for the emotional response. "I am in a state of shock. The injustice and the ruthlessness with which they have planned and executed this is what hurts me the most. For so many years they have plotted behind my back to do me out, and I had no idea. But I don't want to be emotional. I want to take a decision."

The lawyer addressed Krish. "This looks like a joint family situation and, presuming this, let me tell you that she has a legal right undeniable under the Indian system. They have suppressed her existence from the court. She has to get her name added to the family tree in the Ranchi Court. But this is provided the funds are from the grandfather. Can you prove this?"

Arnie shook her head and groaned. She explained her feudal background and the inhumane treatment meted out to her over the years and she could see the lawyer's expression change. His disgust was apparent.

"Even more reason for you to stand up. If I did not see a case for you to fight, I would not recommend that you proceed. But in this case, you have to. Nothing that you have said is new; I have heard tales about your mother's tantrums, her legendary arrogance, and the underhand ways in the corridors of the court. Who is your litigator? And the lawyers?"

Arnie told him that Ramesh had refused to carry on with the case and that she needed another lawyer. Krish and his friend had a discussion and they made a few quick calls as Arnie watched. Everything seemed to happen in slow motion.

"You may be able to get a good litigator," they told her. "But you still need a lawyer who will file the case and make out your statements." Arnie didn't speak, but her expression told the lawyer that she was grateful for his advice.

"So I have a case, and I will fight," she repeated to Krish as the car sped homewards.

The minute they reached home, the kids bounced into the living room, demanding an update. "So how was it? Is that the Ranchi file? Are you going to do this, Mamma?"

Krish talked them through the day. Arnie wanted to be honest and transparent with her children. She looked at them and was moved by their loyalty and concern. "Too young to learn about betrayal and deceit," she told herself, but she knew that their lives had changed forever. Irrespective of the outcome in court, her children had felt the pain of treachery and their innocence had been compromised.

The three of them spoke as Arnie lay down on the carpet and closed her eyes. Then she heard her son's little voice. "Mamma, I have a suggestion. My friend in school, Rishab, his father and grandfather are lawyers. I have their number." Before she could speak, Krish told Shrey that this required a different kind of lawyer. "So then Mamma can speak to Aditya's father. He was in your college and Aditya says he remembers Mamma." Arnie heard the last bit and asked if his friend's father was Vikram and within seconds, she called him.

"Hi Vikram. Hope you remember me, Aditya and Shrey are friends," and without waiting for a response Arnie continued. "A great injustice is being done and I need to stop the sale of the house I lived in; do you remember it?" and she plunged headfirst into the details.

"Slow down, who is selling the house and why the tearing rush? Come and meet me in my office tomorrow."

Before they hung up, Arnie took a deep breath and told him that if he accepted her case, on the other side will be her parents. That they would oppose her with all their might and would use their influence and money.

"Not a problem, we will fight. See you tomorrow."

And that was how it all began.

24

'In order to succeed, we must first believe that we can.'
— Michael Korda

The day flew by and Arnie found herself outside Vikram's office, waiting for him in the reception. The door opened and she was ushered into his room. She looked around as he waved to her, pushing forward a chair as he completed giving instructions to his stenographer.

"Hi, good to see you, long time," he said. "So, you are in trouble? Tell me everything, where have you been since college and what brings you here?"

And over a cup of tea, Arnie took him through the sorry saga.

"Incredible, I frankly haven't seen anything like this in so many years of practice, a mother doing her daughter out. Rarest of the rare. Wasn't Randy in our college?" Arnie nodded. He thought and then whistled. "Aaah, now I get it, he is married to that Alok Punjabi's daughter. Life isn't going to be easy."

Arnie's uneasiness was compounded as Vikram exchanged a knowing glance with his stenographer. "What is it?" she asked, but they shrugged it off saying, "Nothing we can't deal with; her father's reputation precedes him. As you know, we all have close links with the civil service."

"An unsavoury reputation, I presume. Well, Randy and I

were close, very close until he married that man's daughter," Arnie said.

"When did you last see Randy?" asked Vikram, to which Arnie replied quietly. "I last met my brother on the day my nana died. We stood together when the pyre was being lit."

"Got it, so his motivation is . . ."

". . . Money," she added, completing Vikram's sentence. "Whatever I don't get from the inheritance is his for keeps and he has known this for years. Look!" Arnie showed him Randy's signature on the various documents since the filing of the case in Ranchi.

Vikram seemed to read her mind and reassured Arnie. "I accept the brief and will read the papers. Let's meet late evening on Friday."

"Are you sure? There will be pressure; you know my mother. If you accept my case, please be prepared for noise, for calls from the Who's Who."

"We will see you through. Don't worry. Is this my set of documents?"

Arnie nodded and handed them over. As she moved towards the door, she looked back and said, "Thank you, Vikram, thank you."

Finding Vikram was fortunate as she had known him in college and his reputation was outstanding. He was firm and would not be pressurised to do anything that would go against her interest. It also helped that he was friendly with her, and did not like the rest of her family. Several small incidents in the past had convinced him that the Sharmas were not people he wanted to deal with. All in all, Arnie had come to a lawyer who was extremely competent and would stand by her.

Monica called when Arnie was in the car. "What happened? I am worried, what's the scene? Are you sure that you want to do this?" Arnie began filling her in just as the car came to a grinding halt in front of a traffic cop. She was fined for speeding. She called Monica back and they laughed hysterically at the absurdity of the situation. "My life is on a one-way ticket to hell. I will go down in history as the evil daughter who took on her parents."

"Oh yeah, old decrepit parents, right," Monica added, chuckling. "So ill that she can't miss a single Page-3-People party and has to be seen at Polo matches even if she has no idea what a *chakkar* is. And she is old enough to sashay down the ramp without a stick although she has osteoporosis, and is crafty enough to steal from her own daughter and her own grandchildren."

"Hey, we are getting mean here," Arnie tried defending her mother, only to be told sternly, "Shut up! She deserves her brain to crumble like her bones."

"How do you know about the osteoporosis?" Arnie asked, suddenly curious because even she had forgotten.

"I was waiting to see the doctor for my tennis elbow, but madam broke the queue and later, the doctor bitched to me."

"Small world! She will die if only she knew that her secret is no secret," Arnie spluttered, still laughing.

"She has a lot more to die for because I will do a jig and tell everyone I know her age—Sixty-Nine! Also her favourite position! And the bucketful of Botox, not to forget the bit about her being a full blown Cruela. What about the hypocrisy? And that she is the world's biggest miser? And the foul language? I will gladly translate her pet names, *kutiya* and *haramzadi*, for her la-di-la friends. And if I come face-to-face with her or your brother, then I will definitely tell them what I think."

Monica was obviously on Arnie's side. "Monica, it is so good to laugh. My muscles are aching because I haven't laughed like this in ages. I have been drowning in tears." Both stopped laughing and, if it were possible, hugged each other through the phone. "This too shall end, just hang in there," Arnie heard Monica say as she rang off.

The next few days needed to be paced out. Arnie was naturally nervous and on edge, waiting for her next meeting with Vikram. The day arrived.

As she climbed the stairs for the meeting, she bumped into an oily parent who was on the children's school committee. They made polite conversation. "Bagga, love your watch."

"Rolex," he said, rolling the 'R' appreciatively. "My wife bought six of these, for my sons and their wives."

"But your kids are in school!" Arnie stuttered.

"Uff, but they will marry, *na*? But I am a *mazdoor aadmi* and I still have the HMT my father gave me when I got my first job and I wear it all the time," said Bagga, oblivious to the Rolex on his wrist. "And how are you sweetie?" Arnie heard him switch into the all too familiar drawl that made her skin crawl.

"Not so good," she admitted.

"Why love?" and that was enough to get Arnie started. He was told about the rejection, about being done out, but she was suddenly cut short by him. "Darling, let the elders decide, let it be. They don't have to consult you about the sale; they will do what is best."

"Are you for real?" she asked, then brushed past him and entered Vikram's office.

"Elders, sure!" she repeated to herself and then typed a text message to him. "Bagga, it is a bit difficult to talk to the elders as you put it. Both my grandfathers, the elders of my family, are dead." She pressed 'send', irritated beyond words. The advice would have been acceptable if it came from a stranger, but Bagga had seen her struggle; he knew her story. Bagga was like the rest of Delhi, a fair-weather friend, not wanting to annoy the powerful diva, Kamini. The truth and Arnie be damned! A valuable lesson, one Arnie still had to properly learn.

The irritation hung over her like a dark rain cloud and Arnie tried to shrug it off as she walked in for the meeting with

Vikram. Coming straight to the point, Vikram plunged into the legal options. "I have seen the order regarding the disposal of the property and therefore appreciate the urgency. We have looked at the draft you brought us and worked on it. We are ready to file, but once we do so, it is a public document and there is no going back. What do you want to do?"

Arnie looked at him, soaking in the significance of his words. So she was being left out deliberately. There was no mistake.

"Well, I am very hurt, but we are talking about my parents here. Is there no *via media* by which they get to know my intent before I move the court? I mean, despite everything, I am reluctant. I want to give them a chance to sort it out rather than engage in a legal battle. Vikram, I have to live with myself."

"'Fine, then we can serve them unsigned papers and they will have the option of either contacting you or my office."

She nodded. "Yes, I think that is better."

"Okay, we will give them a week before filing, and if they come to the table, it will be delightful."

Vikram looked at Arnie carefully before he spoke again. "Your mother sold her car to the cleaner at the taxi stand near my office. When he went to register the car in his name, he found that there was a small pending tax payment. Peanuts for her, but a huge sum for him. He went to her office several times and was made to wait each time. She never met him until I sent her a legal notice. She is bad with payments and is a bully."

Arnie smiled and left, sad and wistful that she knew so little about her mother. She was grateful that Kamini had kept this huge schism between them. At least Arnie was not going to be painted with the same brush. People gave her a chance despite her mother.

The papers were duly delivered by Vikram's office and a 'receiving' got. The paralegal clerk who delivered them personally regaled the office with a description of what happened. The papers were given to Arnie's father and Kamini had torn the envelope open. Mayhem had broken loose because she had let the dogs on him and thrown him out cursing, "*Haramzada, kameena, tumhari himmat kaise hoi*? Tell that *kutiya*, I will bury her alive."

It was so predictable, the foul language and the desire to bury her daughter alive. "So the papers definitely reached the right person," Arnie joked with her lawyers.

The week was agonising as Arnie stared at both her phones, waiting for them to ring. Ring they did, but the call was never from 'them' or their lawyers. Her phone was always on full charge as she yearned for their number to flash, wishing the nightmare to end. She clutched the phones as she slept and every morning she was disappointed. No text messages and no missed calls. Upset, she checked with the lawyers but they hadn't heard from them either and were just as perplexed.

She told herself to calm down and wait. "You need your job even more now," Arnie told herself every morning, willing her mind to get her body out of bed. "Your salary supports your children and now this." Arnie was not like her mother and she could not default on payments, so she pushed herself to play all the roles that were needed from her at work and at home.

"If only this would ring, if only," she sighed as she checked both her phones to see if the ringer was on full volume for the ninety-ninth time in an hour.

"Why are you making that noise? It looks like you are trying to contact your home planet, shouting for your real parents," said Krish, walking into her home for Sunday morning breakfast.

"Not funny! If we don't hear from them by this evening, we file tomorrow," Arnie replied hoarsely. "So, they hate me so much?" she whispered.

"No, your mother loves money more; it is about power and control. You are the only person who has stood up to Kamini and her instinct is to crush you."

"Bury me alive, as she always said. To do this, when she knows my children depend on me and we have no one else, is ruthless. But Yudi mama will sort it out, Krish, you just wait and see," Arnie said lamely.

"All right. But today, we are going to watch a movie this afternoon, else all of us will go mad staring at your phones." Krish was correct and Arnie readily agreed. The plot of the movie *In Time* was fantastic and she was glad that there was no such thing as buying more life, for Kamini would have ensured her immortality and youth by using money and power recklessly.

Later, back at home, it was decision time. No call had come and no one had contacted Arnie or her lawyers. "We file tomorrow. Decision taken," she told Krish and then called the lawyers.

Vikram, however, wanted to run the motion by a senior colleague and called back soon thereafter.

As if the existing situation was not bad enough, the experienced senior counsel wanted a change in the petition. He believed what had happened was "misrepresentation of material existing fact." It was also, or so it seemed, sounder in law. "It is being filed as an urgent application under the Code of Civil Procedure 1908."

"What do you mean?" Arnie asked, totally at sea.

"Well, although we are well within the time limit for opening up property cases and yes, you are a coparcener by birth in your grandfather's joint family, this has a better chance of surviving in the court. The angle we are using is that their suit is a gross abuse of the process of law."

Her heart dropped like a brick and her spirits crashed as Arnie listened quietly. She didn't know whom to believe or which law to read up on. She was shattered. Keeping the phone down, she locked herself into her bedroom and watched the fan whirl. She contemplated suicide; she wanted to put an end to everything, to escape the ugliness and the rejection.

But then her eyes fell on the photograph of her two children as little babies, a photo that was always with Arnie. It was there as a reminder of how much she meant to her children and they to her. Her resolve to fight renewed itself. "The children need me," she told herself and got up to unlock the door, only to find the three of them waiting right outside her door. "I have decided to fight this injustice and a couple of days will not change anything," she said as they rushed in.

"I know that you are upset and therefore the kids and I sat outside your room," Krish said, "but I just want you to know that we are filing tomorrow and you need to sign the papers before noon."

Arnie nodded, silently mad at herself for being so weak.

So off to the lawyers again the next morning.

"You do realise that they can kill me? What happens next?" Arnie asked Vikram as she signed the legal papers anxiously.

"Court procedure from here onwards; we will try and have it listed as soon as possible," replied Vikram.

"Who is the judge?" asked Krish and Arnie interrupted him rather sharply, "Why does it matter?"

"It does," both men said together and laughed. "You will find out for yourself soon enough. Our chances are better if we get a judge who is a stickler for the law, because our case hinges on a technicality at the first instance. On the other hand, if the other party sways the judge, claiming that you are motivated by greed and are harassing your old parents, then it will get more difficult. Let's see, we will look up the roster."

Arnie left the lawyer's office and just as they began to pull out of the crowded parking, she heard both her mobile phones ring at the same time; on one flashed the lawyer's name and on the other, Chhoti Phua. She took the lawyer's call and was told that she needed to be present in court. Her nervousness and all other arguments were successfully overruled.

"Call Chhoti Phua, it could be something important," Krish said as he reversed the car out of the parking slot.

The all too familiar voice was back on the phone. "*Kaise ho?* Can we meet? You can give me the chocolates and my presents."

"Yes, of course, Chhoti Phua," Arnie replied. "This evening at the Oberoi?"

Chhoti Phua cut her short. "I have to pick up my dry cleaning from the market and you can run into me."

"Run into you? Why?" Arnie asked and was told, "Understand, please." Finding humour from nowhere, she firmly told her aunt, "Okay, I will run into you this evening and we will have chai and samosas."

Krish looked at Arnie and smiled because she was laughing so hard that tears were streaming down her face. "She is the smartest of the pack," he said and left it at that.

"Jaante ho, you look good in red," Chhoti Phua told Arnie over steaming *gulab jamuns* when they met later that evening. "Has my mother told her about the lawyers?" Arnie tried to read her aunt's face, but the expression didn't flicker. "Nice chocolates," she said and they planned to visit Paris together some day.

"What's the gossip, Chhoti Phua?" Arnie asked innocently.

"These days your mother learns dance, Bollywood dance! And also sings. A teacher comes and she wears original designer clothes and not the copies she wore earlier. She has an image consultant and a public relations firm working for her."

"Chhoti Phua, she cannot sing! Remember how even Dadaji used to laugh when she sang the *aarti* on Diwali?"

Chhoti Phua ignored Arnie's interruptions and continued after gulping a generous bite of the *gulab jamun*. "The weather is too hot. Nothing happens here, no change. Jaante ho, your nana's Man Friday?"

After getting back in touch with Chhoti Phua and slipping into a pattern that was once familiar, Arnie was no longer surprised by the abrupt changes in conversation. On the ball, she acknowledged the question, "Yes, Gemini G, named after the legendary film star."

"I hear he died within three days of your grandfather's death."

This was disappointing; Arnie had expected something more fiery and exciting, so she just nodded and agreed. "Hooch poisoning, bad liquor."

"So did he drink single malt before?" she asked innocently as the import of her statement struck home.

"Oh my God, Chhoti Phua, he knew all the family secrets and shameful scandals. He was with them for decades!"

"Yes, the secrets that they wanted people to know and those that they wanted to burn with your nana. Nothing escapes me."

Arnie looked at her, wide-eyed, and muttered that Yudi mama was footing all the bills, looking after the servant's widow and educating his infant child, sending them money regularly.

"A man who supports no charity will not do this without a reason," Chhoti Phua said while digging into the *gulab jamun*. "I am told he rushed Gemini G, as he was fondly called, to the government hospital and was very particular about the death certificate. Standing for hours to complete the formality. Exactly why would a busy man like him do this?" she asked triumphantly, looking into Arnie's eyes.

"Chhoti phua, you mean . . ." Arnie began to ask but her aunt got up and said, "I mean, look after yourself and the children, beta."

And those were her last words to Arnie.

She walked away, waddling quickly on shifty feet, disappearing into the sunset as Arnie stood up and watched. Her gorgeous perfume remained behind, surrounding Arnie and overpowering the rancid smell of oil in the sweet shop, as if to remind her that it was not a dream.

"Love the perfume," said Krish, with his penchant for stating the obvious as he slid into the chair beside Arnie. They ordered a fresh round of eats. She told him what Chhoti Phua had said and they stared at each other. Arnie saw the Sharma *izzat* melting like molten wax in the heat. It was not the weather but the words that fanned the fire.

"Let's go," Krish said as he paid the bill and they walked to the car.

Nervous excitement filled the rest of Arnie's day and then it was morning. Her first hearing in the court. She hadn't slept a wink, she had prayed and meditated. So much depended on the outcome of that first hearing!

25

'Once you make a decision,
the Universe conspires to make it happen.'
– Ralph Waldo Emerson

Chic but simple. That was the look Arnie was advised was the most appropriate for court. She shampooed her hair, dressed carefully, and wore a subdued white *salwar kameez* with small red flowers. A freshly dry-cleaned white *salwar*, because she couldn't help recalling Chhoti Phua's remark about Kamini and grinning to herself. The pearl earrings given by nani, a good luck charm, were worn, prayers were said, and a last sip of some hot chai, and Arnie was ready to leave. She had to make it through the day. If her application was thrown out of court on the first day itself, then it was unlikely that she would have any chance of winning her rights or even stating her case. "Oh God, I have to survive. My mother will bury me alive if I lose today."

"Court number two, gate number seven, and the matter is item number twenty-one. In all likelihood, it will come up at 11.30 a.m., so you should be there at least an hour in advance," had been Vikram's instructions, but Arnie was on the road at 8.30 a.m. Her mind juggled with the possibility of roadblocks, VIP movement, road rage, and all else that could go wrong. It was easier on her fragile mind if she just left earlier.

Entering the court was not easy despite the introduction note from her lawyer and her passport as identification. Arnie was baffled by the various queues that seemed to have lives of their own. And all this just for an entry pass. Having fulfilled the formalities and negotiated the way through two layers of security, she found herself outside the courtroom.

The central well, from where all the courtrooms led off, had a large staircase and several corridors. The waiting area had a growing crowd, even at that early hour. Arnie saw worried litigants, advocates exchanging pleasantries, and junior lawyers and paralegals bustling around with files. She opened the door to one of the courtrooms and peeped inside. It looked like a scene from a Hindi movie, familiar from the screen, just more impersonal and cold. There was an hour or so before the court would be in session and the feeling was one of quiet anticipation, as if something was about to happen.

"Is there anyone as nervous as I am?" Arnie wondered. Her stomach began to cramp and she felt sick watching the sea of people around her.

Courts are adversarial by design in the Anglo-Saxon legal system. Arnie's support base was at the end of a phone, and her mobile phone flashed repeatedly as she received text messages wishing her luck, sending out prayers and encouragement.

A bunch of lawyers represented the other side. They hovered around Arnie and she got hostile looks from them. They nudged and glared, compounding her uneasiness as she waited for her lawyer to join her. She watched them gather in corners, but they scattered like crows as Arnie walked past. Finally, she spotted her lawyer and walked towards him, needing her team around her.

"Their full battalion is here, led by your mother's legal team," Vikram said, pointing towards the aggressive bunch.

"And they seem to be super confident," Arnie added. "All is well, right? You have read the brief?" she asked, her voice trembling. "You have to understand, they will kill me. You have to win for me to live, please," Arnie implored with a quivering voice.

Suddenly, she heard an unfamiliar voice behind her and turned to face Sanjeev, her Ranchi lawyer. He had come to observe how the case would go in Delhi, although he would only be handling matters in Ranchi.

"Don't worry, madam!" he said. "We have a good judge. He will hear the merits of the case and our team is also good. Let us hope for the best," he added, winking at an un-amused Vikram as he lunged forward to touch Arnie's shoulder sleazily.

"She is here," Vikram said, not needing to explain which 'she' he was referring to, and added a "don't worry" to assuage Arnie's fears.

The mobile phone rang; it was Krish, and Arnie began talking before he could say hello. "My mother is here, dressed in white. I can see my dad too. Their lawyers are here. Around fifteen or so are surrounding madam, conferring and exchanging papers. They are giving me the collective death glare," she said, referring to her son's imitation of Darth Vader. "She is talking on the phone. Must be to Randy. Do you think Yudi mama knows?"

"Yes, undoubtedly he does," replied Krish quietly.

"Did you hear that?" Arnie asked him.

"What?" he asked, perplexed.

"My heart splintering; did my heart not make a noise while shattering?"

"Don't be silly! You are going to be okay. Best of luck, there is a God, you will be fine," were his last words as Arnie switched the phone off and moved into the courtroom.

Filled with people, the courtroom looked very different from the empty space she had looked into a short while ago. Arnie sat on the last bench, the seat closest to the door so that she could flee as soon as the hearing was over. She prayed, crossed her fingers, and strained to listen to the proceedings. She was at the end of the room, farthest from the judge. The room was silent but there was a buzz of activity nonetheless.

Suddenly, there was a huge commotion as a statuesque lawyer pulled up a cowering woman, simple and scared. "And this, My Lord, is the real wife, the mother of the dead man's child, the legal heirs to the deceased's property. My client did not divorce the now deceased gentleman, may he rest in peace." Then a pause before a well-heeled buxom woman jumped up, waving a piece of paper dramatically, which purportedly was the wedding certificate, and handed it to the judge. The judge examined the evidence while amused lawyers looked on, tittering on how handling one wife was difficult enough, leave alone dealing with two. "Brave man," they commented, making snide remarks to each other, laughing all the while and covering their mouth to muffle the sound. The scene with the thundering lawyer looking heavenward when appealing for justice, a hapless widow with a young child, and the Other Woman was straight out of a Bollywood movie. Truth is often stranger than fiction. The drama concluded as the judge thundered and passed an order and moved on to the next case.

Kamini sat in front of her daughter by chance and her stiff back reflected her anger. Arnie could tell, because she remembered her mother being like this before she flew into a rage and hit her. Luckily, there was little chance of Kamini sorting things out with a slap today.

"God please, please God, be with me," Arnie muttered and then bent forward to listen as the judge began to speak. "You have come very late. Orders have been passed. Where were you until now?" Was it all over before Arnie had even settled into her seat? Her fifteen seconds of fame?

Arnie's litigator, a well-respected member of the Bar, had not even had time to respond to the curt comments of the Honourable Judge, before a raucous pack of lawyers began shouting in loud voices: "The daughter is a usurper." "She has no rights!" "She is greedy and has no legal position." "She has come late because she smells money." "Her petition is misconceived, mischievous, and mala-fide."

Arnie could identify this group above their well-rehearsed litany as being the lawyers representing her father and controlled by Kamini. They spoke in sequence, seemingly spontaneously, but the flow of their sentences showed that they had practised this before coming to the court. Arnie's ears turned red; she wanted to hide, she wanted to run away and bury herself somewhere.

Then, almost as if he had been expecting this all along, she heard the dignified voice of her lawyer rise above their aggressive cacophony. "My Lordship, a misrepresentation of material fact has been committed on this Honourable Court. Misrepresentations and falsehoods, contrary statements under oath in another court, have been made by the other parties in the case."

She strained to hear the judge and panicked as she heard him say, "You have come very late, the orders have been passed." Undaunted, her litigator continued to argue and his presence seemed to have silenced the shouting legions; it was just his voice and that of the judge now. "But Your Lordship, my rights stem from my descent and ancestry and I have an undeniable right to be impleaded in this matter. It cannot be decided until I am heard."

Kamini chose this moment to swing around and gesticulate like a *kathakali* dancer, making Arnie lose the thread of what was happening in the court. Her mother's heavily kohled eyes flashed with anger and her red lips mouthed familiar abuse. She didn't speak but Arnie got the message and shrank in her seat. She caught her mother's eyes and she saw her mother make the sign of death with her fingers.

Petrified, Arnie stood up and ran to the door. As she closed the door behind her, she heard her litigator say, "I will talk to my father, your Lordship."

The unexpected words left Arnie shaken and confused. Why

218

did they have to talk to the litigator's father? Where did he fit into all of this? As if Arnie didn't have enough problems with her own family, now she had to deal with her litigator's father as well? She ran to her car, breaking the heel of her shoe in the process but not caring, and told the driver to speed homewards, all the while looking over her shoulder in absolute fear.

With trembling fingers, she switched on her phone and received an alert of several missed calls. Before she could read them, Arnie saw her lawyer's name flash on the screen. "Hello," she said nervously.

"Where are you?" he demanded.

"I ran, fled actually," she told him, giving him the details. "What happened, Vikram?" she asked softly.

"We won the round! You are impleaded, subject to your being able to prove your ancestry and that you are the daughter of your parents. Once that happens, you will have won because the sale cannot go ahead without all parties being signatories. You are at risk until you prove that you are their daughter. After that, no one can touch you."

"What?" Arnie squealed. "You mean that I am recognised as a party in the case?"

"Yes," he said. "But you still have to prove that you are the daughter and this court has no time to deal with your ancestry. So, it is still going to be a struggle."

"Awesome, you bought me time. I live," Arnie exclaimed, but the irony was lost even on her lawyer. "What, by the way, was the reason we had to involve our senior counsel, the litigator's father?" she asked, her confidence returning slowly. Vikram was confused and wondered why Arnie was referring to his father, but they sorted out the confusion. It seemed that when the senior counsel had said "my father", he was speaking for Arnie. Simple enough once he had explained it!

Arnie called Krish and the joy in his voice and the "Hurrays!"

from the children filled her heart with undiluted happiness and relief. She saw stars dancing before her eyes. Yes, this was her moment!

"Thank you God, thank you," she repeated, whizzing past the busy streets of Delhi. She saw the gigantic silk cotton trees with their leaves moving gently in the breeze after the monsoon drizzle, the silken flowers crimson red and ready to burst. God, as they say, was in heaven and all was well with the world.

26

'We must accept finite disappointment,
but never lose infinite hope.'
— Martin Luther King Jr.

▼

Nothing in Arnie's life happened easily. After her lawyers had pulled a rabbit out of the hat by getting her through the first round in the High Court, she had presumed that proving her ancestry, that she was the daughter of her parents, would not have taken the Ranchi Court time to even draw breath. However, where would be the drama if that had happened?

How many people remember their birth? Not Arnie and not many do. You do not question who your parents are, particularly if you have known them all your life. It is one of those things that is just there, just so, no questions asked. Wondering about your parentage is, for most people, like wondering whether the sun would rise the next morning or not. Arnie thought that she was part of the fortunate many, fortunate to be the daughter of parents who were with her throughout her childhood and her life.

Surprisingly, she was also part of the fortunate few who had tangible and incontrovertible proof of her birth, with a registered and detailed record, containing her name and that of her parents, in the local registry of the Parisian district where she was born. She had never considered that document to be of any value, for never had she questioned her parentage.

It was therefore unexpected when a strangely jubilant Sanjeev called Arnie from Ranchi to tell her, "Your mother just said that she doesn't remember having you!"

Pin drop silence as she tried to process the statement. "What? Come again," she shouted into the phone. "That is just not possible," she muttered. "And why is my lawyer so happy with this development," she wondered.

"The judge questioned your parents' lawyer when I showed up in court. A former justice appeared for them. No one expected a daughter to appear after so many years, a daughter of whom there has been no mention. The judge looked at me suspiciously as he couldn't believe that new family members were emerging in a matter where there was an unchallenged family tree on record for almost a decade. I stood up and said that I am your lawyer and asked for my application to be admitted."

Arnie's application stated that she was the daughter and part of the family tree, a part of the family that someone had erased and no one had bothered to put back.

Then, after a pause for dramatic effect, Sanjeev continued his narration. "Obviously, the judge was surprised and asked me who my parents were, and then he turned to my father's lawyer."

Court language was still unfamiliar to Arnie and she fell into the same confusion that she had with Vikram in Delhi. Did everyone's father enter this matter? At first, it was the litigator, her senior counsel, and now here was Sanjeev bringing his father into the picture. "Your parents, Sanjeev? Is it a court protocol?" she asked, puzzled.

"Not mine. Yours! That is just legal language; I represent you so that's why the judge asked in this way."

"What did my parents' lawyer say?" she asked impatiently.

"He asked for time and said, *hazoor* after Diwali I will get back to you on whether I have a daughter or not. The judge just exploded in court and gave him an hour to call his client and revert."

"Sanjeev, what happened next?" Arnie implored him. However, enjoying the suspense, he disconnected the call mid-sentence, promising to call her back.

The tension was beginning to get to Arnie and she phoned Krish to tell him the little she knew, but Sanjeev called her again, so she put Krish on hold to hear the rest of the story.

Sanjeev completed his tale and Arnie whistled in disbelief. "Their lawyer said that your father is not well and cannot remember anything as he was under medication and sedated. At which point, the judge, wanting to get to the bottom of the matter, asked whether your mother was available and that the former justice should get her response for the court. You should not feel bad, but she said that she was not a party in this case and that she did not have to tell the court anything."

"What?" Arnie exploded, as this was meandering and going nowhere, at least not in any direction that worked for her.

There would be many occasions in Arnie's legal battle for her rights, when she would be grateful for the sagacity and wisdom of the judges that she encountered. This was one such moment, for the judge in Ranchi, it seemed, had insisted that her mother answer the question put to her, or he would pass an order forcing her to respond.

Kamini was a veteran of court battles, having fought several when usually in the wrong, and she relied on expensive legal teams to confuse and complicate matters until the people against her withdrew due to sheer exhaustion. Delaying answering to a court when she was not even party to the case was child's play for her.

Sanjeev clarified, "'She will try and remember' was her message to the court and she asked for a date several months into the future to respond, citing various legal provisions and excuses that even the judge could not ignore. It seems that your parents are serious when they said that after Diwali they will think and let the court know whether they had a daughter or not. They are trying to buy time, as they know that your impleadment order is dependent on your proving that you are their daughter. They feel that they will complete the sale and dispose off the properties while you are still tied up with minor procedural matters in various courts." He went on, adding ironically, "But don't worry. It is your birthright."

"But Sanjeev, why are you so happy?" Arnie was upset and irritated. "You told me that the court will pass my order immediately, but now what? I kept asking you to file my birth certificate, but you did not attach it with the application. Now look what has happened!"

"Look, this is court strategy. Let them deny that you are their daughter, let them. We will then produce the birth certificate, but they won't risk it and the good news is that the next date is in the coming week and our petition has been admitted. Also, I have information that your brother has attached a death certificate in your name in some court. I am working on that, don't worry. Matter will become criminal as soon as I get that paper. As you can see, I am looking into this myself and not leaving it to my local team. You need to pay me more. It is a small amount for you, but it keeps my interest going in the case. It will be charges for travel and stay and another amount for appearance; my professional fees, as you can see."

As shocked as Arnie was to hear that Randy had signed her death certificate, she was also concerned about the money. Sanjeev was looking after the matter in the Ranchi Court, which was a lower court and he should not be charging more than Vikram and the senior counsel. She needed Sanjeev as the Ranchi Courts could be navigated best by a local lawyer who was accustomed to practicing in those courts, but his fees seemed to keep increasing.

"Sanjeev, I'll have to think about it."

In response, he told Arnie that he was being reasonable as the matter was in an outstation court. She needed to keep her lawyers motivated. "Otherwise, you are free to find someone else to represent you." He disconnected before Arnie could reply, leaving her distraught.

Arnie called Krish and told him what had happened. Complaining bitterly about her life, she asked questions that had no answers, her voice trembling with emotion. "What have I done to her? Why? I have children too! What would make a mother deny the existence of one child? And Randy? He is quiet? Enjoying this while Dolly counts the money?"

Sanjeev had made it sound so simple. "It will be done in a blink," he had assured Arnie. He had wanted her to give him the entire case and do away with Vikram and his team, as he would be able to sort it out in a week, ten days at the most. Luckily, good sense prevailed. "Horses for courses," she had thought. "Vikram for Delhi and Sanjeev for Ranchi would both be needed and so would the excellent but oh-so-expensive senior counsel, the litigator."

It didn't seem quite so simple now. She had never thought that she would need to prove, to show, that she was the daughter of her parents. This had now become her central concern and the focus of her struggle, strange but true.

"Let me get to the bottom of this," said Krish reassuringly when Arnie called him. "Where are you? In the office? Let me make a few calls and then I will ring you."

"Krish, I feel I am in a snake pit. Will I get out alive? Can you come over this evening? I am so confused! Do you think I have done the right thing?"

"Hey, you are in the right," he responded immediately. "Don't question it. I will pick you up from office, so send your driver off."

"That will be nice," thought Arnie as she had started looking forward to him coming around and them meeting up.

Her boss, a German, walked into Arnie's cabin, as always without knocking. "We need to talk now, please come to my room in ten." She nodded and froze. There was something wrong; she could feel it.

The conversation was terse and brief. Arnie had been unceremoniously fired. Just like that, without any reason or explanation.

Stunned. Shocked. Destroyed. Dismayed.

He was speaking in the background, his voice so very far away. "You are fighting a court case and you will have to focus on it, so this is the time to part ways. I do not want any noise in the office."

Arnie's head was churning with panic and inquisitiveness. "You got a call? Was it my powerful family? Is it my mother?" she asked as he showed her to the door impassively.

"How does it matter? Please hand over everything tomorrow."

"But, I need the money. I will work conscientiously. Please!" she begged.

"Tomorrow it is. Some day you will be glad. I have fought battles, wars in court, and it takes over your life. Focus your energy on the case."

Hopeless and helpless, Arnie walked back to her room and waited for Krish. Her mind was blank; yet again she had been dealt a massive blow. The room began to sway. She closed her eyes and prayed, but nothing seemed to help. Nausea overtook her and she was struck by the unfairness of it all. Reverting to the womb, she wanted to be in darkness and in the comfort of nothingness. Switching off the lights in her office cabin, she sat and cried.

She could not stop wondering why all of this was happening. Hearing about her brother signing her death certificate had made her world spin off its axis and now this! Where was she going to find the money for all her expenses? She had worked so hard to support her children, struggled to pay the mortgage, pay for life and still save a little bit, and she was now blowing it all up for an endless, hopeless battle. How could she have thought that she could fight her family in court and even hope to get something out of it? All that she would be left with would be bankruptcy, debts, and disrepute.

"Worthless. I am worthless, because I have bartered my children's future for my battle."

An old conversation with Jaya popped unbidden into her head. Kamini had shouted at her and beaten her up and Arnie had crept under the blankets and whispered to Jaya on the phone.

"Jaya, my mother just told me that I am a worthless kid. How other kids are getting involved in so many productive things and I just sit around talking about clothes. How she is ashamed to have me as a daughter. How I am never going to get into any college because nothing about me is good. And, you know what? She's kinda right. My grades are average. I've never ever come first. No matter how hard I try, I am pathetic at sports. I have no talent. I spend my day watching others walk around on the road and eating. I am plain and useless!"

Jaya did not, all those years ago, let Arnie feel sorry for herself. "Don't let her get to you, okay? Which clothes? The ones you dream about? Because your uniform is torn, buttons are missing, and socks faded? Aunty is awful. Screw it, there is next year. Now listen to me. You are in class eleven. Your grades are fine for that. You will figure it out. You have your life ahead of you."

Kamini had crushed Arnie's fragile self-esteem repeatedly. She remembered crying all the time. "Jaya, but everyone has everything figured out already. I am nowhere."

Jaya had put Arnie back together, piece-by-piece. "You definitely won't get anywhere if you sit around expecting things to come to you." At the time, Arnie had taken out her frustration on Jaya, getting angrier and angrier on the phone. "Don't you think I fucking try? I am not useless. I'd like to believe that if only somebody would believe that! Anyone! My parents, my teachers. Anyone. I am going to study and be the best. I am gonna work like a bitch and some day all this will be behind me."

This was exactly the reaction that Jaya had wanted, to turn Arnie's negative emotions into a force for her growth.

Then, as now, escape had seemed so far away, but Arnie was determined to outrun her fate and prove her mother wrong. Yet again, Kamini had tripped her. Had her mother been right all along? Arnie was without a job. In her mind, she was useless.

Little did Arnie realise that the scars of her childhood were wounds that would continue to ache in different ways for the rest of her life. She could not shut out the abuse that was ringing in her head, or the effect it had on her. It had taken over yet again, reminding Arnie of her lowly status.

"Saving electricity?" she heard Krish say as he walked into her office room.

"Nope," Arnie said, running into his arms as he grabbed her, his surprise apparent at this open display of affection. He held her tight as she sobbed and told him the latest in her unfolding saga. "Hang in there. The darkest hour of the night comes just before dawn," he said, making Arnie get up and refusing to let her feel low. "Let us get out of here and talk. No need to let your boss gloat and see you miserable. Even if you don't care, my ego is kicking in! Pick up your bag and let's leave," he said, nudging Arnie like a collie with its sheep towards the half-open door.

He had parked right in front of the main gate of the office. Grandly opening the door, he tossed Arnie's bags into the boot, made her get in and swung out carefully into the traffic. "Where are we going?" Arnie asked, because he seemed to be working on some plan in his mind.

Krish took Arnie to her favourite sushi bar for an early dinner. "Sit back and relax for now. We will sort it out. The children will panic if they see you like this."

As she sank into the comfortable sofa, Krish ordered her favourite Bento box and a tempura platter for himself. She sipped jasmine tea and described all that had happened in her crazy, crazy day.

Her mother had said that it would take her time to remember if she had a daughter. That the coming of Diwali would somehow bring back her memory. "Have you ever heard something like this?" Arnie asked, her hurt apparent.

"No, this is absurd. I have seen her at her worst, but this is totally unexpected, even from her."

"She should be fed to the pigs," Arnie retorted angrily and then chuckled as she heard Krish's reply.

"Even pigs will turn their nose up at her."

"Seriously! I am stuck now, Krish. I don't know which way to turn or what to do," she said softly.

"The first thing is for you to trust your legal team and no one else. I did check. The court process will take time even in simple matters like adding your name to the family tree. Have some patience, otherwise you will trip up. Your mother will exploit any mistake you make in your filings or arguments in court. Do not sign any paper without referring it to Vikram, your Delhi lawyer. In addition, it would be prudent not to contact your family, and if anyone calls you, maybe now you need to refer them to your legal team. Whatever else you do, please do not have a long conversation with your mother because she always twists things out of context and she can be sinister."

"What do you mean?"

"Remember, she would tape people by getting them to talk and then literally make them eat their words?"

"Yes, she did a lot worse," Arnie added and then turned the conversation to her biggest concern, her job. "What will I do now? How will I run the kitchen and pay for the case? I feel hemmed in. How could my mother call my boss? She needs to jog her fucking memory about me, but what about Sia and Shrey? Unbelievable! How can she be so ruthless? She wants to do what she has always threatened to do. Bury me alive. The child abuse, the relentless beating, nothing prepared me for this. She has now placed her throne on my little chest and narrow shoulders. She is aware that Sia and Shrey depend totally on me and she is effectively destroying them too. Krish, I hate her, I hate her!"

"Don't let hate get the better of you. Focus and let's work on a strategy. This is our only strength, your memory, little one, so think!"

"Okay, I get it. I will not say that again. I believe that the Universe keeps an account of good and bad so her payback will be to the Gods."

They ate quietly and then Krish said, "You have to keep safe. You need to be careful because she has a vindictive nature and a big ego. She can go to any length to get her way and Yudi will help her."

Arnie pushed spoonfuls of soft melon around in her plate nervously and held Krish's gaze as he continued to speak. "I have some news, just a sliver of hope. I was so upset after I heard the crap about her not remembering giving birth to you that I actually went over and met Vikram and told him Sanjeev's news from Ranchi."

"What was his reaction?"

"He was astonished and immediately pulled out your Ranchi case file. As we flipped through the pages, we chanced on statements made on oath by various people in your family. If, just if, we are right in our interpretation, you may have the smoking gun, the proof that you need. The proof that the estate is that of your grandfather and that he intended it to go to all his descendants."

"I don't get it, what does all this mean? What is the breakthrough and why don't you sound as excited as you should be if all you say is true?"

"I don't want to get your hopes up until I am sure," Krish

replied quietly. "We have to get this verified by a forensic expert. I had fixed to meet him tomorrow evening, but will now push for a morning appointment. The file from Ranchi has mostly handwritten records, so we need to be certain of what we say. The writing expert will, I hope, confirm our understanding, and then it will be a breakthrough. We will then get an authorised legal translation from a court-appointed professional to submit it as part of our filings."

"Wow, I can't wait for tomorrow! I'll call my boss and postpone the handing over to the end of the week. Krish, I hope you are right. I need some luck because you know that they will come down heavily on me."

Arnie shuddered as they got up to leave and fear took hold of her again. "There is no margin for error, Krish. My life hangs in the balance."

27

'Every one of us is losing something precious to us. Lost
opportunities, lost possibilities, feelings we can never get back
again. That's what part of it means to be alive.'
– Haruki Murakami

▼

The next morning was a blur; Arnie was excited at the
possibility of a breakthrough that would resolve the
Ranchi matter. Krish came early to take her to Kausambi. It
appeared that this guy was the best in the business and would
only meet at his residence before going off to do whatever
he did with the rest of his day. "We will save ourselves a huge
headache and a lot of time so let's just meet him where he
wants to meet."

Although she woke up early every morning to send the
children to school, she was rarely on the road at this time.
She checked her watch and adjusted the seat, looking out of
the window as she watched Delhi wake up.

The Capital city started its day slowly, emerging gently
into the sunshine, as pavement-dwellers stretched and
brushed their teeth near the road, calling out to each other.
Doodhwallas cycled with milk packets instead of the large
milk-cans that were commonplace until a few years ago.
Mothers with children at bus stops waited impatiently for
school buses that didn't ever seem to arrive on time. The
traffic seemed to increase as they drove on, perhaps because
masses of office-goers were descending on the road in their
urgency to beat the rush hour and creating another one by

their collective action, significantly increasing the noise level by many decibels in their wake. Arnie reached for the audio controls and the soft melody of Simon and Garfunkel's 'Bridge Over Troubled Waters' played gently. She smiled and began to hum.

> *When you're weary*
> *Feeling small*
> *When tears are in your eyes*
> *I will dry them all*
> *I'm on your side*

"I love the last bit, can you rewind it?" and she listened quietly as it played.

> *Sail on Silver Girl,*
> *Sail on by*
> *Your time has come to shine*
> *All your dreams are on their way*

Her cousin, Chhoti Phua's son, had played this song for Arnie and she had been hooked on it ever since she had first heard it. This was her song and this particular part was her chant when she was in senior school. Every single day, it kept telling her that "My time had come to shine and better days were on their way". As she told Krish, "It was part of my survival toolkit, battered though my Walkman was, being itself a cast-down from Randy. I played it to motivate myself after yet another brutal attack. I can't recall what hurt more, the physical assault or the constant abuse crushing my battered self-esteem."

"Walkman, huh? The kids would not even know what it is," added Krish, pulling up in front of a house on a deserted street.

"Yes, this is it. I have the papers. Let's go. Promise not to let slip anything about the case. We want him to just clarify the handwritten papers without getting involved any further. We don't want the other party to find out our strategy." Seeing Arnie's quizzical expression he added, "The world is a small place."

She nodded as they walked into the room and were met by a rather surly man. He didn't look as if he wanted them there. Before they could even sit down, he launched into an explanation of how the Reserve Bank of India, the Prime Minister, and various high-and-mighties relied on his word before taking a decision on the basis of handwritten notes, and how he lectured at universities all over, none of which Arnie had ever heard of. Nevertheless, Krish had found this person from somewhere and she was happy to let the process continue. Looking at his dingy, dusty room with heavy mismatched furniture, she wondered if this was where he met the Prime Minister or did he have different places for different sorts of clients.

He turned out to be as good as his word, reading and deciphering scrawls from the court files that looked nothing other than doodles. He began by clarifying his fees in advance, but once he got going, he was charging ahead. A couple of hours later, he was done. Krish had consciously not drawn his attention to any one part of the documents, and the forensic expert had needed to decipher and re-write about five pages.

"I have translated the pages, and have written it down, word for word, young man," he said, addressing Krish because women, in his world, didn't count for anything. "It was difficult, the bugger's handwriting is awful, but I am a trained and certified professional," he said, exuding importance and extending his hand for his payment.

They sat in the car before Krish read out the relevant sentence to Arnie. "Our family money came from our father, he was the source of all our *zamindari* money. My father, from his funds, bought our property. He was the head of the family, a joint, united family." Krish also told Arnie that Anil Dhari had further gone on to list the family properties bought by Dadaji for the extended family's benefit; a list that included Civil Lines.

Not daring to look up, Arnie had been holding her breath; now subconsciously she bit her lip and swallowed her relief in one gulp. This seemed to be what she needed!

"Woweeeee!" she exclaimed as they hugged each other and Krish began singing,

"Sail on silver girl, sail on by
Your time has come to shine
All your dreams are on their way."

"Krish stop! You are killing the song," she grinned and said with mock irritation as they drove off.

"So what, my brain is sharp, isn't it?" he retorted, as Arnie protested, "Modesty, modesty!"

Both the lawyers needed to be informed but neither seemed to be available. They would be in court by now, busy with the many cases each of them handled every day. Arnie could message this news to them. They would need, in any case, the original translation before they could decide what use to put it to. Essentially, the elders of the extended family, including Arnie's father, had been caught lying.

Her father was totally under the control of Kamini, as Krish reminded Arnie. "It is simple. Your mother doesn't think that you can stand up to her. She believes that she is all powerful and that you are incapable of lasting the course." He was right. She did make Arnie nervous. "But Krish, surely a lie is a lie and who are they to blatantly flout the law? What makes them think they will get away with it?"

His answer hit to the core of the issue. It was not who was right and who was wrong that mattered, merely who could hold their breath for longer under water. "She knows that you are vulnerable, that you struggle to bring up the children and don't know Jharkhand. She is also going to use muscle power and her clout; she believes that decisions are taken in the Chambers and not in the courtroom."

Arnie sat back pensively, lost in thought and very troubled. Who could say what connections are made when thoughts are flying all over the place? "Krish, I remember running as a little girl, running as fast as my little legs would carry me when I heard the loud siren."

It was the time of the 1971 India-Pakistan War. Sirens. A rush to switch off the lights; all the windows and skylights were painted black. The maid would half carry, half drag Arnie into the trenches dug in Civil Lines. Everyone, including Dadaji, would sit in the trenches for what seemed like ages. On one occasion, Dadaji exploded with rage while the family cowered, because Kamini had clutched Randy to her breast and was squeezing Arnie into a corner, covering her with mud, nearly burying her alive. Dadaji had yanked Arnie out because she was stuck in the mud with her face almost covered. Was it an accident or a game? From the expression on the faces of Dadaji and Chhoti Phua, it had been no game.

"And from then onwards," Arnie told Krish, "I have hated covering my face."

Krish's attention was diverted due to the traffic around them and Arnie noticed a message on her phone from Sanjeev, reminding her about a small payment owed to him. She felt like a fish caught in a mesh! "When would this end? My mother knows she is in the wrong and yet she wants to fight; she wants to break my spirit, aware that it is an unequal battle because she holds all the cards in her hands."

There was little sympathy from Krish at this moment because he wanted Arnie to be strong. He could see the long struggle ahead and knew that she had to be resilient like never before. "You have taken it on and are now in it. You need nerves of steel, of titanium."

She nodded mutely, aware that she was up against a wall. "Can you drop me off at my friend's farm? Her astrologer will be there and I need some cheering up." He did, even though Arnie saw that he was not sure how an astrologer was going to get her spirits up.

"Some chai?" her friend asked, welcoming Arnie into her drawing room and introducing the astrologer who was seated with a sheaf of white paper in front of him. Arnie sat before him and he asked for her time and place of birth, a few other questions, and then started to make the familiar charts and calculations. Her family on both sides, the Dharis and the Sharmas, were keen followers of astrology.

After an endless wait, he looked up, peered at Arnie rather sadly, and began his narrative as she got up and moved closer.

"Overall, a lucky horoscope with great education and good children, but a flawed marriage. This period is not good. Loss in everything, litigation, arguments, tension, money problems, problems in job, and a heartache. One year of intense problems that ease in August next year, but better times are only after two years."

Already feeling low, these were not the words Arnie wanted to hear. She was devastated and felt weighed down. Her mind shouted out, "All is lost! Gloom and doom is inevitable." She had not told her friend that she had lost her job, but it seemed that her stars revealed all!

Home. Exhausted. A quick dinner and then bed. Falling asleep, Arnie told herself, as she did so often these days, that tomorrow would be a new day.

But tomorrow never seemed to come!

28

'Being challenged in life is inevitable,
being defeated is optional.'
– Roger Crawford

The ringing of her mobile phone woke Arnie. Half awake and still groggy, she bleated out a faint "Hello?" and nearly got her ear blown off! Now she was completely awake. She could hear Kamini shouting in rage.

"We have to put an end to this! She is becoming a nuisance, Yudi. You have to mobilise your contacts before it is too late. You are responsible, you have been too soft on her and you supported her mad ideas. We have to do what it takes . . ."

The conversation stopped in mid sentence with a sharp click. Was that a recording Arnie had just heard? Another voice broke in, one that she didn't recognise, a man's, deep and sombre. "She came yesterday, your mother, and there were angry words with her brother."

"What? Who are you?" she asked.

"That is not important," the voice said and the phone disconnected, leaving Arnie wide-awake and very scared. There was no number registered on the call. 'Private Number', it read, whatever that might mean.

Terrified and shivering with fright, Arnie shrank involuntarily into the bed, wanting to hide away from the world. "What have I gotten myself into?" The words slowly sank in, heavy with sinister overtones. Her fingers were like fudge, unable to manipulate the buttons on her phone to call anyone. Her voice was trapped in her throat and she couldn't even cry out to Aida. She yearned for the time when ignorance was bliss, a time just a few months ago. She was struggling then, as now, to keep her head above the water, but life was less complicated, less jumbled up and lacked this kind of excitement, an excitement that she could well do without.

Life returned to her fingers and she tried to call Krish, Vikram, and then Jaya and Monica, but she couldn't get through to any of them. Shaken, she poured some chai as Aida got her the newspaper, but her mind was far away as she struggled with the mixed emotions in her head.

Finally, she got through to Krish and was breathless as she relived the horror of the phone call. "Speak with your lawyer immediately," he said.

But try as she might, Arnie could not get through to Vikram. "I must be just another case for him, a number on a file." Desperate, she called Krish again, sobbing as she spoke, "Vikram isn't responding. My life hangs in a balance; the kids are not safe. I am going to the school to pick them up. I am terrified," she told him as he listened in silence and then asked her to remain exactly where she was and that he would take care of things.

Arnie's nerves were raw and vulnerable like a scratched scab. Fear, sorrow, and alarm were stuck in her throat like a fishbone. Vikram did not call back.

She did what she had resolved she would not do. Revealed the sorry litany of her family's past to her lawyer. A complete wreck, she typed an email to Vikram and sent him the documented history of abuse, email correspondence between her mother and her, a chronicle of misery.

Krish, in the meantime, had spoken with Vikram. "We have a meeting in the lawyer's office tomorrow afternoon; all is under control. Relax," he said, trying to sooth her jangled nerves. However, she was on edge. She paced the flat, walked in and out of the children's room even though they were back home, much to their irritation, sat beside them and held them tight, even though she could see that they wanted some space.

Tomorrow was another day, but it was just like the previous one. She dressed the next morning with a heavy heart; it was her last day at work. With as much dignity as she could muster and without any drama, she handed over her files to the assigned person and walked out without a backward glance.

The next few meetings with Vikram were uneventful, but something had changed in their relationship. He had read the emails and finally understood Arnie and where she was coming from. He realised what she was going through and the courage it had taken to stand up for herself. "It is a fight for my dignity as a daughter and granddaughter. It is not only about money, it is a struggle for my rights. Parts of me are being stolen this very minute, as my soul watches in disbelief and despairs," Arnie had told him one evening in his office.

Vikram had something for Arnie to read. It was a news report. "I empathise," he said, as he pushed the paper towards her and he did understand. Arnie was no longer just another case for him.

The report was about another woman, a young girl. As she read, Arnie related to the horror as well as the incredible strength of the girl. Similar, so similar. But strangers attacked her. And she had the support of her father.

Her story was well-known. Taliban gunmen boarded her school bus one day, sought her out, and shot her in the head. Eventually airlifted to a hospital in Britain, she survived her severe wounds. Malala was now a name known not only in her native Pakistan, but also around the world. Hers was an even more moving story, because the saga was not just of a brave young girl, but also of a father willing to risk local opprobrium to raise his daughter, not a son, as a proud example for the world. It was among the most tender stories in the world of conservative Islam.

Krish, Arnie thought, always knew, and Vikram had now figured things out. Watching her closely, both of them spoke as one. "You will not be a statistic. But your family does compare with the regressive Taliban!" Krish guffawed at the comparison and ordered coffee and cake for the entire office. The mood had lightened. Arnie was with people who cared about her.

The office boy interrupted them and handed Vikram a yellow manila envelope that had just been delivered by the courier service. Arnie's name was on it, addressed to her through her lawyers. Vikram and Krish read the papers quietly before handing them to her.

She didn't want to read the papers. "What's happened? Am I finished?" she asked, looking out of the window, her heart sinking with the setting sun.

"Are you crazy, I am one step away from doing the monkey dance," Krish said jubilantly as Arnie's eyebrows flew to the top of her head in surprise.

"Yes, we could not have wished for more," said Vikram and pointed out to a few paragraphs in the statement in front of him. "Anil Dhari has done himself in. He has lied to the court in a sworn affidavit. Arrogance of the old *zamindari* lingers!"

Her uncle had strange logic to his arguments. He had claimed that Aranya, having been born well after the birth and adoption of her grandfather, could have no first hand knowledge of Dadaji's early life and from where he got his wealth. His affidavit before the court certified Aranya's birth and sought to exclude her from giving any evidence or stating any facts that occurred before she was born.

This was patently absurd even to Arnie and she didn't need a lawyer to paraphrase the stupidity in the logic. "Wow," she said, astonished. "So, since I did not see India get independence, are we still under the British rule?" She was relieved and enjoying herself and found the absurdity wildly amusing.

"So what happens now?" she asked, biting into the cake as she skimmed through the papers her uncle had served. "Look, he has attached a copy of *Fringe* magazine with her on the cover. I had totally forgotten about this," Arnie chuckled. "This is interesting; it's going to be my bedtime read."

Bringing her back to the case, Vikram cleared his throat and said, "We are well prepared for the court hearing. As I see it, their statements on oath are going to come back to haunt them. Our strategy is to buy time here until you can get an order from Ranchi recognising you as the daughter of your parents. We need a formal order that proves you are the daughter and that will consolidate our position in this matter significantly. No worries. See you in court. We have a good judge; he has risen from the trial court so he will appreciate the legal point that we will definitely take up."

Arnie toasted her family cheerfully with her cup of coffee. "Here's to another family reunion. I see more of my mother in court than I have for years," and got up to leave, finally seeing humour in the situation.

It bothered Arnie that her parents and uncle were, as usual, not taking her seriously even though they were in court. What had possessed Anil Dhari to file such an absurd reply? Her car followed as Arnie rode with Krish; she wanted to talk to him. The expletives and statements describing her as a usurper and a greedy bitch did hurt. Krish calmed her down and told her to focus on the next day, as she had to be in court to respond to the papers that had been served to her a little while ago.

He told Arnie that she should have faith in the system, that she should believe that she would get the right to reply and have the right to be heard. "While their lawyers will resort to any tricks to destabilise you, this will not work, for the judicial system in India is sound."

"They have so many and such big names with them on their legal team!" Arnie exclaimed.

Krish would have none of it and reminded Arnie that she too, had a great legal team, even if they were not household names and didn't appear every day to make comments on television. He once again reminded Arnie that even the weakest and most vulnerable litigant did get their chance in court; that was the strength of the judicial system. "Of course," he added, "the rich and the powerful have the ability to make better arguments through better lawyers. However, it is a matter of getting a better lawyer, not a more influential one or one better known. And you have very good lawyers with you, so have faith in them and in the system."

Krish asked whether she was ready for the next day. He was asking about her mental state, but Arnie chose to answer more literally as she didn't have an answer for his real question. "Yes, I have shampooed my hair, had a manicure and pedicure. Taken care over my clothes and I am all set. My appearance will ooze confidence. However, I am nowhere near getting the Ranchi Court to recognise me as the daughter of my parents," she said wearily.

"Let it be. Concentrate on getting through this hearing with Vikram so that they cannot sell," Krish told Arnie as he dropped her home.

Sleep eluded Arnie and she walked from room to room, playing musical chair all over the house. She sat on the sofa, then the bed, and then at the children's desk, praying and meditating. Sometime in the morning, the alarm must have rung and the streetlights must have been switched off. Sometime in the morning, she must have seen the children off to school and got herself ready for court. For when she really became aware of her surroundings again, she found that she was sitting in the now familiar hall, outside the courtroom.

The crowds milling around were, like Arnie, anxious and worried as case numbers flashed on the electronic board, like at an airport lounge. Instead of flights, fates were decided there. The courts were progressive; they allowed electronic devices and Arnie had brought her iPod to drown out the noise. She listened to Sufi songs, her special favourite, as the day dragged on and the court broke for lunch.

As the court reassembled, she looked around for Vikram and asked about the senior counsel who was needed for this hearing and he reassured her, but Arnie was worried as she hadn't seen him around. "Vikram, we need him, we are in a strong position."

"Your parents have arrived, they don't look too happy," he said under his breath, and Arnie swung around and spotted them. Tender feelings rushed to her heart when she saw her father and she got teary-eyed yet again. Kamini was standing only a few yards away, presiding over a meeting of lawyers. Her beauty had not diminished, although she had a perpetually stretched, surprised look. Clearly, a plastic surgeon's sleight of hand.

Their case was next. A short wait and then it was Arnie's turn. Vikram was ready; Arnie had managed to convince someone to move and let her sit in her lucky seat. They were like a Formula One pit crew, ready to launch the car into the fray. But there was a problem, for their driver was missing. Her litigator, the senior counsel, had another case at the same time and couldn't make it in time for the hearing.

Vikram did his best and it was just about good enough, but Arnie was bitterly disappointed, for she realised that they had lost an excellent opportunity. "Throw her out; the daughter is greedy, a usurper, and has no rights."

Her fists knotted up tight like her stomach. She saw her mother gloat; after all, it was going well for her. The system worked, however, and the judge refused to throw Arnie out and kept her petition pending, setting an early date instead. She breathed again, lungs full of air, and quickly exited the courtroom.

This time she waited for her lawyer and didn't drive away

as she saw her senior counsel approach. She contained her disappointment as he explained that the hearing clashed with another case. "What next, sir?" Arnie asked politely after Vikram had briefed him.

"Contempt of court; we file immediately. Vikram, meet me tomorrow," he said, disappearing behind a cloud of cigarette smoke as Arnie finally walked to the car and called Krish.

"Come home, I'm waiting here for you. This happens in court matters; there will be good days and bad days."

Exhausted, Arnie sank into the seat and slept on the way back home, not knowing where she stood and whether she was in a good place or not.

29

*'When you come to the end of your rope,
tie a knot and hang on.'*
– Franklin D Roosevelt

The week flew by with endless meetings filled with legal jargon and mountains of papers for Arnie to sign. Contempt of court was not a matter to be trifled with, she realised, and almost pitied her uncle, Anil Dhari, who would have to defend himself against this charge. Her senior counsel had taken umbrage on behalf of the court at what Anil Dhari had filed and would now hold him accountable. This would also have the added benefit of focusing the judge's mind on the merits of Arnie's case, which was her strongest point, as she was in the right.

Arnie's legal team told her that this would shake them up and get them to the table. "In the meanwhile, contact your other cousins and try to get some family support," the senior counsel suggested.

Arnie shook her head, indicating that it was a bad idea. "Only I have been left out of the family tree. These two women, my cousins, are part of the family as per the court record, so they will not support me."

"There are no words to describe your mother. I change channels now if I see her talk about women's rights and gloat about her NGO on the television," were Vikram's parting remarks as they got into their respective cars.

The immediate focus was on the Ranchi Court. It was Arnie's responsibility, through Sanjeev, to get an order from the court declaring that she was the daughter of her parents. This was what was required to make her situation in the Delhi case firm and strong. Time had passed very quickly, as it does when you want it to creep along. How would the judge react to a situation where the sale of Civil Lines was presented before him and Arnie still did not have an order stating that she was their daughter? Would he throw her out, let the sale go ahead, and push the case out of his crowded roster? That was exactly what Arnie would have done if she were in his place, and he appeared to be nobody's fool. He had seen the worth of Arnie's argument and given her a foot in the door by impleading her, but that was all that she had. She had to take matters into her own hands. She had to go to Ranchi, stand before the judge, and prove that she had been born to her mother and her father.

"I will make a short trip," Arnie told Krish over dinner, adding that she would carry her birth certificate, photographs, and other bits of evidence with her to Ranchi. A friend had agreed to let her stay at his parents' apartment for the night so that Arnie could keep her visit very low-key.

"Good idea," Krish said. "I will come with you. No ifs and buts." Before Arnie could stop him, he had called the travel agent and booked the flights. The kids looked at them, their expressions morphed with concern. Arnie's voice sounded unconvincing as she told them that all would be well.

The tension began to corrode Arnie's insides, and in the middle of the night, she woke up in pain and ran to the bathroom. "Damn period again," she cursed under her breath and called her gynaecologist.

"You are bleeding to death," her doctor said. "Every ten days is a bad sign."

"I know, doctor, help me. I have to go to Ranchi for the case tomorrow and I am doubled up with excruciating pain."

"Okay, my dear. But this is the last time that I am giving you medicines, now I need an ultrasound and a pelvic examination. You are killing yourself while that mad woman parties," for she knew of Arnie's life and was aware of her relationship with her mother.

Fortified by her medicine, Arnie buckled into the airline seat, nervously clutching the pillow as the flight took off. She was glad that Krish was there with her.

"Do you remember Ranchi?" he asked.

"Nope, very little, but I do remember the trip to the village and the *pokhri*."

"*Pokhri*?" he asked.

"Our own pond attached to the house," she replied with a tinge of pride. "And the Ram temple."

"Wow! Excited?"

Arnie nodded in response and prayed at the same time.

Sanjeev was surprised when Arnie called him from Ranchi and told him that she would appear in court. "Yes*ji*, very good idea. It is next to the *pulliya*, I mean bridge. This is a surprise. Tomorrow 10 a.m."

Arnie repeated the conversation to Krish and teased him, "Wait until tomorrow. Seeing you will be an even bigger surprise *ji*."

There was a method to the madness in what Arnie had chosen to wear. A spotless white *salwar kameez* with a printed *dupatta* and a big *bindi* in the middle of her forehead. Hair brushed straight until she could feel the static and then she looked the part. "Just like her," she whispered to herself in satisfaction.

"Shit, you spook me! The resemblance is startling," said Krish, getting into the car. They sped to the court and met Sanjeev at the juice shop as planned. Vikram had called a little earlier from Delhi, wishing Arnie luck.

"This is my colleague, Ajeet Singh," said Sanjeev. They stared at a rotund *sardarji* who got up to greet them. "Don't worry, *wahe guru ki kripa.* You just expresso yourself if judge asks you." Arnie nodded as they walked into the small courtroom.

And she stopped. She had gone back in time, into an old Hindi film set, still covered with dust, as if it had been opened only in her honour. The hard wooden benches, the flies and the files, the strong smells that wafted in from the open windows. She felt like the big city girl, out of place in the sticks. Try as she might, she would never fit in here. Arnie discretely sprayed J'Adore but regretted it immediately because it spread and attracted undue attention.

"Relax, you cannot merge into the furniture," said Krish, reading her mind as the judge strode in.

Sanjeev took charge and he seemed to grow in that tiny courtroom. He was in his element and Arnie drew strength from the confidence with which he began talking, putting forward their case. "*Hazoor*, my client, the missing daughter is here and would like to say a few words, with your permission."

Getting a nod from the judge, he pulled Arnie forward and she was now on stage. It was her cue to speak, and caught in the drama of the unreal situation, she parroted her lines perfectly.

"*Hazoor*, I am the daughter. I have come late but want justice. I never knew about all of this. My grandfather was Sir Eshwar Dhari and my father is . . ." Her voice trailed off as she broke down, hit by the cruelty of having to prove her birth, of who she was, standing in court before a judge. Not being able to speak for a moment, she quietly passed her documents and photographs to the judge, photocopies of which were added to the official records of the court.

She spread her *dupatta* and asked for justice, as a daughter, a granddaughter, and as a woman, in the classic pose recognisable anywhere in the country. "*Hazoor*, here is my birth certificate.

Please look at my wedding photographs; my entire family is there. You will recognise my mother . . ." and she let the sentence hang, too embarrassed to draw attention to her mother's escapades. "And those are my children. Your Lordship, in the second photograph, Yudi *mama* is holding my son as my daughter looks on. I am not the neighbour's daughter," she repeated with emotion. "It takes courage to stand up against a powerful family. However, being let down by my own parents, I have no recourse other than your court. Please grant me my rightful position in the family."

"The law is the same for everyone," said the judge, dismissing them.

The harshness and cruelty of it all hit Arnie as she walked out and she wept. "My parents have disowned me, why?" She didn't understand the court process. "It should be so simple, for I do exist; I produced myself before the court. And my birth certificate. And photographs. And other evidence. So, what does it mean that the law is the same for everyone?"

Sanjeev had stayed back in the court as the lawyers were arguing some motions with the judge. He met Arnie at the airport and told her that the judge was a good one and wanted to do the right thing. Sanjeev himself seemed more motivated and sincere after having seen Arnie appear in court.

He cautioned Arnie. "Your mother is ruthless. She will produce another daughter, another girl like you. Or get your birth record removed from the municipal records in Delhi. You know that she is powerful and capable of this." Arnie nodded and told Sanjeev that she was born overseas, in France, so Kamini could not use her Delhi influence to wipe clear the records of Arnie's birth.

The newly motivated Sanjeev said that he had a "short date" and he would try his best to get the order in the next hearing. "We must do so," Arnie thought to herself. "The *Dussehra-Diwali* period is almost upon us and time is passing way too fast while I remain stranded in the same place without making any progress."

Arriving home late at night, Arnie didn't get to speak with the children till they had breakfast together. "When I was a little girl," she told them, "there used to be this big *havan* on the ninth day of the *navratras*, in the aangan. All of us would sit around the fire and watch Dadaji preside over the *puja*. When the *pandit* said '*Swaha*', we would throw *samagri* into the holy fire and chant the *Gayatri Mantra*. After the *havan*, we would have a scrumptious dinner together. This was a family tradition but with time, it changed. Kamini fought with Chhoti Phua and then forced my father to have a separate *puja* room and a different kitchen. From that time onwards, there was only cabbage for me at breakfast, lunch, and dinner."

Their condominium complex, in which Arnie lived, celebrated all festivals with gusto, and *Dussehra* was no exception. Arnie stood with her children in the evening and watched *Ravan* being stuffed with firecrackers. Little Krishang looked up and said, "Aunty, next time we will get *Ravan's* sister."

"Sure, but generally the brothers are burnt along with the effigy of *Ravan*, not the sister," Arnie replied, launching into a lecture but stopped, noticing all the children grinning at her. "What's up?" she asked.

"Well, for starters we have the perfect face for the effigy; we will stand Sia's grandmother next to *Ravan*!"

Arnie burst into peals of laughter as the condominium kids giggled convulsively at their joke. They stood together and watched *Ravan* burn and the crackers burst, as good conquered evil.

"I WILL win," Arnie told the kids as they walked back to their flat.

30

*'The world is round and the place which may seem like
the end may also be only the beginning.'*
– Ivy Baker Priest

Contempt of court was such a serious matter that Vikram
wanted Arnie to be certain before filing the petition.
"You do realise that after this filing, we are going to be at
war; the entire family will be pitted against you since they
have a common goal to sell and you are slowing it down. The
dispute is going to get bloodier."

"Yes, I am aware of this. I know that together they are
formidable; they have money, clout, and a louder voice than
me. For me this is about my dignity, about standing up for
my rights and those of my children. Go ahead and file."

He wanted to file anyway and would have advised
Arnie to do so anyway, but being a good lawyer and now a
friend, he felt that he should caution her. She didn't need
to appear for the hearing, as the matter was one where her
legal team would bring a perceived slight to the dignity of
the court itself to the notice of the judge. This would be
a matter where the court would fight the petition against
her uncle.

The date arrived; Krish as usual followed the proceedings
on the Internet through the court website. Arnie received
various messages and calls from Sanjeev and Vikram
updating her on the general atmosphere, very tense from

what they told her and unusually silent. Her senior counsel was hanging around, very much present as well.

Krish got a call on his mobile. Arnie concentrated on her breathing, feeling the air leave and enter her body slowly. Krish burst into the room with news that he said was good. The judge had admitted the petition of contempt but had not ruled on it. The matter was to be heard the next time the court met. Ten days, she was told.

Disappointment gnawed at Arnie. "I am still not part of the family tree in Ranchi, not even declared the daughter. This was supposed to be easy-peasy! And the contempt matter too, has got postponed to the next hearing." Her lower lip quivered as she spoke. "I have no clout, not with the courts and not with God," she complained bitterly because the pressure was getting to her.

"Listen, I have something for you," Krish said, pulling out an airline ticket.

"Where to?" Arnie asked, puzzled.

"It is your reunion at the University of London, fifteen years since you graduated, and you must go."

"I cannot afford it," Arnie replied lamely.

Krish would have none of it. He had arranged for her to stay with a friend in London, gifted her a ticket, and left her with just enough time to buy some foreign currency from the bank, for she was supposed to leave the next day!

"Shit, departure tomorrow! Wow, thanks," Arnie said and grabbed the ticket. She was so glad for the diversion.

She bustled around, making last minute arrangements and gave a pile of clothes for ironing, her mind on the dress she wanted to wear for the formal sit-down dinner at the Waldorf Hotel. "This one or the other one?" she asked Sia, who hopped from foot to foot, happy to see her mother excited. Shrey was told that Arnie could not promise too many gifts because of the court expenses, but she would get him a Manchester United jacket.

"Just have fun Mamma, just have fun," both told their mother, enveloping her in a bear hug. "And don't catch a chill, be warm. Take cabs, Mamma, because it will be freezing cold," they cautioned her. "We won't have big birthday parties this year because of the case, so don't worry."

And before she knew it, Arnie was on the flight to London.

The next few days were the happiest in a long time. Far away from Delhi, Arnie felt her body relax. Drinks, dinner, and fancy presentations marked the occasion. She looked around at a room full of people and only the odd face seemed somewhat familiar. She took in the receding hairlines and prosperous paunches, the women more chic in their designer suits and clicking heels. "What do you do?" she was asked over a glass of sparkling wine and Arnie was at a loss for words. She tried old party tricks like playing with her glass and tossing a hors d'oeurve into her mouth to get time to think of a response.

Self-justification made Arnie describe her corporate career and then explain that she had recently taken time off to focus on personal matters. "Aah, personal matters," repeated the person next to her annoyingly. Arnie disappeared into the crowd. She didn't want to engage further. "Hey, no offence meant," she heard him say as he followed her and added, "You are connected with me on LinkedIn."

"Is that so?" Arnie made a mental note to delete him immediately from her connections.

"I am the Managing Director of El Grande Corporation," he said, "and I live in this large house in Mumbai, on Napean Sea Road, sea-facing flat." He was trying to impress Arnie, but she took his card and slipped away to the dance floor as the DJ racked up the music to her favourite Black Eyed Peas number. She swayed to the music and enjoyed being in the moment.

I gotta feeling that tonight's gonna be a good night
That tonight's gonna be a good night

Then she totally lost it, dancing with gay abandon. The night extended into frantic clubbing and ended with early morning vodka shots.

The next morning was a rush as Arnie shopped for the children. Her day was spent at Primark as she could not afford much else. She was jostled from counter to counter by the swelling crowd of hysterical shoppers, but was too tired to protest as she moved with the wave and finally stood in a queue for hours to pay, and then in another line to claim VAT, because now every penny counted.

Her head hurt and she wanted to skip the formal dinner. Knowing that her friends would be disappointed, she thought of excuses on the tube ride back to her temporary London home. It began to rain as Arnie walked out of the station, struggling with the packets and feeling the cold even more than the other people around her. It was typical British weather and the evening was dreary. Her friend, also from the University of London, insisted that they had to go and Arnie decided to brave it, although she felt that she might be a little cold in the off-shoulder formal dress that she had chosen for the evening. The look that greeted her when she stood before the mirror made her smile. She looked a million bucks and felt it too. The sequins from the dress sparkled cheerfully as she brushed her hair one last time before they got into the cab.

The ballroom at the Waldorf dazzled, the mirrors reflected their sense of pride, and the speeches tied all of the people present together in a warm fuzzy embrace and broke down the earlier barriers. They all belonged to one 'family' and there was a general bonhomie. Dinner over, they headed for the dance floor and yet again, Arnie found herself face-to-face with the full-of-himself

Managing Director. This time she teased him, "Guess this place does get it wrong. You must have been an admission's mistake." Her humour was lost on him and he started listing symbols of success. A trophy wife, corner office, rich father-in-law in Kolkata. Arnie excused herself hurriedly and escaped to find her friends.

Nothing mattered this evening, neither her case nor her problems. For that one evening, they were just alumni partying together before they flew back to their routine lives the next day.

From Heathrow, Arnie called Krish and spoke with the children. "We are well, just chill," Shrey shouted into the phone as Arnie walked to the departure gate, suddenly weighed down by uncertainties again as she boarded the Virgin Atlantic flight for Delhi.

Her mood changed on the flight itself. From Black Eyed Peas to Gloria Gaynor. 'I will survive, I will.'

At first, I was afraid, I was petrified
Kept thinking, I could never live without you by my side
But then I spent so many nights thinking, how you did me wrong
And I grew strong and I learned how to get along
Oh, as long as I know how to love, I know I'll stay alive
I've got all my life to live, I've got all my love to give
And I'll survive, I will survive

Arnie was back in Delhi. It was time for the next hearing and she was sitting, yet again, outside the same courtroom. Nervous, petrified, and humbled. She had dressed with care; crisp white shirt and a dark suit and she was carrying Shrey's lucky penny. "I will go down fighting," she told herself, "but I will not let her see me as weak."

The song came to an end; Arnie took off the headphones and looked around. Her gaze met that of the person sitting across.

"Here for divorce?" she asked Arnie with an American drawl.

"Nope, what made you think that?" Arnie was a little miffed.

"You have Gloria Gaynor playing on your iPod; every woman's anthem during a break-up."

Arnie smiled broadly and related her story as the woman listened wide-eyed and reached across to hold her hand. "This must be so difficult for you. Don't give up, just don't. I am a Jain and I believe that it is all ordained." Touching her forehead, she said, "It is the writing on the forehead; we come with it."

Tears glistened in the corners of Arnie's eyes as the woman narrated her own emotional trauma. "It was very difficult, but, like you, I am fighting my own brother. I live in America. My sister and I were shocked to receive legal papers from my brother asking us to relinquish our rights to our Greater Kailash house. It is worth a fortune and my sister needs the money. She is handicapped. But his lawyers tell us that we should just let him have it, that we are greedy and materialistic. My son wants me to fight. Six years and there is still no solution in sight. We get one order in our favour, and then my brother appeals. It is like snakes and ladders. However, don't worry; just have patience. And don't let her tire you out," she said and hurried into the courtroom, understanding at once that Arnie's battle was with her mother, and the other protagonists were just playing their part on this stage. A stage that was defining who Kamini had become and was giving Arnie the choice to shape what she would become.

Arnie's case was next. The entire family was here with their lawyers. They looked serious and worried for the first time since this saga had begun. Arnie's senior counsel was speaking to the judge. Their lawyers had glum expressions on their faces and were clearly reluctant to speak or to interrupt her litigator, who was in great form; his deep voice resounded in the courtroom. "Your Lordship, my client seeks leave to bring to the notice of this Honourable Court the false and misleading averments and statements made by the petitioner on oath in this suit. Furthermore, it is submitted that the petitioner has made contrary statements on oath before different courts of law. This is an offence against the court itself and should be treated as such; as contempt of court!"

A pause and silence for a moment. No Oscar-winning director could have asked for a better setting to hold the moment. The pathos and force of her litigator's words settled down in the courtroom and seemed to form a cloak covering the assembly. Little, it seems, remained to be said. Then, a lawyer from the other side spoke, albeit without conviction, "Your Lordship, my client is in hospital with brain haemorrhage, so this matter should be adjourned."

Silly though the argument was, the spell was broken. Although the lawyers opposing Arnie were brilliant and well paid, they couldn't subvert the judicial system that they were a part of and which did work in India. The pile-up of cases and the heavy workload meant that justice was sometimes delayed, but Arnie was to see another side of the system. The side where, when the matter was addressed, the system worked.

The judge's steady glare would have made lesser mortals faint. His expression communicated a lot. "In most such cases," he said sarcastically, "people discover that they are not well and land up in hospital. Your client should have thought of this before . . ." And he stopped, not wanting to pass judgement before the process had been completed, but clearly indicating his mind. "Please accept the notice and file your reply. Your client only has to sign what you prepare. There will be no adjournment of this matter."

It was a turning point, Arnie realised. The first moment was perhaps when the court had impleaded her, but she had believed that to be luck. This was something else. She had seen the battalion of lawyers silenced. She had seen her legal team's argument win the day. She had seen a judge of the High Court stand up and support a single, lonely woman.

Beaming and grinning at everyone outside the courtroom,

Arnie was floating on air. Spotting her senior counsel, she ran to thank him as he beamed beatifically and told Vikram to write to the Land Authority, apprising them of the developments.

"I gotta feeling it is going to be a good *Diwali*," Arnie told the children, hugging their little bodies as they searched her face for reassurance. "And we will celebrate Sia's birthday." She drowned their little protests about money. "We have to be careful, but we still have to live, my little ones," she told them, caught in a group hug.

The *Diwali* lights had been switched on in their condominium. Looking at them, Arnie felt happy and calm. All the buildings were lit and so were the neighbouring colonies and markets. It was time for new beginnings and happiness.

Arnie and her children dressed for the *Diwali* party in the condominium park. "Can I wear the dress you wore at the University of London ball?" Sia asked tentatively.

"Seriously, a dress for *Diwali*? Don't you want to wear something Indian?" Arnie suggested, but gave in. She took out the brightest silk sari in her cupboard and draped the six yards around her.

All set, they joined their extended condominium family to light the crackers, dance, and eat traditional Indian food. As always, the steaming *aloo puris* with gooey *halwa* were delightful, and they tucked in.

31

*'The whales do not sing because they have an answer,
they sing because they have a song.'*
– Gregory Colbert

Money had become tight and job interviews were hard to come by in this stagnating economic climate. "I need a job, I need this job," Arnie repeated to herself as she walked in for an interview with Novella Technologies. As the panel and she exchanged pleasantries, her mobile phone began to vibrate. It was Sanjeev from Ranchi. Focussing on the questions from the panel, she ignored the call. One of the interviewers stepped out to take a call and Arnie made use of the opportunity to read the ten text messages from Sanjeev.

"Take call, your brother standing in court."

Another update read, "They talk amongst themselves, loudly say no daughter."

The third was one word, "Urgent."

The fourth was an ominous one, "Talk now, important."

That was it! Her mood was ruined and she was now completely distracted. When the interviewer came back, she made some half-baked excuses and left the meeting room, rushing past the visibly surprised interviewer.

"What is it Sanjeev?" Arnie hissed into the phone. "You ruined my interview."

"It is very important. They are here creating a scene. What do you want me to do?"

This almost drove Arnie crazy because her lawyer was expected to deal with opposition in the court. What did he expect? That they would lie down and roll over and let him rub their stomachs? "Sanjeev, let them say on oath that I don't exist. I have run out of tears, please go back into the courtroom and this time come back with something," she implored him.

The afternoon dragged on as she waited for news from Ranchi. Arnie had no expectation that anything favourable would happen. Life seemed to be so difficult these days.

Sanjeev called. It was good news. Very good news. The best, in fact!

"We have got the order. You are part of the family tree by court order. The judge saw through their lies and has put on record their opposition to your name being added. Today was tense, but I managed to get my way. I want some bonus for this, you know, to keep me motivated."

Arnie thanked him profusely and he added that the matter should now be completely finished. "This is a matter of a week now; they will come to you. Just keep your mobile on all the time, now all will be sorted out," he said.

Habits of a lifetime kicked in. Arnie chanted her prayers and lit *agarbattis* to record her gratitude. She then plastered her face with Charmis cream and revelled in its greasy sense of wellness. Another old habit and one that reminded her of Chhoti Phua. Arnie could see her slathering cold cream on her face and then wiping it off with soft muslin napkins, stopping only to examine the dirt stains with satisfaction.

Her mind did not want to accept what had happened, for Arnie feared that this might be an illusion and would vanish as soon as she recognised it. Having lived in fear of losing for so long, it had not sunk in that she might have won. She fussed around, arranging and rearranging the cushions, straightening a chair here, and a paper there. She let activity prevent her from thinking about the present. About the possibility, the faint possibility, that something good could actually have happened to her.

Her birth certificate clearly stated it, her passport recognised the same, and she had forever believed it to be true. But it took a judge in a small provincial courtroom to give her dignity. She was a daughter by court order.

Shrey broke into her thoughts. "Wow Mamma, that is brilliant," he said, stopping for a moment on his way to cricket practice. "Awesome! So a pizza from Fat Lulu's tonight?"

Sia too, was delighted with the news. "Relax, we will celebrate your birthday like always, my love. Your little milestones will not go unsung."

For her children, loved and cherished as they were, it had always been difficult to truly understand what Arnie had gone through. It was inconceivable for them that the living breathing person they saw, hugged, and cuddled ceased to exist because someone chose to say so.

Warmth and happiness filled Arnie's heart and her soul. She belonged, if only by court order. She was someone. With an identity. An identity that had never been under any threat until a few months ago when she saw the family tree without her name in it. But today, the loss was not there and she felt whole again.

In the background, she heard Sia plan her party as her little world spun happily on its axis, humming with joy.

"If I call my school friends and the condominium friends, we will need to book the basketball court for my birthday," Sia joked and then added with vehemence, "Wish I could shoot her for spoiling our life!" All of them knew whom she was referring to. There was only one 'she' or 'her' when spoken about in that tone of voice.

Sia's thirteenth birthday needed to be special and Arnie enlisted Krish's enthusiastic help to get it done. Caterers, fairy lights, music, and all her dear and close friends, and some of

Shrey's as well. They tried to keep the arrangements a secret from Sia, but little Miss Nosey-Parker got wind of the plans before the day was out.

Colour, noise, and gawky teenagers running amuck were all that Arnie would remember later. For Sia, it was undiluted bliss. This was a high point for both mother and daughter, as Arnie watched her little Sia, all grown up and radiant in the clothes she got her from the rushed trip to London.

As the sun set, Sia hugged her mother and whispered, "Thank you Mamma." They ran to switch on the fairy lights as the DJ played, 'I Gotta Feeling', and the party moved to the makeshift dance floor on the basketball court.

"Congratulations," said Jaya, resplendent in white. "Sia looks so happy; this is what she will remember years from now."

"I hope so, Jaya. Both these children have gone through so much with the case."

"Oh here, I have something for you, read it. It may help," she said as she handed Arnie a book.

Arnie flipped it open. It was *The Fakir* by Ruzbeh.

"May answer some of your questions and give you the faith to hang in there."

Arnie nodded as they stood near the long table piled with food. Fried toast dripping with saucy baked beans, yellow sponge cake dripping with pastel icing, tiny kebabs served with a fresh mint chutney. She handed Jaya a plateful of food. "They are still kids and the menu reflects their innocence," she apologised for the childish menu, and they asked for some tea and sat down to gossip. Arnie felt more relaxed than she had been in a long time.

Sia looked so happy. In stark contrast to Arnie's memory of her birthdays. Perhaps Kamini thought that by ruining her daughter's birthdays, she could wish away her birth as well. "Remember Jaya, my mother bleached the happiness from my birthdays. Even today I dread the day. Like all children, I too wanted to untie the long ribbon, tear the wrapping paper, and open my presents. Usually I would be greeted with . . . nothing. If it was a lucky year, I was given some used jumpers or old cardigans. It felt wrong," Arnie remarked as they noticed Sia's little mountain of presents lying on the side table. Wrapped in coloured paper and tied with bright ribbons.

It may not have been so bad if Kamini had been even-handed in her neglect. Arnie could then have passed it off as her being too busy to care about such things. But it was not so. "Jaya, I still remember sleeping on the *chowki*, half asleep on the eve of Randy's birthday. My mother would tiptoe in, shake Randy awake, and always give him a big hug. I can, even after so many years, hear loud rips and see shreds of fresh wrapping paper fall to the floor. Loud rustling. The package being opened. And Randy taking out a new beige leather jacket with a grin on his face."

The December air had a chill in it, particularly after the sun went down and Jaya was feeling cold, Arnie could tell. "Can you lend me your *pashmina* shawl?" Jaya requested.

"But of course, let's go in and I will find it for you," Arnie told her and they went up to her flat. She opened her Godrej *almirah* and stood on her toes to reach the topmost shelves. Suddenly some papers dropped out. "Here," Arnie told her, handing over the shawl.

Jaya had bent down to pick up the papers. "Hey. This card is addressed to your mother for some reason." Arnie took it and began to read. Tears clouded her eyes and she quietly handed it back to Jaya. "How did this happen Jaya, what went wrong? What did I do?" Both looked at the words on the card.

My Dear Kamini,
When I read the invitation card for Aranya's wedding, my mind was filled with memories of our college days and a young, slim girl

with her long plait swinging as she walked down the corridor. Sometimes, it seems that it was just the other day when we were all in college together. But of course, it was two decades ago and our children are adults ready to get married. The wedding of one's daughter creates so many mixed feelings, I am sure that it will all go off well. I wish I could have been there, but unfortunately I will be in Coimbatore and will be back only much after. Please tell Aranya that there is a person who she has never met but who wishes her a marriage full of understanding and love. Take care Kamini, will be thinking about you on that day, Vrinda.

"Who is this Vrinda?"

"I don't know," Arnie replied. They wondered what had happened to that simple girl with a long plait, Arnie's mother. "What made her this monster?" Arnie asked Jaya. "If we rub through the layers, will I find the girl with the long plait again? Will she remember having me?"

They went down to the party again, not wanting to be away from Sia and her friends for too long.

"Any news from Yudi mama?" Jaya wanted to change the topic.

"Nope, not even a birthday greeting. I did send him a text message, asking him for his blessings and told him that much progress has been made in the court cases. I still hope that as always, he will be the knight in shining armour and make my mother see sense." Jaya thought Arnie was being a fool and that if he had to do something, he would have done so already. "Maybe he didn't know," Arnie said softly, her words hollow and pathetic, whimpering for attention, his attention.

To lighten the mood, Jaya mentioned the forthcoming winter holidays, and Arnie heard Krish say, "I have booked rooms at the Sula vineyard near Nasik. Then we will head to Mumbai for New Year's Eve."

"What?" Arnie spun around to ask, as he grinned adding, "It is okay, let me handle this. It will be good for the children and we will be back before your next hearing in January."

"Sounds super," she told him as Sia pulled her on to the dance floor.

32

'Out of difficulties grow miracles.'
— Jean de la Bruyere

Driving up to the Sula vineyard, they had this wonderful feeling of driving away and beyond the ordinary. Their rooms overlooked a beautiful lake, and they spent the weekend lazing around the swimming pool. That was when the children were not up to mischief. It was good wine and little food for Arnie. Sia and Shrey spent some of their time playing board games and ordering platefuls of delicious snacks at their camp near the pool. It was relatively stress free because Sia had banned any discussion of court matters and even Arnie had to obey her.

Arnie's room had a balcony. The balcony overlooked the lake and the tranquil vineyard setting was like a balm on her troubled soul. She sat for hours just looking out, preferring to sit quietly while the children took a dip in the vineyard pool and tried their hand at kayaking in the nearby Gangapur Lake. Shrey was excited about the bike rides, but gave up after being chased by stray dogs. So, as the children tramped the woods and waded through the creeks, Arnie basked in contentment.

The private yacht party in Mumbai on the 31st of December was mind blowing. As Arnie looked into the deep waters of the Arabian Sea, she wondered about the numerous dark secrets it had successfully hidden in its vastness. "Happy New Year, Mamma," the children squealed at midnight, holding her in a tight hug as Krish looked on.

"Wish we didn't have to go back," Arnie said wistfully to Krish over a glass of champagne. "Back to Delhi, back to the case. The hearing is next week," she told him as they headed back to the hotel.

The holiday had been good. The sun, the lake, the sea, and the salted mist; all of it had calmed Arnie.

Returning to Delhi, Arnie called the lawyers and arranged to meet them.

"Any news?" Vikram asked hopefully. "No New Year's greeting, no messages?"

She shook her head and replied quietly, "Nope, nothing."

"Ok, not a problem," he encouraged. "Let us go over our strategy for the next hearing. I want you there."

Arnie would be there if he wanted her to be there, of course, but her shoulders slumped as she imagined the case to be endless like the Arabian Sea, dark and mysterious. Suddenly, the happy afterglow of the holiday vanished and she was left staring at the ugly truth. There was still a bitter fight ahead of her. These were times that shook her because she was unhappy in the present and wavered in her decision, in her ability to hang in there. Her status as a daughter in the family of Eshwar Dhari had been established, but what did it mean in the context of the wider court battles that were going on between brothers, cousins, and with the Sharmas butting their noses into matters that were really no concern of theirs?

"Have you read the book I gave you?" Jaya asked on the phone.

"Started," Arnie replied, a bit sullen after leaving the lawyer's office.

"It is written by Ruzbeh; maybe you should go meet him. He channels."

Arnie was not quite sure what channelling was, but she did know that it was related to connecting with the Universe. "And where will I find him? It's a bit like having an audience with God!" she asked, a bit peeved.

"There is a reunion tomorrow; some of us are meeting at the Diva Café. See you then," were Jaya's last words before disconnecting.

"Huh friends and frolic," Arnie muttered to herself. "Wish I had their luck!"

Not really caring one way or another, Arnie struggled to make the effort and dress well in order to lift her spirits. She carefully pulled on her favourite red Burberry trench coat, and wore a smile as she walked into the cafe.

They knew about her court battle. One of them, sitting next to Arnie, offered advice. "It is karma, something from your previous birth. You need to chant, chant for your mother's peace and happiness, for your brother. This is the only way forward. I am a Buddhist and this has helped me." Arnie nodded, wondering whether this was the same type of thinking that Yudi mama wanted her to follow, but it turned out to be very different from his superficial and fanciful adoption of the spiritual trend of the moment.

The friend was more than helpful and she dictated a mobile phone number to Arnie. "It is that of Ruzbeh, my Guru. Send him a message and see if he agrees meet you." Astonished, Arnie asked whether he was the same Ruzbeh, the author of *The Fakir*? Yes, he was, it turned out. Hesitatingly and without any expectation, Arnie sent him a message and asked for a meeting. After a brief moment where their signals were buzzing around electronic circuits, she got a reply! "Meet me just before Republic Day, will give address later. *JAI BABA*!"

"Wow, I believe in miracles," Arnie told her friends, beaming at them. "Next round of drinks is on me," she said happily. "Keep the faith, keep smiling," they told Arnie when they eventually got up to leave.

The court had reopened in January and Arnie had a hearing. She smiled cheerfully for the camera to get the gate pass and walked to the security entrance, happy that despite her family's combined money and influence, she still had her foot wedged firmly in the door. She looked at her shoes, the same pair she had worn for all the hearings until now. She was clad in a smart jacket with a crisp white shirt and tweed trousers. "How many winters will I see?" she wondered, trudging forward to get her bags scanned at the security. "Until your lucky shoes wear out," she told herself and groaned involuntarily.

It was the first working day after the winter break of the court. The place was packed and Arnie felt completely intimidated by the crowds. Lawyers in black robes rushed around, juniors carried files catching up on court gossip, pathetic litigants like her waited for their case, hoping that some luck would shine their way. All thronged outside the courtrooms, waiting, watching.

"There you are!" Arnie heard a loud voice and turned on her heel to see a well-known journalist, a face she watched on television every night. "*Yaar*, I took a trip with your mother, man. We went to Shirdi last week in Rajkumar's personal plane." Getting no response from her, he added, "*Arrey*, the minister. She was with her gorgeous friend. Your mother is strange because within a fortnight, she was on my programme, running Rajkumar down. I don't get her. Apparently, he is miffed after she took a free ride, spoke to him all along in her signature coy style, and then in Delhi she knifed him . . . What's with her?"

"You will find out soon enough," Arnie told him as she moved away.

"So her trips and parties continue; will fill you in with the gossip later," Arnie texted Krish.

"She is here," Sanjeev hissed, suddenly coming up and startling

Arnie. This had become his standard line at every hearing, for Kamini was always present. It was a constant wonder to Arnie that no one questioned Kamini's right to speak for her father. Would he have dealt with the matter in the same way if he had the ability to stand up to her? Moreover, it was not because of his ill health, for he looked fine to everyone, and Kamini would have made a meal of it in court in the event that he had even the slightest ailment. Did she even have a power of attorney document entitling her to represent him, or had she, once again, usurped the authority and shouted louder than anyone else, so as to silence them?

"Today, I feel she is not looking happy. *Kapde bhi* not good." Arnie turned around to look at this woman, her mother, who was fast becoming just Kamini for her. Arnie had started losing the maternal connection with her due to the emotional upheaval of the case. Her mother looked scaly and cool, her skin pale as plaster and lips painted crimson red. Arnie noted with detachment her odd clothes, a western coat and trousers worn with her trademark *bindi*. She felt sad for her mother and for her father sitting with his head bent and eyes closed in prayer. The irony was not lost on Arnie as she watched him. For years, he had prayed for her as his daughter, but he was now praying that she be defeated. "Will it confuse God?" Arnie wondered, rising to enter the court with the others.

Her lucky seat was taken, so she stood next to the door and heard Kamini's lawyers shout along with those representing Bhabhi and Chhoti Phua. Arnie turned and looked at them from across the room, impassive and expressionless as their eyes met. Everyone was very serious today and they didn't smile back, neither with their expressions nor with their eyes. Anil Dhari was absent because of the Damocles Sword hanging above his head; would the court find him guilty of contempt? His lawyer was, however, part of the shouting brigade. Arnie could hear aggression and irritation in their loud arguments and then she cowered as she heard them shout her name, louder and louder, over and over again. She was one person pitted against so many; their collective power intimidated Arnie as she watched from afar.

She strained to hear the judge speak. "It is not for me to tell the Civil Administration how to run their affairs. I will not issue an order against them. You can file a writ against the Government of India if you like; just don't bring this court into the picture. And what about replying to the applicant?" he thundered, the last bit referring to the fact that no one had replied to Arnie's impleadment application, even though he had passed an order on it.

Kamini's lawyer mumbled something to the judge, which got Arnie's senior counsel to his feet, but she couldn't follow what was going on. Then the hearing was over and once again, she had no idea what had actually transpired, so she slid up to her senior counsel as they left the courtroom.

The Universe was smiling down on Arnie! Some government department dealing with land matters had taken notice of the court case and had blocked any further movement on the sale of the Civil Lines property, pending the full disposal of the matter. Furthermore, her father's lawyers had replied to Arnie's petition but marked it to some advocate unconnected to her, for which the judge had held them in breach of court rules and fined them a hefty sum. It seemed Arnie had won the day. As her senior counsel, an avid football fan, had once told her, this was the Barcelona strategy. "Keep the ball with your team and the other side cannot score a goal." If Arnie understood the outcome correctly, her legal team had bought her time and there was little chance of the court allowing the property to be sold. She was well aware that the Ranchi Court had yet to issue formal orders declaring her the daughter of her parents, and until she had that order in her hand, Arnie was vulnerable.

"Sharp tactics, your parents have served the papers to another lawyer. Seems to be your mother from what the opposing counsel tells me. She expected you to crack under pressure over the depressing winter months. She knows all too well that the cold bothers you, so she strategized to trip you up, having successfully blocked all interaction with the rest of your family. It is well thought out," said Arnie's lawyer pensively.

Arnie left the court relieved and called the children. "Order Dominos pizza, I survived today with God's grace. How was school?" she asked. God had truly been with her, for an unknown person in some unknown government office stood up and wanted procedure to be followed and, as a result, Arnie was in a stronger position.

But God gave with one hand and sometimes took with the other. Were the children and Arnie paying too heavy a price in other ways?

"Mamma, do you even know that we have our final examinations next month?" Sia asked, crying into the phone as Arnie listened, suddenly exhausted. "I want my Mamma back. I want you as you were, not like this. I am not eating enough Mamma; I am scared. I get tired in school; even getting through the day is tough. Have you noticed?"

Arnie listened, shocked, and asked her, "But baby, why did you not tell me?"

"Mamma, I tried. But you look so troubled all the time and I did not want to add to it."

"Stay there; don't go anywhere. I am on my way home," Arnie told her. Turning to the driver, she asked him to make the best possible speed in getting them home. Her Sia was hurting and she had to get to her.

Bursting into the house, she held Sia tight and her daughter's anguish was apparent. Arnie clutched Shrey and reassured her children.

"I want to come to court with you; they are so many together

273

and you, Mamma, stand alone by yourself. I want to be there with you," Sia told Arnie and she quickly agreed. Not to be outdone, Shrey extracted the same promise from her. Arnie consoled her little children but her insides cried out for she had no one to console her.

Monica called and Arnie spoke softly, updating her on what had happened. "You have to talk about this publicly, people must know. If she is so ruthless, she can harm you physically." She was right. Arnie's lawyers had repeatedly expressed the same fear. Monica and Arnie decided to spread the word amongst their friends, to let it go viral. With wide knowledge of what was going on would come security, Arnie hoped!

"Hey, have to go. I am getting another call," Arnie told her reluctantly and disconnected to take Krish's call. Apparently, her lawyer had some information and spoke with Krish when he could not get through to Arnie since she was already on the phone with Monica. "Your parents have sent the reply by courier as mandated by the judge. Vikram could not get through to you so he called me. Full of lies. You have to meet him tomorrow."

"Sure, join us for pizza and a movie this evening?" Arnie asked.

"Of course I will come. Did you wear the same shoes?" He loved pulling Arnie's leg and did elicit a laugh.

"Never mind the shoes," she told him. "See you soon. Much to tell you. I won this round."

33

'We are twice armed if we fight with faith.'
– Plato

A rnie was at Vikram's office the next morning and the papers filed by her father were painful, more personal than before. Her mother's language and words were all over the pages.

They had finally taken Arnie seriously, for this legal document was well crafted, though full of lies and misrepresentations. Their legal team began with the normal paragraphs of Arnie's 'abuse of the process of the court' and stated that this was resulting in an injustice. "Look who is talking," Arnie said loudly.

"Shhh, read in silence, there is more," she was told sharply by Krish and Vikram. "They have said that you have come to court with unclean hands and that your impleadment should be immediately reversed."

Kamini had filed an affidavit that Arnie had sent her a text message relinquishing her rights on all family assets from the Dhari side of the family. Complete falsehood! As she looked at the affidavit more carefully, Arnie noted that her mother had attached the phone records showing that a text message from Arnie's phone had been sent to her, but the contents, of course, were unknown. She was so manipulative and such a liar! This was a text message Arnie had sent to

Kamini on her birthday, wishing her a great year ahead. Arnie rapidly looked at her own phone's memory, and sure enough, the date and time matched.

It got better. They had tried to cover up their contradictory statements made in different courts as inadvertent errors. Then came the clincher. They claimed that Arnie's grandfather, Eshwar Dhari, had been corrupt. In their greed, they had not hesitated in tarnishing a dead man's memory too. Kamini, guiding the hand of Arnie's father's lawyers, had pointed out that Dadaji had not inherited his wealth as Arnie had mentioned, and neither had he earned it, as he was an academic, a politician, and held ministerial positions. So, he must have been corrupt, as he could not have earned enough money to purchase these properties from any of his work assignments. This was part of Kamini's revenge on Dadaji, sullying him even in his death.

The reply to Arnie's petition also tugged on the heartstrings. With violins playing in the background, the reply alleged that Arnie's self-centredness was making her grab money from ageing parents and that her intention was to turn them out on the street. Conveniently forgotten was the fact that the family was in court well before Arnie had turned up, and they had decided to sell the family home before she had even known of their plans or intentions.

Conveniently also forgotten was any mention of an inconvenient truth. No one in the Dhari family in her father's generation did any work, so where did the money to buy the family home come from if not from Dadaji, particularly when all but one of the siblings were still in school when the first in the sequence of homes was bought? This was clearly on Kamini's mind, for the legal reply also mentioned her 'illustrious career', a reference that made Krish and Vikram laugh, for they could not understand the context. No one, not even Kamini, would be silly enough to suggest that the Dhari family home had been bought out of her earnings.

What a career it had been, leading up to dancing, while skimpily clad, to the tune of '*Sheila ki Jawani*'. Her mother was all over Page 3 of the daily newspaper, which Arnie had brought with her to show Vikram and Krish. Vikram turned the page back to point out the reference to her own illustrious career, as both men sang '*Sheila ki Jawani*', laughing convulsively and adding hand gestures to their tuneless voices.

"Let it be, there is nothing of substance in this reply. They are just muddying the waters," Vikram assured Arnie and took down some factual details that he wanted to put into the rejoinder. He had news from the legal grapevine that Kamini had been very upset with her lawyers and was pulling in some more heavyweights for the next hearing.

Krish had been jotting down some numbers on a piece of paper while Vikram and Arnie went over the structure of the rejoinder he would file. "Guys, I have something for you. It will make your day. Look at the cheques attached with the sale deed." He had found that the payment details attached to the sale deed were fraudulent and didn't add up. The cheques didn't match what the sale deeds purported to say.

"So who gets the mango tree?" he asked, laughing convulsively as they caught another lie.

"Aaah the mango tree, which stands majestically in the middle of the driveway, another oddity. You know guys," Arnie told them, "it was considered a symbol of prosperity and is so revered that the family chose to negotiate their way around it rather than trim even the branches. Better bang the car than touch the tree. So the meagre amount mentioned as the cash component spent on Civil Lines will certainly not cover the cost of this sacred tree."

Arnie's days were an emotional roller coaster ride, but she left Vikram's office flying high as a kite and upbeat. She promised to sign the papers before she travelled out of town to meet Ruzbeh.

She bounced down the flight of stairs to the car, happy for the moment.

"Give me a lift?" Krish asked, getting into her car as Arnie rolled up the window to drown out the noise. Shrey called and told her that a courier packet had come for her and it was at home. She felt happy and, unlike before, this did not trouble Arnie. She giggled, telling Krish that he must go home with her. "Come over; there may be more fun and games today!"

"Aida, please make us some *elaichi* chai," Arnie requested, taking off her heels as she walked into the flat and settled into her favourite sofa. "Here," said Shrey, handing her an innocuous envelope; it was too small for court papers.

"All yours," she told Krish, asking him to open it. "No, all yours," he said, handing it back to Arnie.

She opened it and stared wide-eyed at the Polaroid photograph of her mother in the arms of a man.

"Shit, it is her *angrez* boyfriend. The one she was going to run away with. Michele or was it Michael?"

"You tell me," he asked, while Arnie looked away.

"Show me, show me," Shrey screamed, wanting to be part of the excitement.

"Nice ass," said Krish, thoroughly enjoying the moment as Arnie began to speak, drawing from the crevices of her mind. "I wonder who took it; there is no address on the envelope. Shit, she does have enemies. I feel sorry for her. This facade of being holier than the rest, more noble and better in every way is being peeled. Layer by layer."

"So this is true, not morphed?" asked Krish.

Arnie held his gaze and answered, "How can you mistake her, the arched back, the long hair, the slim waist and the big *bindi* as she, as she . . ." She broke off, at a loss for words.

Krish completed the sentence for her ". . . as she orgasms. I can almost hear the scream. Man, porno. Where was this taken?"

Arnie looked at it and suddenly exclaimed, for she recognised the room. "In her flat, her pad!"

"You mean the place your nana, Mr Sharma, gave her? That pad with designer furniture where she had all her parties in the heart of the city?"

"Yes, at one point, she was going to move in with this *angrez* into this very flat."

"And then?" asked Krish, intrigued beyond words.

"Well, everyone knew, including her ageing parents and Yudi mama. She ditched him because a quick calculation told her that it was a bad idea. The man on the verandah, my father, won; the scales tilted in favour of his money."

"What happened to the good *angrez*?"

Arnie had to think back but the memories were still there in her mind, because like Chhoti Phua, she seemed to remember so much. He wasn't a prince, as Kamini would have wanted him to be. He married some Thai chic and had kids, even sent her a photograph of his son. Arnie remembered that she had told him Kamini's age, and had got a resounding slap from her mother. "This was two days before we got married. How was I to know that she had convinced the idiot that she had me at ten? I remember her shedding tears and walking around as a widow; always drama. Krish, it was her sex pad. Fuck, how did I not get it? She fooled the entire world with her Mother Teresa in hot pants act. Some woman!" The photograph shocked Arnie, as she had had some inkling of the truth, but had never put the pieces together.

"I wonder what will come in the mail next time!" Krish grinned at her, thoroughly enjoying himself, and asked, "Who took the photograph? Can't be Chhoti Phua? Shit, this is like the leaked Jennifer Lopez sex files. Recording themselves, look at it, man, too hot!"

Distracting him, Arnie changed the subject, as she was still a bit uncomfortable, for this was her mother they were talking about. "On a more serious note, I want to make a day trip to Pune. Will you be in town? I am uneasy about leaving the kids alone. This is to meet Ruzbeh."

He nodded and Arnie firmed up her plans.

Nervous and excited, Arnie rushed from the airport to meet Baba. Ushered into his *puja* room, she was immediately struck by divinity. She sat down as directed and then he spoke, as though reading her mind, and gently told her not to give up. "She will know by tomorrow that you came."

Arnie looked at him in shock! "You know my mother? You will tell her?"

"No, I will not, but she will find out. Her tantric will tell her. I know that life has not been easy for you, but you chose her womb, you are going to get some form of success, as impossible as it sounds, but you have to hang in there."

Arnie looked at him and quietly asked, "Why would I choose the most random and mean person to be my mother?"

He told Arnie that Baba was with her and that she had to do a special *puja* at a temple near Mangalore in order to be further protected. She told him about Kamini's rushed trip to Shirdi and asked if the Gods took sides. Her question was dismissed with a smile.

Arnie got up feeling strangely at peace, the turmoil within her settled, and decided to head off to Mangalore.

"Krish, I need you to stay with the children for a few more days. I need to go South for a certain *puja* to appease my ancestors. Please!" she begged him on the phone.

"Are you sure you want to do this?" he asked, and when Arnie replied in the affirmative, he said that he would look after the kids while she was away.

The Kukke Subramanya Temple was located in the beautiful Western Ghats range of Karnataka and Arnie was taken in by its pristine beauty. She felt blessed to be there. After offering prayers, meals were had together by all the devotees in the common dining area attached to the temple. The priests cooked the food. Arnie took her place, squatting on the floor and eating off a banana leaf; she was certain that no five star hotel or gourmet cook could replicate the taste or the peaceful ambience.

It was Arnie's birthday. A fact she realised only when she stood in line in the morning for her final prayers, after which she had to leave for the airport. Exhausted but happy, she arrived back in Delhi just in time for a family dinner painstakingly prepared by Sia and Shrey. "Love you babies," she told them, pulling both into a hug as she described her pilgrimage.

She was to feel the positive effects of her pilgrimage very soon. Much had happened while she was away, both positive and negative.

The negative first. The Ranchi Court had become embroiled in technicalities as various family members, including her father and brother, had filed objections to the order declaring Arnie as the daughter from being officially passed and recorded. Sanjeev had been to Ranchi ten times, and despite having a good application and Arnie having made a personal appearance, he still had not been able to get the order. Arnie needed the order urgently, for the Civil Lines property could now be sold any time, and they had been saved only due to the letter from some government office preventing the sale from taking place. Sanjeev told her that he was doing his best, but circumstances had been against him. "I rushed to Ranchi but the court was closed today, a lawyer died late last night."

"Bad timing," Arnie muttered insensitively.

A countervailing positive too. Vikram called and told her that there had been a court hearing while Arnie had been away. A short one and the judge had seemed angry, she was told. "They filed a writ petition which came up for hearing while you were away, challenging the letter sent by the Land Authority and asking the court to direct the Government of India to allow the sale of the Civil Lines property."

Arnie, it appeared, did not require to be served a notice for this hearing. The writ petition was before another judge and she was not made a respondent to the matter, so none of her lawyers were present in the court. Completely unopposed and with a junior government lawyer against them, the might and power of Kamini and the Dhari family lawyers tried their best to browbeat the government advocate and the judge to pass an order in their favour. It was not to be. The judge called into question their very ownership rights on the property, dismissed their suit, and passed strictures against them for wasting the time of the court.

And it happened on Arnie's birthday, on the day she was doing the final *puja* in Mangalore.

They, it seemed, continuing the football metaphor of her senior advocate, had scored an own goal!

34

'Any truth creates a scandal.'
— *Marguerite Yourcener*

▼

Krish and Arnie were speaking on the phone when she heard Shrey shouting for her from the other room. Running to him, she found that a woman had called on the intercom. "She is coming up," Shrey said. "She called while you were away and I forgot to tell you."

"Who is she?" Arnie asked as he disappeared into the bathroom.

"*Didi*, there is a madam at the door and she is asking for you," Aida told Arnie as she walked to the front entrance.

"Yes, can I help you?" Arnie asked pleasantly, looking at the woman at the door. She looked strangely familiar.

"I need to talk to you; we are related. I am Fatima Sheikh," she said, asking if she could come in. Intrigued, Arnie nodded and led her to the drawing room, noticing her crepe Patiala *salwar* with delicate embroidery inset with Swarovski crystals and the expensive *jamewaar* shawl. Arnie closed her eyes for a second, but she could not identify her designer perfume, sophisticated and sensual.

They settled down to talk over a coffee and Arnie was curious to know why she had come to meet her. Why did she say they were related? She didn't let on anything and Arnie saw her looking at the photographs on the table. "And this is?" she asked sweetly. "My nana and nani at their wedding. Both dead now."

"So this is him; there is a resemblance," Fatima said, taking out a packet and laying old sepia photographs on the sofa between them. Arnie picked up a few photographs.

"You left these in a yellow envelope some weeks ago. Why?" Arnie asked her. Fatima watched her over the rim of her coffee cup. Her expression changed as the happiness drained from her face; Arnie could almost see it leave, muscle by muscle, as she aged in front of her eyes, and struggled to speak. Whatever she had to say was tormenting her.

Her story, when it finally came out, was riveting and beyond anything that Arnie could have imagined. But she told the story her way; the ending first and then working her way backwards to the beginning. "I want a sample of your blood," she said. "I need it, you understand. It is important." Arnie blinked, not understanding what she was getting at.

It took some time, but Fatima was finally able to explain the story. It seemed that nana's father had had an affair with Fatima's mother in Pakistan around the time of Partition and Fatima was their love child.

"You are nana's sister?" Arnie asked, suddenly agitated but ready to believe anything at this moment, because the past year had been so strange. Her world had caved in and now the hole was just being dug deeper until it reached a pit of shame.

"Yes, *bachche*, I am your nana's half-sister. But I can't prove it without doing a DNA test, so I need your blood. This was a huge scandal in Multan but they skipped to India."

"Who did?" Arnie asked, still confused.

Fatima, her great aunt according to her words, looked only a little older than Kamini, and she was not done yet. This conversation was surreal. Arnie didn't know whether to believe the woman in front of her, or to pinch herself and wake up from a horrible dream. Her frames of reference were being recast with diabolical precision. She had known that nana had been in the police in Pakistan just before Partition and that he had come across the border to India from Multan. However, in her wildest dreams, she could not have imagined the circumstances under which he had returned.

Fatima continued her tale. "At the behest of his father, your nana killed my father and brother in a false encounter and passed them off as terrorists in the files. The police was very powerful in those days. The period leading up to the Partition was one of great violence, murder, and pointless deaths. Ostensibly because of some work, your nana made my father run in an open field and shot him right before the eyes of his young son, my mother's first-born, before turning on him. There were riots all over. Multan was in flames and these were just two more murders in the countless killings of the time."

"My nana shot your father?" Arnie repeated her statement, disbelievingly.

"Yes, to protect his father and the family name," Fatima clarified. "It took us years to rebuild our lives and everyone believed that I was the natural daughter of my mother and her husband."

"Your great-grandfather, your nana's father, then raped an innocent girl, his neighbour's twelve-year-old daughter. The shame of it, raping a young girl, made the local people turn on your family. They would all have been slaughtered, but they managed to escape. Your great-grandfather slinked out of the country first, before the people of my community found out what he had done, otherwise the outcome would have been very different. The bastard went with the womenfolk to India, while your nana took the very last train from Multan like a hero."

The intensity of her gaze burned holes into Arnie's soul. "I never saw my great-grandfather," Arnie told her quietly, wanting to distance herself from the dirty old man. "But my nana was a good man, well respected, honourable. He did a lot for women and children. He founded organisations and ran them until his death. He is well recognised and has won countless awards for his good work. Awards that he stuffed in an old trunk, never displaying them. He was modest about his success."

She defended nana, and through him, the family honour and name. There was no good reason for Arnie to believe Fatima, but there was sincerity in her voice and a look that she could not ignore. If her story were true, nana had murdered half of Fatima's family.

"Yes, I know that you won't accept this," Fatima said matter-of-factly. Arnie watched the diamonds on her finger sparkle as she turned on the lamps. They looked out of the French windows, lost in thought as the crimson sky merged into early evening. If it had been any other time and any other way, Arnie would have turned her out of the house and hurled abuses at her for slandering her family. But she had seen so much over the past year that nothing seemed unbelievable any more. She struggled with the overload of information and the emotions rising due to it.

Arnie remembered her nani's stories about Punjab and their house in Multan. "There was a huge *drakhat*; we had a huge house," she would tell Arnie. They had to leave it all and come away, she would say, sadly shaking her head. Arnie always believed that she missed her old home until now, until she heard Fatima's story. It was only now that Arnie understood that nani was not wistful at all but grateful for the timely escape. She felt ashamed of her family legacy, having been taught all along to learn from their example and acts of moral instruction.

"Do they, I mean my mother and Yudi mama, know? Have you met them?"

"Yes," she answered. "They are in denial. I met them at my nephew Saif's wedding to that movie star. Your mother was very charming to my son, flirting and looking into his eyes and batting her eyelids at him. It sickened me and I dragged my son away. After all, I had seen what the earlier generations had done! All this after that gorgeous Rajput politician told her about his hotel chain.

"We have lived with it too long, watching this *tamaasha* from across the border. The hypocrisy of your family has been too much and I finally made up my mind. I decided to come across for the wedding and use the opportunity to see what can be done. My mother is old but she wants the world to know what happened all those years ago. We have Pathan blood from her and are strong. Allah has been merciful and we are doing well for ourselves in Dubai. But we want to right the wrong done decades ago. She, my mother wants it. She wants me to be able to prove who my real father was."

Fatima reached out to hold Arnie's hand and continued. "At the wedding, I heard what Kamini has done to you. She will do anything for money. She and Yudi are the spawn of evil people!" Her emotions were getting too much for her, and she suddenly got up and thanked Arnie. She had one last request, something she had begun with. "I need a sample of your blood and then I will not trouble you again. This is my personal battle for justice and I will not involve you again."

Arnie was stunned, but she was ready to believe the worst of the Sharma family. She agreed to the blood test and thought that it would either prove Fatima right or put to an end the extraordinary story that she had just heard.

Her liveried driver jumped to open the door as Fatima turned to give Arnie a quick hug. "*Insha Allah, milenge*," she said, pressing a small package into her hands. Arnie hugged her back and wished her well because she identified with the woman's courage. She remembered reading that the pure and simple truth was rarely pure and never simple.

Then she was gone in her gleaming limousine.

"Was that your mother I just saw drive off in a Jaguar?" asked Shrey, running up to Arnie. "Hope it turns into a pumpkin on the National Highway," he muttered, pulling her towards the cricket field. "I am batting at fifty not out," he announced proudly.

"It wasn't her . . ." Arnie managed to mumble before she lost it!

All she could do was stand there, shaking with laughter, not knowing what to believe any more and giving up understanding destiny and the ways of the world.

35

*'It is always wise to look ahead,
but difficult to look further then you can see.'*
– Winston Churchill

The court was in recess for a while; they decided to have a change of scene, and Shrey suggested that they go out for the day. "Let's go to Humayun's Tomb tomorrow for a picnic. The weather is good and Sia can take some photographs for her school project. We can take a picnic hamper," he said, looking at Arnie beseechingly.

"Sure, except let's just pick up the food from somewhere because I am too tired to make it."

Arnie bought a picnic hamper from Wengers, their favourite bakery in Connaught Place. And as they walked into the Humayun's tomb complex, she was struck by its grandeur. The tomb, commissioned by Humayun's wife Hamida Banu Begum in 1562 AD, was the first garden-tomb in the Indian subcontinent. It was also the first structure to use red sandstone on such a scale. It looked beautiful and majestic.

"Let's attack the food," she told the kids. Before she could complete the sentence, they grabbed the picnic basket.

Days passed. The short Easter break was over and her children were moving up to the next class in the new academic year.

The first day of school was special and she watched her children with pride as they left for school the next morning.

She was so proud of them. The way she felt could only be compared to nani's sense of pride in her work. Nani would hug Arnie close and whisper words of encouragement in her ear and reward her in the way she knew best, by cooking a special lunch of *khadi chawal, badi vale chawal,* and black *daal* with her favourite *tadka.*

Waiting for the kids to return home, Arnie grabbed a cup of coffee and picked up her legal file, flipping it open. Something familiar popped up as she randomly opened to a page. It was the old *Fringe* magazine with her mother's oh-so-famous interview.

She read it again after many years. At forty, the size and description of emeralds no longer grabbed her attention. It was the web of deceit and lies that screamed out loud. Grimacing, she read on. *'From Rags to Riches, From Bahenji to Bombshell.'* Her eyes glazed over this, alighting on the graphic description of her mother, so different from Arnie's memory of her at the time of the famous, or should one say infamous, interview.

'Despite her broken English and gaudy, ostentatious jewellery, dramatic big red *bindi* and filmy dialogues, she won me over. Kamini, otherwise known as the successful exporter and supporter of women's causes, candidly revealed details of her hateful marriage and related anecdotes from her childhood days.'

Arnie's mother had described her childhood days as dismal and depressing to the journalist. Their family was simple, poor, and perpetually swimming in debt. Torn shoes and patched clothes were a given. While her friends went on glamorous holidays to Goa and Bombay, Kamini and her family considered themselves lucky if they went on a short road trip.

Arnie paused in her reading and chuckled at the irony of the situation. Despite having all the money, being married into a wealthy family, Kamini had sent Arnie to school in tattered shoes and clothes gaping with holes.

She read on as the journalist went on to tell the reader that Kamini had described her mother as a 'Lalita Pawar'. "'Her snarling tone, crooked eye spewing wrath used to frighten me,' said *bechari* Kamini. In a mixture of Hindi and something which I could not call English, she narrated the ill-treatment meted out to her as a child. She describes her mother as strict, abusive, and heartless. Just to finance her Yudi *bhaiya*'s winter wardrobe, Kamini was deprived of sweaters and had to wear torn socks."

This was not the nani that Arnie remembered. The torn socks were Arnie's and it was she who was sent to school poorly clad by Kamini!

Family values were of utmost importance to the Sharmas. Despite being a die-hard romantic, in her words 'Romeo *aur* Juliet *vala* with sprinkling of Mills and Boon', Kamini claimed she was forced into marriage before she was able to pursue her superstar dreams.

As she read the interview in *Fringe* magazine, Arnie didn't know whether to laugh or cry. Her story sounded only too familiar. It sounded like Arnie's life in print. Why did she leave her own daughter with a similar inferiority complex? Why did she make Arnie the *lal-mirchi* and the *kutiya* despite having suffered herself? Why did Kamini force her to marry before pursuing her education abroad? Why? WHY!

Or had she made it all up for public sympathy? For this article had catapulted her into the spotlight.

Kamini went on to describe her marriage as hateful. She claimed that her in-laws were money-minded and ruthless. She married into a wealthy home, but was robbed of her identity. She was forced to hide and go out for work at odd times so that no one could notice her absence in the household. Further, she found the daily ritual of touching her husband's feet and doing *pranam* as demeaning. She refused to drink the water after she had washed his feet.

Give it a break! Who was she trying to fool!

The room echoed with Arnie's hearty laugh. "Yeah right, Mom!" When did her mother ever do *pranam* to Arnie's England-educated father?

Kamini reiterated that her kids were her world. "Yeah! Lies again," Arnie thought to herself. The article quoted her as saying, "My *chhoti beti* and darling son are my *sab kuch*. I feel guilty that I have not been able to spend more time with them due to my spiralling career." At this point, Arnie was not too sure about which career she was referring to. Surely, must be a backbreaking, time-consuming task holding up those double-D cups along with that career!

As she reached the end of the article, Arnie was left shocked. If she was her mother's '*sab kuch*' then why had she been beaten and flung across on the wall on numerous occasions? Why was she the victim of her filthy abuse? She was never protected, why? Arnie looked at her photograph taken for the article and saw a younger Arnie, more naive and more forgiving.

36

'I am confident that, in the end,
common sense and justice will prevail.'
— Cat Stevens

The phone rang and Arnie ran to answer. It was Deep mama, her mother's cousin calling from Seattle. He had been a big part of her growing up years at nani's house. It had been ages since they had last spoken but she remembered his familiar drawl. "Hi, how are you and the kids?" she asked enthusiastically but was cut short.

"I have heard about the case," and just as she began to explain, he cut her in mid-sentence aggressively. "I am not interested in the merits of the case. Yudi called me yesterday; he wants no noise. We have heard what you are saying and now you listen to me. Fight in court, but do not talk. Protect the family *izzat* or else it will not be good for you or your children."

Arnie took time to speak although the response was clear in her mind. "The time for keeping quiet is gone. *Jo izzat loot rahen hain, un se baat keejiye.* They are the ones lying," she said, disconnecting the phone and then watched as it rang repeatedly, but she did not move an inch towards it.

Court had reopened and Deep mama's call had made her resolve even stronger. "This time, I want one of you to come with me to court," Arnie told her children. "I want you to see it for yourselves. The outcome is not important, but I want you to remember how I stood up against all of them. So who will come?" Shrey jumped up first, with Sia not far behind. Shrey it would be then. "I will glare at them," he said. "Stamp on their feet and stick chewing gum on their seats."

"It can take hours and you get restless. Are you sure?"

"Yes Mamma," he said, wearing his love for Arnie on his sleeve.

Having Shrey with her was annoying but also very entertaining. Arnie was less on edge. Ever so often, he demanded Gummy Bears, then Sour Punk, and then his iPod, then wanted to check out the bathroom. It was impossible to keep up with him and be tense at the same time. "She has come, Mamma," he suddenly said, his voice reduced to a squeak because he was excited. "I can see her, she has 1 . . . 2 . . . 8 . . . 15 lawyers, Mamma. Where are your Vikram and Sanjeev?" he asked, panicking.

"All well, Shrey, relax. They are right here," Arnie told him as he ran to offer them chocolate and wished them luck, a little boy trying to be the man around her.

"Don't expect much to happen today, they will ask for an adjournment," Vikram cautioned her.

"Courts are not the place for children."

Arnie looked up and found herself looking at the beaming face of an old friend, Neeraj. "What brings you here?" As she began to speak, Vikram rushed her into court. She settled into her favourite seat with Shrey and leaned forward to hear what was being said. As they shouted her name, Shrey's grip on Arnie's hand tightened and he told her not to worry.

The matter was adjourned to the next day. Lawyers representing various parts of the family asked for another date as they had no clue about what to do next, for Arnie's petitions had blocked the sale very effectively. Her legal team did not mind an adjournment either; it gave them more time to get the formal order she needed from Ranchi.

Speaking with Krish that evening, Arnie told him that everything changed after nani died. "She held all of us together." She also told Krish that she would be taking Sia to the court the next day.

Sia and Arnie got ready and rushed to the court. They did not speak in the car but Sia held Arnie's hand, aware of her mother's nervousness. "Sia, I do not know the outcome, but I want you to know that I tried very hard and stood up against all odds."

"I know Mamma, I know that your mother used you as a punching bag, but we are together punching her back," she answered, her voice older than her thirteen years as they stood in line for the entry passes to get into court.

Arnie held her daughter's hand as they made it past the entry barricade and walked up the stairs to the court building. "So many people are here, and they all look so worried." They sat down and Arnie said her prayers while holding her baby girl's hand. "Today, they should be worried. Why are you so nervous? Hey little girl, you cannot take the courts for granted and your grandmother has the best lawyers money can buy, and I think I have low BP. Need to have some of that chocolate when we get in." As they settled down, Arnie heard whispers behind her. Her mother's lawyers were supremely confident. They laughed loudly, pointing at her. She could hear them as they referred to her as 'the mad daughter' for taking on such a powerful mother.

"Hi, your daughter today, is it?" Arnie spun around and saw the familiar face of the lawyer friend from yesterday, a senior advocate. "I got her for moral support, I do get nervous."

"Mamma cannot sleep for at least two days before the hearing," her daughter informed him as Arnie grinned.

"Also, I want Sia to see for herself the huge wall I am up against and the number of lawyers that represent my mother, ostensibly my father. Both children must see the courage it has taken to stand up against all odds."

He nodded and added, "It really is amazing. No one can tell from looking at her, and her public image is so different. In fact, your family is well respected. Are they not scared that this will go against them?"

"Nope, look at her team, they are foaming at the mouth like mad dogs. She feels that I am of no consequence and neither is the truth."

Sia gripped her mother's arm and Arnie looked up and saw Kamini walk in. She saw her mother stride across the hall, dressed in white, head thrown back, eyes hidden behind large dark glasses. Arnie looked at her daughter and softly told her, "She was my role model when I was growing up, but now I don't want to be like her and neither should you. Above all, remember that the truth will shoot free like fire, igniting the last threads that hold the family, and I don't know whether she realises that she cannot rely on lies and my ignorance to win."

Then she elaborated because Sia looked puzzled. "She is banking on her political contacts, money, and power and believes that I am not as well networked as her, which may well be true, but I don't have as many enemies either. Sia, just remember that people are not stupid and figure out if you are genuine or not. Even when provoked, try not to be rude and do not curse like she does."

Sanjeev walked across and greeted Arnie with his customary "good morning ji" and a "hello Sia". She shook his hand and congratulated him on his good work in Ranchi. Arnie wanted him to feel motivated and to remove the objections that had been filed. "I have worked very hard, taken personal interest. Your mother has resorted to underhanded games and delaying tactics. Getting all advocates to boycott the court by not appearing or randomly appearing one at a time and then asking for time. But next week, we will get the order."

Sanjeev looked at Kamini and added, "Look, madam is

wearing sunglasses within the building. Maybe the rich feel the glare even in the shade."

"Or she has something to hide," they heard a small voice and all of them smiled at Sia, having forgotten momentarily that she too, was with them.

Arnie heard a commotion and looked up to find her mother staring at her through the dark glasses, but with one lens missing. Trying to conceal a grin, Arnie smiled nonetheless for she looked like a pirate with a patch. Sanjeev caught her eye and got up suddenly, for he was doubling up with laughter. He told Arnie, "She has cello-taped actual power lenses to the back of the dark glasses," as he held up the missing lens, which had dropped near him. "So funny," he said, disappearing behind the pillar to hide his convulsive laughter.

They smiled broadly as Vikram spoke, "Your brother's wife, that Dolly. Did she live in America for a while? And she had a childhood boyfriend whom she wanted to marry?"

"Yes, Dolly was very close to someone but eventually married Randy. Why?"

"Well, I was at a party, mainly people from your college and she came up in conversation. Apparently, she was quite a *cheez*, and found comfort in many arms before landing up with your brother. This friend was at Yale and knows your brother from school. He said that she shacked up with a friend of his and the noise was so much that it could be heard over the Bose speakers. And that she took the term FTW to mean fuck the world a little too literally. Seems that the friend and she are still quite intimate."

Grinning, Arnie replied, "Yes, I have heard similar stories. My brother found a replica of my mother in her, so good luck to them. If I were my mother, I would be careful because Dolly's other great love, beyond even sex, is money! She will not think twice about pulling the plug on my mother if she is in the hospital and Rundee, I mean Randy, will look away."

Arnie and Sia sat directly behind Kamini and Chhoti Phua and watched them. They saw Bhabhi's shifty-eyed lawyer taking instructions from Kamini. This was not the first time; she seemed to have undue influence over him. Arnie looked at him and was reminded of a fat frog in a black coat, big stomach and thin spindly legs. "I must ask Vikram about this," she told herself, making a mental note.

"This daughter is greedy! She has no rights, Your Lordship, and is opportunistic. She smells money. Throw her out," they yelled as Arnie froze. From the corner of her eye, she watched Sia steal a glance at her grandparents, looking here and there at the same time nervously.

The marvellous, wonderful judge and judicial system were not to be cowed down, however. They didn't give any relief to the family pressing for an immediate sale of the Civil Lines property and the court closure for *Holi* gave Arnie yet more time to get the order from Ranchi. The order that would make her whole as a daughter. Albeit, by court order.

Arnie kissed Sia and told her under her breath that they had done well. Her little face lit up as they walked out together, hand in hand, a big smile on their faces.

In the car, Sia snuggled up to her mother, asked the driver to buy them cold drinks, and watched the city flash past as they drove off.

"Well done, Mamma," said Shrey, throwing himself into her arms when Arnie rang the bell of their apartment. "How was court?" he asked Sia and then Arnie noticed her tears.

"Why baby?" she asked, looking deep into her daughter's eyes.

"Mamma, no girl my age has seen the rotten side of her family. Grandmothers hug their grandchildren but mine did not even say hi to me. She has taken away even nana, he is so scared now."

"It is okay, we will survive, Sia. I have developed nerves of steel," Arnie told her. To cheer up her daughter, she added, "You have wanted a makeover of your room. Let's do it before the next court hearing at the end of the month."

"But it cannot become a girly room," objected Shrey, putting his foot down as they burst into giggles. They laughed at the silliest jokes and Arnie was secretly relieved that her son was different from her father and her brother and asserted himself when required.

The next couple of weeks were sheer bliss as Arnie bonded with her children over gallons of Fevicol, hardboard and the Internet. They were on a modest budget, but were determined to make the place look wonderful. They began by making a list of essentials, chuck-ables, and storage items. As expected, Sia and Shrey came up with different items for the chuck-able list. Finally, they settled for an aquamarine, white, and black combination for the room and then fought over which of Sia's paintings to frame.

"I will hang a witch's hat for sure to hex her and you cannot say anything, Mamma," declared Sia, brimming with rebellion. They reached a deadlock over using Shrey's skateboard as a shelf. Arnie left it to them to sort out as they showed each other many websites, almost coming to blows. They argued endlessly, but Arnie did not complain because her life was full of colour and she enjoyed every moment.

They spent the hot summer afternoons relishing good food and chilled *nimbu paani*; they gossiped, giggled, and laughed. Arnie let herself relax, she took in their banter and just held on to the little things that she had forgotten over the tense months. Reaching for the remote, she grinned as Shrey tried to beat her to it so that he could quickly change the channel to sports. Over pizza, they discussed Sia's current 'best friends and worst peeves'. Arnie chuckled because she had heard these stories many times but she loved listening to her daughter's voice. Not to be left out, Shrey piped in with his Manchester United stories as Arnie covered her head and groaned in mock annoyance.

37

*'Strength is looking back and seeing what you have been through
and knowing you were strong enough to make it.'*
– Anonymous

Arnie woke up to *Holi*, an important festival and a holiday
for the children. She made herself a cup of tea for Aida
was on holiday and watched from her apartment balcony as
the children played with their friends. She waved to them.
Then the doorbell rang and she found herself surrounded
by her condominium pals who dragged her down to the
basketball court, the venue for the *Holi* party. The entire
condominium complex celebrated the festival together with
great verve and enthusiasm and the level of craziness had
only increased over the years. Mr Gupta got naughty with
Ms Bhalla, but no one minded as a bucket of coloured water
was poured over them.

There was complete madness as the music started
and the adults surreptitiously drank traditional alcoholic
drinks. Everyone moved to the makeshift dance floor and
the children, not to be left out, elbowed in and danced to
the rhythm of the drums as the latest Bollywood songs
blared on Bose speakers. In the middle of all the dancing,
people left the floor to quickly grab a snack or two and
then came back on to dance. The older grandmothers dried
themselves in the corner. They clucked at the obscenities in
the lyrics of the songs and at the young girls who giggled and

joked with their grown-up grandsons. They sat and enjoyed the traditional eats such as *malpuas* and *mathris*. The little children of the condominium enjoyed the festival as they threw water-filled balloons at passers-by, or drenched themselves with their water missiles, the tiny devils.

Arnie grinned, watching them chase each other across the lawns and looked up at the sky. It was perfect weather; the chill of the winter had finally given way but the hot summer was not quite there.

Struggling later to get the colour off her skin, Arnie caught a glimpse of herself in the mirror and laughed out loud. Her face was dark blue with streaks of pink. Her hair was green, but she didn't complain. It had been so much fun and then she prayed that her struggles would ease.

"Please God," she prayed.

For tomorrow, she was back in court.

Relaxing in the afterglow of the *Holi* celebrations, she opened her laptop and went back to the article open on her screen. The author, Sohaila Abdulali, had written about surviving rape.

'When I look back, it is not the seventeen-year-old me I want to comfort, but my parents. They had the job of picking up the pieces. The week after I was attacked, I heard the story of a woman who was raped in a nearby suburb. She came home, went into the kitchen, set herself on fire, and died. The person who told me the story was full of admiration for her selflessness in preserving her husband's honour. Thanks to my parents, I never did understand this.'

Arnie understood pain and she understood what it was to be violated. For she knew rejection, she wanted to tell Sohaila, but of a different kind. "My own parents are the predators. My own mother leads the attack in what the lawyers call, 'the rarest of the rare cases'."

'Because it is not about honour' the heading of Sohaila's article read. Arnie suddenly understood her purpose. It was a crusade for justice, for her dignity, for a choice she should have. Her mother, the very woman who said feminism and the cause of women's rights were dear to her and shrieked every time a woman was raped, burnt or driven away, had led the pack along with a subjugated husband and son. Led the pack to strip away her daughter's rights and with that, strip the dignity of Arnie's little unit. It was rape of another kind.

Scrolling down, she hoped that, like for Sohaila, the day would come for her as well.

'When one incident is no longer the central focus of your life. One day, you find that you are no longer looking behind you, expecting every group of men to attack. One day, you are not frightened anymore.'

Arnie did not want to be a symbol, but she just wanted to survive. She wanted her children to survive; she wanted to get to the other shore. She wanted to believe that she was equal to her brother and she wanted nothing more.

Sia's books were lying scattered around, and Arnie picked them up and put them away. Her children were precious and she loved them dearly. Thoughts gathered in her head. She needed to change the nominee and guardianship on her dwindling investments, for she no longer wanted the trustee to be Yudi mama, whom she had adored. Her children were minors. "Who? Who, I wonder, is my next of kin? Who can I trust?"

The next day, Arnie dressed for court with care, a little preoccupied, although she had no real reason for concern. The ping on her mobile handset distracted her and she opened the text message that had just come in. Like the ones before, she expected this to be a 'best of luck' message, but her eyebrows furrowed and she felt a lump in her throat as she read the words from a designer and socialite friend:

> I know that you are jobless and lawyers cost a lot of money. The case-related paraphernalia and drama must be a drain.

And another:

> You, poor darling, must not pay when we go out. And though you cannot afford the Leela Hotel, I like going to Le Cirque, which, in your circumstances must be very tough. But darling, I only like eating at the best places, so there is no point in unnecessary castle building from your side. We should therefore meet less often. A Delhi-style drift apart perhaps.

Finally,

> Whichever way you cut it, it is good for both of us in the long run.

She had dropped Arnie from her guest-list because her story was no longer sexy, and her winning millions seemed a distant possibility, an illusion, even to this scatty-brained socialite. Arnie's reply to her was brief and to the point. "Go to hell. I can do without meeting you."

Arnie felt sick, alone, and miserable. Her mind emptied out as she was shaken to the core; she doubted her own decision to fight. "Has my decision to go to court compromised the future of my children? This money earned diligently and saved over years was for them. My 'friend' has cut me off, but this fall is spectacular, a fall from a social and professional hierarchy, where I have been thrust out of a revolving door and on to a pavement, for I no longer belong."

Another ping and this time it was an email from the same friend. She had not taken kindly to being told to 'Go to hell'. This was a lengthy email. She did type fast! Unless she had been drafting this for a long time and had only now thought it fit to send it to Arnie.

She had not finished sticking the knife into Arnie. In true flighty fashion, she was blaming Arnie, forgetting that it was Arnie who had introduced her and given her the break into the corporate circuit by inviting a different crowd for the launch of her summer collection earlier in the year. Now her bloated self-image thought that not dropping Arnie from her guest-list would be virtual murder on the social circuit.

```
Sweetie,
Unpleasant surprise this morning! Obviously
the air between us is far from clear . . . :)
You know absolutely nothing about me or how
I go about my work-related activities. This
is about you and me.
What do you need to prove?
1. That you have friends?
(Heck, I know that. High and mighty ones
too.)
2. That you support people?
(Oh well, I guess I know that too!)
3. That you are helpful, lady?
(This is not about your helpfulness but none
of us are selfless.)
Thank you for your offer, but you owe me no
dinners. You can't afford it!
Are we finished? Finished with this dialogue
and finished with the friendship?
Good day dear!
Rosie G
```

This was followed by yet another text message.

```
You are going nowhere on the social highway.
You, my darling, no longer count. Learn to
be more like your mom.
```

What a great way to start the day, and that too a day when Arnie had a court hearing. But the day had a lot more to offer.

It was blazingly hot, even at nine in the morning. The line at the court entrance was not moving and no one could enter without a gate pass. Then it was announced that the server had crashed and there was total mayhem.

"I will never get in on time for the hearing," Arnie told Krish as they spoke on the phone. "The damn queue is not moving." Just then, it did move. She got her pass and confidently walked through the court gates, sailing through the X-ray checks and the body scans that had once made her nervous. She found her favourite spot in the waiting area and settled down outside the courtroom. Vikram met her and threw the next bombshell.

"I have heard that their senior advocate is ill and can't make it out of bed, let alone stand in court, so they will try and get out of the hearing."

"You mean all fifteen lawyers are mysteriously ill?" Arnie asked wide-eyed.

"Yes, like all leaders of the opposition can fall ill on the same day to avoid a national convention and nothing can be done."

"But Vikram, she is here with a huge file and even Chhoti Phua looks pleased." He told Arnie not to worry as this hearing was after lunch just before the court's summer vacation, and the judge was unlikely to do much.

Arnie's fear was not assuaged. She looked around rather tense and then watched as her mobile rang. It was her bank manager, adding to the pile of straws on the camel's back. Without waiting for a response, she was told that she needed to sign forms to break another investment, and she was told the account balance. Her heart sank because she was going through her savings at breakneck speed.

It was the last straw. The straw that finally broke the camel's back. It hurt and Arnie rushed to the bathroom and sat on the floor, disappointed and discouraged, but she resolved not to give up.

"My silly, stupid, fashion designer ex-friend! What can a privileged bitch like her know of earning and supporting children? What does she know about rejection?" Like a particularly virulent pesticide, she had just killed Arnie, left her for dead on the social highway. And it was true; the bank manager had just confirmed it. Arnie was broke!

Arnie's lawyers called on her mobile phone, telling her that her case was the next one up. She could not go out. She had been crying. They, her mother and the rest of the family, had brought her up and knew that a red nose meant that she had been crying. She could not let them see her like this. She resolved to sell every bit of jewellery and even her flat, but she decided to fight. She would do whatever it took and she would succeed.

"Please come to the courtroom."

She read the curt message from Vikram, hurriedly dabbed some perfume and rushed out, reaching the courtroom just as the hearing was adjourned.

They had been lucky. No change in status until the court reopened after the summer vacation. Arnie nodded as they walked to the canteen for a coffee and Vikram pulled out a cigarette. "Can I have one?" she asked, taking one.

"You cannot behave like you did today. It was not good, you put too much pressure on me," he complained, helping her light up.

She nodded, mumbling her apologies, blowing circles of smoke in the air. From the corner of her eye, she watched Kamini and the rest of the clan pass by, but she didn't stub out the cigarette. She felt free because what they thought of her didn't matter, not any more. As she looked at them, she was reminded of her desperate need to belong.

Ten years ago, Arnie had craved approval when she transferred the mortgage of the flat to her name and successfully resisted its sale, turning it, instead, into a safe haven for her toddlers. She remembered showing her mother the appointment letter as Head of Department, but Kamini told her how well Randy the Dandy, her brother, was doing. Arnie told her how Sia and Shrey had glowing report cards, only to be dismissed and accused of over ambition and warned that they would have nervous breakdowns. Seeing the clan pass by now, all that seemed so distant, so passé.

Arnie walked towards her car, past the tall mulberry trees, their ripe purple fruit scattered on the green lawns, and dialled Krish. "Mixed day, I got anxious," she told him sheepishly on the phone. She described the knots in her stomach and the bloody intuition that had driven her crazy, and of course, the messages and email that had brought it on; her words rushed like water out of an enclosed dam.

She called Jaya and confessed her stupid behaviour to her friend as well.

"Don't be harsh on yourself. Only you know what you are going through, and that designer woman is not worth talking about. She has life dished out on a silver platter. Forget her. Isn't she the one who explained the merits of the two-way social highway? That she wanted to know people for their social trappings and what they can do for her? Without her family label, she will be unable to compete even with your local tailor. All of this has taken a toll and you are just human. You must take a holiday this year."

Jaya cut Arnie short when she said that she could not afford it. She asked Arnie whether she could afford hospitals, because that was where the children and she were headed if they continued this way and didn't release the stress from time to time. And she was right.

So a holiday it would be.

This was the first thing that Arnie told the children when they opened the door for her as she reached home. "We will be going on a holiday, so let's plan."

"Can Papa come with us?" asked Shrey hopefully.

"Yes, if you want him to and if he can take time out," Arnie replied, asking Aida to make her some tea and then lying down, exhausted.

Sia came in and lay close to her, and quietly told her, "It is difficult, Mamma, but we will pull through. I want to tell you something that may cheer you up. My friend, Linda, was with her father at this big party. Her father is this big designer, with a hundred stores and his own label. Your mother walked in and Linda went up to her and told her, 'Your granddaughter is my best friend!' Loudly, so loudly that everyone could hear. Linda also told her that she knew the truth, which caused your mom to scurry away in embarrassment, as Linda started telling her father about the case. The guests at the party quite enjoyed the spectacle. There were whispers, murmurs, and giggles fuelled by the gossip."

"So see Mamma, people are getting to know and Shrey and I will be good kids. You will be proud of us when we grow up," she said, wiping Arnie's tears.

"I am proud of you today and will always be. I love you unconditionally! But you have to live your dreams and not mine," Arnie told her, hugging her back. "I had a terrible childhood and my mother was awful to me. However, I have not allowed a trend to form; there is no reason for me to unleash the same terror and thereby destroy Shrey and your life. By not doing this, I am repaying my *karmic* debt. In turn, you must be good to your children and they to theirs. Sia live in the moment."

Before Arnie could say it, she shouted "Carpe diem" and was joined by Shrey from the other room, "Carpe diem, Carpe diem! We know, we know, that is the way to go!"

38

Goa it was then. Krish had also joined the holiday, but Arnie had many doubts about the wisdom of spending money that she didn't have. "Wish I hadn't bought this damn Rolex," she told him. "For the price I paid for it, I could have funded so many court hearings. But before you say anything, I need the holiday more than anyone else, so let us enjoy it. Please!"

Goa was beautiful. Arnie could gaze at the sea for hours on end, mesmerised by the gorgeous sunset. Seeing her set the alarm for an early morning jog, Sia giggled, "Not happening." Arnie turned to smother her in a hug as her giggles filled the room. Sia and she found themselves glued to the screen watching Madonna's 'WE' on the television, while Shrey swam in the pool with Krish and later played tennis. Meals were the highlight of the holiday; they tried different cuisines and stuffed themselves at the buffet table. Watching the children relish the food, the legendary Chef Rego invited them for a meal cooked specially by him for Shrey, the little foodie. It was a meal fit for the Gods. Finger-licking was just not enough to describe it; it set the benchmark against which Shrey compared food from then onwards.

Arnie, of course, consulted master*ji*, the resident

astrologer. He looked at her intently and then, without a blink, said, "Mother is neurotic, and your life is devoid of praise, I see betrayal. I also see that despite a struggle, the outcome is largely in your favour. Your struggle will not be in vain. I see children, two good children. Coming to the present, the times are difficult, legal hassles, but there is victory. You will see, I give you a year and it will be over within this time."

Arnie rushed to tell Krish, but found him engrossed in a phone conversation. She stood quietly and looked at the sea, but her attention waivered as she heard him talk about the case and he mouthed, "Vikram". Confused, she asked, "Why?" but he gestured for her to be quiet and then finally, concluding the conversation, turned to talk to her.

"Vikram's assistant got a message telling her to tell you, the client, that Kamini has managed to get permission to sell Civil Lines. Vikram and I are trying to figure out if it is a hoax. We have concluded that you are safe. No panic. By the way, he is leaving for Costa Rica for a vacation. Chill and don't look so worried."

"But who sent the message?" Arnie asked, her curiosity getting the better of her.

"Came from some random number, and according to Vikram, we should not engage with the person. Knowing your mother, this can be a trap to find out your strategy. The plot thickens. You have to be very careful. Remember that there will be a backlash and so from now onwards you will have to be extra careful. She will stop at nothing. Damaging your reputation is the easiest, but that hasn't worked, so now there may be physical harm."

"I am back again where I started, and yet it is different." Arnie's eyes sparkled with hope. She paused, took in the magnificent view, and told him quietly but resolutely. "I will not give up the legal battle for my rightful share. This is beyond money. It is for my dignity as a human being and includes a better future for the children and me," she repeated, her eyes bright and burning with determination. "I fly free; I am not bound by their *izzat*. Even Yudi mama is a hypocrite, so stand up I will, even in the face of their power and money. I ain't giving up Krish, oh no, not me!"

Back in Delhi, the children got down to completing holiday homework and sundry chores. Arnie watched Aamir Khan on *Satyamev Jayate*. The episode was on domestic violence and talked about women empowerment, about making daughters strong, about bringing daughters up with *izzat* so that they had self-esteem and could stand up for themselves, just like their brothers, the sons of the family.

The doorbell rang and pulled Arnie's attention away from the programme. Papers from her lawyers. Bills and an affidavit from Sanjeev. "I am taking the morning flight, but have some expenses that you must clear." She quietly signed the cheque and spoke with Sanjeev on the phone, then handed the cheque to his assistant. "You know this is of paramount importance, Sanjeev, we need some relief from the court."

"You now speak our lingo. It is our good luck that the Ranchi Court has not closed over the summer. But the timings are early, it gets too hot." Arnie barely heard him because she was saying a silent prayer. She still hoped and prayed that she would see some goodness in her mother, in her family. She hoped that they would reach out and resolve their differences. She didn't like her mother losing face in court, hanging on to lies, digging her grave deeper as the truth tripped her again and again. "Give up mom, redeem your *izzat*," Arnie prayed.

"Mamma, I am going to try out for the MUN," Sia told her mother, and seeing the puzzled look on her face she added, "Model United Nations. And I want to resume those contemporary dance classes."

Not to be outdone, Shrey said, "And cricket coaching please." Arnie's heart melted as she looked at them, her iron spirit reflected in them as they planned. "Sure, let me work it out," she told them, turning her attention back to the TV.

"Hey, your phone is vibrating," Sia said, as she bent across to pick it up and gave it to Arnie. It was some 'Vikram Assistant'.

Arnie heard something very unexpected. "Your case is listed tomorrow for hearing. Kamini has moved the Vacation Court." She was jolted back to life and screamed, "But this is not possible! What do we do? Can you call the senior counsel? Where is Vikram?"

But the odds were against Arnie and she had finally run out of luck. Vikram was in Costa Rica on vacation. Her regular senior counsel was also away somewhere. However, the other senior advocate she had consulted recently was available. Vikram's assistant told Arnie not to come to court, as she would handle the matter. She told Arnie that she would burst a nerve given how anxious she got. The lawyer wouldn't be able to handle both Arnie and the court matter, so it was better that Arnie stayed away. Kamini, it seemed, had done something extraordinary, for the Vacation Bench of the court handled only matters of life and death.

Arnie prayed, messaged Ruzbeh for protection, and called Krish, Jaya, and Monica, willing to talk to anyone and everyone. Her mother must have somehow found out that Arnie's lawyers were abroad and expected to get an order unopposed. To throw Arnie out of the case and to sell prime property.

Evening comes and night must follow. Her eyelids drooped and were heavy with sleep, but Arnie could not rest. She lay in bed, too exhausted to even sit up. She just heard the ticking of seconds from the mantelpiece and the hourly chiming of the clock.

Then it was morning. Court had opened. Lunch. No news, no messages. Arnie was ready to throw herself off a cliff and it was lucky that there wasn't one available. The children came back from school and tiptoed in as they huddled close. An hour passed and then it was almost four in the afternoon. "The court must be about to close now," Arnie remarked, looking at her gleaming Rolex.

Just then, she got a call and the room fell silent. It was Vikram's assistant.

"We have won! Our litigator was superb; even when the judge and your father's senior counsel pressed him, he stood his ground and did not give in. They muddied the water by saying in court that if you are proven the daughter, then you can approach the court again, but until then, the sale must be allowed to go ahead. Finally, the judge was convinced by our arguments. He said that it is like granting a divorce without an existing marriage. We held our ground and did not concede at all. Your mother was devastated; she was in shock because she must have thought that this would go unopposed."

"Well done," Arnie joyously exclaimed, grateful for her support.

Over a quickly-ordered pizza dinner, Arnie went over the court proceedings with a toothcomb and realised that it was a close shave, a very close shave.

The next hearing and the one after that were write-offs, as their lawyers asked for adjournments. Vikram was back and was very suspicious of what was going on, so he had asked for an inspection of the court file. He called Arnie the day the court gave him permission to see the official case file and asked her to rush to his office. Must be something important and Arnie prayed that it was in her favour.

It wasn't good news. The Land Office that had held up the sale of Civil Lines had changed its mind and filed an affidavit in court that they were no longer opposed to 'disposal of the asset' as they called it.

Arnie was in shock. How had this happened? Events were unfolding far too fast for her and she seemed to be facing new threats from places that she had never even thought she needed protection from. Someone new was guiding her mother's strategy, for now she was fighting Arnie on several fronts. Arnie had no answers to the various attacks that were coming in from all quarters.

Ranchi was still a washout; no order. Arnie met Sanjeev and asked him what they needed to do to consolidate their position. "I have just come back, let me think and tell you. I will talk internally to my team and some known lawyers and get back."

"What next?" Arnie wondered and strategized. She called Vikram and asked if she should fly her friends, teachers, and even an ex-employer to Ranchi to prove that she indeed was the daughter.

"Absolutely not," was his firm answer. "Come and have coffee with me at 11 a.m.," he said.

Over ice-cold mochachino, he told Arnie to relax. Courts didn't work on an emotional track, only on facts and evidence. "But the fact is that I am their daughter and Eshwar Dhari's granddaughter," she told him. "So what is the problem? Why is the court taking so much time over a simple fact?"

"Court procedure," was his two-word reply. They sipped their coffees in silence and then he quietly added, "Judges have seen everything, but always give all parties a chance to respond. Less chance of the order getting challenged."

"Okay, so what must her lawyers be advising her?" Arnie asked.

"It is a poker game, a game of patience. They must be hoping that you blink first, that they can break you down in as many ways as possible, emotionally, psychologically, and most importantly, your spirit, so that you make a mistake, say something that can be used against you or appeal to her as a mother emotionally, but she will use it to her advantage. You must unnerve her because the new you is a person she has not encountered. *Chaliye*, let's go," he said, paying the bill and brushed aside her offer to pay. Her fears assuaged, Arnie watched *Grey's Anatomy* with the kids at night and then fell into a deep sleep.

The phone rang early morning and she leapt to pick it up, having an aversion to such calls because in her experience they were never good news. "Sorry, I know it is early, but there is only one thing left to try. You need to come with me to Ranchi and I will tell you what to say before the Honourable Court. We have to go this evening because the case is listed tomorrow; think about it. If you agree, I will take the afternoon flight and you catch the last flight out," said Sanjeev.

Arnie called Krish, telling him that Sia and Shrey would have to miss school since he was travelling and she didn't want to leave them alone, not even for a day. She bought tickets online and arranged to meet Sanjeev at the airport with the kids. As soon as Sia and Shrey came back from school, she made them pack an overnight bag and hurried them into the car.

Her mobile phone came alive just as they were pulling out of her condominium, and Arnie rummaged through her bag to find it.

"Are you going to Ranchi?" she heard a vaguely familiar voice ask.

"Yes," she replied, adding without thinking, "I have to because I will lose the case if I don't go." The phone crackled as they sped down the highway and then she heard, "If you go, you may lose your life."

With that, the phone was disconnected. She tried to call back but realised that it was an unlisted number. Worried and anxious, she walked through the security check at the airport with the children, but the warning rang in her ear, stinging like a slap. She tried Sanjeev just as they boarded, but she could not get through.

It was just Arnie's luck that the flight was cancelled due to a technical snag. There went her chance of getting something from Ranchi in a hurry!

Sanjeev called in the evening and it turned out that the cancelled flight was amazing good luck. There had been a frightening incident in the Ranchi Court compound. "Good you did not come," he said. "There is a God up there. Today, just as this young woman walked into the court using the same dimly lit corridor, someone threw acid on her. I saw it; it was horrible. I don't want to scare you, but it did cross my mind that she was the same built as you and she was dressed in a white *salwar kameez* with short hair, just like you. The point to note is that we cannot be too careful."

Stress, mortality, fear induced by the acid attack, and worry about whether it was meant for her . . . life, they say, flashes before one's eyes at moments like this. But it didn't really for Arnie. She looked back at her childhood and tried to remember one occasion when her mother had really laughed joyously with her. She could only remember artificial laughter.

"Not like her!" Arnie wanted to stick a Post-It on her forehead and declare to the world. She didn't want the family ills to stick to her. "This is not who I am," she repeated to herself, and then in a moment, realised that she was free. She no longer had this cloying need to belong. She didn't need their approval. She no longer wanted appreciation from either her mother or Yudi Sharma. She didn't care what the Sharmas or the Dharis said any more. She was who she was.

Arnie was free from the confines of their prison because their *izzat* was no longer her identity. She was not perfect but she didn't pretend to be either. She had no image to protect and lived no lies. She was grateful for today and would make the most of tomorrow and that was that. She didn't plan and didn't plot because she believed that her life was like a hiccup, unexpected.

39

'A problem becomes a problem only if you believe it to be so.
And often others see you as you see yourself.'
— Chitra Banerjee Divakaruni

Arnie's life had changed after the acid attack. There was a newfound confidence and she was ready to take on the world like never before. The brutality had set her free and given her courage that she did not know she had.

"You cannot go to Ranchi unless you have decided to kiss your life goodbye," Vikram said firmly at their next meeting.

"I know there is a huge risk, but this is the only way forward and this is my last chance. I have to take the chance and they can't throw acid again," she replied.

"Yeah you are right, could be a bomb blast next," he muttered to her astonishment.

Arnie found herself in Ranchi, in a hotel room. Nervous as hell and spooked by the banging doors. She called friends or they called her to ensure she was safe. Finally, dawn broke and she was glad. She dressed for court, holding on to her *rudraksh* beads bought in Delhi just for this hearing. She needed the order and would get it.

"Ready?" asked Sanjeev, escorting her to the car. She made her way to the courtroom, sighing in relief when she sat down on the hard wooden bench. The raging heat outside did not bother her nor did it bother the stray dog that walked up to sniff around. The villager seated next to her dug his nose and farted, staring at her throughout. She caught his glare and smiled back. A woman in a dirty sari grabbed her hand, admiring the ring Arnie had forgotten to take off, but she smiled back because she was safe as long as they were there next to her. It would need buckets of acid to get to her through this crowd.

There was no pretence any more. Even the court registrar mentioned Kamini by name when announcing that the case was adjourned to after lunch, because Arnie's mother's lawyer was busy. Lunch came and went. The court reassembled. Kamini's lawyer, a junior counsel this time, informed the judge that the senior counsel was with the Chief Justice of the High Court and could not come for another couple of hours. Arnie groaned, nervous and on edge, but also strangely calm. Her friends, the children, Krish and Vikram were all following the developments in this court with the same zeal as the final overs of an India-Pakistan cricket match.

Sanjeev and his assistant lawyer gained confidence from Arnie's attitude and they calmed each other's nerves. Arnie needed the order as her mother and the family would happily lock her into a gas chamber and turn it on if they could, burning her alive. She needed something. "We are aware, do not worry," both lawyers told her as she slumped down, sitting with a thud on the hard bench.

Then her lawyer spoke in a whisper, "If their lawyer doesn't show up, you get up and speak. The court is well within its right to pass the order. We have time." The judge pounded the table, silencing all, like in the movies. However, in the court there would be no retakes if they missed the opportunity. Arnie leant forward, waiting, as the raging sun continued to beat down oppressively and she perspired profusely.

Then she saw him enter. The senior counsel followed by his cronies. His juniors ushered him in, announcing his arrival with much fanfare. They had managed to get it right this time and he was introduced as representing Arnie's father. "Your Lordship, I was in the High Court, with the Chief Justice. I was in his chamber, giving my humble opinion on certain issues. Urgent matter, and was called, therefore not able to come earlier. But *Hazoor*, this daughter is mischievous. He is greedy, My Lord. This application is only his greed, big greed you know, My Lordship."

Arnie watched quietly, itching to tap their senior advocate on the shoulder, just to remind him of her gender, but resisted. As Sanjeev stood up to argue, there was a loud protest from the other side and finally Arnie's local lawyer stood up and she blanked out as the judge began to dictate the order and the pompous senior counsel of her father completed the sentence, looking very pleased. He marched out of the dusty courtroom followed by his cronies and the stray dog.

"Please get up and thank the Lordship, now. Stand up." Arnie nodded and got up and, with her hands folded and head bent, she humbly thanked the judge. As she spoke, she was not sure what she was thanking him for but heard her voice. "Your Lordship, I am a daughter of this state and you have recognised me as the granddaughter of Sir Eshwar Dhari after seeing all the evidence. Despite my parents saying they do not remember having a girl, your court has given me justice. I beg that Your Lordship protects those very rights now and I want to put on record my grateful thanks." Then she was nudged towards the door and they left.

Once safely outside and out of earshot, Sanjeev said, "Thanks to God, all went well."

Arnie looked at him in disbelief, for though she was supremely confident and overdosing on adrenaline, she had absolutely no idea of what actually had happened in court. "But Sanjeev, their senior counsel was jubilant. What was he so happy about? And if he won, then we lost, right?" Arnie was very confused. Handing her a cold drink, both lawyers grinned and told Arnie that she had chosen the wrong moment to faint. "Low BP," she mumbled, still unsure of what had transpired in court.

The judge dictated the order and their senior counsel heard only the beginning and marched out. The first part of the statement by the judge said that the statute of limitations extended to Arnie's application, and that she should have approached the court within three years of the original case, where she had been missed out from the family tree. At this point, their lawyers declared victory and marched out. Like George Bush had declared 'Victory in Afghanistan' while on a US aircraft carrier in the Mediterranean Sea. And just as the US troops who stayed behind understood and recognised that the war was far from over, Arnie's lawyers and she stayed behind in the courtroom and heard the rest of the order.

For the first part had been just a preamble and a qualification to the order itself. The judge went on to explain that misrepresentation of material fact had been carried out and that there was no limitation on seeking redress when an applicant's rights were taken away by an act of misrepresentation. On merits, therefore, he found that Arnie was the daughter of her parents and the granddaughter of Dadaji. A modified family tree would be appended to the original case.

Now truly, and on record, she was a 'Daughter by Court Order'.

"So they cannot lock you in the gas chamber, that is for sure," said a chuffed Sanjeev, walking Arnie to the car. "There is a five-star hotel nearby, let's go and sit there before we go to the airport. We have three hours to kill before the flight." She nodded and followed him around, her head in the clouds and a song on her lips.

They ordered drinks and snacks and talked non-stop. "Sanjeev, we have come a long way from the day my mother asked me to get a piece of paper to show that I exist, huh? Today, not a mango from my grandfather's orchards can be sold without including me in the picture. God has been very kind," she said, picking up her overnight bag as they got into the car en route to the airport.

Seat belt buckled, she took a sip of water and looked out of the window as the flight took off. Arnie chuckled and grinned to herself as the reality of the day sank in.

She rushed through the arrival lounge and ran into the open arms of her beautiful children. Krish grinned at her and gave her a hug saying, "Well done" and then turned to congratulate Sanjeev. "Amazing day, Sanjeev. We were all following it and there were moments when my heart sank. The delays were quite dreadful."

"I told her not to worry," Sanjeev said. "She actually fainted in court as it was so hot and we had to prop her up to speak. But I am satisfied; we will have a certified copy of the order in a week."

Suddenly finding her voice, Arnie asked, "But what will they do now?" and both men answered together, "Not a problem!" Krish added, "You sleep tonight, and tomorrow we will talk to Vikram."

"Happy?" all of them asked Arnie as she sat between her children, holding their hands on the drive home.

"I sent a message to Vikram from Ranchi," she told Krish before falling asleep in the car.

The next day was spent in a flurry of excitement; calls went back and forth and strategy was discussed. "Let's not take calls from their lawyers, we will wait and watch. The shoe is on the other foot now. See you in court tomorrow," said Vikram, signing her court pass with a flourish.

"I am going to get my hair washed and blow dried before I come home," Arnie told Sia on the phone. "Ask Aida to polish my lucky shoes and get my clothes ironed." She walked into the ultra chic saloon. When she left, she had to run to the car because it was drizzling, the monsoons were here; another season had changed. She rolled up the car window, looked out at the passing traffic, and heard the annoyed car horns as traffic piled up.

The driver picked a fight at the toll barrier and Arnie calmed him down. "Don't! I really need to be able to get to the court tomorrow," she told him as they slowly negotiated the potholes on the road to her freedom. "Freedom, huh," she thought to herself. "Where did that come from?"

The next morning, she was at the High Court once again. She went through the motions and completed the security process. Vikram and Sanjeev were standing together.

"They are here in full force," they told her. "Madam is inside and is wearing her dark glasses; she hasn't noticed the season has changed and the sun's glare is not the same." Chuckling to himself, Sanjeev added, "A lot will change for her. We have the order and it has been given to our senior counsel.I have asked both the senior counsels to be here and they know the latest development from Ranchi."

"Sure, let's go in and wait for our case to come up," Arnie told them confidently, leading the way.

"Our case is after the supplementary items, so most probably at noon. But why are all of them looking so happy?" Vikram wondered aloud. "No panic though, we will get to know inside the court. I have to admit, I am surprised at their attitude," Vikram said quietly.

Krish had come with Arnie to court this time, but he stood a little away from them, for this was her fight. Arnie winked at him when it was time to go in. "So this is it, Vikram?" she asked and then she looked around for her litigator.

Her case came up and she heard the judge say that he would hear the matter at a later date. Arnie's lawyers showed urgency, requesting the court to hear the matter. They appealed to the judge saying, "It is a small, simple matter, Your Lordship." The judge snarled back, "It cannot be a simple matter. You are present along with a distinguished panel of senior lawyers. I do not have the time to hear this today." Her senior counsel fought and got the Ranchi order introduced into evidence. Arnie watched in suspended disbelief as her mother's team of senior lawyers thanked the judge with an exaggerated sweep and trooped out of court.

Arnie was demolished; this was her moment, her day in court, but her Ranchi order had gone unsung. She looked towards the opposite side and they grinned cheekily at her. Their happiness was apparent in their body language, which reflected success while her shoulders drooped.

"What happened?" she asked her lawyers, bewildered as they walked up to her. "Shit," she messaged Krish as Vikram walked across and gave him an update.

Arnie's lawyers, meanwhile, were flapping around. The regular senior counsel had vanished. Sanjeev seemed to feel that the family would sell Civil Lines and she would be left with nothing. She would have the satisfaction of being the daughter of the family, but it would be to no avail and the judge had not seemed to want to discuss ownership of Civil Lines. He wanted to get the matter off his list and that would happen only if the property were to be sold quickly. The open issue of Arnie being the daughter had been the only aspect preventing the sale, and now the court was free to recognise the sale as no further questions were pending before the court. In a strange way, it seemed that her winning in Ranchi had screwed Arnie in this case, for now the sale could go ahead. She could not object to it, as she had not filed a property dispute case, merely one of misrepresentation of material fact. The misrepresentation had now been dealt with and Arnie had nothing to show for it.

"The Ranchi order needs clarification."

"We need to act immediately."

"Let's file a property case right away."

"You rush to Ranchi."

"They will sell Civil Lines now. You need to compromise; I can talk if you want. This can carry on for generations, listen to me, wrap it up," Sanjeev told Arnie before rushing to the bathroom.

Krish was still nowhere to be seen. Arnie picked up her BlackBerry and pressed speed dial to speak with her children. The phone rang and was picked up immediately. "Does she see sense?" Arnie heard a voice that she knew so well, that of her mother. It was not her children. Arnie had mistakenly picked up Sanjeev's phone and found her mother on his speed dial list! She was shaken at the betrayal. Sanjeev had walked over, selling her out. Her ears burned, but the best management techniques she had learned, kicked in. She remained calm and reminded herself of tense board meetings where she had successfully negotiated on her terms. "Come on Silver Girl," she told herself as she saw Sanjeev emerge from the washroom. She handed him his phone as he continued to banter, pressing her to compromise with her mother.

Then Arnie got a message from Krish, who had been missing for he had sat down for a coffee with their regular senior counsel, who was a friend of his, and he did not know what the others had been discussing. "Congratulations!"

"For what!" Arnie messaged back angrily, and glared at him as he walked over for it was in moments like this that he could drive her crazy. Krish was confused on seeing their glum faces. "I just spoke with your senior counsel," he told Arnie. "Guys, you have won! Why the sad faces? Don't you get it?"

"Yes, but they are free to conclude the sale now," she told him. "That is our problem."

"But you have won," he irritatingly continued to insist.

"How?" all of them asked, turning aggressively towards him.

"Well, the matter seems to be fairly straightforward. The Ranchi order declares you the daughter of your parents. The High Court has said that once your birth in this family is proven, your impleadment is confirmed and you become party to the case. The original order of sale that your family got from the court states that the sale proceeds will be divided amongst ALL the parties in the case. This now includes you! So now all you need is a formal order from this court, which should not be difficult."

Arnie looked at him and looked away guiltily, wondering if he too, was on her mother's side, but she saw sincerity in his eyes.

Her team of lawyers reflected on what Krish and their senior counsel had concluded. Genius! Sheer genius! It suddenly dawned on Arnie that it was indeed her moment and that victory often did not come with trumpet, song or beating drums . . . it just happened! And sometimes, like her, we are too scared to shout it aloud, to announce it full throttle, afraid that we may wake up.

Jaya was the first to get to know about the hearing from Arnie. "I think I have won, or at least it has gone well, but in court cases you can never tell," she whispered into her mobile, still hesitating to accept Krish and the senior counsel's interpretation. Then she saw another call coming in and her mobile phone rang all afternoon.

They congregated at Vikram's office the same evening and he quickly got the paperwork completed to get certified copies of all the orders. Arnie looked up at his notice board for inspiration and read,

'You can't stop the future,
You can't rewind the past,
The only way to learn the secret
… is to press play.' (Jay Asher)

"Vikram, what will happen next?" she asked as she signed the papers.

"Well, I will file first thing in the morning so that the Ranchi order is on court record. Simultaneously, Sanjeev, as your Ranchi lawyer, will send them a copy of the order from Ranchi. I will also send them a notice telling them that you are now party to the sales proceeds from Civil Lines. Let the action begin!"

"I would rather you handle the entire process yourself and leave Sanjeev out," Arnie almost shouted.

Sensing her resolve, no questions were asked. Arnie said her goodbyes, wishing them luck. They were so close to winning; it finally seemed real.

On the drive back to Noida, she tried to piece together her life.

She remembered running in the aangan as her mother shovelled chicken down Dandy Randy's throat, holding him close to her heart. She remembered begging for some, but was given the leftovers.

On another occasion, Kamini told nani to buy a tricycle for her wonderful son when he could barely walk and it was Arnie's birthday. Her doting father bought apartments in Kamini's name with money saved from UN Peacekeeping Missions so she did not suffer. Arnie's mother had doting parents, so why did she treat her daughter like a leper?

She fawned over Randy's one certificate in Class 3 in school, while Arnie's sheaf of accomplishments and awards was not noticed. Arnie remembered looking at her holding Randy's hand and she hoped that her mother would show the same acceptance and affection for her. Arnie remembered becoming junior school captain and holding her house flag, trying to see if her mother was there in the audience, but only nani was there.

Arnie walked into her flat and the children welcomed her.

The pop of champagne took her back to the huge party her mother had had for Randy at her party pad with mirrors on the ceiling. The champagne flowed that day for Randy, who was clearly happy, and Arnie too, was thrilled for him and proud of him, for it was a celebration, his graduation from university. What a contrast to her own unsung graduation from an equally prestigious academic institution in London. It was the same pattern, repeated again and again; Arnie's children were ignored whereas her mother sung paeans about Randy's infant, ironically giving the speech at Arnie's children's school where she was invited as their grandmother.

Everyone has someone they can turn to in times of crisis, but Arnie's mother let her down each time, every time. She always claimed to be a feminist, but how was she different from an ignorant woman? Like her, they viewed their daughters as a burden and blamed the daughter if she returned to the parent's house, either stuffing her back in the marital home or killing her off. They looked the other way as she suffered. Arnie remembered her mother looking away so many times, gloating at her misfortune. She remembered Kamini telling her how her friend's daughter had killed herself. Was there a hint in her words?

"Krish, I know what I am going to do next. I will live life in a manner that draws inspiration from Dadaji. And I will use my experience to show other women that they can fight injustice in their families, as well." Arnie smiled at Krish as she swirled the champagne in her glass and turned to pick up an olive. "Krish, whatever happens next and no matter how the case pans out, my rights have been established. My family is barbaric; I can see all of them clearly. Had I been uneducated and helpless, they would have cut me out and done me in with the cunning of terrorists who watch helpless people walk into a building, knowing that they will blow it up in a few seconds. My family set me up for failure."

"Let's go out for dinner, I will just change," she told Krish, putting down her glass. As she got up, she smiled and said, "Sweetheart, life has been a long dark tunnel for as long as I remember. I yearned for the day I would get out of it and dance in the sunshine. I undersold myself and did not believe in myself, for Randy was the best. Childhood conditioning! I was happy with second bests, but life had other plans for me."

"So what is the secret? What kept you going?" Krish asked as they got into the car.

"Nothing profound. Even when there was no hope at different points, I just hung on and lived from day to day, hoping, praying for a day when I would be thrown out of the tunnel and into the sunshine. I got sucked into it so I believed that one day, someday, I would get thrown out too. My children and my close friends gave me the courage to carry on."

40

'I will not die an unlived life'
— Dawna Markova

Sanjeev was scandalised. "My lawyer went to deliver the notice and both your mother and your brother were there. She just pounced on him and began to abuse him. *Ram ram*, it is awful to hear abuses like *kutta* and *haramzada* from a woman. My junior is still in shock. She brought out a camera and began to film him. She asked for his identity card and he showed her the pass for the Lower Court as well as High Court. She then lit into him and abused me by referring to me sarcastically and telling him that she had heard about me from the Law Minister of India and that she would report me. I am not scared. My junior told her that he was a representative of the court and handed over the papers."

"What about Randy?" Arnie asked, astonished at the unfolding drama.

"He just bleated and ran alongside his mother. He, according to my junior, was comic. Are you sure that he is not gay, because the junior and the driver are cracking jokes about him."

"Let it be, Sanjeev. What do we do next?" she asked. He told Arnie that he was sitting with Vikram and it would be good if she could join them.

Much had happened since the last court hearing. Arnie's lawyers had filed affidavits and notices in court and delivered copies to all the parties in the case, including the Land Office of the government.

Then they sat back and waited.

After a few days, what they thought would happen, did happen. Her father's lawyers approached Vikram and their senior counsel from Ranchi spoke with Sanjeev. Kamini wanted to do a deal with Arnie.

Perhaps this would be the end of it all. Arnie closed her eyes and prayed for some wisdom, specially hoping that she see some goodness in her family through their behaviour in this last stage of a harrowing process.

"You are very important," said Sanjeev as she walked in.

"Why so?" Arnie asked, surprised.

"*Arre*, now all their lawyers want to speak with you."

"I do not want to speak to anyone directly. I will speak through my lawyers. I will not meet anyone either before the deal is decided," she told them. "Vikram, do you think that my mother will handle this well?" she asked, and then added, "In your experience, what happens now?"

"She has shown little grace until now. If she had any goodness, and maybe even brains, she would not have left it until so late. After all, this is a public loss of face. Most families reconcile, but she is a basket case. I have heard that she doesn't listen to her lawyers and that your brother is a wimp."

"We have your instructions and will act accordingly." Both lawyers reassured Arnie as she paid for the coffee and left. She had clearly told her lawyers that she would only settle for her rightful share, for she did not want to take anyone else's share and neither would she settle for less.

She was poring over Sia's homework at night, when she heard the phone ring. It was Vikram.

"I have Krish on the line," he said. "Your mother's lawyers feel that if they strike a deal with us, you still may not agree to it and they want to talk to you personally."

"Well, tell them that I can ask the same question. What guarantee is there that their client, my mother in actual fact, will honour the commitment they make? I will not speak with them."

"They even asked if you wanted to meet at a third party's place, somewhere neutral and of your choice."

"The answer is no; too little too late," Arnie said firmly. "They are running out of time, not me. Frankly, I am not perturbed."

"*Chaliye*, goodnight," Vikram said, disconnecting the call.

Early morning, the phone rang again and Arnie jumped to answer it. Events were moving quickly. Deals were about to be made. The senior counsel of her father was flying in from Ranchi. A war room had been set up under the control of Kamini and Randy at a centrally located luxury hotel.

A meeting was set up where Arnie would be represented by Vikram and his team. Kamini's lawyers, including the senior lawyer from Ranchi, would be present.

Arnie didn't trust them and told her lawyers so. "Vikram, it won't just be the lawyers, believe me. There will be drama. My mother, brother, and Yudi mama will descend, along with their political contacts and Page 3 friends, if they can manage it. Please do not make any commitments on my behalf without checking with me and do keep me in the loop."

She was right.

"Your mother has arrived" was the first message from Vikram and the second one from his assistant read, "Randy here".

"And now Yudi Sharma has walked in."

Then Arnie got a call from Vikram. "They want us to tell you that they love you very much and are dying to meet you, but they do not know where you live or your mobile number and so want us to tell you."

"Sure, Vikram I get it. Tell them that I have seen their love up, close and personal."

"Also, your mother says that she has no other property and unlike Chhoti Phua gets no rental income, so she will be on the road if you don't back off. They also want you to come for the meeting."

"Vikram, give her the list of three houses and apartments, commercial real estate, and offices that she owns. Her words are complete bullshit!"

"Okay, will tell them our client will not come," said Vikram.

Yudi Sharma, meanwhile, had gone all macho and had just told Vikram that he had a strong handshake. Not one to match Yudi Sharma, of course, as he had broken people, but strong nonetheless. Yudi Sharma then claimed that the Civil Lines property was worthless as there was some architectural peculiarity in the rear portion of the plot. He then rubbished Arnie's valuation of the property, dismissing it as nonsense and pompously citing his own example of getting different quotes whenever he wanted for his businesses. "He has asked us to tell you that it will not auger well for you if you do not come within an hour and quickly accept his offer."

Arnie listened quietly and told Vikram, "Please tell him that he, as a Sharma boy, has no role in my paternal grandfather Eshwar Dhari's property and that I don't need an hour; a moment will do. I turn down his offer and wish him a safe drive home."

There was radio silence from the meeting of the lawyers. Arnie fidgeted and drank endless cups of tea. "I will not undersell myself this time," she told herself.

Vikram called. "Your uncle was very annoyed as he had come on a mission and you undermined his authority. His body shook with rage and disbelief when we conveyed your message. Through his hooded deep-set eyes, he looked piercingly at us. He glared through his glasses and waved his hands about to emphasise his point."

Yudi mama's waving of his hands was one of the oldest memories that Arnie associated with him. Like the Dalai Lama, there was remarkable power in his voice. However, unlike the Dalai Lama, he expressed agitation and anger by waving his hands.

Vikram went on. "According to their calculation, or should I say expectation, you would have fallen at his feet and signed the document that your mother's lawyers were carrying. They had booked two rooms at the hotel and had printers etc. ready, but were absolutely stunned when you did not arrive. We finally told them that we cannot force you to come and left the place. Your mother, she did not offer us even water. Today I know what you have gone through. We spent eight hours with them. Your Yudi mama bats for them, we saw it today. I am sorry."

"I am really grateful to all of you. How did their senior counsel take it?"

"He had come hoping that he would take credit for being the architect of the settlement, having made a mess in Ranchi, and thus resurrect his flagging reputation. As expected, he was very disappointed and your mother openly abused him while your brother pushed him around. Yudi Sharma did not shake hands with him on his way out, so this round has failed."

Arnie felt a twinge of regret, but she was determined not to barter her children's future or her own happiness. She had to stand up for herself and she was responsible for her own happiness, as she told herself and repeated it to Krish later that evening.

Tired, she was close to sleep.

"Another day gone, another one bites the dust," Arnie told Krish as he walked into her room. "So glad you are staying over, Krish."

Time was passing and with it was going the patience of the court. The judge was upset with the entire family. If they could not come to an agreement and settle, the entire court case may get thrown out.

Krish was keeping Arnie's spirits up. "You are good stuff and it takes immense courage to stand up like you have done, despite all odds, and therefore the numbers of the settlement have to make sense to you. What do you want?"

"My rightful share as defined by the law."

"So we know the ball park figures, chill," he said, handing her hot cardamom chai which reminded her of nani; Arnie's affection for her was uncluttered and still unquestioned. She remembered her room always smelt of warm spices mixed with the smell of talcum powder, soft and cloying.

"Yes, she loved you," she heard Krish tell her, as though reading her mind.

There was another call from the lawyers. Arnie had to go for the meeting along with the lawyers; Kamini was insisting upon it. Her messages had been conveyed to them that only the rightful owners, which included her father and his family, should be there to talk to her. "Vikram, I expect my mother will be there. I have to do it, no way out."

"Hi Mom," Arnie said, a little louder than normal, filled with anxiety as she walked up to her mother in the designated area of the hotel.

"Hello," she almost shouted, as Arnie flinched. "This is the last time you call me mom. I am Kamini Dhari and like being called by my name. Why are your lawyers here? I want to talk to you all alone, you so and so." She spoke stiffly and avoided looking at Arnie directly.

"I will not talk to her alone," Arnie told her lawyers.

"But you have to; that's the only way forward," they said to her.

Arnie reluctantly sat down and even before she could sit, her mother snarled. "Do you think I will give you the money just like that? You are really something else, you so and so," she spat out the words, hurling abuses as Arnie's ears turned red and she stared in shock. Kamini threatened her and tried to give her an ultimatum. "I will give the keys," she said, "and I will sell the house by this evening, so unless you agree, you will get nothing. I will not tell you who the buyer is."

"You can no longer bully me," Arnie told her. "You have never told me anything, so that is not new. My lawyers will get the papers from the court and as always I will get to know."

"Talk louder," her mother said, menacingly drawing closer. Arnie sat back in the sofa, trying to remember whether her mother was near-sighted or far-sighted. "I cannot see you," she snapped and gesticulated angrily with her hands.

"There is nothing to see, as long as you can hear me," Arnie replied as the tears glistened in the corner of her eyes, but she brushed them away rebelliously.

Arnie shook her head, indicating that she would not be party to her mother's schemes and then Kamini raged out loud, much to her daughter's utter horror and embarrassment. "Do you think I do not know how you have come so far? You sleep with them, your lawyers," she said, shaking her fist.

Too shocked to react, Arnie just sat there in silence and then got up and looked her mother in the eye. "I have learnt from you," she said calmly and walked across to her lawyers. "I will not speak with her, you have to negotiate with her."

Arnie watched from a safe distance and then ventured to ask her lawyers if they could break for lunch, as there was no service in the lobby.

"Better not to," they texted back. Hours rolled by as they talked to her mother and Arnie sat far away.

Looking at her watch, Arnie realised they had spent five hours and were nowhere near closure. She remembered her childhood and the long lectures, sometimes overnight. Her mother's tantrums could extend for hours until something distracted her.

"Uggggh," she shuddered and got up as Vikram showed her

the proposal from Kamini, exactly half of the figure that Yudi Sharma had offered the previous day. Arnie walked up to her mother and told her, "Your proposal is not acceptable, Mrs Kamini Dhari. I am leaving for the day. I will get the papers regarding my grandfather's house from the court."

Arnie looked her mother in the eye and firmly told her, "I want only my rightful share. I will not stand in the way of anyone who has a right and I do not want a gift. I will get it legally as my share from his estate and I was always a granddaughter, but unlike you, I do not tag my name to his on social media."

"You tamper with my Wiki page," she almost screamed, as Arnie softly but resolutely reminded her that unlike what she thought, Arnie was no fool because cyber activity was simple to track.

"What about me? I deserve something. After all, I fought them for forty years," she asked Arnie as her daughter stared wide-eyed.

"Is that why you did not show me on the family tree?" she asked incredulously.

"What if I am recording this conversation?" Kamini threw back. Undeterred, Arnie asked, "Am I on camera or is it voice? Let me start at the beginning. I, the daughter born to Dad and you, your daughter by court order, want only my rightful share and will not stand in your way. Do get your own share by court order too."

As she spoke, Arnie caught the eye of the concierge, who looked away in embarrassment, having witnessed India's icons fighting in public. Arnie walked across the lobby resolutely.

Arnie concentrated on the chicken sandwiches, which were awesome at the Delhi Gymkhana Club. She got some packed for Vikram and for her children, signed and left, a bit sad at how the day had turned out. Her illusions about Kamini lay shattered like shards of sharp glass in which she saw distorted and frightening images.

Another day went by. Arnie got a call from Krish, for she

was tired and had asked Vikram to keep him informed of the progress. It was excellent news! Arnie had won! She didn't want to rejoice too soon. However, a victory it was, for her mother had caved in and had agreed to give Arnie her rightful share. "I have won and I don't know how to react!"

The next day was a flurry of activity as many calls were made between lawyers and from Arnie's lawyers to her. "After yesterday, I will not be at the same place as her when I need to sign the papers. And the escrow modalities have to be agreed upon beforehand, and there is no question of relinquishing my right on the entire estate. I refuse, let them know."

"I agree," Vikram said. "We will push back and we are also going to make sure that if there are any further costs like dues on the property or if it is appealed, you are protected."

"Thanks Vikram," Arnie said, her voice quivering. "Please, make it watertight."

"I will be in the office all night exchanging emails with their lawyers, but ask Krish to meet me at 8 a.m. sharp. We are running out of time."

"Sure thing," Arnie told him, disconnecting the phone.

Early morning brought further good news. "You will not believe it. Because they cannot handle an escrow account, your parent's lawyers will record the accepting of your status and rights in court tomorrow."

"Yayyyy," Arnie said, lighting *agarbattis*.

Arnie walked into court exactly a year after her first hearing. This time, she walked in with her head held high, knowing that she had won. Her heels clicked on the ground as she walked towards Vikram and his team. "Thank you for making this happen. I had a Cracker-Jack legal team. All of you were amazing, absolutely awesome."

"We did our job, but you have someone up there smiling at you. Civil cases take years despite the best legal teams and you have won in such a short time," they told her as they trooped into the court.

"Beta, thank you," said Chhoti Phua and she grabbed Arnie in a warm embrace. Arnie hugged her back and asked for what she was being thanked. "You have shown me that every *Ravan* has a fall. Kamini has harassed me. She has revelled in my misery, our misery," she said, looking at the rest of the family as they beamed. "She met her match. I am happy that you are different because your brother is a wimp and fit to sit next to his father on the verandah."

"Chhoti Phua, she is watching. She will kill you for speaking with me. I had asked for the original owners to be present at our negotiations, but she came alone and told me that you and the others hate me."

"We hate her, not you, and she is a habitual liar. We did not speak with you because of the case, but it is over now. She cannot touch a hair on my head," Chhoti Phua told Arnie.

Arnie's smile morphed into something wicked, almost mischievous, and giggles bubbled up, rising softly as Arnie was able to breathe again. She looked at Chhoti Phua, nodded and laughed at the same time. "I hope I will see you again soon," Arnie told her, as their lawyers walked up and ushered them into court.

"There is a lot of paperwork and the legal mess has to be untangled. They left it too late, so many orders have been passed," Vikram told Arnie. "We need to unravel so much and the other lawyers are flustered at having lost, as they are getting shouted at by your mother and no one can work under such pressure. But we will get it done in a couple of hours."

It took longer than a couple of hours. At times it felt as if the papers would never be completed. They were told that the judge had been taken ill. Arnie's hopes were dashed as Chhoti Phua clutched her hand. "Beta what will we do? Court closes in an hour and now this."

There was no time to cry; Arnie could not lose now. She ran to Vikram and discussed the options. "There has to be a solution, this cannot be the first time that a judge has had a heart attack in court," Arnie said, all the while holding Chhoti Phua's hand. Sanjeev was hanging around and advised Arnie to settle for less, as nothing had been lost. Even though he was very animated, Arnie chose to ignore his words. She smiled. "The game's up, Sanjeev. We know what is going on, so please save the fine words for another day," she told him.

They moved another court and Arnie's rightful share was given by court order and not because of some lame settlement. She watched Sanjeev shrink as the judge dictated his order. Finally, as Chhoti Phua had pointed out that morning, evil had been defeated.

Bhabhi and the other family members hugged Arnie, while Chhoti Phua winked at her and waved from across the room, despite being wedged in between Arnie's parents. Her parents acknowledged Arnie's presence by glaring sullenly at her.

The buyers were present with their teams of lawyers. Arnie watched Chhoti Phua sign the sale agreement only after receiving her bank draft. The wily old woman would not sign before she held the money in her hand.

She signalled Arnie to sign next. Bhabhi's daughter took a photograph while Arnie signed her name with a flourish. Then the buyer's lawyers passed over an envelope to her. Arnie had her inheritance in her hand.

Holding Arnie's hand, Chhoti Phua addressed the girl's father. "Aranya is right. I kept quiet during the case but I am happy for her. Our father left enough so that his grandchildren could have a nest egg. This belonged to our father, not to your father-in-law," she spat out the words while Arnie's father cowered and her mother stared back darkly.

Arnie walked out of the court with dignity and pride.

Her children had a future. No glass ceiling, but a blue sky of opportunity. She looked up at the sky. The buttercup yellow sun shone happily and she spotted a lone eagle soaring high. She smiled to herself because she had won in the court where her nana was a legend. She could feel her Dadaji smiling at her and his presence enveloped Arnie in a big hug.

"I will see you in the car," Arnie told Vikram, walking out to her freedom. She beamed with happiness and confidence, glad that she had stood up for herself and yet again moved by the simple gesture made by her father's family. Amused that the Sharma's had joined hands over something that never belonged to them.

Getting into the car, Arnie saw that Vikram was still very agitated. "That woman is mad! She was complaining about you being a greedy daughter to the Court Commissioner. Even he told me that you were very dignified and that he has watched you in court. She lit into me and accused me of going out of my way for you and Randy shouted at me. He said that he would see me outside. What does that mean? You are so different from the rest of them. How did you survive? I have so much respect for you. I have small children and I think about how you brought yours up without any support. You have had the courage to stand up, litigate, and have carried your legal team. Kamini Dhari's lawyers dislike her intensely and were so relieved that the case is over."

This she wouldn't admit to anyone, but Arnie was in a state of shock. For almost the first time, she saw the world as a bigger place than the one she had been born into. What had been her whole world suddenly seemed small. She was the person no one would take a punt on because her chances of winning were negligible. She had no papers, she did not have even a room under her occupation in Civil Lines or a locked cupboard for which she had to hand over a key. Yet, she needed to sign for the sale to be completed. She felt like a poor waif from Bihar who had suddenly won a gold medal at the Olympics! Stunned but exhilarated.

ONE DAY. ONE MOMENT. LIFE STARTS.

'Destiny is strong and swift.
You cannot trick it so easily.'
– Chitra Banerjee Divakaruni

Arnie pulled up in front of the Chief Minister's house for a lunch to celebrate India's Independence Day. As she walked in, she was greeted with "Happy Independence Day" greetings and she smiled. "It is your independence too," a friend walked up and told her, as the CM's son, a friend from college, smiled.

"Indeed," Arnie replied and turned to ask, "It concluded last evening, so how do you know?"

"We know everything," Ravi told her. "Many of us from college have been rooting for you."

As she skipped joyfully to her car after a delightful afternoon amongst friends, Arnie was happy and she saw a new world opening up for her.

Five Years Later

Arnie smiled as she sipped champagne and looked out at the beautiful skyline from her sprawling penthouse. It had been five years to the day and so much had happened. Her life, like her career, had taken off. Krish was doing well. Their friendship had strengthened. Sia was at RISD in Rhode Island and Shrey was in Class 12. Arnie knew he would do well and follow his dreams.

She got up and put the books she had bought for Sia into her suitcase. These included *The Fakir* and *The Dalai Lama's Cat*. The books were different and yet so alike. She hurriedly packed the *salwar kameez* for Fatima; they were friends now.

The ringing phone got her attention. It was the principal of Queen's College, Arnie's alma mater, telling her that yet again her mother and uncle had tried to create noise. They tried to scuttle the scholarships she ran in memory of her grandfathers, saying that her grandfathers had not studied at Queen's College. They implored the principal to cancel the scholarships. They were agitated and aggressive, offering money, five times more than Arnie's scholarship amount. Then they dropped names and tried to exert influence. "When nothing worked," he told Arnie, "They said that you were not a direct relative. But this time I had them. For you are, as I told them, the Daughter by Court Order and justice has been served."